Ships in the Night

BELL FYFE

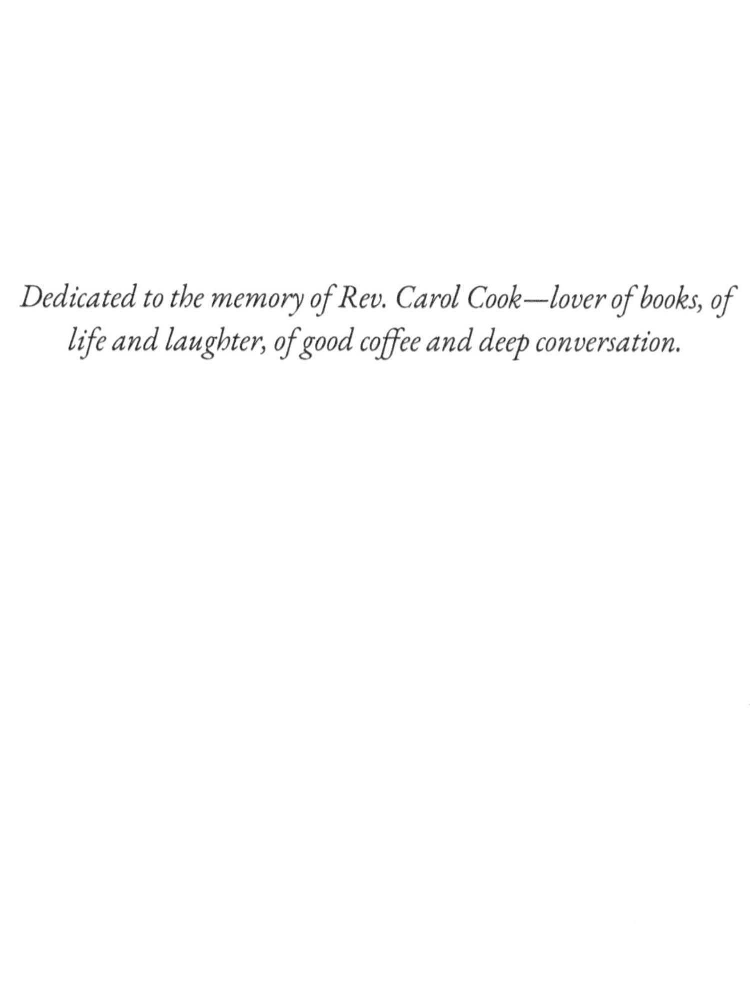

Dedicated to the memory of Rev. Carol Cook—lover of books, of life and laughter, of good coffee and deep conversation.

Chapter One

"It is a truth universally acknowledged," the gangly girl with sideswept bangs and vintage brown suede knee boots intoned, "that a clergyman in possession of a modest parsonage, must be in want of a wealthy patroness."

Abby Reilly rolled her eyes in the direction of Selwyn Sherman, in whose company she'd silently critiqued every Ships in the Night performance for the past eighteen months. So far, five of the eight contestants had started with variations of the same line, and sure, the first line of *Pride and Prejudice* was among the best-known of all time...but come on.

As usual, Selwyn had no comment.

Abby turned her attention back to the stage, reminding herself that the girl at the mic deserved credit for entering her work in The City Bookmark's renowned fanfic event. As a fellow aspiring author, Abby knew how hard it was to read your work to a crowd, even one as enthusiastic as the rowdy group that jammed into the bookstore every first and third Friday night of the month.

"'You've made great improvements to Hunsford Parsonage,' Lady Catherine de Bourgh said, heaping praise on Mr. Collins, 'but I'm afraid I won't be satisfied until you muster the vigor to squeeze a little more shelving deep into this closet.'"

The line earned a smattering of laughter, which the author acknowledged with a smirking mock curtsy before continuing.

"Mr. Collins' eyes widened as the highborn lady bent low, offering her round, matronly rump for his consideration. Extra shelving wasn't all he hoped to squeeze in there."

More hoots and a drunken catcall. Abby joined in the applause out of politeness, gauging the crowd's reaction. There had been bigger laughs tonight, but then again, there had been better jokes.

Despite the sold-out crowd and the book sales they would generate, tonight's event didn't hold a candle to the earliest days of Ships in the Night when it was just Abby, her best friend Stephanie, the shop's owner Ben, and a motley scattering of friends and bookstore patrons who happened to be browsing at the time.

Back then, the three friends lit each other up like a string of firecrackers, chasing each other's doctored prose and ad-libbed dialog, cheering each other on and rarely stumbling. They'd stuck to the classics, casting their favorite characters in sexual tableaus as ribald as they were outrageous, awarding each other points for wordplay and novelty.

But this batch of contestants lacked nuance and, frankly,

even a hint of the truly erotic. Lady Catherine and Mr. Collins? It was one step up from imagining your parents going at it.

Abby generally tried not to be overly critical of the Ships in the Night contestants. Without them, this thing that had started out as a few laughs between friends would never have grown into a consistently sold out event that might well have saved one of the few remaining independent bookstores in San Francisco's North Beach neighborhood.

Besides, what right did she have to judge? The prose tonight might be tired and uninspired, but at least these authors had the guts to stand in the spotlight—unlike Abby, who was hiding out in the travel section with a plastic cup of cheap, warm chardonnay for company.

And Selwyn.

God bless you, Selwyn, Abby thought, giving his spine an affectionate pat and straightening his neighbors.

Week after week, month after month, Selwyn and his *Shoestring Guide to the Wonders of Egypt* were always there for her. Once, during a particularly painful mangling of *The Scarlet Pimpernel* featuring Mr. Jellyband and three nubile fishwives, Abby had taken Selwyn's book from the shelf and checked out the author photo on the back: salt-and-pepper beard, bow tie, retro black-framed glasses, and one slightly, skeptically raised eyebrow.

Now, there was a man who saw the world as Abby did. Too bad he'd probably be in his eighties now, judging by the seventies-era polyester sport coat he wore in the photo.

The woman onstage wrapped up with Mr. Collins

declaring his newfound love of carpentry as he "hammered his joint home."

Pretty clever, Abby admitted to herself as she joined in the applause.

Ben leapt nimbly up on the little plywood stage and took back the mic as the author dipped another deep curtsy. "Folks, that was Molly Wasyl with 'A True Proficient.' Grab a drink, help yourself to the refreshments, and we'll be back in a few minutes with lots more of what you came for!"

While the audience cheered, a man making a beeline for the cheap boxed wine stepped on Abby's foot as he squeezed past her.

"Oh," he said, barely glancing at her. "Didn't see you."

Abby huffed in annoyance. It was a common occurrence, but a baffling one all the same. Just another of the unwritten rules for fat girls that Abby knew all too well: the fatter a girl is, the more invisible she becomes.

Hey, that would make a pretty good book, she thought. *The Unwritten Rules for Fat Girls*, in which she'd compile the thousand subtle snubs and judgments and criticisms she'd dealt with for most of her life, the ones that formed the invisible boundaries which girls like her were forbidden to breech.

Like the one that had Abby lurking in the Travel section in the first place: No Folding Chairs.

Contrary to popular belief, it wasn't a fear of collapse that made fat women avoid such seats but the barely disguised annoyance of the people seated on either side, when no matter how tightly a woman squeezed their arms and legs, a bit of thigh or upper arm inevitably brushed against their neighbors.

Maybe if Abby had been born braver, if she had more of the moxie her grandfather claimed she'd inherited from him, she could have overcome her fear of judgment and insisted on her right to take up public space. Instead, she made sure to get to the bookstore early enough to claim her spot in the back.

It was also why Abby would never actually write a book like *The Unwritten Rules*. The same reason that she'd long ago given up appearing on the Ships in the Night stage.

If the event didn't bring in so much business for Ben, Abby might wish it had never caught on. Its meteoric rise had begun almost by accident when Abby's twin brother, Owen, had tried to convince Ben to lend him the bookstore's Classic Mystery table for their family's pub half a block up the street.

"It's the only table big enough for McNickles," Owen cajoled. Her brother had enough of Grandpa's moxie to try to pass off his version of Quarters as a genuine Irish drinking game.

"You know I hate to say no," Ben said, an obvious lie since he'd been the voice of reason ever since they were kids and Owen was constantly trying to rope him into misadventures. "But as you can see, it's currently in use."

"It's only for a couple hours. It's not like hordes of customers are going to show up looking for—" Owen picked up the nearest book and made a face. "*And Then There Were None*. Sounds dead boring."

"It's a classic," Ben said sternly.

"Does it have sex scenes?"

"Of course not! It's Agatha Christie."

"Whatever. Trust me, no one's interested."

Five minutes later, Owen and a couple of pub employees were carrying the table down the street.

"What if your brother's right?" Ben said with the long-suffering scowl of a man who'd been losing arguments with Owen for more than two decades. "What if no one cares about the classics, and they only want smut? I mean, this quarter's sales..."

Abby wanted to reassure Ben that the sanctity of the written word would never be in danger, but she knew he was barely keeping the shop afloat since taking it over from his aunt and uncle a few years earlier.

Steph poked her head out from the Romance section. "So then give them what they want, Ben."

"How am I supposed to do that? Rewrite *And Then There Were None* so people get killed during a blindfolded key party?"

Steph grinned. "Why not? Each of us could write a scene and—and *perform* it," she said, picking up steam. "We could make it into a whole fanfic night. Put that on The City Bookmark's socials, and I guarantee you'll move every copy you have in stock."

"You're ridiculous," Abby scoffed, though if anyone could pull off such a scheme it would be Steph. As a freelance consultant for some of the biggest nonprofit organizations in the city, she routinely coordinated fundraisers for hundreds of their most prominent and wealthy patrons.

"I'm not a writer," Ben said flatly.

"I'm not either," Steph said. "Only Abby is, but I don't see why that should stop us. Know what I think? You're scared."

"Of *you*?" Ben pushed up his tortoiseshell glasses and made a show of looking Steph up and down, taking in her striped tights, chunky black work boots, glittery pink miniskirt and vintage paisley pussy-bow blouse. "I bet you don't even weigh a hundred pounds soaking wet. Fine—I'm in, and I'll even throw in the prize."

So it was that on the following Friday night, Abby's "And Then There Was Cum" took first place to the enthusiastic applause of Owen, his best friend Dex, and a handful of patrons who'd seen the posts Steph had designed for the shop's media accounts. Steph's piece—in which the missing supply boat reaches the island with a cargo of sex toys—was voted second place, and while Ben's half-hearted effort to kill General MacArthur with a blow job rather than a blow to the head was booed off the stage, he awarded the prize, a chipped, decade-old tennis trophy, with grace.

"I'm going to need this back," he told Abby sheepishly. "It's the only time I ever placed. If we do this again, I'll get a real one made."

"What's it say?" Steph asked, peering over Abby's shoulder as Ben excused himself to help ring up the line of customers that had formed at the counter.

"'Fourth place, Malden Community Junior Classic, 11–12 years old,'" Abby read fondly. "Oh, Ben."

Steph giggled. "Can you imagine him at twelve? With braces and one of those shirts with the little penguin?"

"You were right," Abby admitted. "He's selling out of Agatha Christie."

"Yep," Steph smirked. "Looks like we'll be doing this again."

And so Ships in the Night was born.

The second event, a ribald homage to *Don Quixote*, was met with a surge of interest. Half a dozen bookstore regulars not only submitted entries but brought their friends. By the end of the night, all the slots on the signup clipboard were full, and by the two-month mark Ben had to buy another dozen folding chairs.

Soon after, Ben was forced to start selling tickets in advance so they didn't exceed the fire code limit, but that didn't come close to quashing the show's popularity. Dex built a portable plywood stage, Steph snagged an old podium from one of her clients, and Ben invested in AV tech, first to launch a podcast and then to capture video and upload it online. Steph took over Ben's social media, and around the six-month mark the bookstore's following exploded after a wildly popular wellness influencer tweeted that she was fan of the show.

That was when Abby stepped away from the stage. She'd been fighting the urge to quit ever since reading the comments on the first live-streamed event. The jerk who'd stepped on her toes was a goddamn prince compared to the casual cruelty of the fat-shaming trolls who ruined the otherwise glowing praise with their venom.

Not that anyone would ever know the real reason Abby left the spotlight. Her friends and family accepted her stage-fright excuse at face value. Why wouldn't they? It was quiet little Abby, after all, the moxie-less Reilly twin.

But quitting didn't mean that Abby stopped writing.

"Next up is Stephanie Tran with 'Mary's Pressing Question,'" Ben announced once everyone was back in their seats. Applause broke out as Steph took the mic from Ben with a winsome smile. She slid on a pair of vintage crystal-studded cat-eye glasses and held up her phone to read.

Abby twisted her hands nervously with familiar trepidation at hearing her words being read aloud. It had seemed like a natural transition when, almost a year ago, she and Steph agreed on their new roles. Steph was a born performer but a lackluster writer, and Abby still had the itch to write.

They struck a deal in secret: Steph would submit and perform the pieces Abby wrote. Technically, it was against the rules, but no one was the wiser. Not even Ben knew.

"Mary Bennet melted into a dark corner of the stable, her plain woolen dress the same drab brown as the rough wooden walls," Steph read in what Abby thought of as her shaking-the-money-tree voice, the cultured tone that got donors to double their pledges over cocktails at Novela or The Armory Club. Tonight Steph was wearing a jade silk smoking jacket belted over vintage Pucci shorts and orange patent stilettos. "The handsome groom, the one Mary secretly watched from her window, didn't look up from his work. It wasn't surprising: of the five Bennet sisters, Mary was the one best described as literally blending into the woodwork."

Abby resisted the urge to silently mouth the words along with Steph. Not that anyone would notice; the audience was riveted by Steph, as always. In addition to her arresting appearance, Steph's natural charisma effortlessly kept them in her thrall.

"'I was hoping you could help me with a quandary,' Mary said timidly. 'You see, no one in the house will answer my questions, and I am desperate to know why my sister Lydia ran off with Mr. Wickham. Maybe you can tell me—what he could possibly offer a lady that would induce her to risk public scorn?'"

Steph favored the crowd with a saucy wink before delivering the lines Abby had stayed up until the wee hours polishing. "Even in the dim light of the stables, Mary could see the groom's muscles rippling as he pulled off a shirt soiled from hard work. He laid his rough, callused hands on the walls on either side of Mary and gazed into her eyes.

"'I could tell you, Miss...but wouldn't you rather I show you?'"

Chapter Two

"Third place?" Owen crowed, setting the round of drinks on the table and leaning down to take a better look at the trophy. "Now you're sucking diesel!"

Abby rolled her eyes at her twin brother. Not because of his questionable Irish slang or the ridiculous Lucky Charms leprechaun accent he used at work, which barely even registered anymore, but at his blatant ogling of the bronze statuette of a curvy girl in a St. Pauli Girl-style bustier pole-dancing on the mast of a ship.

True to his word, when Ships became a regularly scheduled event, Ben had commissioned custom trophies for the top three places. The trophies shared a nautical theme, with a pair of deckhands shackled together for second place and an anatomically impossible Captain Hook for first, inspiring some pretty creative selfies.

The winners got to keep the trophies only until the next event, but in the meantime they posed with them in social media posts that tagged the bookstore. Since the #ShipsInTheNight hashtag began trending, the bookstore's follower count had steadily risen.

"Pull it together, Owen," Abby growled. "You're drooling on Steph's trophy."

He straightened and looked around the table. "Only the three of you tonight? Where's Jan?"

"Jane," Ben corrected him. Abby and Steph exchanged a worried glance. "She skipped tonight's performance."

"She sick?"

"Of me, maybe. We broke up."

"Sorry to hear it, boyo," Owen said cheerfully, not being the long-term commitment type...or the short-term type, for that matter. "Look on the bright side—it's a great night to find yerself single. Look around, the place is packed with bonnie lasses."

"That's enough out of you, Darby O'Gill," Abby snapped. "Time to shuffle back behind the bar."

Owen shook his head sadly at her. "I see how it is. This is the thanks I get for trying to cheer up my fellow man." He'd retreated only a few steps before being distracted by a table full of female revelers.

"Ah, lassies! 'Tis a pity, all these empty glasses!"

"I swear," Steph marveled as the girls swooned. "Owen becomes more like your gramps every time I see him."

"I know," Abby said. "He keeps finding ways to up the ante. Next he'll start wearing a green suit and carrying a shillelagh."

She waited for the din of the bar to swell again before

putting her hand on Ben's arm. "How you doing, buddy?" she asked quietly.

"Fine." Ben tried to tug his arm back, but Abby dug in her fingers. "Honestly, Abs. I'm *fine*."

"You don't have to be, though," Steph piped up. Her exquisite hearing made it difficult to leave her out of conversations. "Not around us, anyway. We're your *friends*."

"I don't think he wants to talk about it," Abby murmured. She knew Steph was trying to be kind, but as nice as it was to know your friends had your back, you never wanted to become a burden.

"The weird thing is, I *am* fine," Ben said. "The breakup was actually pretty amicable."

Steph wasn't buying it. "We *are* talking about the same Jane, right? Jane *Silverstein-Warren* from *Upper Westborough*?"

Ben winced. Jane was from a humble part of South San Francisco, but she didn't like to admit to it. She'd refined her origin story to signal how much more refined she was than everyone else, but Abby and Steph had done their best to pretend to like her until now, for Ben's sake.

"She wasn't that bad," Ben countered. "Just opinionated. A lot like you, actually."

Steph's eyes widened, trying to decide whether to take offense. Abby gave a subtle shake of her head.

Ben was right, but in all other ways, the two women couldn't be more different. Steph was a Ships favorite, while Jane had to work harder for laughs, probably because she was so determined to project the image of a *serious* writer. She wore owlish glasses and scant makeup beyond a slash of brick-red lipstick, Indian cotton skirts and high lace-up boots and carried a stiff canvas messenger bag covered with earnest political pins. Her long hair was so straight and colorless that Abby suspected that Jane ironed it into submission on a board. And it was a rare conversation into which Jane couldn't find a way to insert her MFA from Wellesley.

Still, it was true that she and Steph were both passionate in pursuit of their goals. Abby had privately wondered if that similarity was what had attracted Ben to Jane in the first place.

Steph decided to let his comment pass. "Anyway, for probably the first time ever, I have to agree with Owen. There are plenty of other women in the world, and you're too much of a catch to stay single for long."

"I agree," Abby said, raising her beer for a toast. Ben reluctantly clinked mugs, but his eyes never left Steph's face.

The poor guy had it bad. Abby had witnessed his unrequited longing for Steph for years...all the way back to their freshman year at San Francisco State, when Abby had brought Steph to the pub for her grandparents' fiftieth anniversary party. There, she introduced her roommate to her childhood friend who'd spent his summers at his aunt and uncle's bookshop a few doors down.

Abby didn't believe in love at first sight. Relationships were built on complex dynamics that took time to develop and cement. But if anything could have changed her mind, it was the look on Ben Kantor's face when he first laid eyes on Stephanie Tran.

And if Abby's intuition was right, his love hadn't flagged in the decade since. If anything, it was both brighter and more bittersweet than ever. Yet Steph remained oblivious. It was as though her first impression of Ben as the comfortable old friend had stuck, and she was incapable of seeing him in any other light.

She occasionally considered telling Steph about Ben's crush, but Abby had a firm belief that love should grow naturally between two people, indifferent to the tides of public opinion and cultural norms and biological clocks and tax advantages and every other factor. The only thing that mattered was the way two people felt in each other's presence. To Abby, love was the only arena where the words "meant to be" rang true, an opinion she'd never had the courage to explore further.

Which was part of the reason she'd never said a word. Not to Ben and definitely not to Steph.

"So now that you two have broken up, does that mean I have one less competitor to worry about?" Steph asked lightly.

"You wish," Ben said, grinning. "Jane *loves* Ships. She only skipped this week because she thinks Austen is over-rated, but there's no way in hell she'll miss the next one."

"Yeah? Who'd you pick?"

Ben took a folded piece of paper from his pocket and laid it flat on the table. It was the cover page of a press kit for a new book.

Steph shrieked. "Isaac Ferrer? Are you serious?"

Abby barely got a look before Steph grabbed the paper and clutched it to her chest. "Uh, who is Isaac Ferrer?"

Steph slapped her arm. "*Evernight*? The TV series?"

Abby looked at her blankly. She could count the number

of times she'd turned on the television in the last year on one hand. "I thought the books had to be in the public domain," she said to Ben. "So you don't get sued."

"That's only if I don't have written permission from the author," Ben said smugly.

"Wait—you *talked* to Isaac Ferrer?" Steph demanded breathlessly. "*The* Isaac Ferrer?"

"I did. And two weeks from now, you can too. Because Isaac didn't just grant permission to use the book, he's signed on to be a guest judge."

Steph looked as though she might faint. "Oh. My. God. How did you manage it, you magnificent man?"

Ben gave a modest shrug. "He's a local now. He moved to the Bay Area a few months ago and came in to sign books for pre-orders last week. Turns out he's a fan of the podcast. He told me he's listened to every episode."

Steph's mouth fell open. "And you didn't *call* me?"

"Didn't want to ruin the surprise. Besides, how was I to know you were into epic fantasy?"

"Who isn't?"

Abby meekly raised her hand.

Steph turned on her. "Oh come on, Abby, he's like a cultural *phenomenon*. You must have heard of him."

"Who hasn't my hermit sister heard of now?" Owen had appeared again with a tray full of empties. "Last week Dex was talking about Sonic Youth, and she thought they were a soccer league."

"Isaac Ferrer."

"Really? Come on, Abs. Even I know who that is. Dex loves *Evernight*—watches it every week." Dex, Owen's best friend since kindergarten, was also his roommate in the apartment above the pub.

"That tells me everything I need to know," Abby said. Dex was a nice guy, a hell of a lot of fun in the right situation, but his taste was notoriously lowbrow. "Let me ask you this: How many of the female characters get to wear clothes in this 'cultural phenomenon' of a show?"

"Some...do," Owen said uncertainly.

"But not all of the male characters do, either," Steph added gleefully. "It's gender-equitable."

"Do you even *hear* yourself?"

"Something tells me that this show is going to be our biggest ever," Ben said, ignoring their bickering.

"I can guarantee you right now that *my* entry is going to blow Isaac Ferrer away," Steph announced, sliding Abby a glance.

Oh, great. Abby covered her dismay by taking a big gulp of her beer, thinking she was going to have to switch to something stronger if she was going to have to come up with a worthy takeoff of this guy's work.

She could always beg off, claim to be too busy at work, but Abby couldn't bear to douse the excitement in Steph's eyes.

Besides, for an author who had single-handedly turned an Agatha Christie classic into an orgy, a cast comprised of hot naked characters was going to be a walk in the park.

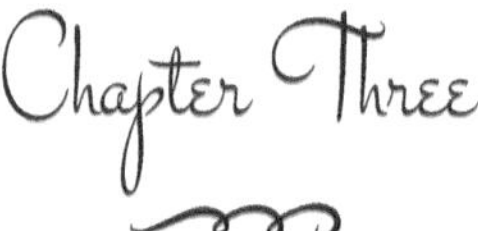

Chapter Three

Theoden Dryllis leaned against the glistening marble column behind him, stroking the long, smooth shaft with his strong archer's hand. "I maybe half-elf, Mistress Grey, but I assure you, I am all man."

Blech.

Abby backspaced over the paragraph she'd just typed and shoved the laptop aside. Time for a break—and the teapot had begun to whistle on the stove.

Abby got up from the kitchen table and fetched a mug from the cupboard. The words "Murphy's Irish Red" and the red-and-gold logo of the brewer were worn away in places. It had been Gramps's favorite, and even though it was just swag from a distributor and Gram had tried to sneak it into the trash a thousand times, the mug was one of Abby's prized possessions.

Still, as she sipped from the steaming mug, it was Gram's presence that filled up every corner of the room. The rest of the tidy, careworn bungalow held memories of both her grandparents, but the kitchen had been Gram's domain, and Abby had spent many happy hours here.

When Abby was in high school, she'd helped Gram perfect new dishes, like the apple dumplings and baked pub cheese dip for the bar. They were still crowd favorites—even though Gramps wasn't around anymore to swear that the recipes came from his mam back in the old country.

Abby had made a few updates to the house since she'd inherited it, replacing the worn-out plumbing and ripping up the carpet to expose the beautiful hardwood floors, but she hadn't touched the kitchen. It had barely changed since her grandparents bought the place. For years, there had been no money to remodel, and by the time they could afford it, Gram couldn't overcome her natural thriftiness. She'd been raised poor but resourceful, and she knew how to take care of things and make them last.

The original gas stove still worked perfectly, the pine cabinets with their scalloped trim were polished until they gleamed, and the old telephone nook—where Gram still used their landline long after most of the world had switched to mobile—now held a printer and client folders for Abby's freelance work. Other than a new set of café curtains to replace the threadbare ones Gram had washed and starched every few months, it still felt like Gram might walk in at any moment, take her apron from the hook, and get to work.

Abby and Steph had been living in a cramped two-bedroom apartment in the trendy Dogpatch neighborhood of San Francisco when Gramps died less than two years after Gram passed, and left Abby the house. Owen was more than happy to keep living above the bar that had been his portion of their inheritance, so Abby invited Steph to move in.

They shared the expense of upkeep on the house, but no longer having to worry about scraping together their exorbitant rent each month changed both of their lives. Steph was able to quit her cross-town, seventy-hour-a-week job at a giant publicity firm, and take a position with a nearby theater company housed in what had once been a dance hall. Only a few months later, she'd created enough connections and word-of-mouth interest to start her own business.

Abby was nowhere near that brave. She held tight to her unremarkable technical writing gig for a midsized software company headquartered in the Financial District, but at least now she could treat it like the boring 9-to-5 gig it was rather than living in constant fear of being laid off. Not having to worry about the sky-high price of housing in San Francisco meant she could take a breath and enjoy her time off, helping out at O'Reilly's Pub or working on her pieces for Ships every week.

Abby's favorite place to write was here in the kitchen where her grandmother's presence served as comfort and inspiration...though Gram would have a fit if she knew what Abby was currently writing.

Sorry, Gram.

Abby stared gloomily at the stack of Isaac Ferrer books Steph had lent her, heavy hardbacks with lurid foil covers hinting at the darkness within the pages. For the life of her, Abby couldn't imagine shelling out twenty-five bucks, much less waiting in line for hours as Ferrer's fans were wont to do whenever there was a new release.

Abby had tried her best, but after slogging through a third of *Crystal Cataclysm*, the first book in the series, she'd given up. The writing wasn't the problem: the narrative was competent; the prose was engaging, sometimes even lyrical.

But the story itself was so painfully bleak—brutal, even —that Abby's instinct was to turn away to keep the joy from being sucked out of her. Virgins sacrificed! Child kings ripped from their mothers' breasts! Why on earth did people subject themselves to this stuff?

Abby prided herself on reading all kinds of things— historical fiction, mysteries, biographies—but she was always happiest with a lighthearted romance. Everyday life was hard enough; when she curled up in Gramps' old recliner with the quilt Gram made her for her sixteenth birthday (the pattern was Irish Chain, obviously), she just wanted to leave her problems behind and enter a world where people found happiness and love triumphed.

This, in fact, was one of the reasons why Abby couldn't tear herself away from Ships. There was only so much a person could take of the self-importantly dense books featured on The City Bookmark's Staff Picks shelf.

Abby understood wanting to be taken seriously, and no one wanted to be taken seriously more than Vaughn, the most prolific staff contributor, who wore vintage tweed jackets and little gold-rimmed glasses and smoked French cigarettes moodily in the alley on his breaks. Abby had once been like Vaughn, back when she'd been working on her degree in English Literature and wrote poetry during the biology class that she had to take twice.

But if she read one more blurb on the cover of a book

claiming the author was One of the Most Important Voices in American Literature, she was going to scream. These books had no plots! The protagonists were thinly veiled extensions of the (all-too-frequently-white-old-and-male) author's failed aspirations!

At least these Ferrer books had a story—a dark, bloody, miserable story, but a story nonetheless.

And apparently people ate them up. The back cover of the most recent book boasted of over eight million copies sold, along with a list of awards the series had racked up, and fulsome praise from those Important Voices, who were probably tearing themselves apart with envy. Ben could barely keep the books in stock.

Abby flipped the cover of *Crystal Cataclysm* so she could study the inner flap of the dust jacket...again. The photo of the brooding author was already seared into her brain, and Abby would be lying if she denied that she found him attractive. Who wouldn't?

That thick, inky black hair...that rock-hard, sculpted jaw...the shadow of a beard and skin burnished as though he wrote under a Mediterranean sun and dove in the ocean for his dinner. The photo made it clear that Ferrer's obsidian eyes were windows into a tortured soul and those generous lips were incapable of forming a smile.

If it wasn't for this photo, Abby might have actually finished reading the book last night. Instead, she kept getting distracted by Ferrer's resemblance to one of his characters, the half-dark elf Theoden she'd decided write about, a battle-hardened mercenary with a rigid and consuming moral compass. Abby could almost imagine Isaac Ferrer in the shadows of the magical Mistress Grey's keep, transfixed by her arresting beauty.

Only when Abby envisioned Mistress Gray discovering she was being watched, it wasn't the wispy, blue-skinned woman sprung from Ferrer's pages whose heart raced or whose lip quivered...but her own.

Abby was gazing at the photo, lost in her fantasy, when the front door opened.

Startled, she dropped the book on the floor, mortified at being caught daydreaming about elves and witches, and attempted to nudge it under the table with her foot.

"What the hell, Abby?" Steph clomped into the kitchen in yellow platform sneakers, her eyes wide with indignation, the effect underscored by glittering purple false eyelashes. "That's a first edition!"

"I'm sorry," Abby said hastily. "I was, uh, caught up in the story and I didn't hear you come in." Not entirely a lie.

Steph set down her bag and slid into the chair across from Abby. "Does that mean the story is going well?"

"Afraid not." Abby sighed. There was no way to tiptoe around the truth. "These books just aren't my thing. And there are so *many* of them."

Six, in all, five in a stack that teetered next to the coffee maker, and one under the table.

"So why are you torturing yourself? It's just a silly fanfic competition. No one takes it seriously. Just pick a few characters at random and throw them together in a stable."

"I can't. We did a stable last week, remember?"

"Oh, yeah." Sometimes Abby wondered if Steph even paid any attention to the pieces she read. She had always thrived in the spotlight, which was one of the things that made their friendship work—Steph pushed Abby to overcome her introversion enough to venture out into the world, and Abby provided the peaceful, nurturing space for Steph to relax.

But the colorful, performative ebullience that helped Steph coax huge contributions from donors tended to take all the air from the room. It wasn't a problem at work, where Steph was expected to focus the attention on herself and her message, or even at Ships, where her presence was arguably just as key to their success as the entries themselves. But it did mean that Steph wasn't exactly fully engaged.

"How about if you put them in a dungeon?" she suggested. "Really, no one cares where the characters are as long as they get down and dirty."

Abby got up to make more tea so Steph wouldn't see her roll her eyes. Steph might be right, but to Abby, that kind of authorial laziness—when a Ships contestant didn't even read the book—ought to be disqualifying. She could always tell: they might get the characters' names right, but their motivation was all wrong, the chemistry nonexistent. It was just bad dialog and awkward sexual scenarios that were adolescent in their prurience and often anatomically impossible.

If Abby were a less generous person, she might even speculate that the entries reflected a lack of experience in such matters.

The image of brooding, scowling Isaac Ferrer flashed through Abby's mind. *No lack of experience there!*—she'd bet her salary on it.

"*I* care," she said. "I don't want to just phone it in.

Wasn't that the whole reason we started this? To do something better—wittier—than the usual fare?"

"Yeah, you're right. And you are way better than the usual fare." Steph gave her a grin that showed off the little gap between her front teeth. "In fact, we should have won first place last time. So knock yourself out. Only, at least give yourself a break and watch a few episodes of *Evernight* instead of forcing yourself to finish an eight-hundred-page book you hate."

"A TV show isn't a book," Abby said primly.

Steph laughed. "And fanfic isn't exactly highbrow literature. As good as you are, I doubt Michiko Kakutani is going to review you in the *Times* anytime soon."

Steph was right, of course. And Abby didn't mind. *Add us together, and we make one perfect woman*—wasn't that what they always said? Steph's outgoing nature and Abby's sensitivity. Steph's spontaneity and Abby's attention to detail. Steph's impulsive generosity and Abby's grace under fire. Abby provided structure that Steph badly needed, and Steph saved Abby from taking herself too seriously.

Still...for some reason, the comment stung.

Steph grabbed a seltzer from the fridge and headed up to her room, and Abby shut down her laptop and moved to the living room. Steph's arrival home from work signaled quitting time, which was a good thing since Abby often lost track of time when she was working. She picked up the remote and settled into the recliner, and—why not?—clicked around until she found the show.

There were two seasons of *Evernight* already, and a teaser

for the third. At the bottom of the screen was a bunch of bonus material, including an interview with the author.

The scowling, brooding, wickedly hot Isaac Ferrer.

Abby clicked.

The screen filled with a close-up of her half-dark elf with the piercing coal-black eyes. So it wasn't one of those posed, photoshopped, airbrushed author photos that could make a dowager writer of cozy mysteries look like a come-hither temptress with a quill pen.

And then Isaac Ferrer opened his mouth and started to speak—and Abby was a goner.

Chapter Four

eing nervous before Ships in the Night wasn't new to
Abby. When she read her first piece aloud, back
when it was just the three of them and a few friends,
she had to compete with the din of the who-do-you-think-
you-are voice in her head, the same inner critic that kept her
from finishing her novel.

When Steph took her place at the mic, Abby's nerves
receded but didn't vanish. No matter how well her work was
received, the cheers and applause never overcame her clammy
hands and pounding heart. Still, nothing could compete for
sheer terror of the early days of the Ships juggernaut, when
her nerves had given way to flat-out terror.

On a night when she'd worn a new sweater purchased for
the occasion, a soft brick-colored cardigan that comple-
mented her fair skin and strawberry blond curls, the tender
shoots of her hopeful courage were crushed when a guy in
skinny jeans snapped her picture from the front row. Abby
instantly lost her composure, stumbling over her words and

as he tapped away at his phone, knowing he was uploading the photo to some social media, tagging it so that the store's thousands of followers would see it.

The post was even worse than she feared, catching Abby with her mouth unflatteringly open and captioned "Moby Dick at #ShipsInTheNight & looks like the whale showed up to read."

Abby tried to convince herself that it didn't matter. She didn't know those people, and besides, anything that brought Ben more business was a good thing.

This became Abby's mantra—*you're doing this for Ben*—when he launched the podcast, and she doubled down on it when the live-streaming began. But it didn't take long for Abby to reach a tipping point. As the audience increased, so did the trolls in the comment section...and there were only so many times Abby could endure being called a "disgusting cow" or a "sad fatty who only writes smut because she can't get a man."

It was a chilly May Friday night when Ben greeted the crowd with the news that the #ShipsInTheNight hashtag was trending because of an influencer fan. Abby barely made it to the restroom before losing her dinner. She passed it off as a case of food poisoning, made her apologies, and slunk out the back, pale-faced and sweaty.

It was the last time Abby Reilly ever entered under her own name. Two weeks later, Stephanie Tran received her first standing ovation for her take on Ibsen's *A Doll's House,* "Nora Fulfills Her Contract."

Abby had been afraid people would wonder why Steph's voice had evolved so dramatically precisely when Abby departed. She needn't have worried. If anyone noticed, it was soon forgotten when Steph placed three times in a row, a veritable Ships in the Night sensation.

A year had passed since then, and Abby's chronic show-night jitters were a small price to pay for the luxury of writing whatever she liked while being able to hide in the shadows.

Things might have gone on that way indefinitely if Isaac Ferrer hadn't crashed the party.

At least no one was paying any attention to her. The store was no more packed than usual, owing to the fire code restrictions, but the mood inside The City Bookmark was electric, the audience buzzing with anticipation.

Abby didn't like it, not one bit.

She reached for Selwyn's spine and stroked it like a security blanket. *It's okay*, she tried to convince herself. *Lots of people get nervous around celebrities, and you're not here to see him anyway.*

Yeah, right! scoffed her inner critic, who all too often weighed in on matters outside of Abby's writing. *That's why you've watched every Isaac Ferrer video you could find online.*

A sudden hush fell over the crowd and everyone shifted to watch Ben greeting Isaac at the door, then burst into spontaneous applause while Ben showed him to the folding table that held what passed for refreshments at Ships in the Night. Abby's heart raced and her throat constricted as Isaac Ferrer walked past. She wouldn't have thought it possible, but the man looked even better in person.

Abby would never admit how many times she'd watched Isaac's interviews in the privacy of her bedroom, propped up on a pile of pillows under her blankets. She'd memorized the intensity of his obsidian eyes, that five-o'clock shadow on his burnished jaw, the wide shoulders that suggested a longshoreman's build under his cashmere sweaters. It was ridiculous, really. Why were his arms so muscular, if all he did was write? Weren't those good looks wasted on someone who lived in self-imposed exile save for the occasional book tour?

Though that was dangerous territory. Abby knew what it was like to be someone who didn't match people's expectations. People who knew her brother wanted Abby to be just as outgoing and funny. People who knew Stephanie thought Abby would be stylish and svelte. Then there was the marketing director whose emails took on an increasingly flirtatious tone until Abby was invited to meet with his team in person...and his stammered "I didn't recognize you" failed to conceal the distaste in his eyes.

(After that, Abby replaced her online avatar photo. She'd chosen it specifically because it made her look thinner, after reading somewhere that fat people were much less likely to land an interview. The new photo concealed nothing—better to lose out on an opportunity than to go through that kind of humiliation again.)

As thrilling as Isaac Ferrer was to look at, he was even better to listen to.

Considering that men had been allowed to be "leg guys" or "boob guys" for decades, Abby was surely entitled to this one private fetish. Maybe it was weird that a guy's voice was the thing that set her aquiver, but Abby didn't care. She would happily make love with Mr. Peanut if he sounded as gruff and sensual as Isaac Ferrer (though she didn't recall noticing so much as a bulge in his nubby yellow groin).

Abby knew better than to go down that rabbit hole, but she'd been up past midnight listening raptly to him discussing his books and which authors he'd invite to his perfect dinner party (Tolstoy, Ursula Le Guin, Iain Banks). She didn't even care that he recycled his material, that the discussion of his mentors and formative events never seemed to change. He was tight-lipped about his childhood in a working-class Cuban neighborhood in South Florida, and had little to say about his education at a small liberal-arts college somewhere in New England, giving the impression that the former had been difficult and the latter had stunted his creative development until he'd left to follow his muse.

Abby spent so much time watching and listening to Isaac online that little time remained once she started on her piece. She was left with no choice but to take Steph's advice—not about watching the TV show (no show had ever been better than a book in Abby's opinion, and it wasn't much of a book to start with) but about not worrying about characters' back-stories and just writing whatever came into her mind.

Which was how she ended up writing a blisteringly hot scene between Theoden and Mistress Grey...except in her mind it wasn't the dark elf and the blue-skinned temptress, but Isaac and her.

And *damn* if the words didn't flow.

Abby felt slightly sordid when she turned in the piece. The scenes she'd been inspired to write were downright filthy, much more so than her usual fare. Hell, the thing with the bewitched shackles had caused Steph to gasp before bursting into laughter. Abby had come very close to begging Steph to withdraw the entry, and the only thing keeping her in her seat now was the knowledge that no one would ever know who the true author had been.

Which, in truth, was yet another of Abby's qualms. It wasn't like she had to beg Steph to get up there and read every time—Steph loved the attention—but it still felt...inauthentic.

Ha! scoffed her inner critic. There was nothing authentic about any of this. No reading between the lines of the chosen books suggested the almost-never-credible pairings between characters; and, it was hard to believe that any of her competition had experienced the vigorous and imaginative couplings they so enthusiastically described. Nonetheless, every time Steph walked confidently up to the mic, Abby couldn't banish the feeling that she was throwing her best friend under the bus.

Ben seated Isaac next to the podium, giving Abby an unobstructed view. She paid no attention to Ben's intro and studied Isaac instead. He was dressed, as always, in black—structured T-shirt, linen trousers, Italian boots...and yet there was something different about him.

Isaac's in-person energy was entirely different to the controlled vibe he gave off in every video Abby had watched. It was almost as though he'd hit his head on the way over and woken up with a new identity. His body language was relaxed, and he grinned as Ben ribbed him about the TV series' success. When the audience laughed, Isaac laughed right along, and when Ben landed a zinger, Isaac lifted his palms with a "who, me?" expression that was both genuine and adorable.

But then Jane—as Ben predicted, she couldn't stay away

from Ships, especially given the presence of a celebrity—crept out in front of the podium waving her phone. "May I take a few photos?" she asked in a syrupy tone. "For the store's media accounts?"

Abby's irritation gave way to surprise at Isaac's reaction. Abruptly, all that relaxed good humor vanished as he rose to stand stiffly next to Ben, scowling with his hands jammed in his pockets. He was as immobile as a statue while Jane snapped away, and yet the instant she put the phone away, Isaac smiled at her and dropped back into his seat with a modest smile.

Interesting. Abby, who had grown up in the theater of her grandfather's pub, knew instantly what she'd just witnessed: a fellow chameleon transforming. The question was which version was the real one—and why someone like Isaac Ferrer, with all his fame and wealth, needed to pretend to be anything other than himself.

"First up this evening for your listening pleasure is Dominick Schwartz, a second-time entrant from Emeryville, with 'Jorrgan's Balls At the Dragon's Ball.'"

The crowd hooted as a young guy in a button-down and loosened tie bounded up to the podium. As the young man cleared his throat and began to read, it was safe to say that Abby had never been more riveted...even if her eyes weren't on the performance.

Chapter Five

"Theoden stalked across the drawing room, his gaze never leaving Mistress Grey's."

Steph was pitch-perfect tonight, her voice throaty and silken, her long-lashed gaze dipping only occasionally to her phone before returning to the rapt audience.

Abby took a covert look around. Clustered near the front were a handful of regular entrants who she and Steph had privately nicknamed "the Strivers." Most of them had placed at least once, and they had formed an alliance, *Survivor*-style, whose purpose seemed to be to intimidate the competition. Jane, naturally, was among them.

Then there were Steph's admirers—she attracted plenty, of all genders—and a few people (Marin County interlopers, Abby suspected) who seemed stunned into a stupor by her outfit: an ecru lace slip dress topped by a shiny jacket silk-screened with the entire Beverly Hills 90210 cast and long, dangling feather earrings.

Then there was Isaac, leaning forward in his chair, riveted.

"She found herself transfixed—nay, bewitched—unable to move, barely able to breathe. Mistress Gray half expected an act of sorcery from the dark elf, perhaps vanishing into a cloud of smoke and reappearing in another corner of the room."

A snort came from one of the Strivers, but Steph didn't bat an eye. "For the first time, she was in the presence of one even more entrancing than she, a roiling storm of sensual need raging in his eyes—and Mistress Gray didn't know if she should flee, fight..."—long pause for Steph to scan the audience, letting her gaze linger on the Strivers until they started to squirm—"or submit."

Abby was as breathless as Mistress Gray, her fingernails digging into her palms. But why? She knew exactly what happened next—she'd written the damn thing. And her biggest fear, that Isaac Ferrer would be just as dismissive and caustic as his author photo would lead one to believe, had faded the first time he smiled.

In fact, the longer she watched the handsome author from her safe little corner, the more he resembled a regular guy. An extremely hot one, to be sure, but down-to-earth and possessing a sense of humor, especially where his own work was concerned. He'd laughed and cheered even the most middling attempts, and appeared amused, even charmed by the liberties the entrants had taken with his prose.

It was impossible to reconcile this good-natured guy with the dark, violent, disturbing worlds he created in his books.

But even that added to Isaac's appeal, somehow. Maybe because the only thing hotter than a man of mystery was a man of mystery who could take a joke.

In fact, the contradiction sent a little shiver down Abby's spine, directly to the happy place that had been starved of attention for too long.

Was it Abby's imagination, or was Isaac's smile just a bit broader as he watched Steph perform? The solar flare of happiness expanded into another sensation, one that made Abby sit up a little straighter. *Pride*, that's what that was, because this famous author seemed to be genuinely enjoying something that she'd written—and not in the too-frequent ironic, mocking way that Ships entries were often received.

"Mistress Gray stumbled backward into her alchemy table, catching herself with both hands before she fell. She gripped the edge of the cool marble with trembling fingers. 'Every time I see you, Theoden, you wear a scowl upon your face. A lady might begin to wonder if her company displeased you.'

"'Far from it, Mistress,' Theoden growled. Oh, that deep, melodious elfin timbre, which could stir the senses of anyone who came near. 'Some nights, when I find myself alone in the woods, the thought of your...company is the only thing that brings me pleasure.'"

Abby was horrified to feel her cheeks flushed with heat. *Oh God—not now*, not in front of all these people. A Reilly blush was stunning to behold, bright red like a warning flare.

No one is paying any attention to you, she reminded herself as she tried to wedge even further into the corner. It was true: Every eye in the room was fixed on Steph, even

Jane's. But Abby knew what was coming next, and she for damn sure wasn't about to look at Isaac as Steph read the rest of the scene.

What have I done, Selwyn?

"Mistress Gray perched on the edge of the table, delicately sweeping her skirts to expose a bit of ankle, and drew her shoulders back to give Theoden the best possible view of her bosom swelling over the constricting bodice of her dress. 'Then why do you look as if you've just tasted the bitter winterbane root?'

"'Perhaps some was slipped into my drink at the revels,' Theoden rumbled, taking a step closer and not even bothering to pretend he wasn't staring at her nipples, hard as rubies under the silk.

"'Perhaps,' Mistress Gray agreed in her most sultry tone, knowing it had the power to harden the steel of Theoden's sword. 'If so, there's only one antidote.'

"'The nectar of the sweetest fruit in the land.' Theoden's eyes were bright and flinty and boring into her own. 'Is such a potion among your stores?'

"It was, of course, impossible to win a staring contest with an elf, so Mistress Gray let her eyelashes flutter as she eased her legs apart, tugging her skirts slowly up to expose her shapely shins. 'No, but I have something far sweeter for you.'"

The crowd erupted in a roar of approval, but all Abby felt was a desire for the floor to open and swallow her up. What was she thinking, writing such a steamy scene when she knew full well that Hottie McHottie-Pants was going to be in the audience?

She couldn't look. Could she? But Abby's need to know was even stronger than her mortification...

Isaac was laughing along with everyone else.

In fact, he was laughing harder than everyone else, wiping at his eyes with the heel of his hand and shaking his head.

He probably thinks it's ridiculous, Abby suggested to Selwyn, whose lack of response forced her to reconsider. Men didn't fake a laugh like that, not in her experience, and as Abby watched him carefully while Steph concluded the reading, Isaac looked like he was having the time of his life.

Steph finished with an exaggerated curtsy to applause that threatened to bring down the house, and people were still clapping when Ben tried to introduce the next contestant. He had to tap the mic to settle everyone down enough to get through the final two entries.

Abby barely paid attention, her focus split between Isaac and the strange combination of mortification and exhilaration swirling inside her. When Isaac—still grinning and loose-limbed like he felt perfectly at home—loped onstage to announce the winners, he had to wait through a burst of applause that was almost as enthusiastic as the one Steph received.

"Third place goes to Terrence Beale," he said—aka Sleepy, who was suddenly wide awake. "Nice work with the demi-goblins, by the way. Second place to Barbara Chen, with a shout-out to your use of alliteration—'curiously captivating cobalt cleavage,' I think it was?"

Isaac didn't drag it out like Ben did, playing the moment for drama, and his praise seemed genuine. Abby had suspected that no one stood a chance against Jane, who'd outdone herself this week with an Anais Nin–style reflection on the inner versus outer worlds...of a Sky Warrior in heat. Still, she felt disappointed that Steph had been passed over, especially since Isaac had seemed to enjoy her reading so much.

It had been a long shot. Ben had received a record number of entries this time, including one from an Oakland poet of some renown who'd never deigned to attend before. Ships in the Night was moving up in the literary world, it seemed.

"And first place goes to Stephanie Tran, not least for her beautiful prose. Really remarkable."

What?

Abby forgot not to gape, her eyes wide with shock as Steph bounced out of her seat, twirling to make her skirts swirl around her hips before taking Isaac's hand and giving him a coquettish kiss on the cheek.

They'd won. She and Steph had actually won Isaac Ferrer's Ships in the Night.

Abby tried to dial back her dopey, delighted grin, but it was impossible. And really, why shouldn't she give herself over to this one magical moment of pure joy? True, she couldn't have done it without Steph, but just for tonight Abby was determined to ignore the inner critic who even now was trying to suggest that the win had more to do with Steph's short skirt than the entry itself.

Ben handed Isaac the trophy, and he pretended to almost drop it—Captain Hook was surprisingly heavy—before presenting it to Steph.

"Let it be known," he said, not bothering with the mic

since the audience quieted down at his commanding, deep voice, "that on this twentieth day of February, the title of Ships in the Night champion is conferred upon...Miss? Mrs.? Ms.? Madame?"

Steph giggled, cradling the trophy in her arms, as Abby's critic guffawed. *He's not even pretending he's not flirting with her.*

"Miss is just fine," Steph said. "I'm single."

"Miss Tran, then." Isaac put his arm around Steph, but assumed his glowering alter-ego before people started snapping photos.

We still won, Abby told Selwyn, though the victory had shrunk a little.

Ben joined the others up front and thanked the audience for coming, noting that Isaac had signed the stack of hardbacks at the register. As the audience started queuing up, Steph grabbed the microphone to make herself heard.

"Abby! Come over here and meet Isaac!"

Chapter Six

I t was the worst thing Steph could have done, and she knew it—or should have, anyway, since Abby's discomfort with the spotlight was the reason that Steph was up there in the first place.

Still, blaming Steph felt like a cop-out, and Abby swallowed down her fear as she made her way to the front with a forced smile.

Ben threw an arm around her shoulders. "Isaac, this is Abby Reilly, one of the founders of Ships in the Night and also a good friend."

"And my roommate!" Steph added brightly. She was standing very close to Isaac.

Abby had lost the power of speech so she just nodded and smiled, her mouth feeling stretched and unnatural.

"Great to meet you!" Isaac seized her hand and gave it a squeeze.

Oh, my...that was certainly a large...warm hand. Abby's palm tingled when he let go.

The three of them returned to their lively, intelligent conversation, while Abby stood silent. As the minutes ticked by, Steph began shooting her pointed looks—*say something* —and Abby prayed for an earthquake. Just a small one, a floor rattler that didn't do any damage. (Or if it reduced Bespoke Bitters next door—seriously, an entire shop devoted to mixers—to rubble, that would be okay too.) Anything, really, to end the torture of standing close enough to Isaac Ferrer to catch his woodsy, limey scent while her face was locked in a frozen rictus.

It wasn't the first time Abby had met a famous person, but she had definitely established a pattern. There was the time she asked a stranger in an elevator what floor she was on, only to realize it was a famous actress—and was so flummoxed that she hit the wrong button, and then another wrong button trying to fix the mistake. The actress had glowered at her until they reached her floor.

And that time when a hugely popular chef grabbed Abby's suitcase off the carousel by mistake, and Abby chased him out of the airport, tongue-tied, until he finally turned around and asked how he could help her in a tone that made it clear he thought she was a stalker.

Isaac was probably wondering the same thing. Damn it, all Abby had to do was make some harmless comment, or even agree with something one of them said, or—

"So, what's up next?" Isaac asked.

Steph didn't miss a beat. "O'Reilly's! We always do a post-show wrap-up there."

"Great little bar," Ben added generously. "Abby's family owns it, in fact."

All three of them looked at her, and Abby swallowed. "Well...technically my brother Owen owns it, but it's still our family name outside...sort of..."

Oh God. Why did Steph have to invite Isaac? There was no way that Abby could go with them, and the wrap-up was her favorite part of the night, the three of them revisiting the funniest moments and making plans for the next event. Also, if Owen caught her behaving this way, all flustered and tongue-tied, there would be no end to the shit he would give her. Especially if he figured out that Isaac was the reason.

"Great!" Steph said. "Let's get Owen to mix up a pitcher of Sex On The Bogs."

"What's that?" Isaac asked.

"Secret family recipe," Steph quipped. "Drink two and you start seeing faeries."

"Intriguing. Here, let me carry that stupendous trophy," he said gallantly, tucking it under one arm. "Lead the way."

"Um, I...can't," Abby squeaked. "I think I'm getting a headache." She gave her temples a vigorous rub for authenticity.

Steph looked crestfallen. "Abby, you have to! You know Owen won't give us the family discount unless you're there. He's such an asshole."

That wasn't the real reason, Abby knew (although it was true, Owen being as much of a skinflint as Gramps). Steph wanted her there because she needed a wingwoman, not the third wheel that Ben would be on his own.

"Tonight's on me," Isaac said firmly, "in appreciation for the wonderful time I had. And I'd love it if you would join us for even a little while, Abby."

He offered her his arm.

Abby stared at it a moment too long, trying to process the ecstasy of hearing that voice say her name. Panic threatened to overtake her as she studied the fine black knit stretching over Isaac's bicep.

Tentatively, Abby slipped her hand under his elbow. *Oh! Wow!* The sweater was soft, but the arm underneath was taut and warm, and when Isaac gave her a reassuring smile, she floated along beside him out the door and down the street, certain her feet had left the ground.

Steph kept up a steady flow of chatter, saving Abby from having to make conversation as they walked down the street. The bar was already packed with Friday night revelers, but their usual table had a Reserved sign scrawled in Owen's blocky handwriting and Abby felt a rush of affection for her brother.

Maybe one of his employees had called in sick, she thought hopefully, and she would have to go help behind the bar...but no, Owen gave them a cheerful wave while Gwen carried a tray of empty glasses and Dmitri served a trio of heavily made-up interns at the end of the bar.

There were only three chairs at the table, suggesting that Owen hoped that Jane's absence was permanent.

"I can stand," Abby said hastily, adding "I *want* to stand," before anyone got any chivalrous ideas. Because if she sat down, the construction of the sticky wooden chairs Gramps had purchased in the early eighties was such that her tummy would push out in the least flattering way possible, something she had never much minded when it was just her and her friends.

But Abby's home away from home had suffered a breach in the form of a literary Adonis in whose presence Abby was reduced to jelly. And if four people tried to crowd around the small table, her arms and thighs would inevitably squish up against those on either side, which again would be fine if it was Steph and Ben—but even now Isaac was carrying a chair high above the crowd, his sweater pulling up above his jeans to reveal an inch of smooth skin dusted with a hint of dark-brown hair.

Abby swallowed as he set the chair down and gestured to it with a smile. "Indulge me," he said. "Please? We haven't had a chance to have a conversation yet."

Abby glanced at Ben and Steph, who were no help at all, smirking on the other side of the table as if they were enjoying her torment.

"Thank you," she said stiffly.

She had barely sat down when Owen appeared, dressed in a T-shirt featuring a faded green Gumby stretched a little too tight over his belly, camo board shorts and an ancient pair of Converse sneakers. It was so unfair—Abby was pretty certain Owen dressed in the dark and hadn't updated his wardrobe in a decade, but no one ever judged him for what he had on or how it fit.

"There are my lovely dossers!" Owen said cheerfully. "All done with yer blarney and ready to get fluttered, I imagine."

Steph rolled her eyes. "Sometimes I don't think you know what you're saying."

"You might be right," Owen said good-naturedly. "But admit it, you love the way I say it." He offered his hand to

Isaac. "Owen Reilly. Sorry my sister's too starstruck to introduce us."

"Isaac Ferrer."

"So I gathered. These three wouldn't shut up about you all week."

Isaac looked slightly abashed. "Well, it's a pleasure to meet you, and I'd be obliged if you'll open a tab."

Owen raised his eyebrows and whistled at the matte black credit card Isaac handed over. "Don't think I've ever seen one of these before. How rich do you have to be to get one? *Ow!*"

"Owen!" Steph scolded after Abby kicked his shin. "Don't be crass!"

"It's not crass to admire another gentleman's good fortune," Owen protested. "And under the circumstances, I wouldn't think of insulting you by offering the family discount."

Isaac laughed. "Of course not. I hear you make a drink called Sex on the Bogs. Would you mind bringing us a round?"

"I'd love nothing more!" Owen said, giving Isaac a conspiratorial slap on the back. "I'll even use decent gin."

"*Owen,*" Abby muttered through clenched teeth. She couldn't really blame her brother. He was only repeating the schtick that had kept the pitchers of green beer flowing for over five decades. But there was only so much family humiliation a woman could take. "If you don't go away right now, I will tell everyone in this bar what you dressed up as for Halloween in fourth grade."

"Right." Owen backed away, chastened. "I'll be back with those Bogs in a bit."

"Sorry about that," Abby mumbled. "My brother can be a little much sometimes."

Isaac seemed confused. "Did I notice...an Irish accent?"

Steph snorted. "Please. Owen sounds like the Lucky Charms leprechaun."

"Who?" Ben asked.

"From the TV commercial?" Steph said, exasperated. "You know, the cereal?"

Ben reddened slightly. "My parents didn't let us watch TV growing up," he explained to Isaac.

"Ben comes from a family of huge book nerds," Steph teased. "Anyway, the thing you have to understand about O'Reilly's is that it's all a facade. It's not even their real name."

"It's true," Abby reluctantly admitted when all eyes turned to her. "This whole place is a sham. When our grandparents bought the place in the seventies, it was just a dusty corner bar. Gramps changed the name to Reilly's, but it wasn't bringing in much money at first. So he decided to turn it into an old-fashioned Irish pub. Reilly's became O'Reilly's and it just kind of snowballed from there."

"Grandpa Fergus was the one who started the fake-accent thing," Steph chimed in, having heard the story a thousand times.

"They bought some Guinness signs, slapped some shamrocks on the walls and windows, and damn if business didn't pick up," Ben continued. "The more over the top it got, the more people loved it."

"And no one minded that it was all fake?" Isaac asked.

"It's not *all* fake," Abby said. "We are Irish...mostly. At least Gram was—she came here as a child. Gramps was from Cleveland and was half Italian."

"With a name like Fergus?"

"Well, he was born Fred Reilly," Abby said. "'Fergus' was part of the rebranding.

"Oh man, remember your grandmother's Irish stew?" Ben sighed dreamily. "Damn, I miss that stuff."

Abby did too. The memory of a steaming bowl with a slab of soda bread fresh out of the oven took right back to her childhood, to the chilly San Francisco summers when Ben was visiting from Boston and tagging along for dinner at their grandparents'. Only a year older than Owen and Abby, the three became inseparable for the season, reading in the bookstore, playing in the apartment above the bar where the twins lived with their mom, doing odd jobs for the Grant Avenue merchants for pocket money.

She was so lost in the memory that she didn't notice Isaac's soft gaze focused on her face until he spoke. "It sounds wonderful."

Abby instantly came to her senses and pushed back her chair. She thought she could handle this like a normal person, but she couldn't. "Those drinks are taking too long," she stammered. "I better go see what's keeping them."

"Abby—" Steph looked alarmed.

"It's cool." Abby forced a smile that felt like a grimace. "Owen's probably just slammed. Be right back."

She took off before anyone else could try to talk her out of it—but not fast enough to miss Steph's next words.

"Don't take it personally. Abby's just really shy, especially around new people."

God in heaven, just strike me dead now.

Chapter Seven

Owen seized a paring knife when Abby pushed behind the bar and stabbed at the air in her direction. "If you ever tell anyone about the Halloween costume—"

"Then I guess you better behave."

Really, Owen's gullibility was a beautiful thing.

In 1999, when the Reilly twins were in kindergarten, Gramps had taken them to see *Passport to Paris* one night when their mom was working late. The movie featured twelve-year-old twins Mary-Kate and Ashley Olsen and a very thin plot involving the girls visiting their grandfather in France.

Abby had fallen asleep during the previews, but five-year-old Owen had been so besotted with the film that he insisted that all three of them reenact it for Halloween, and Gram had stayed up late sewing matching gingham sundresses with coordinating head kerchiefs (which were apparently a thing back then). Gramps found heart-shaped sunglasses with pink lenses to complete their outfits and even borrowed a tux to play their ambassador grandfather, and it was safe to say that the Reillys were the hit of the neighborhood that year.

A few years later, Owen, already submerged deep into toxic masculinity, had destroyed every photo that Gram had taken—except for one, which Abby kept in a shoebox in the back of the closet, and had used to keep her brother in line for years.

"What's gotten into you, anyway?" Owen demanded. "He seems like a nice guy, Abs, even if he is a writer."

"He *is* a nice guy. Which is why I was hoping you could at least try to make a good impression for once."

Owen snorted. "I make a *great* impression. Mom thinks I should run for office because I'm so *poised*, whatever that means. Oh, she wants to know if you're screening her calls."

"Of course I am!" Just like the rest of the family, Peggy Reilly had been heavy her whole life, but had never made peace with the reality of her size. Every time they spoke, her mother had some new fad diet or weight loss advice to pass along—but only to Abby, never Owen.

At least Owen had the self-awareness to recognize it. "I know, I know—just passing along the message. She's still doing that stupid sap cleanse, so I'd give her a week or two before you call her back. Hey, if you're going to hide back here, can you at least do the limes?"

Abby's zesting skills were uncontested, so she took the knife and set to work. "Do I get a cut of tonight's tips?"

"Not a chance. How about an apology for embarrassing me in front of your crush instead?"

"*What?* No. I do not have a crush on Isaac Ferrer."

"Abby has the hots for Isaac Ferrer?" Dex piped up from his stool at the end of the bar, and Abby groaned. Of course her brother's best friend would be here tonight just to make everything all that much more awkward. "Is that him? The guy in the turtleneck?"

"It's a mock-neck!" she hissed. "And it's cashmere!"

Dex smirked and raised his beer bottle in her direction. "Whatever floats your boat. Love is love, am I right?"

"Not that you would know," Abby said, kicking herself for taking Dex's bait. "Besides, I don't need your approval because I don't have the hots for him."

"Yeah, you do," Owen insisted as he poured a variety of alcohol into the shaker. "I know you, Abby. You're acting all nervous. And the last time you offered to help me back here was the night Steph brought that English guy you were drooling over."

"He was Scottish," Abby mumbled, powerless in the face of this double assault of bro boundary-crossing, "and I wasn't drooling over him."

"Yeah, you were," Dex said.

"Stay out of this."

"The point," Owen said patiently, "is that you have a tell, Abs. Whenever you fancy a fella, you do everything you can to put distance between you and him."

Abby felt the pink heat rising in her face again. "What I'd really like is to put some distance between me and this conversation right now."

"It's true," Dex said matter-of-factly.

"Don't you have anything better to do, Dex? There's a bunch of Australian tourists over there who'd probably love to know where they can get a super awesome tattoo like yours."

Dex's face fell. The tattoo on his forearm, an ill-considered and not-very-well-executed mermaid he'd gotten on a bachelor party weekend in Cabo, was a sore spot. "Low blow, Abs."

"Then maybe you'll think twice before you start giving me shit next time."

"We're just looking out for you," Dex said, putting on his wounded look, the one that was like catnip for girls on the lookout for a man they could fix.

"We're family," Owen added. "We're supposed to give you shit."

It was a trump card that Owen never got tired of playing. As for Dex, he might not technically be related to Abby, but he was close enough, since he'd been hanging around their house for as far back as she could remember.

"Can you just concentrate on the drinks, please?"

"Genius takes time," Owen said, sprinkling a few flakes of red pepper into the shaker. "So what's your move with this guy? How are you going to get him home tonight?"

"Owen, please stop. I'm not going home with anyone. Especially not Isaac Ferrer."

"Not with that attitude you're not," Dex said.

"Dex—"

"What my friend here is trying to say is that you've got to think positive, or you'll never make it into a guy's pants," Owen said. "There's an old Gretzky quote about missing one hundred percent of the shots you don't take—"

"The Great One!" Dex brightened. "Dude spoke the truth, Abs. Owen's right—you've got to at least try."

"No. I really don't." Abby shoved the cutting board over to Owen and turned on the tap to wash her hands.

"Give me one good reason why not," Dex said stubbornly.

Abby rubbed at her forehead, the headache she had faked earlier settling in as punishment for engaging with these two. She didn't have the energy to keep up the verbal sparring. "Listen, I don't expect you guys to understand. But things are different for men and women."

"You worry too much," Dex said. "Guys aren't that complicated. You have to know that—I've seen you reel in plenty of guys."

Abby groaned. One more comment like that and this night would surely go down in the books as the most humiliating of her life. It didn't matter that Dex had a point. Despite the world's love of publicly fat-shaming women, Abby had never had trouble catching a D when she really wanted to.

But this was different. *Isaac* was different. So far out of her league that it wasn't even worth considering. Besides, even if by some miracle she had a chance with him, she wasn't looking for a quick hookup. Unlike Dex and her brother, she wanted more than a quick shag and a pizza from a relationship.

What she'd really meant was that things were different for *fat* men and *fat* women.

Though both big guys, Owen and Dex had no problem getting girls—in fact, the thing they struggled with most was disentangling themselves from the ones who wanted to get serious, since they apparently planned to live above the bar in bachelor bliss for the rest of their lives. Abby, on the other hand, emerged from most one-night stands without so much as a text to say goodbye.

"Dex is right," Owen said, taking her silence for doubt. "Most times we'll take whatever is in front of us. I mean, take this nasty bar mix that's been sitting in the storeroom for two years—if it's all there is, guys will eat it."

"Let me get this straight," Abby said. "In this scenario, I'm the stale bar mix?"

"It's not like that, dude!" As if to prove his point, Dex grabbed a handful and shoved it in his mouth. "Mmmm! Seriously, Abs, I know guys can be jerks, but when it comes to seduction, we don't care all that much about things like high heels or a pretty face. We're not picky."

"Hang on. Did you just call my sister ugly?"

Abby and Dex both turned to look at Owen, startled by his tone. The only time Owen forgot his Irish accent in the bar was when he was well and truly pissed.

"No way," Dex said quickly. "I just meant—"

"You know what? I'm good," Abby said before either of them could accidentally insult her or each other again. "But seriously, you can drop it because I'm not seducing anyone."

"Who is Abby trying to seduce?"

Great—now Gwen had overheard. If she picked up on the thread it would be all over the bar.

"No one," Abby said a little too forcefully. "Here, I'll take those empties."

"The guy sitting next to Steph," Owen said, tilting his head toward their table.

"The dark-haired one, not the prissy one," Dex clarified. "Or the less prissy one, anyway."

"Holy shit—" Gwen's eyes widened. "Is that Isaac Ferrer?"

Abby winced as the people around her turned to look.

"Don't get too excited, Gwen," Dex said. "Abby already called dibs."

Oh God. Abby had to get out of there fast, before things spiraled out of control. "Shut it down, Dex, I mean it. Dibs is for the last beer in the fridge, not people. And no one is seducing anyone."

"Are you sure?" Gwen said. "Because if I were you I would totally—"

"Damn sure." Abby cut her off before she could get too far along that thought. Gwen had broad tastes among both men and women, and with her wild corkscrew curls and dancer's body, she rarely missed her mark.

Abby grabbed the tray of cloudy yellowish drinks and held it high above her head to save it from jostling, a skill she and Owen had both perfected long before they'd turned twenty-one. "Now listen up, all of you, because I'm giving you fair warning. If any of you come within ten feet of the table, I'll break your damn legs. Got it?"

Three solemn nods.

But as Abby wangled her way into the crowd, Gwen's voice trailed after her.

"Yeah, she's totally got the hots for him."

Chapter Eight

Abby's heart sank as she reached the table. Four tall, lanky girls who had to be on a basketball team had taken over the neighboring table, long legs sprawled everywhere, leaving Abby no way to avoid brushing against Isaac. Her hip bumped against his arm, and she was painfully aware that her breasts were only inches from his face when she reached across the table to set down the others' drinks.

"Be right back," she muttered, her face on fire. She took several deep breaths as she carried the empty tray to the bar cart, and when she returned, executed a tortured limbo-like move to slide into her seat so as to avoid sending Sex on the Bogs into her friends' laps.

Isaac gave her a warm smile and leaned in conspiratorially. "Steph won't tell me what's in those drinks. I think she's trying to get me drunk."

Abby almost snorted the dainty sip she'd been in the

process of taking. "She doesn't know," she said, furiously dabbing at her face with a bar napkin. "*I* don't even know. It's Owen's secret recipe. But I'd definitely stop at one if I were you."

"Commander Sphere was the one who double-crossed the Efflugian spy, right?" Steph asked loudly, tugging on Isaac's sleeve. "I've got five bucks riding on this."

"It wasn't Sphere, it was her concubine. In *Dragon's Solace*," Ben said smugly. "Come on, Steph, I own a bookstore. I mean, I'm happy to take your money, but you're punching above your weight."

Ben and Steph turned to Isaac for the final word.

"Sorry, but that was three books ago," Isaac said apologetically. "I don't remember. I'd have to check the bible."

"The...what?" Steph asked.

"Sorry, that's the name of the document writers create to keep track of all the details of a series," Isaac explained. "There are too many pieces to keep track of. If I didn't write it all down somewhere, I'd get murdered in the reviews for putting horns on a Water Calmer or something."

"Never," Steph gasped. "I can't imagine anyone giving you anything but glowing reviews."

"You don't have to imagine. Just check out any online bookseller," Isaac said good-naturedly. "There are plenty of folks who think my books are a steaming pile of crap."

"The curse of the Internet age," Ben said with feeling.

"Honestly, it's fine. I know I'm not everyone's taste. I just write the books that make me happy, meet my deadlines, show up where the marketing team sends me, and stay away from controversy. You know the drill."

There was silence as everyone tried to absorb this. Ben looked like he was trying to fit Isaac into a slot labeled Best-Selling Author; Steph had her chin in her hands and heart-eyes. But Abby was suspicious—was she really supposed to believe that the man Booklist had called "the bard of this generation's cultural apocalypse" didn't obsess about how he was being received?

"Anyway," Isaac said, tossing a pretzel into his mouth, "enough work talk. Does this neighborhood have a name? I thought this was North Beach, but my driver said it's Russian Hill."

"It's confusing," Steph said. "I blame the realtors. Every time they slap a new name on a few square blocks, they add a hundred thousand dollars to the listing price. Everyone always called this North Beach but now they split it up. You've got Telegraph Hill, North Waterfront—hell, Abby's house is right on the edge between Pac Heights and Cow Hollow. Just the other day I heard someone call it Presidio East."

The astronomical cost of real estate was an evergreen topic in San Francisco, and as Ben and Steph warmed to the subject, trying to outdo each other with outrageous examples of gentrification, Abby eased out of the conversation. She was happy to be free of the spotlight of Isaac's attention, and it had the added benefit of giving her an opportunity to watch him undetected.

Abby was a world-class wallflower. In fact, she'd always thought it silly that the word was considered an insult, since the skill was so handy. How better to study people, to discern their motivations and character, the quirky details that made them different from every other human on the planet, than to fade into the background and become invisible?

And Abby had been a student of human nature since way back. Once, when the twins were in third grade, their teacher sent a note home suggesting that that their mother might consider taking Abby to a counselor to deal with her "shyness problem" and to "help her bloom" as Owen already had. While their mother wrung her hands over the situation, Abby's Gram took action.

The next day, Gram walked Abby into the classroom clutching the teacher's crumpled note. It was the only time Abby had seen her gram's fiery Irish temper on full display.

Brigid Reilly informed the teacher in her genuine County Sligo accent that Abby was just fine exactly the way she was. That where she came from, modesty and reserve were considered virtues, and did she have any idea how many books Abby had read? In fact, Abby probably ought to be teaching the class, and if this was what passed for an education in their district, there was a city councilman who just might be getting a call from blah blah blah, until the teacher was falling all over herself apologizing and promising to find books advanced enough for Abby's obviously superior intellect.

There was another advantage to fading into the background...it made it a lot easier to sneak out without calling attention to oneself. Though it was certainly pleasant to gaze upon Isaac in profile, feasting her eyes on his granite-like jaw with that sexy stubble and the glossy black hair that curled against his neck, the tiny lines that appeared at the corners of his dark, soulful eyes every time he laughed—it was best to get out before anyone started teasing her again.

And yet, the human chronicler in Abby couldn't resist lingering. She was fascinated by the juxtaposition of this affable, laid-back Isaac with the one the world knew, the one she'd watched in online videos, who glowered from the back cover of those eight million books.

In Abby's experience, few people could pull off maintaining conflicting identities. And as a Reilly, she should know. Her family was more successful than most at keeping up the illusion. And even though Abby refused to put on the "O'Reilly" brogue when in the pub, she was hardly living what could be described as an authentic life. She still switched back and forth between plenty of masks: the competent, no-nonsense professional who turned in her work early coexisted with the fun-loving, mischievous person who came to life with her friends, and both of those selves gave cover to the one Abby did her best to hide from the world, the one plagued by insecurities and shame.

Unlike Isaac, who appeared perfectly at ease in both his personas.

"...did you?—Abby?"

Too late, Abby realized that Steph had been talking to her, and now all three of them were watching her expectantly. She'd been so caught up in the conundrum that was Isaac Ferrer that she hadn't been paying attention to the conversation.

"Uh, sorry," she stammered. "I was lost in thought."

"We were just saying that we hadn't realized that Isaac

lived in San Francisco until he showed up in the store last week," Ben said. "Your press kit still says you're in New York."

Isaac grimaced. "Between us, I was never really in New York full-time. It's not my speed. For the last six months, one of my nieces and her friends have been living in my apartment there—they're just starting out as social workers and the pay is peanuts—while I crashed with my sister back in Florida."

"So how long have you been here?" Steph asked.

Isaac looked at his watch—a surprisingly modest, battered old Timex. "Two months, four days and about five hours."

"Wow! And you were in Florida before that?"

"Yeah, just outside Miami. Most of my family's there."

A surprised laugh burbled out of Abby, and everyone turned to look at her, as if they'd almost forgotten that she was there. "South Florida and San Francisco," she explained. "I can't imagine two places that have less in common with each other. It must have been quite the culture shock."

"It was," Isaac said. "It is. But in a good way. I mean, I did my research, and I've been here for a few events in the past. It's not like I picked this city at random. But living here? It's a whole different story. I've spent most of the time just walking around, taking it all in. I've barely started to unpack. There's too much to see."

"New York's a big city," Abby pointed out. "There's a lot to see there, too."

"Sure," Isaac said. "And there are parts of it I love. I'd kill for an onion bialy, and it never gets old, taking my nieces and nephews to the public transit museum and the Long Island Ferry. But San Francisco's different." He paused to think, his eyes going unfocused, and when he didn't say anything for a while Ben and Steph started talking about something else.

But Abby knew that look. When the images in your mind are more real than what is in front of you. When a story blossoms from the smallest detail. It was the engine behind her best writing days, the ones when she triumphed over her fears and made steady progress on her novel.

I see you, Isaac Ferrer, she thought with a wonderful little shiver—and then she realized how ridiculous she was being, in danger of turning into just another excitable fangirl.

"This city—she's a chameleon," Isaac said suddenly, looking directly into her eyes. "Early in the morning, she sends fog up from the piers and wraps it around everyone on their way to work, shopkeepers sweeping the streets, guys making deliveries. She blurs the skyline and muffles the sound of traffic and gives you cover as you're waking up to your day. She's always there around you, but never crowding you. Never pressing down on you, like New York does sometimes. You can breathe here—the bay, I don't even know how to describe that smell. It's different from the Atlantic, you know. And then when the sun sets, she lights up like a woman in love, like she can't believe the sheer buoyant gorgeousness is really her, but she also can't wait to show it off." Isaac paused, suddenly bashful. "Sorry. I'm not sure that last one worked," he admitted.

Abby couldn't believe what she was hearing—it was exactly how she felt about her city, only she'd never had words like these to describe it. Maybe it took a newcomer's perspective—a newcomer with a gift for language.

"No, it's beautiful," she assured him. The description reminded her of the most lyrical passages in Isaac's books, where it almost seemed like he'd forgotten himself in the sheer joy of painting with words. Of course, those were the same passages that readers occasionally complained were boring. Frankly, Abby was surprised that no one had edited them out.

But maybe that was what fame got you. After all, what editor was going to tell the publisher's biggest cash cow he was wrong?

"I mean, I get what you're saying," Abby quickly amended, embarrassed by her earnestness. "But doesn't fame get in the way of everyday life? Like—I don't know, enjoying a walk out on the piers? I could only imagine how hard it would be for someone as—" Abby bit her tongue before the word "hot" slipped out. "—well-known as you to go anywhere incognito."

"You'd think so, right?" Isaac asked without a trace of self-consciousness. "But here's the thing. Until tonight, anyway, Isaac Ferrer—the character, the brand—hasn't shown up anywhere in San Francisco. He's been back in New York, or wherever people imagine him. And the real me, the regular Joe—well, no one pays any attention to him."

Abby knew for a fact that wasn't true. Just look at Gwen, who kept peeking over at them with a feral grin. But Abby knew what he meant.

"So your whole persona, the tortured-artist thing—it's all

for show?" Steph asked. "The person you are in interviews, at public events—it's not really you?"

"It is and it isn't. It's a part of me...but not all of me. I'm sure Abby gets it."

"Me?" Abby blinked.

"Sure. I made up Isaac Ferrer the persona to do a part of the job I have no interest in, but can't get out of. Like how those neon signs sell a lot of Jameson and Tullamore Dew."

"So dressing in black and brooding in your photos—that sells a lot of dark fantasy books," she said softly.

"But your writing is so...I mean, it's dark—really dark—and it came from the real you, right?" Steph asked.

"First, thank you. And yeah, I wrote it. It came from my brain. But when I'm not writing, I'm thinking about, I don't know, regular stuff. What's for lunch and where I left my umbrella and whether dogs fall in love. The rest is just marketing."

"So, Isaac," Ben said. "You know this doesn't have to be your last event at The City Bookmark. You're welcome any time—even if you want to come incognito. We won't tell anyone."

"Or you could keep judging," Steph suggested enthusiastically. "We're doing Gatsby next, right, Ben?"

"I'd better not," Isaac said with a smile. "If your next piece is as good as this week's, I'll have to give you top prize again and then I'll be accused of bias, when your work totally stands on its own. What you did up there? It was magic, Steph. You've got a gift."

Even though that sterling compliment was directed at her

best friend, Abby felt a bright blossoming of pride, because she knew it was her words that had won Isaac's praise.

But then he covered Steph's hand with his, still holding her gaze, and a simmering look passed between them. And Abby's lovely sparkling feeling was carried away as if by the deadly winds of Arcturus IV.

Chapter Nine

Abby and Steph first met on a social media group for incoming San Francisco State freshmen. Discovering they were both majoring in English—Steph with a concentration in literature, Abby in writing—they struck up a conversation that led to deciding to room together.

The apartment Abby found for them was cramped, shabby and still the most they could afford. The first night, they stayed up until two in the morning talking and discovering how much they had in common. Both came from working-class families—Steph's dad owned a small construction firm and her mom was a receptionist at a Ford dealership, while Abby's mom had worked in a bank until her retirement—both were the first generation in their families to go to college, and both were bookworms. Both of them loved the city of San Francisco, though Steph had only been there once before, on a family vacation when she was eleven and decided on the spot that she would move there the minute she could. Both came from loving, multigenerational families, both had played softball, and neither had dated much in high school.

They even had the same pet peeves: people who leave globs of toothpaste on the sink, strangers who tell you to smile when you're minding your own business—and women backstabbing each other over guys.

"It's not exactly like they're an endangered species," Steph observed, lolling on one end of the sectional they'd bought for forty bucks off Craigslist.

"And what are the odds it would be worth it?" Abby, dressed in the old O'Reilly's T-shirt that she wore to bed, curled up at the other end, a stain shaped like the state of Florida on the cushion between them. "I mean, it's definitely not worth losing a friend over."

Until tonight, this agreement had never posed a problem, as the two of them usually preferred different guys. Steph went for tycoon types—tailored suits and expensive haircuts and luxury cars (having grown up in Akron, Ohio, it took a while for her to warm up to the idea of public transportation). Abby, on the other hand, was a sucker for starving artists with soulful eyes.

Isaac Ferrer didn't fit neatly into either of those categories, but that hadn't stopped Steph from talking about him since the moment they left the bar.

"I'm in love, Abby," she declared as they got into their ride share. "It's the real thing this time."

Abby unsuccessfully hid a snort, and Steph had the grace to look slightly embarrassed.

"I know, I know, but I swear to you that the moment

Isaac smiled at me, I felt like...like I'd been hit by a very small bolt of lightning. Like from a triple-A battery, maybe."

"That's a terrible metaphor," Abby observed. "At least go for a nine-volt."

"I can't help it!" Steph threw her head back dramatically against the beige upholstery of the sedan, earning a worried look from the driver. "Isaac has stolen my focus along with my heart!"

"You're not in love. You're just drunk," Abby told her, then leaned forward to reassure the driver. "I promise she won't puke in your car."

"She'd better not," the driver muttered. Judging from the cloying smell of air freshener, she wouldn't be the first.

Steph ignored the exchange. "Did you see the way he was looking at me, Abs? I've already started designing my wedding dress."

"That's nice." Abby couldn't really blame Steph. Hell, though Isaac's attention had been focused on her for only a few minutes, she too had been afflicted with a military-grade crush.

Not that she'd ever admit it.

Because despite all they had in common, she and Steph differed in some key ways. For instance, Steph thought nothing of baring her soul in the presence of strangers, while Abby couldn't imagine anything more mortifying. Steph rarely gave a second thought to the impression she made with her fanciful outfits and arresting presence, while Abby could spend hours worrying what others thought of her. She had been working on it—there were half a dozen books on her shelf with titles like *An Introvert's Guide to Connecting* and

Finding Your Voice When No One is Listening—but it was safe to say she'd always be happiest out of the spotlight.

"It was the most amazing night of my life," Steph proclaimed earnestly. "It's like we already knew each other before we, like, got to know each other."

"And to think people open up their checkbooks after a night of listening to you," Abby marveled. What she didn't say, because she wouldn't dream of raining on her best friend's parade, was that odds were they'd never see Isaac Ferrer again after tonight.

It wasn't that she thought the man was out of Steph's league—though he was so clearly out of her own that it barely counted as the same sport. No, Steph was attractive enough to appeal to every heterosexual male author currently on the NYT bestseller list. But attraction wasn't the same as sincere interest.

Isaac Ferrer was an actual celebrity. He'd come to their event tonight for a few laughs, and accepted Ben's invitation for drinks because he was bored, but his dance card would soon fill up with whatever rich and famous people did—cocktail parties in Nob Hill mansions, black-tie fundraisers at the Palace Hotel, sailing the crystalline waters of the bay. Steph was pretty and charismatic, but she was also loud, impulsive, and boisterous. And while those qualities had endeared her to Ben, Abby, and just about every regular in The City Bookmark and O'Reilly's combined, they generally weren't the attributes prized by the upper echelons of society.

To put it simply—Isaac Ferrer just wasn't their people.

He wouldn't return to the bookstore for the next Ships

in the Night, or the one after that. He wouldn't be popping into O'Reilly's for another round of Sex on the Bogs—in fact, he'd probably regale his new friends with tales of his evening spent slumming at the fake-Irish tourist trap while sipping cognac at the Bohemian Club.

Or maybe not: Isaac seemed thoroughly decent, not the type to flaunt his status by putting other people down. But Abby had already seen two of his selves—the one scowling out from the screen and the laid-back guy who'd showed up tonight—and it wouldn't surprise her if there was another who was even now handing his keys to the valet at whatever luxury high-rise he now called home.

Which meant that the version that Steph had fallen for was probably as inauthentic as the characters in Isaac's books.

There was a part of Abby that wanted to pop Steph's sparkly bubble, to force her to come down to the same reality that everyone else had to occupy. But few people knew the real reason that Steph went after rich, successful men who were on the fast track at their law firms and hedge funds and tech companies, something that Steph had confided one night their senior year after she'd broken up with yet another boyfriend.

"I have to be with someone who *matters*," she'd sniffled, most of the way through a bottle of cheap merlot. "And I know how awful that sounds. But I watched my parents scrape to get by for years before they saved up enough for Dad to go out on his own. I saw the way sales clerks treated my mom, the way they looked down on her out-of-date clothes and vinyl purse. Mom and Dad never went on a vacation until I was in college. When they finally bought their first new car, they only got eight hundred dollars trade-in for the old one." A tear meandered slowly down Steph's cheek as she gulped the last of the wine. "That's not going to happen to me, Abs," she said fiercely.

No wonder she'd fallen so hard for Isaac. A man with his wealth could ensure that Steph would never worry about money again. She could fly to visit her folks any time she wanted. Hell, she could buy them a mansion—Abby was pretty sure the cost of housing in Akron was nothing like the Bay Area.

And what harm was there, really, in letting Steph dream a little? Abby knew what it was like to have a crush on someone who didn't really exist. Some of her greatest love affairs had been with her literary heroes, who never took the low road or used up all the half-and-half or forgot an anniversary. Whose eyes were as dark as obsidian and dangerous as quicksand, whose voice rumbled through her body like distant thunder during a storm...

Abby abruptly banished the thought, realizing she'd gone skipping down the same path as Steph. At least she was still solidly grounded in reality, whereas Steph had spent the evening in the irresistible thrall of Isaac's flirtation, so captivated that Abby had started to feel bad for Ben. The poor guy had been denied the well-earned chance to bask in Ships' success and the coup he'd pulled off by landing a visit from such a popular author, instead having to watch the woman he loved charmed right out from under his nose.

"Mrs. Stephanie Ferrer," Steph was saying dreamily. She had traced her new monogram in the condensation on the window. "Doesn't that sound nice?"

"I'm sure you'll be very happy together." They were only a few blocks from home, but as far as she was concerned this night couldn't end soon enough.

Steph fell silent, and Abby turned to see if she was all right. Steph was gazing at her sadly. "Don't worry," she murmured.

"Worry? I'm not worried. What would I be worrying about?"

Steph tilted her head and patted Abby's hand gently. "I'm sure we'll still be roomies for a while. Until the end of the year at least."

"Wait...what?"

"Isaac's the kind of man who moves fast when he wants something, you know? I could see him popping the question as soon as he's sure, and given the fireworks between us, I mean..."

The car came to a stop in front of the house, and Abby caught the driver watching them in the rearview mirror. Instead of looking away, he bobbed his brows suggestively.

Abby looked away and scooted across the backseat, following Steph out. She'd just slammed the car door behind her when the front window lowered and the driver called, "Hey, beautiful, when it doesn't work out with Prince Charming, give me a call. I can think of plenty of ways to cheer you up."

Steph spun around on the sidewalk, wobbling on her heels while Abby was instantly electrified with fury. Nobody talked to her best friend that way and got away with it.

"What did you say?" she demanded, leaning down to the window to address the driver, who was around their age with a nasty smirk and thinning pale hair in need of a cut.

"I wasn't talking to you, fat ass," the driver snorted. "Nobody's ever talking to you."

He peeled away before Abby could respond, and she had to lunge for Steph to keep her from falling as she teetered into the street, holding both middle fingers high above her head.

"Go fuck yourself, ashhole!" Steph slurred at the disappearing taillights. "You're getting one star and no tip!"

Another perfect ending to another magical night, Abby thought as she pulled Steph back onto the sidewalk and up the stairs before Mrs. Vittadini next door could peer between her drapes to see who was bringing down the neighborhood.

Chapter Ten

"Thank heavens," Abby muttered to Selwyn. "The last thing any of us need is another mob scene."

Selwyn might be too considerate to say anything, but Abby was pretty sure that she'd done a poor job of disguising her true feelings about the fact that Isaac had failed to show up tonight.

She turned her attention back to the contestant currently at the podium, who was nervously jiggling the watch chain hanging from the pocket of his woolen vest as a standing-room-only crowd hung onto his every Fitzgerald-inspired word.

It was true that Isaac's presence would have been disruptive, since he couldn't exactly sneak into a crowd like this; he'd be noticed immediately and surrounded by rowdy fans. But it was hard to see a problem with that scenario, which was pretty much all upside for Ben, who'd sold out his entire stock of Isaac's books last time.

Even if he had shown up, it wasn't as if he would have

remembered Abby. Which was for the best, since she'd be so flustered to see him again that she'd make a hash of the conversation, and the experience would only leave her feeling worse about herself.

And that was something Abby could accomplish all on her own, thank you very much. Even coming here tonight felt a little like marching to the gallows, since she had a pretty good idea of how this week's entry would be received.

But there was a stubborn, naïve part of Abby that couldn't be talked out of hoping to see Isaac again. That longed for another peek at those ripped forearms and unexpectedly callused hands, the thick black hair curling against his neck, the way his brown eyes lit up when he laughed. That wanted—even for a moment—to feel the warmth of his attention focused on her alone.

"I mean, we're already pushing the fire code with this crowd," Abby told Selwyn. "One more body would probably get Ben get cited."

A woman a few feet in front of her turned to glare, so Abby directed a scowl at the couple to her left before giving the woman a conspiratorial shrug. *Some people*, she mouthed.

The truth was that she wasn't all that embarrassed about being caught talking to herself. She'd spent so much time in her little corner of the bookstore, unnoticed and anonymous, that it had come to feel like a safe zone where she could let her guard down.

Unlike Steph, who flitted around before the performance like a butterfly in a flowerbed. Right now, she was sitting in the front row between an elderly couple who were among her biggest fans, drinking cheap wine, dressed in an eighties vintage chartreuse cocktail dress with a weird poufy skirt. Meanwhile, Ben gazed adoringly at her from his post halfway between the podium and the cash register.

Ordinarily, Steph kept an eagle eye on the competition, making mental notes to entertain Abby with later. But tonight she kept checking the door, fidgeting in her seat, doing everything but holding up a sign reading PICK ME ISAAC like a tourist at the *Good Morning America* taping in Times Square. Even now, twenty minutes after the show started, Steph still hadn't given up, and the hope on her face was almost painful to see.

Steph had always been the type to throw herself into her whims. It sometimes seemed to Abby that Steph had only two speeds, reverse and full steam ahead, while Abby spent a lot of time idling in neutral. By nature or practice, however, Steph had developed a thick skin when it came to rejections and plans falling through, while Abby seemed to take every disappointment harder than most.

Coming to terms with Isaac's disinterest now was for the best. Abby could only imagine what a little encouragement would do to Steph's full-bloom crush, making the inevitable rejection all the more painful. Better to rip off the Band-Aid in one go than little by little.

Abby ought to know.

"Hey."

Abby whipped around, startled to hear the whisper from Selwyn's direction. Isaac had somehow managed not only to sneak in unnoticed but to squeeze himself into her little niche.

"Isaac," she whispered, trying to rearrange her features into mild boredom. "Um, hi."

Isaac was doing a pretty convincing version of incognito. He'd ditched the all-black getup for a Fort Myers Mighty Mussels T-shirt and a faded pink baseball cap, paired with cargo shorts and hiking sandals that gave off a distinctive "suburban dad" vibe. Somehow, Isaac had managed to make himself look almost forgettable.

Well, not exactly forgettable. Looks like Isaac's—seventy percent classic heartthrob, twenty percent dangerous mystery and ten percent nerd (unless his current outfit was purely camouflage)—would never go unnoticed.

Especially when he was standing as close as he was now.

"What did I miss?" Even whispering, Isaac's voice stayed solidly in the lower registers, all rumbly and compelling.

"Just the first three stories." Abby pretended to be engrossed by the performance so she wouldn't have to look at him. "It's Gatsby tonight."

"Right. I might have guessed." More than a few of the contestants had come in costume, sporting bow ties and suspenders and flapper dresses. "How were they?"

"About what you'd expect. Two Jay and Nick stories, and one Myrtle and Daisy."

"Hmm. I guess the homoerotic overtones make sense, considering the material. Has Steph had her turn yet?"

Abby kept her smile fixed in place, despite the little stab of chagrin. Of course that was what Isaac was interested in. "No, she drew the fifth slot tonight. She's sitting up there in front."

"Ah. I'm glad I'll get to see her. I meant to slip in right after the show started, but I'm not used to the traffic yet."

"Mmm." Traffic was one of those evergreen San Francisco topics that required only commiseration.

Instead of wandering off to get a better view of the podium, Isaac stayed put, evidently comfortable with a lot less personal space than Abby. Onstage, the guy with the watch chain wrapped up his entry with a zinger.

"'I know you've already been introduced to West Egg, Nick, but I think it's time you meet my East Egg as well,' Gatsby said, pulling his trousers down."

Abby joined in the polite applause as the contestant exited the stage, wondering how many more times she'd hear some version of that egg/testicle joke tonight.

"Not a fan?" Isaac asked.

"Oh, it's...fine." Abby shrugged, not realizing she'd let her opinion show. Ordinarily she kept her thoughts to herself, having learned that it was best to be Switzerland at these events. But something about Isaac standing so close to her made it hard to keep her guard up. "I mean, I'm just not much of a Fitzgerald fan in general."

Isaac snickered. "I don't think you're allowed to say that in a bookstore. They'll sic the literary police on you."

"That's why I stick to the edges of the crowd." Abby gestured at the traffic jam of people taking advantage of the break between contestants to refill their wine. "It's easier in case I need to make a quick getaway."

"Ah, that explains it. I wondered why you hide out back here."

"I'm not hiding," Abby protested, her embarrassment

tempered by the pleasant surprise that Isaac had taken note of where she'd been standing last time.

Which didn't mean anything, of course.

"I heard you might be shy," Isaac continued teasingly. "But it turns out you're a rebel. It's a nice twist."

"You're on to me. I'm secretly a bad influence." Abby tried to match his tone, giving her hair a little flip for good measure. "I don't know how you managed to figure it out. You're the first, you know—I've had the rest of these guys fooled for ages."

A woman in a shiny red fringed dress took the podium and unfolded several sheets of paper as Ben clapped to get the audience's attention. The woman in front of Abby turned to glare at her again, changing her mind when she caught an eyeful of Isaac.

"You're already getting me in trouble," Isaac whispered, leaning in so close that his stubble brushed Abby's jaw, sending a shiver through her. "I like it."

Abby raised a triumphant eyebrow at the woman, who turned around huffily. It was amazing, although also more than a little disturbing, to experience the power conferred on a girl just by having a hot guy at her side.

Although that flirty "I like it" murmured in her ear was an even more powerful force, making Abby feel like she might spontaneously combust.

It was only a joke, though. Isaac was clearly here to see Steph. He just happened to recognize Abby in the back of the crowd and joined her to be polite...or because he was trying to get into Steph's pants.

It was another one of those unwritten rules that Abby

had learned the hard way—if a hot guy is talking to a fat girl it's because he's trying to impress her attractive friend.

The buoyant feeling sparked by Isaac's arrival continued to erode while the red-dress woman read her entry, which featured a three-way scene between Tom, Nick, and Myrtle. And then it was Steph's turn, the crowd falling silent as she made her way to the podium in her pointy heels and eye-popping dress. She had taken to skipping the microphone in favor of belting out their entry in her all-eyes-on-me voice.

"Wow," Isaac observed, though it wasn't clear whether he was reacting to the dress or to such a big sound coming from such a diminutive person. Abby tensed as she always did when her work was read, Isaac's presence making her anxiety much worse.

"The green light bore witness to everything," Steph began, sweeping the audience with a sultry look before continuing. "All of West Egg's secrets; all its affairs. It saw every excess and slight, every indulgence and flirtation. It heard every whispered endearment and ecstatic cry and accusation. Truth and lies, courage and cowardice, sacrifice and betrayal, tragedy and redemption—all of life played out before it.

"There was nothing that light didn't see...especially among the frenzied hedonists who flocked to the glittering summer evenings that Jay Gatsby hosted at Pembrooke."

"Fifth place to, um, Amory Blaine?" Ben announced. "I see what you did there, buddy. Nice."

"Pffft," Abby scoffed to Selwyn. Now that it was just the two of them, she was feeling considerably more relaxed. After being recognized on his way to the restroom, Isaac had decided to slip out before the last contestant had finished his piece to avoid stealing anyone's thunder. "Assuming the name of the protagonist of Fitzgerald's second-most-famous novel isn't exactly a tour de force."

The increasingly rowdy crowd disagreed, however, sending up a raucous cheer for "Blaine." As Ben continued down the list of winners, Abby's heart sank a little. The truth, however, was that she should have seen this coming.

"...and seventh place goes to local favorite Stephanie Tran for 'The Mistress's Menage.'"

Steph bounced up from her seat and performed a graceful bow, even as Ben raced through the last few runners-up. He'd been opposed to increasing the number of winners from three to ten until Steph pointed out that the opportunity for glory was one of the factors behind the event's wild success.

"Does the National Book Award have nine runners-up?" he'd argued. "The Pulitzer? The Booker Prize? Besides, half the crowd is drunk on box wine by the time I announce the winners."

Steph had rolled her heavily made-up eyes. "Walk it back, Harold Bloom. Think of Ships as a preschool T-ball match. Everybody gets a prize."

That was figurative, of course; though the top three place trophies were still passed from winner to winner with great enthusiasm, the rest of the runners-up received coupons for 15% off a bookstore purchase. The coupons had been designed by Minerva, who was an aspiring manga artist on the side, and featured an illustration of a naked woman with a suspicious resemblance to a certain fifty-something bookstore employee reading a book while lashed to a ship deck. Few winners ever redeemed the certificates, and one had recently sold online for three hundred dollars.

Once Ben finished reading the winners, people started gathering their things and taking their purchases to the register, and Steph headed straight for Abby with a look of irritation on her face.

"Seventh? Really?" she fumed. "And on the night that Jane won? That witch is never going to let me live that down."

"Steph!" Abby chided in a harsh whisper. The last thing they needed was to be heard bad-mouthing the competition

—especially Ben's ex. Some of the regulars had groused that Ben played favorites with his friends.

"Just kidding," Steph said as an afterthought, already scanning the crowd for a certain familiar face.

"You can't be too careful," Abby fretted. "Though I guess we should have seen this coming. People come to Ships in the Night for testicle jokes, not—"

"Subtly cynical commentary on Fitzgerald's misogyny?" Stephanie suggested. "Critiques of the decadence inherent in the wealth divide of the twenties?"

So she *had* been paying attention. "You could have pointed that out when I gave you the rough draft last week," she said crossly, even though Steph was right. Hell, Abby had known it even while she was composing her entry, larding it with jokes to disguise the fact that she'd never been a Fitzgerald fan.

"At least Isaac wasn't here to see me bomb like that," Steph said, touching up her purple-orchid lipstick in a tiny purse mirror.

"You did great," Abby assured her. If it hadn't been for Steph's arresting stage presence and her little group of hard-core and very vocal fans, their entry might have come in dead last. "It was the material that bombed. And Isaac *was* here. He came in late and hid out back here with me."

Steph looked up, her lips in a pouty purple *o*. "Really? Or are you just trying to make me feel better?"

Abby laughed, but it came out hollow. "Really."

Steph instantly brightened. "But where—"

"He's grabbing a table at the bar."

"Well, fuck me!" Steph exclaimed. "I guess it's my lucky night after all."

And Isaac's lucky night as well, Abby thought grumpily—then stopped herself.

Jealousy was not okay. It was Abby's firm belief that life offered a bounty to those of generous spirit, that jealousy was counting others' blessings instead of your own, that the jealous are consumed as rust eats away at iron, blah blah blah. (What had she ever done without Instagram to provide a moral compass?)

"I'm happy for you," she said, as warmly as she could manage.

"Did he say anything about the story?" Steph asked hopefully.

"No, but he also left before the winners were announced, so…"

So Abby was spared hearing his opinion, thank God. After the crowd's lukewarm reaction, hearing it from Isaac too would have been too much.

"Okay, I'll go grab Ben, and we can head over to the pub and find out!"

"Steph, look at the line—it'll be ages before Ben can get out of here."

"Uh-uh. Minerva can totally handle it by herself."

Abby sighed in defeat. Steph was right—Minerva was ringing up customers, autographing the winners' coupons, and reminding everyone to return for the next Ships in the Night, all without skipping a beat.

But Abby was in no mood for a repeat of the last Ships. She had no appetite for Owen's killer cocktails and no desire to watch Steph and Isaac gaze into each other's eyes, lost in a private, amorous cloud.

Handling her feelings of jealousy was the mature thing to do, but that didn't mean Abby had to sign up to be a front-row spectator for Steph's grand seduction. Especially since she was going to have to hear all about it when Steph got home.

And that wasn't the only thing keeping Abby away from O'Reilly's. There was also the matter of Owen and Dex and their "humor" at her expense. Teasing was one thing—the three of them had been doing it nonstop since grade school—but lately the taunts had more bite. Or maybe Abby was becoming more sensitive. Either way, she was going to have to have a talk with the two of them...just not tonight.

Which left her with the problem of how to bow out gracefully. If it was anyone else, Abby would claim a headache or wretched cramps, but Steph would see right through the excuse.

"I wish I could come with you guys," she said, gathering up empty cups so she wouldn't have to look at Steph, and crossing her fingers so the lie wouldn't count. "But you know the project definition statement I was working on? The Vancouver office wants to shift the deliverable timetable, which means I have to redo the whole thing."

Steph waved her hand impatiently. "I know what you're doing. You just don't want to come, so you use all that jargon because you know I don't understand any of it."

"Steph!" Abby affected a hurt look. "The Vancouver office doesn't mess around–I can't screw this up."

That, at least, was true. Unlike her relatively laid-back

colleagues in the San Francisco headquarters, the Vancouver department head loved nothing more than finding fault with her work.

Steph's expression softened. "Oh, I get it. You're upset about coming in seventh."

Abby figured she'd done enough lying for one night, so she gave a noncommittal shrug. She didn't have to search Instagram to know that not saying anything wasn't the same as making shit up. In fact, it could even be considered a thoughtful gesture if it allowed the other person to believe the story that made them the most comfortable...right?

"Oh, honey," Steph said, putting her arm around Abby. "I know it's been a while since we've placed so low, but it's going to happen from time to time. If we always won, it would get boring, right? Besides, I know how you feel about F. Scott Fitzgerald. It makes sense that you didn't give it your all. Next time will be different."

She gave Abby a conspiratorial wink, and Abby knew she was expected to drag the news out of her. "Why? Did Ben pick the book already?"

"Yup. He's not announcing it until Monday, but he just told me...it's *Dracula*!"

Abby tried to look enthusiastic as Steph beamed at her. Sure, ordinarily she'd be delighted, being a big fan of nineteenth-century Gothic horror. But she was still stuck on tonight's failure to reach the audience, despite having given it her best effort, staying up late two nights in a row and going through half a dozen drafts. Abby had known that the final version wouldn't be as well received as her usual entries...but for some reason she'd gone ahead and written it to please herself.

She'd enjoyed every minute she spent working on it, finding subtle ways to slip in messages about the book's heavy-handed symbolism and emotional emptiness while making the most of the iconic characters. It was tempting to blame the audience for being too dense to get it, but the truth was that they were expecting a lighthearted romp and she'd delivered a literary brick.

That...and she lacked the inspiration that last week's hero had provided. There was simply no way to fit her fantasy version of Isaac into a Gatsby-shaped template.

Bram Stroker's masterpiece, however, was a whole other matter. Count Dracula, that brooding undead soldier, statesman, and student of alchemy... Yeah, that could definitely work.

Abby was waiting outside for her ride-share, head pleasantly spinning with thoughts of Transylvanian castles and abbeys in ruins, when Steph and Ben emerged from the bookstore.

"You sure you can't come for just one?" Ben coaxed.

"Yeah, just one!" Steph echoed half-heartedly. Not only did she know Abby could out-stubborn her, her mind was obviously already on what—and who—was waiting for her at the bar. "Paying full price for drinks is going to tank my budget."

"But you've got a sugar daddy now."

The words were out of Abby's mouth before she could stop them. Ben looked taken aback, then increasingly grim as he took in the full weight of what she'd said. Abby didn't blame him: spending the evening with Steph and her crush was going to be as painful for Ben as it would have been for her, if not more so. After all, her crush was only a week old, while Ben had been in love with Steph for years.

And yet he had found the courage to keep showing up and being a good friend, while Abby was about to slink home with her cowardly tail tucked between her legs.

Chapter Twelve

Abby knew Steph was home well before she walked in the door. Not many cars dared to idle on the narrow residential streets of their neighborhood, laid out in the nineteenth century when no one could have imagined the traffic that would make its residents pull out their hair a century and a half later. But drivers delivering Steph tended to chance it. She had that effect on people, especially men.

Abby was working at the kitchen table when she heard the car door slam. She'd left the bookstore planning to crawl into bed and crack open the latest Fredrik Backman novel, but by the time she got home, she was bubbling over with vampiric inspiration.

Because the only thing sexier than a mysterious man whispering in a woman's ear would be for that woman to find herself lost in the labyrinthine halls of a Gothic castle when the stranger made his appearance. She'd have time only to notice his mysterious stare and elegant bearing before being drawn into his swirling, midnight-black cape. Startled, she'd stumble into his arms only to feel them encircle her, his lips against her ear muttering "I like it" just before his needle-sharp teeth pierced her pale neck.

...Or something like that. Abby was going to have to be careful with her dialog and physical descriptions if she didn't want people catching on, even if it was only her friends.

Especially if it was her friends. It was bad enough trying to convince Dex and Owen that she hadn't been trying to jump Isaac's bones a couple of weeks ago. But if Ben figured out she was nursing a stupid, impossible crush, she'd be mortified. And if Steph ever realized... Oh God, she didn't want to think about it. Abby couldn't bear for things to get weird between her and her best friend, even if Steph's flirtation with Isaac never went anywhere.

So as her fingers flew over the keyboard, Abby was drafting not the scene that she longed to write but her distant second choice: a scene in which the Dutch doctor Van Helsing's attempts to exorcize the demons from young Lucy take a raunchy turn. Abby hadn't become a successful corporate writer without learning fierce discipline, and she drew on those reserves now to strike the right tone: while the piece wouldn't win any points for originality, the repartee was witty, the jokes snappy, and the double entendres daringly risqué. All in all, it was shaking out to be a crowd-pleaser.

"Oh, Van Helsing, your crucifix may be diminutive," Lucy cried, "but your enormous stake will surely pierce me all the way through."

Abby finished typing the sentence just as Steph came through the door calling, "You missed one hell of a night!"

She walked into the kitchen barefoot, carrying her stilettos in one hand and a bunch of wilting dyed-green chrysanthemums in the other.

"I'm glad you had a good time."

The words came out more stiffly than Abby intended, but Steph didn't seem to notice. She dropped into the chair across from Abby, her skirt pouffing up around her like a tutu. There was a smear of something yellow on the bodice and one of the straps had broken, but she was beaming.

"I didn't even get annoyed when Jane showed up and took your seat at the table. She made a fool out of herself, of course, gushing over her win and fawning all over Isaac. And right in front of Ben! She was *shameless*, Abs."

A glance at the clock revealed it was almost 2:30. "You all stayed until closing time?"

"Nah, Ben only stayed for one drink, and Jane tried to keep up with us, but she left around midnight. After that, Isaac and I were hungry so we got sausages."

"Mustard?" Abby guessed, indicating the stain. Steph looked at it as though just now noticing it.

"It must be. You ever notice how amazing roasted meat tastes when you've been drinking? Anyway, the whole night was magical."

Steph sighed happily, her eyes lit with that same faraway, distant sparkle Abby recognized from last week. But it was the fact that Steph wasn't freaking out about her ruined dress that convinced Abby that Steph was even more into Isaac than she'd suspected.

"So...sausages, huh?"

"Yeah, and onion rings! See?" Steph blew a tipsy breath.

"Oh. Wow. That's oniony, all right."

"Which is strange because you know I'd never order something like that on a normal date, but with Isaac...it's like I've known him forever. Like we went straight to being completely comfortable with each other without all that getting-to-know-you awkwardness."

Yeah, that *was* strange. In all the time they'd known each other, Steph only ordered bland, light, easy-to-manage fare in public, saving pizza and nachos and her favorite messy Cuban sandwiches for takeout nights at home with Abby.

"Nice," she said woodenly. "So what did you talk about?"

"I don't really remember. Isn't that funny?"

"Hysterical. Exactly how many Sex on the Bogs did you have tonight?"

"The whole damn pitcher," Steph said, nearly toppling out of her seat as she threw her arms out wide.

Ah. There was the answer to Steph's sudden loss of culinary inhibitions. Owen's signature drink had a way of stripping away even the most stubborn self-consciousness. There was a reason her brother liked to call the cocktail "the great liquid equalizer."

"I remember Dex sat with us for a while," Steph continued. "He and Owen got into an argument about some bad call at the Giants game, and then Isaac was telling them about the Cuban National Baseball Series. Did you know they have seventeen teams, one for every province and one just for Havana?"

"I did not."

"Isaac's team is Villa Clara."

"*Villa Clara.*"

"That's what I said."

"No, it's…oh, never mind." This didn't seem like the time to work on Steph's terrible accent.

"Anyway, isn't this great? The guys all get along—Isaac invited them over to watch a game next week—and we totally missed you, obviously. We're all going to be best friends!"

"It's—a nice thought," Abby mumbled.

"Nice? *Nice?*" Steph said in boozy outrage. She reached across the table and grabbed at Abby's hand, missing it on the first try. "Abby. Listen. We are blessed to have such good friends. Blessed."

"You're right," Abby said, pretending to study her screen. "Honey, shouldn't you call it a night?"

"Oh, I do remember something," Steph exclaimed, releasing Abby abruptly and attempting to snap her fingers. "Owen wanted me to tell you 'nice try' but you can't avoid him that easily."

"I wasn't—"

"He's gonna call you tomorrow to give you shit for being a coward," Steph said, carefully enunciating the message as one does when drunk. "Whatever that means."

Abby groaned inwardly, even as she dismissed her brother's threat. She was an expert at avoiding phone conversations, as the three unanswered messages from her mother currently in her voice mail could attest.

"And I didn't even tell you the best part!" Steph crowed. The slippery fabric of her dress had caused her to slide down in her chair, but now she sat up so fast it was as though she'd received an electric shock. "Isaac loved the story. He really, really, really did." She gave Abby a triumphant grin.

"That's nice," Abby said, rereading the last line she'd typed.

"He wasn't just being nice, Abby. He went on this whole big tangent about how it subtly critiques...something, like it embraced the, um, aesthetic? Was that it? Like the aesthetic of excess, or the excessive aesthetics, or whatever, while it refuses to acknowledge the, uh...something else. Strata. I'm pretty sure he used the word strata. God, Abby, until Isaac started talking about it, I never considered that smut could be brainy."

Abby glanced up sharply. "He called it 'smut'?"

"No, he said the piece was 'damn sexy.' Can you believe it?" Steph gave a dramatic sigh. "And that's when I started designing your bridesmaid dress. I'm thinking periwinkle, but like a grayish periwinkle. Not too blue, you know? But seriously, can you imagine anything hotter than Isaac Ferrer calling your words 'damn sexy'?"

No...Abby could not. Especially since they were *her* words.

Steph was the one who read them, and she'd done a fine job. Much better than Abby could do on her best day. And no one could blame Isaac for not knowing the truth.

But it still smarted, a private, acute kind of pain that Abby had never experienced before. No one had ever described her work that way, and it seemed tragic that she might never experience the praise in person. That she'd never hear it from Isaac himself.

But it was still an unexpected gift, one that Abby would cherish. "I hope you didn't get so carried away that you proposed on the spot," she said lightly.

"Ha." Steph seemed to catch herself, and her cheeks turned a rosy pink. "But that reminds me. I wanted to ask you about something."

This couldn't be good. "Oh?"

"So it's, um, super obvious that Isaac really likes your writing," Steph said in a rush. "I mean, he gave us first place last week, and tonight he couldn't stop talking about the story, even though everyone else hated it!"

Wow, Abby thought. *Hated*? Even though it was the truth, Steph's bluntness still stung.

"So I was hoping that whatever you've been doing different with the stories the last couple of weeks, that you could keep doing it? When you write the next one? I mean, make it like the others?"

"In what way?" Abby knew, of course. But she wanted to make Steph say it.

"Maybe even dial it up a little," Steph suggested eagerly.

"Dial what up, exactly?"

"You know." Steph made a slicing motion that could have meant *Back up a little further* or *Damn that stove is hot* or a hundred other things. "More...I mean not boring but, like, more intellectual? But also sexy?... Not so much, 'ha ha he whipped out his dick,' but with the big words and the...allegories?"

And to think that Steph had graduated cum laude.

"Ah. I see," Abby said slowly. What Steph was struggling to describe—less parody, more earnest exploration—was exactly what Abby wanted to write. Even if Steph had declared it a total fail just hours earlier. "Are you sure, though? That stuff won't ever win unless Isaac's the judge."

"I'm not saying we'll do it that way forever," Steph said. Her eyelids had begun to drift down, and her butt was sliding off the chair again. A few more minutes and she'd be fast asleep on the kitchen floor. "Just long enough to convince Isaac that he should ask me out."

And there we have it, ladies and gentlemen, Abby thought. There was the shiny trophy that Steph really had her eye on. Never mind Abby's own wishes, or the satisfaction she took from pleasing the crowd. Abby's best friend was asking her to be her personal Cyrano.

"But you two already went out tonight," Abby side-stepped.

Steph waved her hand dismissively. "That was just sausages and onion rings. I'm talking about a real date at a real restaurant—preferably one with white tablecloths. The kind of place a man could get down on one knee and—"

"Look, Steph," Abby cut Steph off. "There's nothing I can write that will convince Isaac Ferrer to fall in love with you."

"Don't sell yourself short, Abby!" Steph said earnestly. "You're amazing. You should have heard Isaac going on and on about your story tonight. It was like he was describing some—some incredible Italian sports car, or some really old, expensive Scotch."

Abby raised an eyebrow, but given the type of guy Steph usually dated, she could see where that was the highest praise that came to mind.

Still, it was hard to believe that Isaac loved her writing as much as he loved Steph's performance—or her bare shoulders and long legs.

But what did it matter? Even if Abby was careless enough to fall head over heels in love with Isaac, that love would always be one-sided. Even Steph was going to have a hard time holding the interest of a gorgeous, rich, kind, fascinating bachelor for long. Because despite the fact that men had been falling over themselves to capture Steph's heart for years, none of them had been on Isaac's level.

Which meant that she and Steph ought to enjoy his friendship (and in Steph's case, the mutual attraction between them) while they could, as long as they kept in mind that it would only last as long as it took for Isaac to find his real people.

Steph might end up with her hopes dashed and her heart broken, but she'd survive. Abby, a realist, knew there was one way that she could be as intimate as she wanted with Isaac, and that was through her stories.

Steph could flirt. Abby could dream. And the beauty of it was that Steph would never find out how Abby really felt.

Was it ideal? Hell no.

But Abby knew it was as good as it was ever going to get.

"Okay. I'm in," she told Steph. "No promises, but I'll give it a shot."

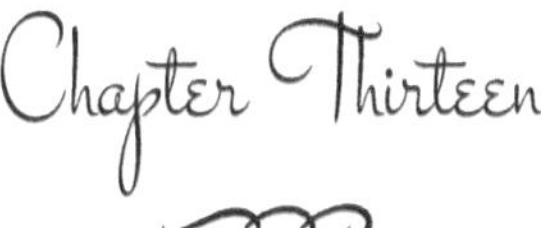

Chapter Thirteen

"People speak of your virtue and modesty," the Count murmured, his cold, waxy lips only inches from Mina's ear. "They call you dutiful and sweet. But I know better."

A thrill of rebellion laced the rapid pounding of Mina's heart. "Virtue and duty mean little when a woman dreams of the world beyond her door. I would be known not for my sweetness but for the depth and breadth of my mind."

"I see the twilight in your eyes and the long shadow that eclipses your heart," the Count said, his words caressing her like vining tendrils. "You may be Jonathan Harker's little virgin, but I long to taste the darkness inside you. I can make you bloom like a..."

Abby stopped typing and took a sip of coffee, wincing to discover that it had gone cold. What was that night-blooming flower called? Steph would probably know—but Steph was back at the house knee-deep in mimosas and *croque monsieurs* and gossip.

"...bloom like a xx."

Abby moved on, the x's a reminder to look up the name of the flower later. O'Reilly's Wi-Fi was pretty good, but she'd turned it off, the better to concentrate. She only had a couple more hours before the bar opened, and she wanted to make the most of it.

It was easy to get lost in the dark, atmospheric world of Victorian London, and Abby was so deep in the character of the seductive vampire as he toyed with the proper Mina Murray that she failed to notice her brother looming until he slapped a soggy towel on the polished mahogany bar next to her laptop, making her jump.

"*Fuck*! Damn it, Owen, I'm trying to work!"

"Oh, is that what we're calling it now?" Owen didn't bother with the accent since there were no customers to impress. "I'm all for you making more of an effort to get out there. Gotta check those traps, right?"

"I don't have traps." Too late, Abby realized she'd missed an opportunity to get her brother to back off. Better to let him think she was on an online dating site—"checking their traps" was his and Dex's charming phrase for seeing if they'd received any replies to the messages they'd sent women—than to have to talk about what she was really up to.

"Jeez, Abs. You're turning into a hermit. You've been ignoring everyone's calls and texts—"

"Not everyone's, just yours. I finally called Mom back," she added defensively.

"How'd that go?"

"About like you'd expect. Lots of unsolicited dieting and fashion advice. Oh, and she mentioned she asked you if you could set me up with any of your friends."

Owen winced. "Sorry. I'd say she means well—"

"It's fine. I told her one of them gave me chlamydia but I wasn't sure which one it was. That shut her up."

There was a startled silence, and Abby relented. "Kidding. Look, I'm only here because it was Steph's turn to host brunch with her work friends, and it's impossible to concentrate with all of them getting drunk on champagne and complaining about whoever didn't show up."

That part was true. Steph threw a hell of a party—hell, it was in her job description—but between the noise and the fog of perfume, Abby would never have been able to finish her Ships entry at home.

Luckily, there was always her second home. There were few places as quiet as the pub on a Sunday morning, and she'd been making great progress, nearly finishing her first draft, until Owen showed up. Now she just had to figure out how to get him to leave her alone.

Owen spun her laptop around so he could see the screen, and a brief tug-of-war ensued before he held it over the sink. Abby gave up. She was pretty sure he wouldn't stoop so low as to drop it in the soapy water...but he could be unpredictable.

"You're writing vampire romance now?" he said. "I hate to tell you, but Twilight's been over for years. Besides, when exactly did that become 'work'? You don't get paid for this crap, do you?"

"I've never been paid for helping you out around here either. And don't call this crap. It's a labor of love."

Owen raised an eyebrow, then read from the screen. "'The undead wound his long, elegant fingers in his inamorata's chestnut hair, lifting it from her milky throat. A delicate moan issued from her carmine lips.' Well, assuming an inamor-whatever is a woman and 'carmine' means 'wet and ready,' then yeah, I'd say there's plenty of 'love' going on there."

"Oh, shut up and let me work," Abby snapped. She knew damn well that her brother only played the fool to get on her nerves; he'd won the spelling bee twice in elementary school, defending his nerdy victory by telling his friends he only did it to keep Abby from getting too full of herself.

Abby grabbed her computer and turned it back around, vowing to be more careful. Ordinarily, she enjoyed shooting the shit with Owen. Maybe it was because they were twins, but no one—not even Steph—had ever really understood her the way he did. At times it was almost as if they could see into each other's minds.

But the downside was that Abby couldn't turn the connection off when she wanted to keep something private.

Owen held up his hands defensively. "I didn't say it was bad! It's probably pretty good—for the right audience."

Abby's fingers stilled on the keyboard. "But...?"

Owen gazed at the randy toucan in a vintage Guinness poster as if the bird might provide the answer. "I just wonder..."

Abby jabbed him with her pen. "What?"

"Look, Abs, when are you going to stop dicking around

and start writing what you love? I mean, really put your heart in it?"

The better question was when she'd learn not to give her brother an opening unless she was sure she was going to like the answer. Owen considered himself the expert in all aspects of her life, and when she gave him an inch, he gave her a lecture.

"Never mind." Abby pretended to have had an inspiration, furiously typing the opening stanza of Tennyson's "The Charge of the Light Brigade."

Owen wasn't fooled. He reached over the laptop and tapped random keys until she stopped. "I'm being serious."

"Okay, fine. I like writing this stuff."

"I know."

"And I already have a job."

"I know."

"A writing job, I'll remind you."

"What was it that you called technical writing again?" Owen said, pretending to rack his brain. "Oh, yeah... 'writing with all the joy sucked out.'"

As usual, he'd backed Abby into a corner, but the last thing she wanted to discuss was the novel she'd been working on for years. She'd held onto the dream long after most English majors gave up, which usually coincided with their first student loan payment coming due. Everyone knew that it was impossible to pay the bills with a publishing career.

Unless you were Isaac Ferrer, of course.

"Look, Owen, how do you know this isn't exactly what I want to be doing?" she tried. "You wanted to be an aerial firefighter, if I'm remembering correctly, so why aren't you jumping out of a helicopter right now?"

"That's not how aerial firefighting works."

"Damn it, Owen...look, I'm fine, end of story. So bug off."

Owen went quiet, and Abby went back to her work. But he kept watching her with an unhappy expression.

"I'm fine," she repeated.

Owen's frown deepened.

"For Pete's sake, Owen. Let's just say that you're right, and I'm yearning to spend my days writing great literature. So what? It's not like publishers would be lining up to buy it, and I'd still have all the same bills to pay. Not all of us can breeze through life like you and Dex—most people have to take what they can get."

"Wait one damn minute," Owen said hotly. "You call running this business singlehandedly 'breezing through life'?"

A clatter of feet on the stairs was followed by two attractive young women emerging from the upstairs apartment. They were giggling and leaning on each other, dressed in last night's going-out clothes.

Dex was right behind them, wearing only a pair of boxer shorts. "You sure you ladies don't want to stay for breakfast?" he was saying. "Owen makes a mean corned beef omelet."

The change in Owen was instant. He straightened up to his full height and gave a little bow. "It would be me honor, ladies," he said in his work accent.

More giggling. "Maybe next time," the short one said sweetly.

Dex made a big show of kissing their hands, then held the door for them as they stood blinking in the sunshine of a new day. Once they were gone, he slid onto his favorite stool with a huge grin on his face.

"Did you hear that, buddy? 'Next time!' I ain't gonna lie, I'd take another scoop of that in a heartbeat."

Abby shook her head. "You were right, Owen. I don't know what I was thinking. Your life is obviously much harder than everyone else's. I'm amazed you haven't thrown out your back, what with these constant orgies."

Owen scowled. "That was just bad timing. It doesn't change the fact—"

"Wait, what's this about constant orgies?" Dex piped up.

Owen ignored him. "I'm not going to apologize for enjoying my life, Abby. I work my ass off, and I deserve to have a little fun."

"Of course you do. Me too—but in my own way, not what you think I should be doing. Just think of this as my version of a one-night stand."

"Holy shit," Dex exclaimed. "If that's what it's like, I've really got to make it over to Ships one of these Fridays."

Abby froze, icy fingers of horror jabbing her in the heart. Had Dex really figured out her secret? "I don't know what you're talking about."

Dex made a face. "Sure you do. You write the stories, and Steph reads them."

Abby felt like she might be sick. Owen gave her a weak punch on the shoulder, his version of a concerned hug.

"Did you really think we didn't know?" he said kindly.

"Come on, Abs, it didn't exactly take a genius to figure it out."

Oh, God—this couldn't be happening. "Does anyone else know?"

Owen shrugged. "No idea. If the regulars have suspicions, they haven't said anything about it in the bar."

Abby's sense of relief was short-lived. If Owen and Dex had figured out their game, it was only a matter of time before everyone else did too. "How long have you known?"

Owen and Dex looked at each other.

"The first night Steph walked in with a trophy," Dex said.

"Yeah. Like we're supposed to believe she suddenly turned into Harper Lee at the exact same time you quit submitting?" Owen added.

Abby dug her fingernails into her thighs, aware she was about to make her humiliation ten times worse. "Please, please tell me that you didn't tell Isaac," she whispered.

Instantly, Owen's expression changed. "Of course not. I may give you shit, but I'll always have your back. Always."

"Me too," Dex said earnestly. "Which is why I hate watching you waste your life hiding in the shadows."

Abby felt the unwelcome sting of tears and hurriedly brushed them away. "You guys are starting to sound like Mom," she mumbled.

"Ouch," Owen said, wincing. "But have you ever stopped to think that maybe she's right? About this, anyway."

"I'm not wasting anything," Abby protested. "Nobody's twisting my arm. I'm doing exactly what I want."

"Right," Owen said, his voice dangerously calm. "So, last

Friday you *wanted* to run away and hide at home by yourself instead of hanging out with your friends and the guy you really like. Because you'd had all the fun you could handle watching a bunch of strangers geek out over some random book and drinking shit wine. Tell me I'm wrong, Abs. Tell me that it was one hundred percent not because you were afraid."

Abby snapped her laptop closed, suddenly shaking with rage. "I can't think here. I'm going home to work."

"I thought Steph—"

"Screw Steph and her damn brunch!"

Abby's words hung in the air as she threw her things into her bag and got up to leave.

"Abby, wait." Owen was twisting the bar rag in his hands, looking distraught. "I'm not trying to piss you off, I swear. I only want you to be happy. *Really* happy, not this...whatever this shit is that you've settled for."

Abby nodded, knowing that if she didn't leave now, she was going to cry for real. Because Owen was right. For all his faults, her brother always had her back...even when that was the last thing she wanted.

"See you guys around," she blurted as she opened the door, instantly overwhelmed by the bright sun.

"You can't keep running away your whole life," Owen yelled as the door closed behind her.

Oh yeah?

"Watch me," Abby said to the empty sidewalk.

Chapter Fourteen

Hey, you going to Ships tonight?

Who is this?

It's Isaac. Steph gave me your number

Abby stared at her phone, her thumb frozen over the screen in shock. Isaac Ferrer had her number. Not only that, he'd asked for it...and now he wanted to know her plans.

It was an easy question. *Answer him!* her inner critic prodded frantically.

"Hey, Reilly." Chetan Patel poked his head over Abby's cubical wall, bringing her crashing back to reality. "Sharon told me to remind you she needs to look over your copy for the announcement before the meeting."

"Yeah, okay," Abby said, nodding without looking up. "Got it. Thanks."

She waited until he was gone to start typing.

> Not sure, still swamped at work

Abby stared at her reply for a moment before screwing up the courage to hit send. It wasn't a lie, technically. But she could finish the edits in less than hour, and there was nothing else pressing on her to-do list...which made her a yellow-bellied coward.

> Too bad. I was looking forward to hanging out with you again.

Uh...*what*? Abby's hand began to tremble violently as a sickening, clammy pall overtook her.

It should have been wonderful news that Isaac was looking forward to anything at all having to do with her. But Abby possessed very limited reserves of social energy, and the prospect of "hanging out with" Isaac, no matter how casually, sent her into paroxysms of anxiety.

This facet of Abby was almost impossible to explain to extroverts, especially since she was perfectly capable of braving the Ships crowd and going to O'Reilly's afterward when she was with her best friends.

But every interaction with a stranger or acquaintance, no matter how pleasant, added to the weight of what Abby privately thought of as her Social Bucket. When it was filled, she was done, and only a lovely stretch of solitude could restore her.

Abby imagined her Bucket to be a big old-fashioned tin sand pail. Casual interactions were like polished river stones, and she could fit quite a few of them in the bucket. Pushy people with no respect for personal boundaries were heavy rocks that quickly filled it up. Ordinarily the people she was closest to were pebbles who took up very little room, but even they could weigh her down eventually.

She still wasn't sure which one Isaac would turn out to be—big rock or tiny pebble. Or if he might be something altogether different. There had been moments with Isaac when Abby had forgotten to be nervous, when it almost felt like he was lightening her bucket instead of adding to it.

Concentrating fiercely, Abby gripped the phone in both hands to steady it and banished her inner critic. Then she quickly typed a text and sent it before she could reconsider.

> But I think I can meet you at the pub after the show

She held her breath as the three dots pulsed.

. . .

:)

Abby stared at the emoticon, a rush of warmth making her feel both faint and delicious, until the voices of her colleagues filtered into her consciousness and she stuffed the phone back in her pocket.

The thoughts she was on the verge of having were definitely NSFW.

Abby slipped into O'Reilly's a half an hour before Ships' usual ending time. Owen was busy with TGIF revelers when she arrived, but he sent her a wink when she slid into a stool at the far end of the bar.

"I'm here," she announced when he got a break, "so you can stop calling me a coward. And make me an End of the Rainbow while you're at it."

"End of the Rainbow?" Owen echoed in his ersatz accent. It was the strongest of their grandfather's signature drinks, featuring chartreuse and apricot liqueur and a healthy pour of single malt Irish whiskey. "Well, all right then, Leannán Sídhe, liquid courage coming right up!"

The ears of a trio of giggling young women perked up, and the boldest leaned across the bar. Too late, Abby remembered the dangers of provoking her brother's curiosity in public. "'Lemon Shee?' What's that mean, Owen?"

"Aah, lassie," he said with a wink. "In Irish folklore, the leannán sídhe is a famous seductress, is she not? But she is also a fae muse and a slayer of men. Now, don't let my sister's unassuming demeanor fool you, for she can be the deadliest heartbreaker this fair city has ever known."

Abby studied her phone, feigning fierce concentration while the girls shot her skeptical looks. "Okay...and what's an End of the Rainbow?" another asked.

"It's just for family," Owen told them solemnly, though Abby would bet her salary he would end up serving them a round and charging top dollar. "Only those with true Irish blood can handle it, and it's only for situations requiring great courage. My sister is—"

"Going to find a table," Abby interrupted firmly before Owen could tell everyone in the bar about her crush.

"I didn't tell them about your future boyfriend, so you can relax," he said when he brought her the drink a few minutes later. "But where is everyone else?"

"They'll be here in a few minutes," Abby said, not meeting his eyes.

There was an accusatory pause. "You didn't even go, did you?"

"I'm here, aren't I? It was a long day, Owen. I'm pacing myself."

"And avoiding Isaac. Admit it, Abs!"

"If that's what I was doing, I'd be home in my pajamas instead of sitting here talking to you."

Owen stared at her suspiciously for a moment before

returning to the bar, but Abby refused to give. At least the drink was delicious, going down so easily that Abby was thinking of ordering another one when the first of the Ships crowd started coming through the doors...and all thoughts other than Isaac flew out of her mind.

"Hey, you're already here!" Steph waved a hand gloved in red silk that matched her lipstick. She was sporting a simple black vest and tuxedo pants and no jewelry unless you counted the huge faux ruby in her turban. "And you got us a table! I was afraid you'd ditched out right after the show again."

"Abby wasn't there tonight," Isaac said, giving her a warm smile.

"Why not?" Ben seemed genuinely surprised.

"Yeah, why not?" Steph echoed.

"It's no big deal," Abby said briskly. "I got caught up in a thing for work. I just got here."

"Oh, that's too bad," Steph said, signaling for Gwen, who'd just started her shift and was pulling on her kelly-green apron. Steph reached into her bag. "Okay, Abs, since you weren't there to see it in person..." She pulled out the third-place trophy, setting it on the table with a triumphant flourish. "Total redemption! Seventh place, my ass!"

"Perhaps now the furor in the international literary community will die down," Ben observed drily.

"Well, I thought your story was brilliant last time," Isaac said.

For a moment Abby allowed herself to pretend that his praise was actually directed at her. She let her eyelids flutter down halfway and basked in the warmth of the fantasy, the feeling like floating in a bath of honey and sunshine. Being the recipient of that kind of affirmation from someone like Isaac—well, it was easy to see why Steph couldn't get enough. That and the way his velvety brown eyes brimmed with sincerity and dark promises at the same time.

"What did you think of this week's story?" she asked before she could stop herself.

Isaac shifted his attention to Abby. In a voice she could have sworn was an octave lower, he rumbled, "This week's was even better."

Warmth crept up Abby's neck, undoubtedly turning her skin the dreaded scarlet. Luckily, Steph and Isaac seemed locked in a staring contest and Ben was still trying to get Gwen's attention.

Isaac liked her work. *Really* liked it, so much that even the mention of it unleashed the hungry *mmm-hmmm* feeling. Maybe Steph's attractiveness and bubbly personality had something to do with it, but Abby knew firsthand the power of the written word over the heart and soul of a writer.

Hell, her high school crush had been *The Count of Monte Cristo*'s Edmond Dantès, with Gilbert Blythe from *Anne of Green Gables* a close runner-up. She wondered if Isaac ever mooned over a literary character...someone intelligent and bookish, perhaps? Strong, independent, loyal...with eyes that had been called sapphire blue (if only by her grandmother) and long, thick curly hair that was often admired by perfect strangers and...

"Abby, you're back."

The pleasant fantasy shattered at the sound of a most unwelcome voice. Abby turned in her chair and found herself at eye level with the leather buckle of a braided hemp belt.

"Jane," she said, reluctantly looking up. "Hello."

"I didn't expect to see you after you ditched out on us last week," Jane said frostily. "Do you mind making room?"

Abby certainly did mind, but she was in no position to do battle. She gave a resigned sigh as she scooted her chair as far as she could at the cramped table. Jane dragged over a chair and wedged it next to Isaac. "So what did I miss?" she crooned in his direction.

Gwen showed up at that moment and started taking drink orders. "And how about you, heartbreaker?" she asked slyly when she got to Abby.

Damn it, Owen, Abby thought furiously. Of course her brother couldn't keep his mouth shut, not when it came to her crush. And Gwen had about as much tact as a badger.

"I'll have another End of the Rainbow."

Gwen looked taken aback. "You sure?"

Abby folded her arms and met her gaze. "Damn sure."

Gwen gave her a mock salute. "All righty, then. Back in a flash, gang."

"'Another'?" Ben said. "I thought you said—"

"What were you working on tonight, Abby?" Isaac interrupted—which made him either extremely perceptive, or genuinely clueless. "It must have been important to keep you away from the show. Steph says you're her most loyal fan."

Steph gave a faint shrug of apology.

"Oh, I was...working on a rollout announcement," Abby said, painfully aware of how boring her job sounded. "I work for a tech company, and they're updating the client interface for a new release of their risk management application and—"

"She's a writer," Ben cut in sternly. Steph had obviously recruited him into her pressure campaign to get Abby back to work on her novel.

"Is that true?" Isaac asked.

Abby shifted uncomfortably. "Ben is giving me too much credit. It's true that writing is technically a part of my job, but it's nothing like what you do."

"Don't do that, Abby," Jane said sharply.

Abby glanced at her in astonishment. Jane had managed to inch even closer to Isaac. "Do what?"

"Put yourself down that way," Jane said pityingly. "So what if you don't have an MFA from Wellesley? You still make your living writing, and that's a huge accomplishment."

"Don't you have an MFA from Wellesley, Jane?" Steph asked in the sweet tone that she used to hide her sharp shark-like bite.

"Why don't you write something for Ships, Abby?" Isaac cut in hastily. Was he trying to change the subject because he could sense the blood in the water or because he was genuinely curious?

"I do, in fact, Stephanie," Jane said coldly. "I graduated from Oberlin *cum laude*, and then—"

"Abby used to write for Ships," Ben said loudly. "She was good, too. But she stopped before it really became a thing."

"Why did you stop?"

All eyes were on Abby—other than Jane, who was busy sulking—and she found herself at a loss for words. Or maybe it was the pressure of realizing that Isaac was truly interested in her answer.

"I, um..."

"Abby doesn't like the spotlight," Steph explained. "She breaks out in hives whenever Ben starts livestreaming. It's why she always stands in the back."

Abby started to protest, but there didn't seem to be much point, especially since Steph probably thought she was helping. Besides, successfully speaking over anyone in this group was nothing short of a Herculean task.

Keep doing what you've always done, and you'll keep getting what you always got, the little voice in her head pointed out darkly.

"I don't know about that," Isaac said easily, adding a conspiratorial wink. "I recently learned that Abby isn't as shy as she lets on."

Oh God.

"What does that mean?" Steph asked.

"Just that Abby and I had a chance to talk at the last Ships," Isaac said, "and I got a glimpse of her rebellious streak."

"*What* rebellious streak?" Jane scoffed.

Naturally, this was when Owen showed up with their drinks. "If you don't know tha', you've not been looking close enough, mate," he said, clapping Abby on the shoulder affectionately. "I could tell you stories from when we were bairns that would—"

"But you won't," Abby said sharply. "Not unless you want me telling every single woman in the bar what you got up to as a *wee lad*."

Owen gave a good-natured shrug. "See what I mean?"

"It's the quiet ones that you've got to watch out for," Isaac said as he helped pass out the drinks. "Isn't that what they say? But Abby, seriously, I would love to hear your work one of these nights."

A silence followed Isaac's words. Steph's tight smile was accompanied by a barely perceptible shake of her head—as if she was afraid Abby might actually say yes.

Fat chance! Abby would sooner sign up for a triple root canal than face a room full of people, not to mention thousands of podcast listeners and YouTube subscribers. Hell, it could be millions by now, for all she knew, since she'd forbidden Steph and Ben from talking about the show's popularity around her—otherwise, she'd never be able to walk into The City Bookmark on a Friday night again.

To buy time, Abby picked up her drink and took a big sip. The End of the Rainbow might've been the most potent cocktail in the pub, but it was far from the tastiest. The liquor scorched her tongue and throat, burning away some more of her inhibitions while it was at it.

"Maybe someday," she rasped. "But Steph, I want to hear more about *your* big victory. What was your story about? And yours too, of course, Jane. I certainly didn't mean to imply that, just because you didn't win, it was..."

"Crap?" Owen suggested innocently, his hand still on Abby's shoulder.

Steph launched into an enthusiastic retelling as Owen returned to the bar and Jane stewed. Isaac broke in with praise for lines he especially admired, and Abby let herself drift off into that warm-honey place again, where men fell in love with women for their words, just as Abby once fell in love with Dan Chaon after devouring his short stories.

But who was she kidding? Abby never really loved Chaon—she didn't know the first thing about him. A literary crush wasn't real; it was just a yearning to share the magnificence of brilliant phrasing, the shiver of recognition of a beautifully expressed truth.

Or something like that.

What it wasn't—what a literary crush could never be—was reflected in the electric tension arcing between Isaac and Abby's best friend the world. No matter how much praise he heaped on the words that she had written, it could never make up for the cold reality that Isaac Ferrer would never look at her the way he was looking at Steph.

Chapter Fifteen

Nothing in life was free.

Every moment of contentment, every glimpse of beauty, every chance encounter with joy had to be paid for in the coin of its opposite. If something good happened, something bad was waiting just around the bend to even it out.

This cosmic balancing of scales wasn't a theory that Abby had come to through reason. Despite having an English degree, she'd always enjoyed her STEM classes, and she knew damn well that the nature of the universe was random and chaotic.

Nonetheless, her lived experience upheld the equation every time. Good hair day? Break a heel getting off the bus. Cute guy at the corner store winks as he hands over your bagel? Inattentive driver nearly kills you in a crosswalk.

Never was the principle of payback more in evidence than on the rare mornings when Abby woke to a massive, blinding hangover. The splitting headache, nausea, and general clammy misery arrived without fail every time she drank too much. This time, however, she almost welcomed her punishment: given her sins of the night before, absolution through divine retribution seemed more than fair.

Because Abby had been a coward.

Few things earned her scorn as much as cowardice. Reillys were made of audacious grit—how else would Gramps have had the guts to put every cent he owned into a failing bar? How would Gram have defied her family to marry a penniless American with a big mouth? Abby herself would never have gotten as far as she had without a thick skin and resilience. *No Quittin'*, as a sign above the bar read, *and no Bitchin'*.

But there was a reason Abby was sprawled sideways on top of the bedcovers wearing her clothes from the night before. Instead of dealing with her problems like a grownup, she'd made the weak and gutless decision to drink too many End of the Rainbows.

God, what had she been thinking? Nothing, by the end of the second one. Everything after that was a blur.

Abby groaned, burying her face in her pillow. She knew better. Growing up in a bar meant watching people attempt to drink their problems away every night of the week...and it never worked. So she'd vowed that she would never be the person sobbing and raging as she was stuffed into the back of a cab at closing time.

It was possible that vow had been broken last night. Abby's memory grew increasingly fuzzy as the night wore on. She fervently prayed that the door to her secrets had remained firmly locked, and she hadn't let anything slip about the true author of the Ships stories, or Ben's crush on Steph, or her own on Isaac.

She concentrated on reaching for her phone, earning a fresh wave of nausea for the effort. Holy cow—it was almost noon. She really needed to get up. Eat something. Greet the day.

Abby sat up and was rewarded by a seismic shift in her stomach. Okay—no breakfast. She'd start with a glass of water. Maybe ease her way into crackers after she'd been vertical for a while, and see how that went.

Abby rose from bed like a zombie, staggering and holding onto the furniture as she stumbled out of her bedroom and into the painful morning light.

She shrieked and covered her eyes to protect them from the cruel apocalyptic sunlight streaming in from the bay windows. Where the hell was the reliable San Francisco fog when she needed it?

"Hey, you're finally awake!" Steph sounded much too cheery. "We'd just about given up on you getting up in time."

"Not...up," Abby croaked, each syllable a struggle. "Changed my mind. Bad idea."

She tried to turn back, but the floor of the apartment chose that moment to lurch sideways, and she had to grab the door frame for support.

Hang the heck on. We...?

"Bad morning?" a familiar voice called. "I can't say I'm surprised. You put us all to shame last night."

Abby stifled a groan. Of course Isaac would be in her living room. She made a rapid assessment of her appearance

—bloated, bleary-eyed, crusty—and her breath, for which she had no words.

"Oh, hi," she croaked, wobbling into the room. Though slightly blurry, Isaac Ferrer was decidedly real and sitting very close to Steph on the couch. "What are you doing here?"

Abby instantly regretted the question. What if he'd spent the night? Somehow, she would have to muster friendly endorsement—or at the very least, indifference—to the romance blooming right under her nose.

Steph frowned. "Don't tell me you forgot."

"Um...?"

"You invited Isaac to come to the farmer's market with us."

This was news to Abby...and didn't answer the question of where Isaac had spent the night.

No. Do not think about that.

"Oh yeah," Abby said in a painful attempt at breezy cheer. "Farmer's market. Right. Sorry, I'm...just a little under the weather."

"If you're not up to it," Steph said, skewering Abby with a pointed stop-before-you-hurt-yourself look, "Isaac and I can go alone."

"No way!" Isaac said cheerfully. Either he was oblivious to the conversational undercurrents, or he was a goddamn sadist. "I need to try those ruby ginger truffles you were talking about. I woke up thinking about them."

She had? He did?

Not a sadist then...a sensualist. That treacherous warm feeling was back, deepening as Isaac came into focus in all his stubbly, masculine glory. No, for the love of God, it wasn't fair. Leave it to the man to look even better in stubble, an old T-shirt, and well-worn jeans.

"I don't know," Steph said doubtfully. "She seems pretty hungover."

"Not a problem." Isaac got up from the couch, rubbing his hands together. "There's no hangover in the world that can survive the Ferrer family cure."

"The what, now?"

"You'll see. C'mon, Steph, let's run to the store—unless you've got clam juice and horseradish on hand."

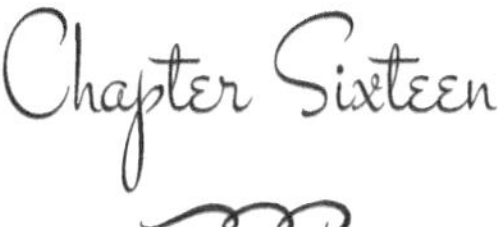

Chapter Sixteen

Isaac's homemade hangover remedy tasted like hell—burning, nasty, salty—but it worked like a charm. After splashing cold water on her face and running a comb through her hair, Abby was feeling well enough to throw on a sweater and jeans. Oversized sunglasses and a wide-brimmed hat completed her outfit.

It was probably for the best that there wasn't time for makeup and figuring out a flattering outfit. If Abby felt pretty, she risked getting sucked into the wretched cycle of hope and despair, thinking that maybe, just maybe, Isaac liked her...that way.

Abby knew better. Besides, she was supposed to be acting as Steph's wingman.

"Have you been to the Ferry building, Isaac?" she asked on the way over.

"Of course he has," Steph said. "Everyone's been to the Ferry building, even day-trippers."

"Actually..." Isaac said, looking adorably abashed, "I've

walked past it a couple dozen times but I haven't gone inside yet."

Steph's conversational U-turn was a thing of beauty, the kind of interactional fillip that was key to her success. "Then it's high time we take you there! Not to brag, but between Abby and me, you're in expert hands."

She launched seamlessly into a description of the Beaux Arts beauty that anchored the San Francisco waterfront like the jewel in a tiara, how it had survived earthquakes that leveled the rest of the city, how its former pedestrian bridge had been dismantled to supply scrap metal for WWII.

Abby knew that Steph had learned all this in preparation for a gala in the building's Great Nave. The research was part of her job—but it still made her seem cultured and brilliant.

Which she was! Steph was great! Abby was happy for her —no, *delighted* that her best friend had found such a great guy. Which was why it caught her off-guard when Steph checked her watch and let out an impatient huff as she was getting out of their ride share.

"Are...we in a rush?" Abby ventured.

Steph sighed. "Well, we got a late start. Not blaming you, just—everything is going to be picked over by the time we get there."

Abby rolled her eyes behind her dark glasses. It wasn't as if she and Steph were foodies. They mostly survived on takeout and microwave meals and coffee. Fresh produce rarely figured into the menu—in fact, the last time Abby bought bananas, they sat untouched on the kitchen counter, turning from green to yellow to black before she threw them out.

And besides, it wasn't Steph who'd come up with this idea, Abby reminded herself. She alone was to blame for her own suffering...on so many levels.

Owen had been right: she really did need help.

Abby was obviously a third wheel. Why had she agreed to come along? She could have been back in bed right now, sipping flat ginger ale and wallowing in self-pity. It was obvious that Steph had hoped a solo outing would take her relationship with Isaac to the next level.

Bullshit!

Abby winced at the judgment of her inner arbiter. It would have been nice to keep pretending, but the reason she was here had everything to do with the way Isaac's face lit up when she'd wavered. *I woke up thinking about them*, he'd said, and for a split second Abby had allowed herself to imagine that it wasn't a chocolate truffle he'd been thinking about.

Steph linked arms with Isaac and rushed to cross Embarcadero Street, and Abby decided to get some distance from her bad decision, letting the crowd of pedestrians swallow her.

Breakfast. That's what she needed, Abby decided as tantalizing aromas spilled out of the food stalls. She bypassed picture-perfect artichokes, glistening fish on beds of ice, and gorgeous homemade jams and soaps to join the line at a popular empanada stand. Next was a gallon-sized cup of coffee, and then Abby found a bench overlooking the water and settled in to watch the sailboats gliding serenely under the Bay Bridge.

Even with the tourists swarming the ferries and the dull throbbing in her head, Abby felt herself relax. She took a bite of her empanada and sighed contentedly at the warm, flaky goodness.

"Am I interrupting? Or would you like company?"

Abby nearly dropped the pastry. "Sure!" she said with her mouth full, scooting over to make room for Isaac—but it was still such a tight squeeze that their thighs pressed together. "Where's Steph?"

"High stakes negotiations with one of the merchants over cabbage, from what I could tell."

"Ah, it must be kimchi-making time." Steph had actually only made the dish once, when her mother came to visit. But because she was supposed to be helping, Abby added, "Her grandmother's recipe is really good. I'm sure you'll like it."

"No doubt." Isaac stretched out his long legs. "We were getting hungry, so I said I'd get some snacks. Looks like great minds think alike."

He held up a white paper bag just like her own, and Abby couldn't help but smile. The man had some sort of good-taste radar. "What kind did you get?"

He opened the bag and peered inside. "Let's see. Spicy carne, pollo, and dulce de leche."

"Oh, save the dulce for Steph. She loves those."

"What did you get?"

"One ham, one veggie." Abby surreptitiously brushed crumbs from her sweater. "I'm saving the veggie one for later."

"Then you've got more willpower than me. I'm always ravenous after a big night of drinking."

"Oh, trust me. So am I."

Isaac gave her a curious look. "Then why are you saving it?"

Why, indeed? Abby wished she could walk back her mistake. Ordinarily she never voiced thoughts like that, instead shoving them deep down in the shame bog.

But there was something about Isaac that made her feel... relaxed. Like she could let her defenses down a little. Besides, what was she worried about? There was no point in trying to impress Isaac. And in her role as a wingman, a bit of self-deprecation might make Steph look even better by comparison.

It might even be for the best if Abby held nothing back until she managed to drive Isaac away. At least then she could finally get him out of her mind.

"Okay," she said, taking a deep breath. "Basically, there's an unspoken rule that women—especially *fat* women—shouldn't be seen enjoying food in public. And if we do, if we order pie or eat a cheeseburger or something, then we have to apologize."

Isaac seemed taken aback. "Whose stupid rule is that?"

"Everyone's," Abby said, shrugging. "Society's. I guess you could blame American culture's weird puritanism—it's like every pleasure or indulgence has to be scrutinized through a moral lens."

Belatedly, Abby realized that Isaac hadn't responded with the universal protest—*but you're not fat*—spoken earnestly, even desperately, with a faint tinge of resentment that the taboo topic had even been raised.

A rush of unexpected gratitude swelled in her...because the truth was she *was* fat. Every time someone tried to deny it, no matter how well-meaning, they only reinforced the idea that being fat was shameful.

But there was no judgment in Isaac's warm brown eyes, his sexy grin. "Fascinating," he said. "Well, then society can to go to hell. If you're hungry, eat. Besides, I'm going to need help with these." He pointed to a white paper box decorated with the patisserie's famous pink stripe. "The way you described these truffles last night, I'm expecting a transformational experience."

Abby's blush deepened. "I guess I really ran my mouth last night. Sorry about that."

"Don't apologize. It was nice to see you open up."

"You're very diplomatic," she mumbled, digging into her second empanada.

As they ate, silence stretched between them, one which Isaac seemed to find perfectly comfortable. It was actually kind of nice, once Abby relaxed enough to enjoy her late breakfast. Isaac laughed at the seagulls hopping around hoping for crumbs and again when the ferry blew its horn and Abby gave a startled squeak.

It felt...companionable, sitting together like this, enjoying a beautiful day. For a moment, Abby let herself imagine that they were sitting together because they *were* together. It felt very nice.

Too nice. Fantasies were dangerous; they made reality all the more painful. Abby decided to nip this one in the bud.

"So! Things seem to be going well with you and Steph."

"What things?"

"Um...you know. What with you coming to see her at Ships every week, and the bar after, and...last night."

Isaac frowned slightly. "What happened last night?"

And there it was, the moment that always came when Isaac was present, when Abby wished the earth would open up and swallow her. "Nothing! I wasn't thinking anything."

She crammed the rest of the empanada in her mouth so that she would be forced to stop talking.

"Oh, no you don't." Mirth sparkled in Isaac's smile. "Now you have to tell me. What do you think happened?"

Abby swallowed with effort. "We've already established that I was drunk. I wasn't thinking clearly."

"And..."

There was going to be no mercy for her. Abby resisted squirming, acutely aware of Isaac's thigh against hers. "You have to realize that I don't even remember coming home last night."

"And..."

"And since you were in the apartment when I woke up this morning, I just kind of figured..."

"That I spent the night with Steph?"

"Oh God, I'm sorry I brought it up." Abby covered her face with her hands. "It's none of my business. I didn't mean to offend you."

"You didn't offend me, Abby."

She peeked through the gaps in her fingers. Sure enough, Isaac's eyes crinkled with amusement.

"I hate to burst your bubble," he said, "but I left the bar an hour after you did. And I didn't get to your house until right before you got up this morning."

"Oh."

"Does that...disappoint you?"

"No. It's not like that. Like I said, it's none of my business. It's just—never mind."

"Abby…"

Heaven help her, just hearing Isaac say her name was enough to cause her heart to start pounding. "It's just that Steph is my friend, and I would do anything to protect her."

Isaac nodded slowly. "Is this the part where you tell me you'll break my knee caps if I hurt your best friend?"

"Something like that," Abby admitted sheepishly. "You're a big deal, Isaac—an actual celebrity. People look at you a certain way. They can get wrapped up in their own fantasies about you, and that can lead to—"

"—ending up with a broken heart when reality doesn't match their expectations?"

"Exactly."

"I understand." Isaac covered her hand with his own, and Abby nearly fell over from the shock. Instead, she tried to ignore the delicious warm feeling while pretending it was normal. Totally normal for gorgeous men to hold hands with her in public; happened every day.

"But you don't have to worry," Isaac continued gravely, "because—"

And that was when Steph showed up, striding toward them in her white skinny jeans, holding a beautiful cabbage and six perfect peonies tied with a pale pink ribbon.

"Empanadas? Sweet!" she gushed—then nearly tripped over her own feet when she spotted Isaac's hand on Abby's.

Chapter Seventeen

Abby's family had always taken fierce pride in their Irish ancestry, and she was no exception. As a little kid, she loved being introduced to Grandpa's regulars as his "little shamrock," and was secretly pleased when he started calling her his "Celtic tiger" after a customer left her a twenty-dollar tip.

But that cherished identity came with one serious downside: a complexion that could be described as rosy at best, but which Abby more often thought of as ruddy. She'd spent a small fortune on primers and concealers and foundations over the years, but nothing could completely hide the florid patches that appeared on her face in a disheartening variety of circumstances.

Tired? Twin purple shadows under her eyes.

Too much to drink? A nose as bright as Rudolph's.

The worst by far was embarrassment, which resulted in an all-over tinge that, depending on the depth of Abby's mortification, ranged from a shell pink to an angry red. And right now, she was pretty sure her whole damn face was lit up like a traffic signal.

She'd yanked her hand back the moment she caught sight of Steph's stricken expression, feeling suddenly mortified, as if she'd been caught engaging in some forbidden taboo.

Steph's smile tightened. "Am I interrupting something?"

"No. Of course not," Abby stammered, tripping over her own words. "We were just talking."

"Oh?" Steph imbued that single syllable with chilly skepticism. "About what?"

"Snacks," Isaac said genially. "We both got empanadas. I saved you the dulce de leche. Here, we can make room."

He patted the bench and squeezed even more firmly against Abby. Instincts forged long ago prompted her to make herself smaller, but she'd already shrunk as far from Isaac as she could...and so with nowhere else to go, Abby shot up from the bench and retreated to the railing overlooking the water lapping gently against the pier.

Steph took the spot Abby had vacated and dug into the bag. "I know I'm being bad, but I just can't resist these."

"Funny you should say that," Isaac remarked. "That's what Abby and I were talking about."

"How sinful these dulce empanadas are?"

"How women are expected to apologize for enjoying their food."

"Huh." Steph unfolded a napkin daintily on her lap. "I've never really thought about it, but, yeah, I guess it's true. And I'm sure it worse for you, Abby. That must be hard."

The shift from skepticism to sympathy caused Abby to tighten her hands on the railing. Steph probably thought Isaac had been holding her hand out of pity.

He probably *had* been pitying her. Abby replayed their conversation, and it suddenly seemed obvious. Being nice to the fat friend—wasn't that what the heroes in romantic stories did?

When Isaac smiled at Steph, when his thigh was pressed against hers, it held another was another meaning entirely. *Obviously*.

Abby tried to ignore the leaden feeling of jealousy that settled into her, pretending to gaze at the sailboats bobbing in the bay. As much as it hurt to watch Steph swoop in and casually take Abby's place next to Isaac, maybe this time she would learn. Maybe this was the reminder she needed that unattainable crushes were best dismantled and forgotten.

Like the quirky, fat best friend in a novel, the most she could hope for was to be a supporting character. Her job was to show up and comfort the heroine at her darkest moment, dust her off, and get her back in the game. Any love interest would be played for comic effect—the awkward tech support guy; the bumbling, shy groomsman; the fat bro the hero went to college with—and their romance would be treated as just another joke.

And if it was a story like the ones Abby wrote for Ships... well, she could bring down the house, make the audience laugh and cry, win that damn trophy every time, but she would never get the credit.

Because that was the way you wanted it, Abby reminded

herself with a ferocity that bordered on vicious. *You're allergic to attention. You hate having people's eyes on you.*

Except that the rules seemed to change when they were Isaac's eyes, those depthless, wise, sexy eyes the shade of burnt umber.

Abby glanced over her shoulder to see Steph pop the last bite into her mouth, making a show of chewing with undisguised rapture, then double down and slowly lick each fingertip, never taking her eyes off Isaac. For a moment, he watched with a startled expression—and then burst out laughing.

Steph had never been subtle, that was for sure—but she also never took herself too seriously, one of the many qualities Abby loved about her. Steph saw life as a stage, an endless opportunity to perform. And yet she wasn't pretending, could never be described as fake. Her love of attention didn't spring from neediness, but from—well, Abby wasn't sure where it came from, only that it was genuine and generous and fun to be around, a perfect complement to her own sense of reserve.

But there was another side to Steph, one that sprang from her own deepest insecurities, and like Abby, she was masterful at hiding it. That shame was the one taboo subject between them wasn't really surprising. But while Steph had never noticed when Abby froze up, the reverse wasn't true... there were moments like this one when Abby caught the briefest glimpse of distress in Steph's eyes before her glossy smile slid smoothly back into place.

"Well, I hope you've still got an appetite," Isaac said,

opening the pink and white box. "Because these are begin-ning to melt. There's no way they'll make it home."

"Mmmm," Steph murmured, giving her stomach an exaggerated comic rub. *Just kidding around,* the gesture said, the companion to the you-didn't-think-I-was-serious-did-you excuse that Steph was never without.

(Oh, no—you thought I was trying to seduce you? Hilarious!)

Then her face fell in playful dismay. "I can't take another bite."

"Can't or shouldn't?" Isaac asked with genuine curiosity.

"Come on," Steph hedged, proving that those unwritten rules were just as ingrained in her. "There's got to be, like, a million calories in those."

"You'd seriously deny yourself when Abby swears these are the best chocolates in the world?"

Steph's smile turned brittle. "Another time."

"How about you, Abby?" Isaac held out the box.

Abby hesitated, old habits warring with a delicate vein of courage that Isaac had helped to create. She'd done so much pretending lately, as Ships' success put her ever more squarely in the crosshairs of the conflict between wanting too much and the pain of disappointment.

Abby was no stranger to denying herself, but lately the cost had somehow mushroomed, a staggering weight she couldn't bear much longer before something gave way.

She watched with a strange detachment as her hand shot out and plucked the biggest, most delectable cocoa-dusted confection from the box and popped it into her mouth. She let her eyelids flutter closed and surrendered to the satiny, chocolaty bliss.

So. Damn. Good. Abby chewed slowly, savoring every blessed bit.

When she opened her eyes... Isaac was watching her with a look of sheer delight.

Chapter Eighteen

Steph's mood soured as soon as their ride pulled away from the curb, Isaac disappearing into the throng of people waiting for the traffic light in front of the Ferry Building.

Abby's friendship with Steph didn't require them to fill every little silence with conversation. Today, however, Steph's nonverbal communication seemed louder than the din of the crowd they'd just left—from sighing to fiddling with her bangle bracelets to clearing her throat.

They were nearly home when Abby couldn't bear it anymore. "Are you going to tell me what's eating at you, or do I have to guess?"

Steph gave her a look that was both guilty and accusatory. "I can't believe you ate that fucking chocolate."

Abby blinked. "I can't believe you turned it down," she said with an awkward little laugh.

"That's not what I'm talking about, and you know it." Steph's voice took on an edge. "You left me hanging out there. You were supposed to be my wingman, but instead of backing me up, you made me look like a jackass."

"All I did was eat a piece of chocolate," Abby said, her hackles rising.

"Yeah, *after* setting it up as a test of virtue."

Abby couldn't believe this. "What the hell are you talking about?"

"'Women who apologize for not wanting to stuff their faces are the worst,'" Steph said in a mocking voice.

"I didn't say that. I would *never* say anything like that, and you know it!"

"Okay, sorry." Steph was obviously not the least bit sorry. "But that's what Isaac took away from your conversation."

Stung, Abby was torn between hurling Steph's words back at her and apologizing. But she hadn't done anything wrong. Not only that, it was slowly dawning on Abby that she was witnessing a temper tantrum, a rare display of insecurity from someone who was used to being able to control every narrative.

She took a deep breath before choosing her words with care. "I really don't think it was," she said, laying a sympathetic hand on Steph's shoulder. "And I know for a fact he doesn't think you're a jackass."

A bit of the tension drained from Steph's face. "How do you know? Did he say something about me?"

"Mmm...sort of."

"What do you mean, 'sort of'?"

"Look, Steph...I may have been a little confused this morning when I got up and Isaac was already in the house."

"Oh, no. What did you say?"

"Just that, uh…I thought he spent the night with you."

"*Abby!*" Her snit forgotten, Steph grabbed Abby's arm. "What did *he* say?"

"That he hated to burst my bubble, but he didn't."

After a long moment, Steph released Abby's arm and started thoughtfully fiddling with her bracelet. "Burst your bubble…" she repeated. "What am I supposed to read into that?"

Abby wondered if she should share the exact words Isaac had used: *Does that…disappoint you?*

She didn't think she'd ever forget the way he looked at her, the sound of his rumbling voice as he asked her that question. She'd been too shocked in the moment to realize that there was another way to hear Isaac's words, one that might never have occurred to her if Steph hadn't challenged her.

Because if Steph was truly confident in Isaac's attraction to her, she wouldn't give Abby's interactions with him a second thought.

And there had been a—well, a *suggestiveness* in the way Isaac spoke. As if he was intrigued…maybe even hoping there was another answer.

Abby pushed down the thought. She was being ridiculous again, letting her fantasies get in the way of good sense.

"I was talking about what came after that," Abby clarified. "When I gave Isaac the whole 'don't even think about breaking my best friend's heart' routine."

Steph's expression softened. "You don't need to protect me like that, Abby."

"Wait, listen. Right after that, Isaac told me that I didn't have to worry because he has nothing but honorable intentions toward you.”

Steph’s eyes widened. “He said that?”

“Pretty much,” Abby admitted. “He was just getting to the honorable intentions part when you walked up.”

“Oh…*Oh!*”

Emotions raced across Steph’s face as she reconsidered the conversation. She took Abby’s hands as the car slowed to a stop in front of the house. “Oh my God, Abs. I’ve been such a jerk. I’m so sorry.”

“We’re here,” the driver announced unnecessarily.

“It’s really fine,” Abby said.

“No, it isn’t.”

“It *is*. But let’s talk about this later, okay?”

There was frank curiosity in the driver’s expression reflected in the rearview mirror. Soon there wouldn’t be a driver left in all of San Francisco who didn’t know the sad state of Abby’s love life. She was starting to think that prurient curiosity was a requirement for the job. She scooted out of the car before he could enjoy any more of the free show.

Steph followed right behind, opening her arms for a hug. “I’m sorry, Abs. I don’t think you’re a terrible wingman.”

As if that had been the most demeaning part of their argument. “I already told you it’s fine,” Abby said with a touch of annoyance.

Steph dropped her arms. “Yeah, but you’re saying it in that *voice*. You know, the one where you’re still really annoyed with me but you hate conflict so you pretend you’re not.”

Abby seethed. That was the problem with arguing with your best friend—she knew every one of your tells.

"*Fine*," she blurted. "You want to know what I'm really upset over? That you and I are arguing over a guy. That's not our thing—we don't *do* that."

Steph's expression underwent a complicated adjustment. "You're right," she finally said. "I never should have made this about Isaac. It's just that today was just...well, we probably should have talked about it first. But you are the world's greatest ghostwriter, and that's what I need you to be right now, Abby. The face-to-face stuff I can handle on my own."

Abby's emotions made a U-turn of their own. "Hold on a minute," she said as Steph headed for their front door.

Steph looked up from digging around her purse for her key, masking a frisson of impatience with a smile. "Hmm?"

Abby forced the words out, her heart thumping wildly. "Are you saying that you didn't want me to come along today?"

"Of course not," Steph said too quickly. "Well...yeah, actually."

Even though she'd suspected it, hearing Steph confirm it felt like a slap.

"Oh, come on, Abby, don't get all offended," Steph protested. "I tried dropping hints before we left."

"Yeah. You did." Abby didn't bother trying to keep the edge out of her voice. "But what about what *I* wanted?"

The confusion in Steph's eyes took too long to resolve. "But...you were hung over."

Abby knew she should drop it. They were out on the sidewalk with Saturday afternoon traffic walking by. Besides, there was nothing Steph could say now that would make her feel any better. But... "And so were you last weekend, remember? But that didn't stop you from coming out to lunch with Owen and Dex and me."

"Yeah, but that—it's not the same. That was just your brother and his friend."

"And Isaac is *my* friend."

Steph's eyes narrowed slightly. "Ri-i-i-ght."

It was only one word, spoken softly enough to let Steph pretend she'd said nothing at all. And yet never in the history of their friendship had Abby felt the sharp arrow of pain that pierced her heart.

It must have shown on her face, because Steph was instantly remorseful. "Abby, I'm sorry. I didn't mean it like that."

Except she did.

Abby felt her mouth flatten into a hard line. Maybe it was all that horseradish in Isaac's hangover cure that had lit a fire in her, but she couldn't seem to let it drop. "Then tell me, Steph...how exactly did you mean it?"

"I just—I didn't—" Steph stammered before opening the door and holding it open with a pleading look. "Wouldn't you rather talk about this inside?"

Abby was stunned. Steph never cared who heard what came out of her mouth, no matter how outrageous. It was part of her charm, her brand—but at the moment she looked utterly miserable, ducking her chin and staring at the ground.

Well, chagrin was a good start, but it wouldn't come close to making up for Steph's cutting words. So Abby planted her feet and crossed her arms. A young mother shot her a dirty look as she maneuvered a stroller around her on the cracked sidewalk.

"Right here's fine. Go ahead and tell me whatever you have to say."

"It's just...well," Steph mumbled. "I assumed you didn't like Isaac because you never talk to him. Until today, anyway."

Now it was Abby's turn to squirm, because Steph was right—Abby couldn't put enough distance between herself and Isaac in front of her friends and family.

But Abby bit back the automatic apology that followed her rare fibs—because Steph's crime was worse. That muttered "right" might have been a toss-away comment, but it revealed what Abby had suspected all along—that not only did Steph think she'd never have a shot at a relationship with a guy like Isaac, but she also couldn't imagine him even wanting to be friends with Abby.

Her anger went from a simmer to a boil, and it took a mighty effort to shove it back down deep inside with the rest of her miserable secrets. It was a hell of a lot easier to be angry with Steph—or Owen or Dex, or literally anyone else—than with herself. Because while Steph's thoughtless aside had missed the mark—it wasn't by much.

Sure, Isaac and Abby were friendly.

But that didn't make them friends.

"I talk to him," she insisted grimly. "At Ships, at the pub. Yesterday we were texting while I was at work. Just because I don't fangirl all over him, doesn't mean—"

"You think I'm a fangirl?"

Shit. Now Steph was the one who sounded hurt. Really hurt.

"No, Steph, I..."Abby forced herself to take a breath. "What I think is that we are both hotheaded and acting like assholes right now. Maybe it's because we're tired or hung over, but I think the best thing for me is to go for a walk and cool down a little before continuing this conversation."

Before Steph could try to talk her out of it, Abby hurried down the street, tears gathering in her eyes. In all their years of friendship, there had been maybe half a dozen times when Abby had lost her temper with Steph, leaving her more startled than dismayed. Then Steph would walk on eggshells for a few days, until things slowly settled back to normal between them.

Steph hadn't come from a talk-things-through kind of family. As close-knit as the Trans were, they weren't big on discussing feelings. Which generally suited Abby fine, since her own family—her mom, grandfather, and brother, anyway—tended to blurt out whatever they were feeling without pausing to consider how it would land.

Except for when they were angry. That was the one emotion that was off-limits among the Reillys, the one realm where they didn't dare tread. Over time, Abby had pieced together the reason; though her grandmother never talked about it, she'd grown up in the chaos and fury of an alcoholic household, and couldn't bear even a hint of an argument. It was a testament to Grandpa's love for his wife that he managed to reign in his larger-than-life personality for her— by going for walks until his temper had cooled, even if that meant staying away for hours.

And so Abby and Owen had learned to act as if nothing bothered them, to apply their famous Reilly grit to every problem. Abby could still remember Grandpa's forced cheer in response to every setback and slight: "Nothing a little elbow grease can't fix," he'd say, or "Why get mad when you can get even?"—the latter delivered with a wink to show he was kidding.

Getting upset meant you were weak. Despite the fact that Abby and Owen were grown-ass adults now, neither of them had been able to escape that toxic family myth. Owen funneled his rages into working on the bar, even if it meant fixing things that weren't broken—but Abby turned hers inward.

But San Francisco on a sunny Saturday afternoon, when the entire city seemed to be out, wasn't great for wallowing in misery. Her vision blurred by tears, Abby nearly collided with a guy carrying a pizza, earning a dirty look.

Abby wasn't having it, not today. "Watch where you're going!" she snarled.

It felt great to be the asshole for once, like pent-up steam released from a valve. But the feeling only lasted a few seconds, replaced by a wave of regret.

She'd lost control. She'd let her anger slip—and worse yet, she'd taken it out on some poor guy who was just minding his business.

"Sorry," she called over her shoulder, then picked up her pace again, as hell-for-leather as any of Grandpa's bad moods. And just like him, Abby paid no attention to where she was headed, mile after mile until her feet ached and she suddenly found herself standing in front of O'Reilly's.

Abby closed her eyes and waited for her pulse to slow, her shirt stuck to her back with sweat. Damn, she was predictable. Every crisis brought her running right back to where she started.

Except she wasn't a kid with a skinned knee anymore, and Grandma wasn't waiting inside with a Band-Aid and a plate of cookies. And Abby was in no mood for Owen and his unvarnished opinions, no matter how well-meaning.

So instead, Abby walked two doors down to The City Bookmark, her sanctuary since childhood.

Because even your worst problems couldn't follow you into a good book.

Chapter Nineteen

As Abby entered the bookstore, she was greeted by the comforting chime of the bronze tingsha meditation bells hanging from the door.

Ben's aunt and uncle had brought the bells back from a trip to Tibet years ago, and the sound of them announcing customers' arrival always took Abby back to childhood. She'd come so often that Mr. and Mrs. Kantor had a running joke about whether the title of official City Bookmark mascot should go to Abby or Tiffy, the big ginger cat who lived in the shop.

Tiffy had retired to Florida with the Kantors when Ben took over, so Abby supposed she'd won the honor by default, especially since Ben certainly treated her like family. But despite their close friendship—or perhaps because of it—she was glad to see that it was Minerva who was manning the shop today.

"Hi, Minerva," Abby called, some of the tension leaving her shoulders. The last thing she needed right now was Ben rehashing last night—especially since he was a pot calling a kettle black. Ben had been right beside Abby while she'd attempted to drink her troubles into oblivion, and if memory served, he'd matched her drink for drink. He was probably home nursing a hangover of his own.

"Hey, Abby." Minerva looked up from her latest project, a length of shimmering fuchsia silk embroidered in tiny geometric stitches.

"What are you working on?" Instantly, Abby realized her mistake, but it was too late to take back her words.

Minerva's eyes took on the gleam of a zealot. "This is a kutch-work potli bag," she said reverently. "Want to see?"

Abby blanched. "I, um…maybe later."

"I'm using a pattern from the seventeenth century that was originally designed to embellish ornamental silk slippers," Minerva continued. "It's a fascinating story, really. There's historic evidence that the tradition comes from the mochis, or shoemakers, working in Sindh at the time. Though recently an argument has come to light that its roots may actually—"

"That is fascinating," Abby managed to interject, the hangover hammer in her head pounding away. "But I'll have to ask you about it another time. I'm just here to browse—and to be honest, spend a little time alone."

Minerva nodded benignly and picked up her needle. Fortunately, she was almost impossible to offend. "Say no more. And you picked a good day for it. The morning after Ships is always quiet."

Bullet dodged. Buoyed by relief, Abby entered the peaceful sanctuary of the bookshelves.

In a great stroke of luck, the Kantors had purchased the entire building for a song in the seventies, and earned enough from renting the apartments above the store to more than make up for the profits they sacrificed by refusing to subdivide the store. There was room for several comfortable old upholstered chairs that offered people a cozy spot to browse, an extensive labyrinthine cat tree that was once exclusively Tiffy's domain and now held cards and mugs and calendars, and the space in back where Ships in the Night shared a rotation with author visits, children's story time, and community events.

Abby's favorite feature, however, were the ancient oak shelves that Aaron Kantor had picked up cheap when nearby Merritt College demolished their old library. Abby knew exactly where Owen and Dex had carved their initials, where a much-thumbed copy of the Kama Sutra had once been shelved, and where she'd discovered an anonymous love letter addressed to a long-ago shop employee, a young man with dreamy eyes and dark ringlets springing out from his head. (Abby had put the letter back where she found it.)

Today, however, she was seeking comfort rather than mystery. She browsed aimlessly, greeting old friends tucked into the shelves, straightening them and patting their spines affectionately. Abby could hear Minerva mumbling to herself as she worked ("one, two, skip two—wait, is that buttonhole or herringbone? Maybe I should knot off first..."), which made it easy to do the same, speaking out loud the conversations that usually took place in her head.

Selwyn was her longest-running friendship, but far from the only one. Ben and his employees might spend more time in the shop, but Abby had them beat in longevity, and searching for her favorite books felt like visiting old friends... the kind of friends she could truly count on.

Friends who would never embarrass or shame her. Who were solid and dependable and unchanging, other than the occasional updated cover. Who wouldn't dream of suggesting that Abby was a coward for not pursuing her crush.

Though actually...

Reading wasn't the domain of the passive, as contemporary culture too often suggested. Not every bookworm was mild-mannered. In fact, the best books were full of conflict and drama; they challenged and provoked; they were sometimes downright subversive.

Abby had been shaken up countless times by the books she read, her world turned upside down and inside out. Sometimes she felt as though she'd run a marathon or detonated explosives or participated in heresy by the final page.

And books had honed the rough outlines of the social and moral codes established by Abby's family. There was a shocking amount of wisdom to be found in the pages of forgotten books, even after the winds of change had surely rendered the world unrecognizable to their long-dead authors.

Not all of them, of course. For every literary pearl of wisdom there were dozens of dated or offensive or disproven passages, entire books devoted to preaching unthinkable attitudes about people of color, queer and nonbinary folks, the neurodivergent—seemingly everyone but the overwhelmingly privileged white men who'd authored them.

It was no surprise that many of Abby's old favorites had been penned by women at a time when doing so was unheard of. Like that lovely faded green hardback on the bottom shelf, a lone copy of *The Tenant of Wildfell Hall*. Unlike the books by her sisters Charlotte and Emily, which Ben kept on near-constant reorder, Anne Bronte's second novel had gone unsold for years.

Abby knelt and ran a fingertip down its gold-embossed spine. Anne never got the love her sisters did, even though her novels packed just as much of a punch as Charlotte's *Jane Eyre* or Emily's *Wuthering Heights*.

At its core, the game-changing feminist novel wove a powerful lesson through its pages—that a quiet, private life truly lived on your own terms could be one of the most subversive things in the world. But it was a secondary theme, that unchecked wish fulfillment led to ruined lives and relationships, that felt stingingly personal today.

"You get it, don't you, Anne?" Abby murmured, positioning the book to stand out among its flashier neighbors. Many of her favorite books could be interpreted on multiple levels, their themes applied to myriad real-life circumstances. But today the lesson that had always seemed meant for people like Steph and Owen—those who had no trouble going after what they wanted—seemed to have turned its spotlight on her. "But what am I supposed to do when the things I want are at odds with each other?"

"Excuse me, miss," a deep voice intoned, "but if you persist in bothering the authors, I'm going to have to ask you to leave."

Abby jumped to her feet to find Ben grinning down from the other side of the shelf.

"I didn't think you were here today," she stammered, smoothing the hem of her blouse.

Ben shrugged. "It's the end of the month. Hangover be damned, payroll won't run itself. You're blushing," he added, delighted. "It's not like this is the first time I've caught you talking to the merchandise."

Abby ignored that. "I...sympathize," she said stiffly. "About the hangover, I mean."

"Yeah, I'm kind of surprised to see you in here, given how you were throwing them back last night. Minerva said you wanted to be alone, but...you know." Abby nodded; it was common knowledge that Minerva wasn't exactly a master of conversational nuance. "And then I saw you chatting it up with the Bronte sisters and figured you wouldn't mind me poking my head in."

Abby held her hands up in surrender. "I grant you permission to come aboard," she told Ben, finding that she actually meant it. Self-exile got old quickly, and Ben was the least abrasive of her friends, thoughtful and courteous and gentle in contrast to the general air of blunt jocularity around Owen and Dex and Steph.

God knew Abby could use a little of what Ben had to offer right now. She didn't even mind when he peered around her hopefully.

"Is Steph with you?"

"Sorry...just me today." Abby wished she had better news to offer him. Wished Steph would finally wake up and see what she was missing.

"Oh, well. Her loss."

It was surprising to Abby that Ben's crush had survived so many years of watching Steph's love life from the sidelines, but he always rebounded cheerfully enough. If only she could do the same. "Ben..." she started, then got stuck.

"Yeah?" He took Abby's elbow and steered her toward the back of the store. "Spit it out, Abby, and I'll make you a cup of tea."

"Not that horrible green stuff," she said with a shudder. And then, so she wouldn't lose her nerve, she blurted "How do you do it?"

Ben gave her a sidelong look. "Do what?"

Abby groaned softly. She'd wanted to ask him forever, but it had seemed rude. Presumptuous, even. But now she needed to know.

In fact, Abby suddenly realized that it was no accident that her aimless wandering had brought her here. Her subconscious mind had decided it was time to learn the truth, and now it was too late to back down.

"How do you stand it? How can you keep seeing Steph week after week, joking around with her, drinking with her, knowing that she's not..."

Abby couldn't bring herself to spell it out—but Ben was made of tougher stuff than she. As understanding dawned in his eyes, any hint of the casual banter of the last few minutes vanished, and for a fraction of a second Abby glimpsed the hurt he usually hid so well.

But it was quickly replaced by a kind smile.

"Steph is...well, I know what she isn't, Abby. She's not a trophy to be won or lost from week to week. She's as complex and unpredictable as anyone I've ever known. And yeah, I'll admit that I wish I was the one who…" He cleared his throat, focusing on the floor for a moment "But anyway, so far it hasn't worked out that way. Maybe someday it will, and maybe it won't, but when you're really into someone—" He gave a what're-you-gonna-do shrug. "You just want them to be happy, you know? It doesn't even matter if they choose you."

Abby's heart broke hearing Ben's words, and not just because she felt them down to her core. For the first time all day—for the first time in a while, if she was being honest—she wasn't indulging in self-pity. The sorrow she felt was for Steph.

Her best friend had no idea what she was missing. For years, she'd had a smart, funny, interesting man right in front of her. One who adored her just the way she was. One she would never have to deceive in order to capture his attention. Steph deserved that kind of unconditional love and affection. She deserved the happiness that went along with it.

They'd arrived at the door to the office, and Abby took a shaky breath while Ben punched in the code. "Do you really believe that?"

"I don't know," Ben admitted, flashing her a smile tinged with sadness. "It sounds good, anyway. And it beats trying to drown my loneliness and longing in so many End of the Rainbows that I end up stumbling around a bookstore and talking to myself the next day."

So he knew—he'd probably known all along. But being Ben, he didn't mention Isaac's name, or say anything more about it. Only Ben could make silence feel like a hug.

"I wasn't talking to myself, Ben. I was talking to Anne Bronte."

"Yeah? Did she answer you?"

"She did. She...implied that I'm a whiner."

Ben raised his eyebrows. "She could cut you some slack. That bit about wanting the people you love to be happy? That included you too."

"I *am* happy," Abby insisted too quickly.

"Right." Ben's echoed Steph's skepticism from earlier that day, but unlike Steph, he didn't leave it there. "But have you ever thought that, just maybe, you could be happier?"

She had, of course. Wasn't that what all these ridiculous daydreams about Isaac Ferrer were about? Fantasizing over a sweeping romance, heated passion, and a partnership of equals?

"Of course, you're always welcome to hang out with us slackers while you think about it," Ben said fondly, giving Abby a little shove toward the tatty old sofa and starting to fill the kettle. "If you play your cards right, I'll let you hide out back here all afternoon and read."

"Deal," Abby sighed, sinking into the ancient down cushions and closing her eyes. After a moment, though, she opened one eye. "You know, Ben...someday you should tell Steph how you really feel about her."

"I'm sure I will," Ben said easily, dropping into his desk chair. "One day, when the time is right."

"Right." It was finally Abby's turn to mutter the word of the day before closing her eyes again.

Chapter Twenty

Why did her friends have to be so damn smart? Abby's attempt to while away the afternoon reading lasted only a couple of hours. Not even an advance copy of the latest Emma Straub novel, a prize she would have ordinarily traded an arm for, could hold her attention.

She was plagued with racing thoughts, her mind going over and over the morning's events—the time she'd spent with Isaac and her argument with Steph. Once she finally gave up and set down her book, she remembered something Ben had said earlier about Steph.

She's not a trophy to be won or lost.

He was right—and not just about Steph, but about people in general. Attraction, affection, love could be fought for, but never guaranteed. And somewhere along the line, both Abby and Steph had lost sight of that.

Each of them had imagined Isaac into her own ideal man,

and now they were fighting over him like children. It wasn't fair to any of them, and it needed to stop.

It shouldn't be hard. For Abby's part, she'd never harbored any real hope that a romance with Isaac would come to be. In fact, it might even be the fantasy that was making her so miserable. The futility of wishing for the unattainable crushed the soul slowly, but just as surely, as a decisive rejection.

Yes, Ben had longed for Steph for years, but the situation was different. Abby and Isaac weren't perfectly matched lovers who just needed a little push, but worlds apart. So unalike that those closest to her thought of Abby and Isaac as mere acquaintances.

It was past time to accept reality.

Steph might not be so easy to convince, especially after today's fireworks. It would take subtle persuasion to guide her away from her infatuation and toward the wonderful man who'd been there all along. Though it wasn't really any of Abby's business. Better to stay in her own lane and—

An idea popped up in Abby's mind, scattering her good sense like marbles. Writing for Ships had been like a master class in setting up scenes of erotic seduction. She'd managed to conjure believable heat between the unlikeliest of literary pairs—compared to that, nudging her dear friends together ought to be a piece of cake.

Abby leaned back on the sofa in the now empty office as she came up with a plan. Ben, who had gone out on the floor to cover Minerva's break, had already set the stage by choosing *A Tale of Two Cities* for the next event. It was easy to imagine him in role of Sydney Carton, trading his life for the happiness of his true love.

Sure, it would be hard to outdo a line as iconic as *It is a far, far better thing that I do, than I have ever done; it is a far, far better rest I go to than I have ever known.* But *She's not a trophy* was still pretty damn good.

Abby's excitement grew as she composed the piece in her mind. Steph might have missed the longing in Ben's eyes, but Abby could make her see, through the story. She could depict Ben's loyalty, his steadfastness and character in a way that Steph was sure to recognize. The features she'd become so accustomed to that she didn't see them anymore? Ben's classical good looks, his dimpled grin and untamable thick hair that he was constantly pushing out of his face, the muscles he'd earned practicing his passion for the nerdiest sport in the world—fencing? Abby would paint them vividly so that Steph would see him as for the very first time.

And once Steph realized that her Prince Charming had been in front of her the whole time, she'd forget all about Isaac, and Abby could stop worrying about being her wingman and go back to writing silly Ships stories filled with the usual, expected dick jokes.

"You didn't like it?" Ben stood in the doorway, pointing at the novel she'd tossed aside. "The reviews have been amazing."

"No, I've just got my mind on other things," Abby hedged. "Work's been ridiculous. The minute I turned in that release announcement, the marketing department decided to shift the entire focus of the campaign."

"Hmm." Ben was too polite to challenge the fib. "Can I give you a lift?"

"If you really don't mind, I'd love that."

Ben was the best kind of generous: one hundred percent reliable in an emergency, but the rest of time he'd let you know if a favor was an inconvenience. He never played games, never let resentment brew. Just another wonderful quality that Steph failed to appreciate.

Once Ben dropped her off, Abby was relieved to find the house empty. She walked into the kitchen to make tea, and stopped short at the sight of a big pink box from Stella Pastry sitting in the middle of the table, her name written in Steph's familiar looping cursive on the top.

Abby untied the twine and lifted the lid to discover what was surely one of God's most exalted gifts to the world, Stella's tiramisu layer cake. Professionally piped in creamy mascarpone icing were the words *Sorry I'm an Asshole.*

Abby burst out laughing, the tension she hadn't noticed she'd been carrying evaporating from her body. "Don't mind if I do," she said out loud, then fetched Gram's old silver-plated cake knife and cut a generous slice. Maybe the fact that it was a peace offering made the cake even more delicious, or maybe it was imagining Steph dictating the phrase to the cashier, but whatever the reason, her fist bite was pure heaven.

Once she'd polished off the slice, Abby wrote *Sorry I'm an Asshole Too* on a piece of paper, folded it into a neat square, and carefully tucked the edge into the cake so it stood upright.

Then she took out her laptop and positioned herself at

the kitchen table so that she couldn't see the clock. That way, she couldn't keep checking it and wondering what Steph was doing and who she was doing it with.

Abby was brimming with ideas she'd brainstormed during the ride home while Ben held a one-sided conversation about how the Giants' season was going. She opened a new document and hit the ground running, crafting the fate of good ol' Sydney so that instead of meeting his end at the guillotine, he would end up with the love of his life, Lucie—who bore much more than a passing resemblance to Steph.

Her fingers flew, the shadows cast by the sun moved slowly across the room, and Abby could barely keep up with the story unfolding in her mind. Her focus narrowed to encompass only the torrent of words she was creating, fleshing out the narrative that had seemed to arrive fully formed in her head.

Like it was preordained...like it was meant to be.

Ben might be content to wait on the sidelines for his happily ever after to arrive, but Abby knew that wasn't how life worked. Gramps had taught her that perfect moments didn't magically appear. You either had to make them happen or give up on them completely.

Isaac had, in the end, been the give-up-on variety of fantasy. But Abby was certain that Steph-and-Ben was not.

By the time the sun sank below the horizon, she had completed a rough draft—a damn good one. It still needed some polishing, but that could wait until tomorrow.

Abby closed her laptop, rubbed her stiff fingers and stretched luxuriously. She had started the kettle for tea and was cutting herself another slice of celebratory cake when Steph walked in.

Catching sight of the sign stuck into the cake, Steph set down her purse and gave Abby a hopeful look. "Does this mean I'm forgiven?"

Instead of answering, Abby wrapped her arms around Steph and they shared a long, tearful hug that ended in laughter. Then Abby finished cutting two slices of cake and poured two cups of steaming tea.

And never even thought to ask Steph where she'd been.

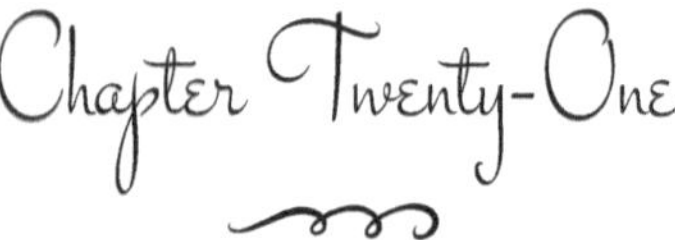

Abby barely registered the conclusion of the night's third performance. The forty-something woman with the expensive haircut and tasteful wool cardigan blushed furiously and dashed off the stage, and Abby clapped extra hard, since it wasn't every day that busy moms from upscale East Bay suburbs found the courage to swerve so far out of their comfort zone.

"That was Brooke Gallagher from Orinda, folks," Ben said, taking the mic with a flourish. He'd relaxed into his emcee role over the last year and wasn't above hamming it up from time to time. "Let's give her some love for coming all this way! You're really making progress, Brooke, you almost got her hand in his pants this time! Take five, folks, grab a snack, say hi to your neighbor, and we'll be back with lots more Ships."

Abby hadn't been paying attention because Steph was up next, and she was plagued with second thoughts. But it was too late to stop her now. That ship had sailed.

Ha, Abby said weakly to Selwyn, who didn't seem too impressed with the quip.

"You okay?"

As usual, Isaac was standing way too close, close enough that she could feel his breath tickling the hair curling at her neck. Abby's stiff posture owed only partly to her nervousness; it was still a challenge to relax when she was pressed up against that damn man. Unfortunately, the more time Isaac spent with the friend group, the more easily he read her moods and emotions, and he'd definitely clued in to the fact that something was off.

"Yeah, fine," Abby mumbled. "Just a little on edge—work stuff."

Which was mostly true. Other than the heart-skittering effect of Isaac standing only inches away—the heady mixture of soft cashmere, hard-muscled shoulders, his chest-rumbling voice and lime-and-leather scent—Abby was downright almost-comfortable around him. Swearing off her crush on Isaac had turned out to be surprisingly liberating, and Abby had stopped worrying about embarrassing herself or saying the wrong thing. If he didn't like her, who cared? Abby had nothing to lose.

Still, it wasn't work on her mind but the story Steph was about to read, the one Abby had been obsessing over for the last two weeks. Never had she labored over a Ships piece as she had this one, worrying over every word, trying to bend each phrase to make it perfect. The future happiness of her friends depended on its success, after all.

"Anything I can do to make you feel better?" Isaac pressed, failing to pick up on her please-drop-it vibes.

What a question—one that risked opening the gates to all the feelings Abby had sworn off. "I'm really okay. If you weren't here, I'd be bitching and moaning to Selwyn, but—"

"Selwyn?"

Why had she said that? It was one thing to feel comfortable around Isaac, another admit to having an imaginary friend. Not even Steph or Ben knew about Selwyn. Abby briefly considered lying, but that was the kind of thing people did when they were trying save face—and Abby didn't do that anymore, at least not with Isaac.

Resigned, she tapped the faded spine of *The Shoestring Guide to the Wonders of Egypt*. "Isaac Ferrer, allow me to introduce you to Selwyn Sherman, reliable Ships date and keeper of all my secrets."

Isaac's confusion gave way to his lopsided grin. "And here I thought *I* was your date."

"Sorry, Selwyn beat you to that honor by about a year," Abby said lightly, bailing water furiously in a sinking rowboat.

"Lucky guy. At least it's encouraging to know you have a thing for authors."

"Don't get your hopes up," Abby said, forcing a laugh. "Selwyn and I are together out of convenience. I was alone since Ben and Steph are busy on Ships nights, and he wasn't doing anything other than gathering dust."

"A fairy-tale love story if ever I've heard one." Isaac was teasing, something he enjoyed a little too much.

"Steph's up," Abby said, hushing him. She watched Isaac out of the corner of her eye, knowing she shouldn't, knowing it would sting to see him brighten at the sight of her best friend bounding up to the stage. Steph was wearing a tight lemon-yellow vintage sweater with a wide sweetheart neckline and a tulle pink skirt, looking like a music box dancer with a Joan Jett haircut.

If the combination of Steph's charm and Abby's words couldn't convince Ben to make his move, nothing would.

Steph cleared her throat dramatically, peeking up at the audience with a sly smile. "Sydney Carton may have loved Lucie Manette with his whole heart, but what good was love from a man with a soul as tattered as his?"

As Steph continued, the audience fell uncharacteristically silent. Unlike Abby's usual fare, this story contained no wicked entendres, no cleverly cast menages, no riotous sexual farce. It was a love story...and a sweet one at that.

It was obvious in minutes that they weren't going to place this week. Which was fine; Abby hadn't been trying to write a crowd-pleaser, not with so much at stake.

"'What would I have done if your plan had succeeded?' Lucie cried. 'How would I have gone on without you?'

"'You would have had Charles. You would have had a long, happy life together.'

"Lucie flinched at the emptiness of his words, so at odds with the torment in his eyes. 'You fool! I am a woman with a heart and a soul, not a trophy to be passed from one man to the next!'"

That was when Abby noticed Ben frozen at the edge of the stage, as if Steph's words had turned him to stone. Very slowly, he turned and sought Abby in the crowd, mindless of the painful glare of the spotlights.

Abby's stomach twisted as his eyes locked with hers. *Shit, oh shit, oh shit.*

She'd gone back and forth about removing that trophy line a thousand times while polishing the piece. In the end, she'd decided it was too damn good to cut. Besides, how likely was it that Ben would remember a throwaway line he said two whole weeks ago?

Apparently, *very* likely.

Haste is a poor counselor. The words of Alexandre Dumas came to Abby like a dress arriving a day after the party she'd ordered it for. But unlike the Count of Monte Cristo, Abby's intentions had been purely good. All she was trying to do was nudge two dear friends in a direction that would make them happy.

Ben's face tightened into fury as he stared at Abby, and she was desperate to escape. "I need some coffee," she muttered as she pushed past Isaac.

Unfortunately, he followed her to the drinks table. "I thought you said you wanted coffee," he said when she queued up for wine.

"I changed my mind." Naturally, on the night she *needed* a drink, only a few drops dribbled out of the box. Abby shook the empty cardboard container at Minerva, knowing how rude she must seem. "Do you have any more back there?"

"Sorry," Minerva said placidly, straightening a platter of stale crackers. "Only red left."

Abby made for the red wine like Caesar storming the Gauls, cutting in front of a couple of the Strivers and filling her plastic cup up almost to the top. Isaac looked slightly taken aback as he followed her back to her corner, just as Steph neared the conclusion of the piece.

"I...take it you aren't enjoying Steph's entry this week," Isaac whispered.

"Something like that."

Ben was *still* staring at her with murder in his eyes. Abby downed half the wine in one gulp.

"Lucie knew that Charles Darnay was a brave man," Steph read, "...a good man, but it was Sydney she loved. Now that she had seen the fire in his heart, her own would burn for him forever."

There was a moment of silence, then a smattering of confused, tepid applause. It seemed to take forever for Steph to find her seat, Abby imprisoned between the gazes of two men, wishing the floor would open up and swallow her.

"I don't know," Isaac mused when the applause died away. "I thought it had a lot of heart. Sure, it was a little cheesy, a little...lachrymose, I suppose, but sometimes I like that."

Abby tried to ignore the shiver that was her body's automatic response to Isaac's vocabulary. She had bigger fish to fry. Calamity-sized fish.

Why hadn't she come up with a plan, a defense, an apology instead of pounding that swill?—and was there time to get more?

But someone was jostling their way into the corner. Someone tall and sharp-elbowed and patchouli-smelling.

"Isaac!" Jane beamed, ignoring Abby. "You're here! I've

been hoping to get a few more pictures of you...for the store's Insta, of course. Oh, hi, Abby."

Jane didn't so much nudge as shove Abby aside. On any other night, in any other circumstance, Abby would probably have let it slide.

But not tonight. "What the hell, Jane? I'm standing right here."

Jane lifted her eyebrows in a parody of surprise. "Sorry," she said, in a tone that made it clear she wasn't. "You were standing in the best light. For the *photo*."

As if she was stupid, in addition to being a massive obstacle Jane was burdened with dealing with. Abby dug her fingernails into her palms and counted to five. *Let it go.*

Except that Abby wasn't the only person to take note of Jane's rudeness. As Jane snapped away, Isaac looked decidedly uncomfortable, his smile strained and unconvincing.

"That's enough," he said quietly. He was probably used to encounters like this—fawning fans cornering him, demanding photos and autographs, peppering him with invasive questions. Abby didn't know how he could stand it.

"Just a couple more?" Jane didn't wait for an answer, inclining her head coquettishly as she kept tapping her phone.

And Abby snapped. Between the tension and the wine and the shit-show brewing with Ben, she just wasn't having it. She stepped in front of Jane's camera, blocking the shot.

"He *said* enough, Jane. That means stop."

Jane's eyes went wide with shock, and then her expression fast-forwarded straight to pissed off. Abby knew what

she was thinking: no one had a right to talk to her that way…
especially not Abby.

"Seriously," she snapped. "What is up with you tonight,
Abby?"

Abby didn't have an answer. She was just as surprised to
discover who she turned into when she officially ran out of
shits to give. Which made it all the more surprising when
Isaac took her hand and pointedly turned his back on Jane,
reclaiming their spot.

Their…spot.

Abby was only dimly aware of Molly Wasyl—the gangly
girl from *Pride and Prejudice* night—embarking on a tale of
Madame Defarge and an entire army of executioners. The
audience regained their enthusiasm; orgies were always
crowd-pleasers.

Isaac leaned in so that his lips nearly brushed against her
ear. "That was the sexiest thing I've ever seen."

Of course he'd turn it into a joke, trying to lighten the
sting of the encounter. Still, Abby couldn't stop the flush of
heat creeping up her neck. "Don't tease me. I was trying to
stand up for you."

Isaac looked surprised. "But I'm not kidding, Abby. That
was awesome."

"I don't know what came over me," Abby whispered
despairingly. "You know Jane is never going to let me live that
down, right? Is she still looking at us?"

"I'd bet my next royalty check that she is," Isaac said,
obviously not appreciating the gravity of the situation. "Not
to mention everyone else who was watching you take her
down. A few of them even got pictures."

"Oh, God." Abby turned away, horrified at the thought of strangers sharing her photo all over social media.

Isaac's face fell when he finally realized she was serious, and he put his hands on her shoulders. "Don't hide, Abby. It makes you look guilty—PR 101. If you don't want them to get a shot of your face, just..." He turned her smoothly so that she was facing him, his eyes holding a sincere apology. "Now I'm blocking you."

Abby couldn't believe it. What unicorn of a man was that kind and decent? But Isaac wasn't finished. He caressed her cheek, shifting her hair so that it would hide her face from the most determined would-be paparazzo.

"Knock-knock," he murmured, and Abby gave herself up to the moment.

"Who's there?"

"A little old lady."

"A little old lady who?"

"Damn," Isaac said, resting his forehead against hers. "You're smart, you're fun—and you can yodel."

Abby laughed at the cheesy joke. She couldn't help it, even if it broke the lovely moment.

"Sorry," Isaac said a little sheepishly. "That's what happens when you have three nephews under ten."

Out of the corner of her eye, Abby could see that no one was watching them anymore, everyone's attention glued to the stage. *All clear.* She reluctantly disentangled herself, trying to hold on to the memory of the moment, the warmth of him, his hands on her face, in her hair. Because it wouldn't last.

It was only a lovely little dream.

Unlike what waited for her when she turned around. It wasn't just Ben staring at her like something stuck to the bottom of his shoe.

Jane was giving him a run for his money.

Chapter Twenty-Two

When Abby and Owen were in second grade, their music teacher chose *The Wizard of Oz* for their spring musical performance. Abby was happy to be cast as one of the tower guards, because it meant she would get to pop out of the refrigerator box perched on top of a ladder and painted to look like brick—until Owen scored the part of the cowardly lion.

Everyone knew that the lion costume, with its silky yellow fake fur around the face and a tail you could bend into any shape you liked, was the best one. Not only that, you got to roar as loud as you wanted, and even at the age of seven Abby thought Mr. Ibrahim's decision showed lazy typecasting.

Now that she'd made her bravest, boldest play of all time, however, Abby realized that courage was overrated. If only there was a refrigerator box, she'd be more than happy to crawl into it and hide. Her grand gesture had not only fallen flat, it had left a smoking crater whose toxic aftermath made this one of the worst days in history.

Okay, maybe that was a little dramatic, Abby scolded herself. She'd had plenty of shittier days, like her grandparents' funerals and the day she received a rejection from the Iowa Writers' Workshop and that time the boyfriend who'd just dumped her had given her chlamydia and—

Whack.

One of the hipsters in line behind her slammed into Abby with his oversized messenger bag, knocking her into a table stacked with new releases and nearly toppling the pyramid of books. Worse yet, the guy didn't even seem to notice, much less stop to apologize.

Abby knew she should never have gone rogue with this week's entry. Thanks to her clever scheme, she'd managed to piss off both of Ben and his ex, for different reasons. Unflattering photos of her were likely to be posted on social media by strangers bent on shaming her for the crime of playing out of her league, even though Isaac's flirtation was strictly for show.

If only she'd stayed in her lane, the one she'd inhabited all of her life, and let Steph, Ben, Owen, and even Dex roar past her in the fast lane. Though they deserved some of the blame, too—if they hadn't been trying so hard to drag Abby out of her shell, none of this would ever have happened.

Shells—the kind women like her took comfort inside— got a bad rap. They served as a solid defense against unwanted attention and unasked-for advice, and a perfectly serviceable place to hide if a person wanted to read in peace, for instance, or avoid drunk loudmouths at parties. Sure, the scenery could get a little monotonous—boring, even—when you never left your comfort zone, but at least you were saved from having to listen to the judgment of others.

On the other hand, if Abby hadn't taken a chance and ventured out, she would never have known what she was missing. Never got to spend an hour or two next to Isaac Ferrer on Friday nights. Never become his friend.

Funny, how the friendship that would have once seemed like a dizzying pinnacle, a stroke of unbelievable luck, now left a bittersweet taste in Abby's mouth.

"How about one more hand for all of our brave contestants?" Ben was saying from behind the podium, having just awarded the first place trophy to Alice, a septuagenarian regular who could be counted on for the most imaginative submissions.

Ben waited for the applause to die down before reminding people to mark their calendars for the next show in two weeks and making a pitch for upcoming author visits and signings. People started gathering their things and taking their purchases to the register, and Abby's dread crept upward at the prospect of the inevitable confrontation that was now only moments away.

But then Isaac appeared, glowering at the messenger bag guy as he pushed his way toward the door. "What was his problem?"

"Oh, it was nothing," Abby said automatically. "It's gotten so crowded back here, especially since Ben ordered all these new chairs."

Isaac looked unconvinced, as if he was considering going after the guy—but instead he steered Abby back to their corner.

"So tell me, Abby. I get why you decided to stop submitting pieces for Ships. Believe me, I know not everyone craves the spotlight." He was giving her the full-bore velvety brown gaze, and Abby felt herself melting until he added, "But why did you stop writing?"

Nope. Uh-uh. Questions about her dreams and fears were the sprinkles on the crap cupcake that this night had officially turned into. Abby cast about for a blithe little fib to put Isaac off, some sort of deflection having to do with work taking up her time or being inspired by some new hobby or even waiting for inspiration to strike. (As if. Abby would never be able to write all her ideas for stories if she lived to be a hundred.)

Abby usually found it easy to throw her family and friends off the scent when they dug into her psyche. They might not fully believe her doctored versions of uncomfortable truths, but they were generally willing to go along with them. Questioning her pretenses would mean questioning the roles they themselves had conferred on her.

But this was different, for reasons she didn't care to delve too deeply into. Abby didn't want to lie to Isaac—no more than she had to, anyway.

"I haven't," she said softly, forcing herself to maintain eye contact.

Even Isaac's perplexity, the tiny line that appeared between his brows, was dead sexy. "You lied," he growled, with the conspiratorial wink of a partner in crime.

"I concealed," she corrected lightly, attempting to play

along. "And now you're trying to muddy the situation with semantics."

That got her a good-natured shrug. It occurred to Abby that Isaac might be the only person in the room who wasn't currently mad at her.

"I still write," she said, relenting. "I just don't talk about it. And it's just playing around. I haven't finished a novel, not even a draft. And I'm not trying to get published."

"Why not?"

"I'm...just not interested. I'm happy just writing for me."

Which wasn't quite true. Abby had loved to write stories since she was a child. Inventing adventures for her imaginary characters fulfilled some part of her that couldn't be satisfied in any other way. Whether she was scribbling in her notebook or tapping away at her laptop, Abby felt more like herself in those moments—more confident and assured—than in any other part of her life.

But the thought of other people reading her words, seeing into the intimate process that even Abby didn't completely understand, terrified her. If she submitted her work, it might be accepted. If it was accepted, it would someday be published. And once that happened, total strangers would see inside Abby as surely as if she sliced herself open on a stage.

On the other hand...she couldn't deny that she'd thought about it. That she experienced a thrill every time the Ships crowd reacted to the words—*her* words, even if they didn't know it. That sometimes she craved an audience, the knowledge that her stories were taking flight in the wider world.

That was why her deal with Steph had been so perfect.

Abby's stories got to be shared, and Steph soaked up the attention and admiration. It had worked wonderfully, right up until the moment when they each wanted something more.

Until they both wanted the *same* something more...in the form of a sexy, witty, charming man.

And there it came to a full stop.

No. Abby wasn't doing this. It didn't matter that her attempt to push Steph and Ben together tonight had crashed and burned. She had still sworn off her feelings for Isaac. Nothing good could from them—nothing but venom that threatened to poison her friendship with Steph forever.

While Abby's mind raced around this familiar track, Isaac never took his eyes off her. "Well..." he said slowly, "if you ever change your mind, I'd love to read some of your stuff."

"Oh God, no." The words shot out of Abby's mouth before she could stop them, followed by a nervous, high-pitched giggle. "I would rather strip naked up in front of a full Ships crowd than let you read my work."

Isaac grinned. "Both options sound intriguing...but you do realize that only makes me want to read it more, right? Now I'm wondering what secrets you're hiding. What you don't want to reveal."

"No secrets," Abby said, too quickly. So much for her vow of honesty. "Just—you know, boring little stories."

"I very much doubt that." Isaac was certainly growly tonight, as if he was on the verge of a cold or—but no. It was only Abby's thirsty imagination that cast his innocent words as suggestive, though that didn't stop her knees from going weak. "In fact—"

"Hey, guys!" Steph appeared between them, a frothy pink buzzkill to Abby's fantasy. She stood up on her tiptoes and planted a kiss on Isaac's cheek, leaving a perfect fuchsia lip print, then laughingly wiping it off with her thumb. She turned to Abby. "Are you using that?"

Abby looked down at the napkin she'd wrapped around her empty plastic cup. "It's all yours," she sighed, then scolded herself for begrudging her best friend a used napkin.

Steph wiped the lipstick from her thumb, then wadded up the napkin and tossed it on the table. "So, thanks for coming out again tonight, Isaac."

He smiled down at her. "Wouldn't miss it for anything."

"You know, I was thinking," Steph continued, tapping a finger to her brow. "I know your publisher doesn't allow you to write fiction for anyone else, but what if you wrote under a pen name and we got Dex to read it on stage for you? It could be our dirty little secret."

Abby blushed. Only Steph could make a reading sound so salacious.

"There's just one little problem with that, Steph." Ben's icy voice came from behind Abby, making her jump. "It's against the rules. Which you both should know, since you helped me write them."

"Oh, you know I'm just kidding," Steph said airily. "Besides, even if I wanted to play the rogue, Isaac and Abby are too honorable to follow along."

Ben wasn't fooled. "Good to hear," he said sarcastically.

Abby felt as though she was being buffeted by a storm of

emotional crosscurrents. The amount of damage control that lay ahead of her tonight was staggering.

"So, Isaac," Steph purred, laying a hand on his arm. "I happened to land two courtside tickets to the Warriors game."

Ben's head whipped around, his ire forgotten for the moment, and Abby sagged with relief. Steph had managed to bring up the one topic that could distract him from Abby's betrayal. Ben's love for basketball was second only to his passion for baseball, rivaling Owen and Dex in his fanatic devotion to the hometown teams. "How the hell did you score those?"

Steph fluttered her fingers. "One of the MoAD board members sent them as a thank-you after the spring gala. Apparently, he wanted me to know that my hard work was appreciated." She giggled as though she'd told a dirty joke. "Would you like to come with me, Isaac?"

"To the MoAD? I'd love to," he said enthusiastically. "Ever since I learned there was a museum of the African Diaspora here I've been wanting to go."

Steph's smile slipped. "I meant, to the Warriors' game."

"Oh...I'm afraid it would be wasted on me," Isaac said sheepishly. "I'm not a basketball fan. My love of sports only extends to baseball and my nieces' and nephews' peewee soccer league."

Steph gave him a blank look, but she wasn't ready to give up yet. "That's because you've never gone to a game with me," she wheedled. "Trust me, I can make any event fun."

And the thing was—it was true. There was a reason that Steph had rival organizations beating the door down to hire her. She made sure donors had so much fun at her events that they happily parted with big piles of cash.

But that didn't ease the ache in Abby's heart. Steph hadn't thrown down that gauntlet to prove a point or crush Abby's spirit or remind her of her place. The thought would never even have occurred to her.

No, Steph had tossed out that brazen line because brazen-line-tossing was what she did. It was as much a part of her as the outrageous outfits and the life-of-the-party sparkle that never seemed to dim, and Abby had seen her do it with cabbies and sales clerks and the neighbor's kid who came to the door to sell Girl Scout cookies.

The fact that Isaac was the one on the receiving end of the dazzle meant a lot less than Steph's other tell, the one you had to know her for a long time to recognize...and that was the way she was twisting her right foot on the pointed toe of her pump. Such a little fidgety motion to contain the depths of Steph's passion, but there it was. Abby had seen her do it while waiting to hear back from a job interview, a room assignment in their dorm days...and every week when the Ships winners were announced.

Abby had always thought she was the only one who knew about Steph's little giveaway. But the expression on Ben's face told her she'd been wrong. As Ben watched Steph's jittering shoe, the anger drained from his face...and gave way to the kind of heartache that Abby knew all too well.

The pain of the one not chosen. The overlooked. The one who goes home alone.

"Well, then I'd be a fool to say no, wouldn't I?" Isaac finally responded, accepting the date.

Abby looked away, suddenly weary to the bones. All she wanted was to get home, put on her pajamas, and put this night behind her.

So much for attempting to bring people together. Abby was hanging up the matchmaker hat for good.

Chapter Twenty-Three

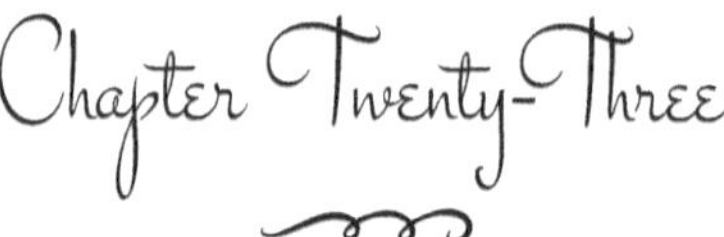

"I mean, what the hell were you *thinking?*"

Abby rolled her eyes in the semidarkness. Asked and answered, she felt like snapping, but since Ben was the aggrieved party and he had offered her a ride home—though "guilted her into" would be more accurate—she figured he was entitled to bitch a little longer. And since late-night construction on Vallejo Street meant the traffic was especially heavy, she could look forward to at least another fifteen minutes of this.

"I wasn't," she repeated tiredly for the second or third time. "You're right. I should have known better."

Gloomy silence fell once again in Ben's ancient, wheezing woody wagon. He'd inherited the 1970 Ford Country Squire from his aunt and uncle along with the shop, and it still smelled faintly of old-lady perfume and weed, which the Kantors had gleefully embraced long before it had been legalized. Ruth and Aaron bought themselves his-and-hers

Priuses when they retired to Florida, but Ben was nearly as devoted to the old beast as to the shop.

"What hurts the most is I thought we were close. I thought we looked out for each other. And now I find out you've been sneaking around behind my back, cheating."

This was starting to get old. "Come on, Ben. You make it sound like I've committed adultery."

"Close enough. Ships in the Night was *our* thing—yours, mine, and Steph's. We were *partners*."

Jeez, he was really determined to make her pay. Abby had known that Ben would figure out what she and Steph were up to eventually, which begged the question of why she'd thought it was such a hot idea in the first place. Luckily, Moody Ben always gave way to Sunny Ben after a sulk.

All would be forgiven...as soon as he judged that she'd groveled enough. Which was why Abby hadn't tried harder to get out of it when Ben offered her a ride home—it was better to just get the whole mea culpa thing over with, but no matter how hard she tried to muster up even a few more drops of contrition, the well had gone dry.

"I am a terrible friend," she said with an exaggerated sigh. "You've been nothing but kind to me since the moment we met, and I've repaid you by spilling the very lifeblood of the most important literary movement of the new century, endangering the reimagined canon and wiping out the gains of—"

"Cut the shit, Abby. Jane was right—you're being kind of a bitch tonight."

Great. He'd been talking to Jane, the last person Abby wanted to hear about. "Listen, Ben. I don't know what you want to hear. There's only so many times I can say I'm sorry."

"Well, you'd better keep saying it until you make me believe it," he said. "Because even if I could forgive you for meddling in my personal life—which I'm not sure I can— you've put me in a no-win situation by breaking the rules of the contest."

"Oh, stop clutching your pearls, Ben," Abby snapped. "If Owen and Dex could figure out that Steph and I were working together then there's no way you didn't know."

Ben shot her an aggrieved glance. "I had *suspicions*. That's different. I hoped I was wrong."

"Really? What did you think, that it was pure coincidence that Steph's writing improved dramatically the very same week I stopped submitting?"

Ben steamed in silence before muttering, "Her writing wasn't bad before."

Abby snorted with laughter. Steph possessed an embarrassment of talents, but fiction writing wasn't one of them. "That's bullshit, Ben, and you know it."

"Wow. Now you're dissing Steph?"

"Oh, come off it. She'd tell you the same thing." Which Ben also knew very well, and since Abby figured she'd taken enough hits for one night, she went for the jugular. "And don't pretend the only reason that stupid rule exists isn't because you knew it meant you were guaranteed to see Steph twice a month."

Ben gripped the steering wheel so tightly Abby thought he might break it. She'd never seen him this upset. Annoyed, sure—the man could out-mope Morrissey when he had the mind to—but the kind of energy he was giving off now was new.

Then again, Abby had never really pushed back before. Never defended herself or her talents. But lately, her confidence had ticked up a few notches, growing too big to be stuffed back into the know-your-place box.

"That's not fair," Ben said in a wounded tone.

"Fair?" Abby echoed incredulously. What made Ben—and every other guy she knew—think they were entitled to *fair*, when women like her got the short end of the stick day after day? The hot, prickly sensation creeping up Abby's neck was so unfamiliar that she barely recognized it for what it was—anger of her own, the kind that refused to keep quiet. "I'll tell you what's not fair—having to hide in the back every week while someone else gets credit for your words."

"Nothing's stopping you from getting back up on that stage, Abby," Ben shot back.

"Is that what you think?" She let out a bitter laugh. "Have you ever read the comments from the first Ships livestream?"

The question was met with silence, just as she expected.

"A third of them are about me, Ben. Not my story, not my jokes—just my *size*. They're brutal. One said it was amazing I was able to write a competent sex scene since no one in their right mind would ever want to fuck me. Another said they were afraid I was going to eat the other authors. And one asshole—"

"Okay, okay," Ben interrupted. "I get it. But that's just how people on the internet are, Abby. You can't let it get to you."

Abby felt like putting her fist through the passenger window. "What great advice. I've never heard it before. Tell me, when did you develop this stunning new philosophy about letting shitty things roll off your back? Was it before or after you ditched out on drinks tonight because you didn't want to hear your crush talk about how much fun she's going to have on her date with a celebrity?"

"Really not fair," Ben mumbled.

"Life's not fair. Don't let it get to you."

The woody wagon had come to a standstill, wedged in a traffic backup caused by a hulking machine marooned in the intersection, ringed by workers in reflective vests who appeared to be taking a break. At this pace, it would be faster to walk.

"Screw this," Abby said, making a snap decision. "I'm getting out."

"Abby. Don't be like this." Ben sounded more hurt than angry. Hurt...and vulnerable.

Which was also new, and bore looking at, especially since Abby was also feeling raw from watching Isaac and Steph set up a date right in front of them.

But not now. Abby wasn't in the mood to take care of Ben at the moment. She wasn't up for sorting through anyone's feelings, not even her own.

"I'm fine, Ben," she said firmly, opening the door. "And so are you. We both just need some time apart to cool down before either of us says something we really regret."

As she got out, the car in front of Ben's moved a few inches and those behind them sent up a volley of honking. Without even thinking, Abby held up a finger at the car behind them, a move that only made the prick at the wheel lean on his horn.

She bent down to the window. "Call me in a few days, and we'll talk."

They'd be fine...but Abby wasn't ready to let go of her anger yet. There was something strangely energizing about it, as if her blood had been pumped full of adrenaline, caffeine, and the sugar rush of a double-shot caramel macchiato all at once.

The asshole in the car behind Ben's rolled down his window. "Fuck you, lady!"

Abby turned around, and her body took over, a marionette defying its strings. Her feet planted wide, she flipped him off with both hands. "Yeah, you fucking wish!"

Abby knew the shocked silence that greeted her words wouldn't last, and she hightailed it around the corner before her heckler could remind her that when it came to women like her taking up space, they hardly ever got the last word.

Chapter Twenty-Four

"I miss the old couch."

There was no one around to hear Abby's declaration, and therefore no reason to feel defensive about it, but Abby defended it nevertheless. After all, what was the point of talking to yourself if you couldn't steer the conversation?

"We never should have thrown it out. It wasn't old; it was vintage. And the taupe went with everything."

Well, that might be a stretch—not only had her grandparents' couch aged to a color that was more dirt-brown than taupe by the time Abby hauled it to the dump, it also had springs poking through the thin spots in the cushions. Nevertheless, Abby still had fond memories of watching Warriors games on that old couch on nights her mom had to work late, a bowl of popcorn between her and Owen while Gramps yelled at the television from his recliner.

It wasn't the same watching tonight's game from the

newer sectional. That had to be why she couldn't seem to settle in and watch the pregame show.

"Aw, hell," Abby sighed, because in a one-sided conversation you had to call bullshit on yourself. And the truth was that though she'd planned on spending the evening clearing out her work email inbox, the only thing she'd had her eyes on was the television. Squirming in her seat, she scanned the stadium for Steph and Isaac.

If only she had a Ships story to work on. But a week after the last disastrous show, neither she nor Steph had heard from Ben, and Abby could only assume they had been banned.

Steph was taking it surprisingly well. When Abby had filled her in on the argument she and Ben had on the way home—without mentioning how Ben had made the connection—Steph hadn't seemed overly concerned.

"Oh, Abs, sweetie," she'd said. "Don't worry. Ben isn't the kind to stay angry long. I'm sure after he calms down, I can sweet-talk him into letting us compete again."

"I don't know," Abby hedged. Steph hadn't seen just how upset—and hurt—he'd been.

"Trust me." Steph was undaunted. "We'll let him stew until after the Warriors game. By then, I'm sure he'll be begging us to come back."

Well, at least one of them was staying optimistic. Abby, on the other hand, was miserable. Not only had she been a total ass to one of her closest friends, she'd also thrown away one of the few things that brought her real joy—writing for Ships.

Naturally, the next show was themed around one of

Abby's all-time favorite authors—Edith Wharton. She couldn't help believing Ben had made the choice out of spite, knowing how disappointed Abby would be to miss out.

If that was his plan, it had worked. All week long, Abby couldn't stop thinking up great scenes that would never see the light of day. In her favorite, Countess Olenski's carriage flipped over into a ditch, leaving her to the mercy of her maid Nastasia's four strapping brothers...

Abby was about to force herself back to email tedium when the TV zoomed in on a black-clad man squiring a beautiful woman in a cropped Warriors sweatshirt and a long, glossy ponytail to her seat.

The announcer wasn't far behind. "—another sold-out game tonight. I see a few familiar famous faces in the crowd tonight. There's Santana, and Guy Fieri—he hasn't missed a game all season—and—hey, isn't that the author of the smash-hit television series *Evernight*? Isaac Ferrer, with a very lovely lady on his arm."

"Isaac Ferrer grew up in Miami, Chuck, but the West Coast was happy to have him when he put down roots in San Francisco last year. Maybe we'll see more of him when the Warriors face the Heat in—"

Abby grabbed the remote and hit Mute. Watching Isaac and Steph onscreen, impervious to the big screens broadcasting their image high overhead, appearing to be completely absorbed in each other, was bad enough without the gushing commentary.

What she ought to do was to turn off the TV and move to the kitchen. The front room, with its bay window overlooking the busy street and windows open to the sounds of the neighborhood, was far too distracting for work.

But Abby was a glutton for punishment when it came to Isaac. Watching him on TV wasn't all that different from standing in the back of the bookshop with him. Either way, he was the center of attention, with Steph the beautiful planet in his orbit—making Abby the dust behind a comet in that awkward analogy.

The last thing Abby wanted was to feel jealous of her best friend. Because she wasn't, not really. She was well aware of how pretty Steph was, how charismatic and charming, with a style all her own and the confidence to carry it off.

But Abby had strengths of her own. Her creativity was a rare gift; she was the heart of her circle of loved ones; she was envied for her organization and steadfastness.

Which was why it was pointless to compare herself to Steph. It would be like comparing apples to machine screws —Abby and Steph could no more fill each other's shoes than you could eat a machine screw or fasten a metal plate with an apple. And contrary to every rom-com ever made, Steph never made her feel like the wallflower friend and Abby didn't secretly long for Steph's life.

And yet there she stayed, lolling on the disappointingly non-pokey sofa deep into the third quarter, struggling to respond to the legal department's inquiry about deliverable timeframe windows, and glancing up every few minutes to catch a glimpse of her friends snuggling in front of the whole damn world.

Only...things weren't exactly as they seemed, even if Abby was the only one who knew it. For one thing, Isaac was dressed as his public persona: black cashmere sweater, black jeans, black Italian leather shoes. Expensive, tasteful watch and not a hair out of place, gaze somewhere in the middle distance no matter what was happening on the court.

And Steph was his perfect complement, just edgy enough to offer lively contrast to his elegance. She'd foregone the thrift store vintage pieces and outrageous accessories tonight in favor of oversized black-framed glasses and a fair-trade handbag woven from recycled plastics by Peruvian artisans, and now the two of them were chatting like old friends while Isaac maintained his enigmatic reserve.

As Abby watched, she realized that Isaac looked a lot like he did around his fans. She remembered his beseeching expression when cornered by Jane at the refreshments table... and something clicked into place.

Maybe it took one to know one, but Abby was certain that Isaac was a fish out of water in that packed arena. The painstaking camouflage he'd slipped into was the suit of armor meant to shield and protect him from the attention that other celebrities craved. This public Isaac was dashing, sophisticated, as unlikely to make an off-color remark as the Warriors were to lose to the Houston Rockets...but the Isaac Abby knew favored outdated Bermuda shorts and made hangover remedies with ungodly amounts of horseradish. And that person would never make an appearance in the public eye.

She and Isaac had bonded over that, hadn't they? Neither felt the need to name it out loud, but they recognized in each other the care each took to deflect public scrutiny, the relief that came when they were finally able to slip out of view. Call it introversion, social anxiety, shyness—Abby had heard them all, but none of those words really fit.

Not for public consumption—the first time Abby heard that phrase, she'd privately adopted it as her own. Just as some wines were too subtle to serve at a barbecue, people like her and Isaac were best appreciated away from the clamor. And it was never more apparent than in the shadow of Steph's flamboyance, a generous and comfortable place that both of them had happily gravitated to.

In that instant, the jealousy Abby had been working so hard to deny simply vanished. The shimmering gloss of perfection lifted and she saw straight through to the real Steph, with her startling guffaw and mismatched socks and habit of leaving the cap off the toothpaste. Someone she loved, not a stranger she envied.

It all made sense now. Of course Isaac had accepted Steph's invitation. The man had to face his public sometime, and who better to step into the fray alongside him than Steph—the perfect shield, the talented go-getter who'd always navigated the world with an ease Abby would never master, no matter how hard she tried.

They were perfect together, and Abby would be an ass to begrudge either of them the match. She picked up the remote and turned off the TV, folded the afghan her grandmother had crocheted, and headed into the kitchen. It was time to call off her one-woman pity party and get back to work.

Because her damn inbox wasn't going to empty itself.

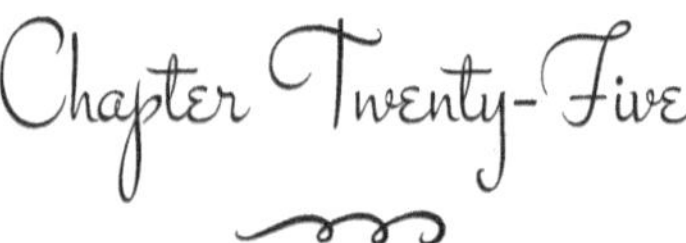

Chapter Twenty-Five

S omething heavy crashed onto the bed next to Abby.
"What the—"

"Are you awake?"

"I am now," she mumbled, prying open her eyelids to find Steph cradling a foam #1 finger like a baby and reeking of alcohol. Abby switched on the lamp and checked the clock on her nightstand: half past two in the morning, meaning Steph had closed down the bars.

This wasn't good.

Steph and Abby were both social drinkers, but very different kinds. On a Friday night, Steph could drink everyone under the table, but that was because she only felt comfortable tying one on when she was surrounded by her support system—Abby, Ben, Owen, even Dex. But plop her down in a formal situation—a date, gala, or professional fundraiser—and she would nurse a single glass of champagne all night long.

Steph didn't need to drink for false courage or to grease

the wheels of social interaction, and her rare benders were usually an attempt to numb the sting of emotions and situations she hadn't mastered—like rejection and failure.

"Oh, God, Abby, it was horrible," Steph sobbed, rolling toward her so she was more or less lying on top of her.

"What was?"

"My date with Isaac."

"Oh, sweetie," Abby said, stifling a yawn as she gently tugged at a big clump of Steph's hair which had escaped her ponytail and was plastered to her cheek. "It couldn't have been that bad. I saw you on TV—both of you looked like you were having a great time."

"*Looked* like." Steph wiped her nose on Abby's SF State nightshirt. "The whole night it was like we were both doing our best to look like we were having a good time, but it was all an act."

"Are you sure you're not just overthinking it?" That was something Abby knew all about. She tended to dissect every social interaction afterward—especially romantic ones. Those could sidetrack her for days, replaying every word and gesture over and over until she had no idea if she'd made a good impression or a giant ass of herself.

But Steph never did that. At least not until now, when she seemed more invested in Isaac than any guy Abby could remember.

"No way," Steph was saying. "Trust me—I know these things. It's my job to know when people are being sincere and when they're just being polite. I know a fake smile from a real one. And I can tell when someone is counting the minutes until they can get away."

"But this is Isaac we're talking about," Abby protested. "He adores you. I've seen the way he hangs onto your every word at Ships."

Steph peered up at her with red-rimmed eyes. "Maybe, but tonight wasn't Ships. I didn't have your words, or Ben to make me look good, or all of us sitting together at the bar. It was just me and Isaac across the table from each other, and...and..."

A tear trailed a sooty mascara-stained path down Steph's cheek, and Abby could feel her heart breaking for her best friend. She was an old hand at being rejected, so much so that she'd developed a few tricks to survive the sting.

But Steph was new at this. In the nearly three decades she'd spent on earth, matters of the heart had always came easily to her. No wonder the hurt was so raw.

Abby put her arms around Steph and gave her a full-body hug while she said out loud what was too painful for Steph to admit. "And now you're afraid he doesn't like you."

But Steph surprised her by rolling away and sitting up, shaking her head. "Oh, Abby, it's so much worse than that. It's not just that Isaac isn't interested in me—it's that I don't think I like him that way."

Abby blinked. "We're still talking about Isaac Ferrer, right?"

"Mmm."

"Steph, you've been obsessed with him for months now. You *love* him."

"I know, I know..." Steph said almost apologetically. "I do adore Isaac. When he showed up tonight looking just like his author photo, I thought—I mean, everyone in the restaurant was staring at us. And I could see the cameras pointing at us during the game. It was heaven."

Abby was having a little trouble following. "So that's... good, right?"

"Sure, until the game ended. I mean, eventually it was going to happen, you know? The moment when it was just us two alone, without any of his fans or whatever, and it never even occurred to me that we might have nothing to talk about."

"Nothing? Come on, Steph, I've seen you work a room. You can talk to anyone."

"Well, yeah. But I meant, we didn't *agree* on anything. He kept asking me my opinions about books I haven't read, asking me who my influences are, and I'm like—I was really struggling, Abs. I tried to shift the conversation toward that idea you and Ben have about the modern fascination with fanfic being a return to Classical Greek storytelling or whatever."

"Roman," Abby corrected her automatically. "The Romans just filed the serial numbers off what the Greeks did. I mean, just look at Virgil's Aeneid. If that doesn't count as fanfic, I don't know—"

"See?" Steph wailed. "You should have been the one having dinner with him tonight, not me."

"Oh, no way—all those people looking at me? Forget it." Abby shuddered. "But things got better at the game, right?"

"Not really," Steph said morosely. "I mean, Isaac was perfectly polite, but I could tell he hated it. And I tried every-thing, Abby—but he refused chant or cheer along with the crowd. He just sat there."

Abby grimaced. "He's not really the jump up and cheer type, is he?"

"Exactly." Steph fell backward dramatically, her splayed limbs taking up most of the bed. "I offered to ditch the game at halftime and take him to that karaoke place in the Castro where we went for Dex's birthday last year, but he wasn't interested. And when the game was over, he said he had to get home because of some deadline that's coming up."

"It's probably true," Abby offered. "He does write for a living."

Steph made a face. "Of course you'd side with him. You always use the same excuse."

"It's not an excuse," Abby said patiently. "It's simply the truth."

"Like I said. You should have been the one there tonight, not me." Steph sighed, clasping her hands behind her head. "You could have talked boring writing stuff all through dinner and then...I don't know, what do you people find romantic?—stroll down the Embarcadero, taking in the view, before doing that whole awkward 'do you want to come up for a cup of coffee' thing."

Steph made it sound like a joke, but to Abby it sounded like a lovely way to spend an evening. Though it still didn't bear thinking about. Just because things hadn't worked out for Isaac and Steph, the idea of Abby ending up with him was still laughably far-fetched.

"I'm sorry that you didn't have a good time tonight," Abby said gently, watching Steph's eyelashes flutter down, her breathing becoming slow and regular.

It looked like Abby was going to have company in bed

tonight…though not exactly the person she'd choose. Steph woke herself up with a little snort and rolled onto her side.

"Thanks, Abs," she mumbled. "I feel better."

"I'm glad," Abby said, and she was…mostly. She was good at making other people feel better.

It just didn't feel like enough anymore.

Chapter Twenty-Six

Of all Steph's enviable qualities, there was one that Abby coveted more than all the rest. Though she would have loved to be able to walk effortlessly in stilettos or charm an entire room with a single smile, Abby would have traded her right arm for Steph's ability to bounce back from setbacks like she was made of rubber, wasting no time on regrets and processing her emotions at lightning speed.

By the time Abby woke the next morning, the house was filled with the sound of K-pop beats emanating from the kitchen, which could mean only one thing: Steph was cooking. And Steph only cooked when she was in a good mood, turning it into a one-woman dance party with a spatula for a mic.

Sure enough, Steph was wriggling her hips in front of the stove in time to "Wa da da."

"I'm making breakfast to say thank you for listening last night," she said with a grin, looking not the least bit hung over. "Scrambled eggs okay? I was going for omelets but when I tried to fold like Kardea Brown...well, let's just say I switched to plan B."

That was Steph in a nutshell: on to plan B, no looking back.

"Smells amazing," Abby said, helping herself to coffee. "But you don't have to thank me. It's not exactly a one-way street, you know. How many nights have we stayed up late commiserating about men?"

"Too many to count," Steph said wryly. "But at least this time, I figured my shit out before I let things get out of hand, you know? And it's a good thing because now I don't have to throw the man out with the bathwater."

Abby snorted. "That's a hell of an image."

She knew what Steph meant, though—when her best friend slept with a man and it didn't work out, then he was out of her life. Steph believed in cutting the tether completely so she never had to deal with the we-can-still-be-friends drama.

"I just meant that even though I don't want to bag him anymore, he's still a friend. One of the good ones."

"Mm-hmm," Abby murmured, so that she wouldn't give away her relief that the two hadn't had sex. Just as when she'd mistakenly thought Isaac had spent the night, she'd tried to tell herself that she'd be happy for Steph if things worked out between them...and discovered that she was much, much happier that it hadn't.

"I mean, what are the odds?" Steph continued, liberally grinding pepper over the pan. "Dex and Owen, and now Isaac. Like, women are always complaining that there aren't any decent men in this town who aren't married or gay, but—"

"You forgot Ben," Abby pointed out.

Steph froze—only for a second, but Abby didn't miss the slightly strained note in her voice when she said, "Yeah, of course, Ben too."

As a pink-faced Steph busied herself with getting plates and cutlery and napkins, Abby took advantage of the break in the conversation to get her laptop and start a new document, ready to begin writing a story about Newland Archer and Countess Olenska scaling ribald carnal heights on the settee in the Welland house while May surreptitiously watched through the keyhole. But then she remembered her argument with Ben, and the fact that anything taking place in the Welland house would be written by others.

"Make room?" Steph hovered above Abby, holding a steaming plate.

Abby slowly closed her laptop and pushed it out of the way. "Looks delicious. So listen, Steph...I think we have to talk about what we want to do about Ships now that Ben knows."

Steph plopped her own plate down and tucked her napkin into the neckline of her shirt, one of the habits she'd inherited from her dad but only indulged in the privacy of their home.

"I'll definitely still go, if that's what you're asking."

"Yeah, of course," Abby said as if she hadn't lain awake wondering if she would even be allowed back inside The City Bookmark. "But what about writing and performing?"

She was surprised by the rush of emotion that accompanied the question. It was one thing for Steph to abandon Ships and set her sights on the next shiny object that caught her eye. But the weekly performances, the hours and hours of hard work that went into every story, were much harder for Abby to let go of—for a variety of reasons she didn't feel like untangling.

"I can't think of any reason not to," Steph said. "I know I'm not half the writer you are, so I won't win as much—or ever, probably. But since I'm not trying to impress Isaac anymore, who cares? Honestly, I'm kind of glad things worked out like this. You can write whatever you want, and I'll get to cheer for you for a change."

"Yeah...great." Abby tried to inject enthusiasm into her voice, though the thought of performing her own work filled her with trepidation to the point of nausea.

And yet...just a moment ago she'd felt so excited about the story she'd been working on last night. In fact, Abby had loved working on every single piece they'd entered into Ships In the Night.

Which was sort of a startling revelation. For the last few years, Abby had begun a total of three different novels, getting twenty or thirty thousand words into them before realizing that all of her earnest hard work hadn't led anywhere she wanted to go. The ideas that seemed promising on page one felt leaden and...inauthentic, somehow, even though she was writing *fiction* so that didn't even make sense.

But these raunchy, satirical amuse-bouches captivated her imagination. They excited her, and without even knowing it Abby had slipped into the comfort and ease of her true style from day one, freed as she was from impressing some imaginary reader or critic, from the confines imposed by her professors' beliefs about what constituted good writing, what merited inclusion in the canon.

Fuck the canon!—a rebellious voice piped up, the same one that whispered dirty jokes and suggestive turns of phrases in Abby's ear while she wrote. But...that voice was *her*. The funny bits came from her own rowdy sense of humor, the twists and reversals from her own delight in the unexpected.

Abby's dreams went beyond bawdy fanfic, to be sure... but not too far. Because when she thought about the thunderous applause, the laughter, the compliments Steph passed along, the conclusion was inescapable: that shit was good.

For now, Abby was working in borrowed worlds, using beloved, timeless characters to tell the stories inside her. But those characters, she realized now, were mere templates to hang her own scenarios on, pre-established reference points that let her jump in and deliver a satisfying story arc in the thousand-word limit.

The audience knew it, too. Sure, they enjoyed the cameos of their literary favorites, but they applauded because the stories were *real*. Because Abby's words touched them, speaking to their own secret longings and fears and dreams, even those they hadn't yet admitted to themselves.

Abby didn't want to stop. Which meant she had a very big problem to face.

She set down her fork, suddenly not hungry. "Steph," she said slowly, "do we still have that bottle of Courvoisier that your grandma sent last Christmas?"

"Yup." Steph polished off the last of her eggs and helped

herself to a triangle of Abby's toast. "We've been waiting for a special occasion, remember?"

"Right...well, I think we might need to use it today."

"Really? What for?"

"To beg forgiveness," Abby said, "and bribe our way back into the show while we're at it."

Chapter Twenty-Seven

"Here goes nothing," Abby muttered before pushing open the door to Ben's office at the back of the store, Steph hot on her heels.

Ben was hunched over the stack of invoices, one hand on the ancient adding machine he insisted on using to double-check the data produced by the shop's state-of-the-art accounting software. All he needed was a green eyeshade and he could have passed for his uncle, circa 1975.

Abby plonked the bottle of Courvoisier down on top of the invoices. "I'm a total ass," she announced as the dusty red-and-green bow detached from the cap and drifted onto the desk.

Ben gave the bottle a dispassionate glance, then allowed his gaze to travel up to take in Abby's attempt at penitence, which involved ducking her chin and wringing her hands as if she was waiting for her turn in the confessional back before Gram gave up on the twins' souls. Next to her, Steph made a sound that was much too close to an impatient sigh.

Ben picked up the bottle and used his sleeve to wipe the dust off the label. "The cognac of Napoleon," he observed.

Abby exchanged a confused glance with Steph. "Umm…"

"He insisted that a ration of Courvoisier be served to his regiments during the wars." He skewered Abby with a sharp look. "He also once said that a soldier will fight long and hard for a bit of colored ribbon. That they'd trade their blood for a trifle, as it were."

"That's not a trifle," Steph objected. "It cost like eighty bucks."

"And you even had it gift wrapped," Ben said drily.

"Okay, fine, my grandmother sent it to me for Christmas. Though I think she regifted it. Anyway, don't blame me— this was *her* idea."

"The…total ass."

Abby sighed. "Yes. A very remorseful total ass."

Ben was silent as he sustained painfully direct eye contact with her. He really was very good at this. "Keep going."

"Okay, fine, Ben. I was wrong. W-R-O-N-G. And you were right. Do you want me to go out there and yell it in the street? Because I will, if that's what it takes. Abigail Margaret Reilly was wrong and Benjamin Stick-up-his-butt Kantor was right."

Ben scratched the back of his neck, the corners of his mouth twitching. "Tempting," he said, "but I feel like that could upset the balance of the universe. I mean, what's next —are you going to admit that you cheat at Scrabble, too?"

"I *never*—"

"Fine, fine," Ben said, waving off Abby's heartfelt denial. "I accept your peace offering."

Abby felt the tension leave her body as if someone had loosened the strings holding her rigidly in place. She hadn't realized until this moment just how anxious she'd been about the friction between her and Ben since the disastrous ride home.

"I'm sorry that I didn't reach out to you in the last few days," she blurted.

Instantly, Stick-up-his-butt-Ben vanished in a wave of chagrin. "I'm sorry I didn't, either," Ben admitted. "I have a feeling we both wish we could take back some of the things we said."

"Oooh, like what?" Steph piped up, suddenly interested now that the awkward part was over.

"Mm-mm." Ben opened his desk drawer and pulled out three crystal tumblers. "That conversation was for total asses only. But everyone gets to drink."

"Wait—are those Waterford?" Steph asked, picking up one of the glasses and weighing it in her hand. "And since when do you keep cocktail provisions in your office?"

"I keep all kinds of things around," Ben said mysteriously. He tucked the bottle in the drawer, only to pull out its half-full twin. "You don't know everything about me, Miss Tran."

There was something new in Ben's voice, a descent into a lower register lined with velvet. From the expression on Steph's face, she'd noticed it too.

Damn, Abby thought. She wouldn't have guessed he had it in him, and yet Ben wielded this new, dangerous edge like a master. In fact, while the two women gaped at him, he nonchalantly turned away and started pouring, going so far as to whistle a few tuneless notes.

Steph managed to get hold of herself and dropped into one of the mismatched chairs, her skirt riding up to reveal her knees, obviously determined to regain the upper hand.

"A stack of plastic cups I could understand," Steph said. "But those are *vintage*. They're probably worth hundreds of dollars each."

Ben frowned at the one he was holding. "No shit? But they're so ugly. They look like something Shrek would use."

"Ben!" Steph yelped. "Oh my God."

"'Course, they were probably a lot cheaper back when Ruth and Aaron got married," Ben said. "Aunt Ruth didn't want to take any of her old stuff down to Florida, but I didn't want to just throw them out, so..." He handed Steph the glass. "Anyway. Cheers."

"Just promise me you won't throw out any of the rest of her stuff without asking me," Steph said. "You could always donate it to one of my clients."

"Noted." He handed Abby a glass and raised his own. "Anyway, here's to good friends. Speaking of which, I saw you and Isaac on TV last night, Steph. Looked like you were enjoying the game more than he was, though."

Twin pink dots had appeared in Steph's cheeks. "You... could tell?"

Ben shrugged. "The man never stood up, even after Curry made that three-pointer at the buzzer. While you had the crinkle smile going the whole time."

"Hang on," Abby interjected, beginning to feel like a third wheel. "What is her 'crinkle smile'?"

Ben gave the point of his nose a push. "You know, when she gets really excited about something and her nose crinkles up."

Ah...*that* smile. Abby knew exactly what Ben meant, and he was almost right. Because Steph didn't only do it when she was excited...but also when she was nervous. Which Ben wouldn't know because when was Steph ever nervous around Ben?

"You're doing it now," he said mildly. "You must be pretty excited about drinking Cognac at ten in the morning."

Steph ignored that. "I was excited about the game, yes. I mean, how often do you get courtside tickets?"

"Damn straight." Ben watched her steadily over the rim of his glass, tipping back slightly in his chair, which gave him a sort of rakish Tom-Wolfe-in-his-prime air. "When an opportunity like that comes along, you gotta seize it."

"That's—that's what *I* said." Steph put her hand to her chest, apparently overcome by the coincidence. "When the game was over, I wanted to go to that karaoke bar you took us to that one time, but Isaac said he couldn't."

"You should have called me," Ben offered, though he sounded almost bored. "I'm usually down for karaoke."

"Next time...perhaps."

Jeez, Abby thought, had they crossed into some strange dimension? Steph looked like she was about to crawl across the desk and into Ben's lap, while he was checking his watch and drumming his fingers on the desk.

Abby tried to keep her expression neutral, but it wasn't easy. All those years, she'd been trying to force the stars to align…when in reality, it couldn't be done. They had to come into each other's orbit on their own.

Or maybe that was planets. Hell, it might be comets—whatever. Abby wasn't a scientist—just one very gobsmacked failed matchmaker.

It seemed obvious now that she never had the ability to make Steph see Ben for who really was, the man behind the dopey-looking glasses and the literary-pun T-shirts. Not the buzzkill she routinely accused him of being, or the entrepreneur who'd found a way to bring a new generation of readers into the shop, or even the dependable friend who always showed up when he was needed.

Because Ben was all of those things…but in Steph's presence he became something even more. His sarcastic wit faded to reveal a capacity for resounding emotional depth; his aloofness gave way to his single-minded passion. Ben didn't bother trying to impress anyone because, in the end, there had only ever been one person whose favor he yearned for.

A lovely warmth bloomed in Abby's heart, a genuine, uncomplicated delight. She didn't have to force herself to be happy for Ben and Steph…she simply was.

The two of them silently mooned over each other a little longer before Ben turned back to Abby.

"Hey, you okay? You haven't touched your drink."

Embarrassed, Abby took a sip and nearly gagged. Did people really pay good money for that shit? "Sorry—I was, um, lost in my thoughts."

"Sure you were," he murmured.

"So does this mean we're forgiven?" she asked, just to make sure.

Ben tipped his chair back again and surveyed the two of them. "Forgiven? Yes. I understand why you two have been partnering up on your Ships pieces. But it's still against the rules, and it can't continue. It wouldn't be fair to the other contestants."

"So..."

"So if either of you want to continue, you'll have to do it on your own."

Abby nodded. That was fair. Though the thought of getting up on that stage again was enough to make her gulp down more of the swill.

"There's something I still don't get," Steph said. "How did you figure out it was Abby writing my stuff?"

Abby shot Ben a pleading look, but she needn't have worried.

"I've had my suspicions for a while," he said easily. "Abby has a very distinct voice. Certain turns of phrases, the way she describes things...what she leaves out as much as what she puts in."

"I guess that makes sense." Steph grinned at Abby. "We had a good run, but I guess it was only a matter of time before we got caught."

"So how about it," Ben said after tossing back the last of his drink. "Are you both going to continue?"

"Why not? I can't pound out an entry every two weeks the way Abby does, especially since I'm rusty. But I'll do my best."

Ben turned to Abby. "How about you?"

She knew what they wanted to hear, but she couldn't

quite bring herself to say yes. "You know how I feel about being on stage," she hedged.

"Oh, come on, Abby," Steph cajoled. "It's not so bad. I can coach you if you want."

Abby winced. Not helpful. Anything Steph tried to teach her would only highlight the gap between their skills. "I'll think about it," Abby said, with enough of an edge that Steph didn't push any further.

"Just don't think too long," Ben said. "I was recently given a useful bit of advice—something about not letting my fears get in the way of what I really want."

Abby let the comment pass, turning away so her friends didn't see her grimace. Because even though the advice seemed solid, it had come from a total ass.

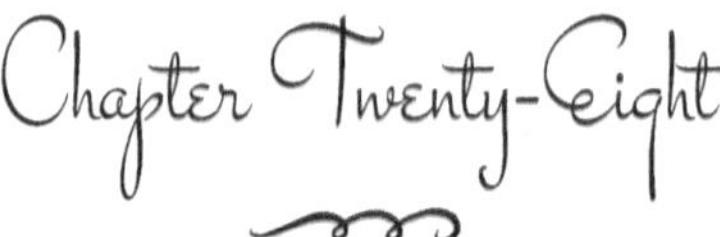

Chapter Twenty-Eight

"This place is starting to go to the dogs," Abby mumbled sotto voce, pressing herself into the corner.

Though he didn't say so, Abby was pretty sure that Selwyn concurred. The man described in the blurb on the dust jacket as bringing "a singular and considered perspective" to touring the Egyptian desert would surely be no happier to see their quiet, contemplative spot in the bookstore overrun by enthusiastic would-be literati than she.

Especially since the throng surrounding them tonight included not just Isaac and Steph but also Dex, who'd ambled over from the bar to watch the show. Abby had tried to pin him down on why the least bookish person she'd ever met had finally deigned to join them, but Dex seemed as infuriatingly at ease in this crowd as he was pounding beers and yelling at the TVs in O'Reilly's.

"You do know that the only alcohol Ben serves is wine,

right?" she asked him, a bit more abrasively than she meant to.

Dex shuddered, but then he angled his hip to show her the top of his flask peeking from his cargo pocket. "'S all good. Maybe next time I can get Owen to send over a pony keg."

"Oh, so you're planning to make this a regular thing? Maybe you should see if you can follow along first."

"Ow." Dex peered at Abby with interest, and she realized she'd made her classic mistake of giving him an opening, one he'd share with Owen and the two of them would keep poking at her until they got to the bottom of it. "You're the one who keeps giving us shit about not showing up."

Abby took a breath, then forced an apologetic smile. "I'm sorry, Dex, you're right. I'm glad you're here. I'm just on edge because of, ah, a deadline thing."

"No worries, bruh." He slung his arm around her, nearly knocking her sideways on her heels. "By the way, you look nice."

"Thanks, bruh," Abby mumbled.

She did look nice—and that was a problem. It was an unseasonably warm May evening, and she'd worn her favorite red sandals and a retro dress with a sweetheart neckline and a swing skirt that swirled around her legs.

Back at the house while she was getting ready, Abby had managed to convince herself that it was a matter of comfort, that the girlish flutter sleeves and above-the-knee hemline were a nod to the fact that the bookstore wasn't air-conditioned. The only trouble was that for everyone other than

Steph, Ships tended to be an exceedingly casual event—and so she stood out like Clifford the Big Red Dog.

"Did you dress up for anyone in particular?" Dex continued slyly.

Abby brought her stacked-leather heel down squarely on his instep. "Shut it," she growled. "You never answered me about why you finally decided to come tonight."

"The thing is," he said quietly, some of his eternal confidence slipping, "a person...who I know...said I needed more culture. So what do you say, Abs, do you think this sort of thing would count?"

"Damn straight." Isaac lifted his plastic cup, not so much joining the conversation as never having left it, since Dex's "quiet voice" was louder than most. "The story, in all its forms—you might say it's the foundation upon which all cultural experiences are built. Even preliterate societies prize and pass down stories as a means of preserving their histories and values."

"Cool!" Dex said, brightening. "Could you maybe say that again in, like, less words?"

"Why?" Abby said suspiciously. "Who exactly have you been talking to?"

Dex shrugged and gazed at the wall of books. "Just some girl I know."

"Some...girl?" Abby echoed.

Having known Dex half her life, she felt qualified to describe him as not the world's most eloquent man. Dex had little to say about experiences that inspired others to rhapsody—as when he'd pronounced a brilliant sunrise that lit every window on the street a shimmering rose gold "dope" or described dinner at the French Laundry on his parents' anniversary as "okay, but I was hungry an hour later."

But there was one subject that turned Dex into a veritable fountain of long-winded praise, and that was women... especially those he'd been or expected or hoped to be on intimate terms with.

Dex was a cheerful sensualist, a lover of food and music and art, at least the kind spray-painted on the sides of buildings. But though he drank deep of life, his highest praise for most of it was "cool" or "fire" or whatever hipsters were saying at the time. Unless he was describing a woman, in which case it was "a blazing hot blond with curves more dangerous than Highway 1" or a "damned killer in the sack with thighs strong enough to squeeze you like a boa constrictor and make you forget your own name."

Never, ever, just "some girl."

It was the reason Abby had always thought he'd enjoy Ships in the Night, with its over-the-top, florid prose and sexually explicit scenes.

And it was also why his uncharacteristic reticence about this mysterious friend piqued her curiosity. "Does she have a name?"

Dex rolled his eyes. "Of course she does, Abby. Jeez." He dropped his arm from her shoulders and turned his back on her. "Hey Isaac, man, do you mind if I get a selfie with you? I kinda told this girl that I know you, and I'm not sure she believes me."

"No problem. Just—gimme a minute—"

Isaac cleared his throat and shook out his arms as if he was preparing to lift a dumbbell, then slipped on his dark, brooding dust-jacket-photo face. Abby watched, astonished, as Dex threw his arm around Isaac and mugged happily while snapping photo after photo.

Wow. Dex felt the need to prove himself to this mystery woman. This merited further exploration for sure, and Abby would find the perfect moment to drag it out of him.

"Thanks, man," Dex said, punching Isaac lightly on the arm. "I owe you one."

"Noted," Isaac said, grinning. "I look forward to calling in that favor."

"That was sweet of you," Abby said as Dex ambled over to the refreshment table, where the usual toothpick-skewered cheese cubes and stale crackers were on offer.

"Not really," Isaac said. "That's definitely a guy to have on your side in a pinch."

"You guys have been hanging out?" Abby tried to mask her surprise.

"Yeah, Owen and your brother caught the last few games at my place. I've got a little more room, so—"

"Uh-huh," Abby broke in, determined to act like it was no big deal. Because it wasn't. It was totally fine that her brother and Dex and Isaac had become one happy little bromance throuple. Next, pigs would start flying. "It's just... I've never seen him like this."

"Well, love makes us all do strange things."

Abby flushed. "Love? Are you sure we're talking about the same Dex?"

"Most people have hidden depths. If you give them a chance, they'll surprise you." Isaac gave her a look that seemed to bore straight to her very soul and Abby wished she hadn't spoken. "Look at you, for example. Your clothes are usually...tasteful, but is it okay I say 'bland'? I had no idea you were hiding such a beautiful dress in your closet."

Hearing Isaac say the word "beautiful" when addressing her threatened to make Abby's cheeks turn the color of her shoes. "Thanks. I decided to do something different tonight. Though between you and me, it was easier to be brave at home. Now that I'm here, I feel as subtle as a parade float."

Isaac smiled. "No wonder I like it. Those are two of my favorite things—parades and you."

Oh, God. Could that be true? Abby pretended to become very interested in an R.L. Stine *Goosebumps* poster, as she tried to discern if he was being polite or sincere. Luckily, not long after, Steph appeared with a glass of wine in her hand.

"I don't get why you guys always stay back here, Abby. Don't you get tired of standing all night?"

"I like it here," Abby said primly.

"But there are still seats in the front row," Steph cajoled. "Come sit with me."

Abby didn't have to guess why. The camera setup used to live-stream events caught only the first couple rows of the audience ...and Steph was never happier than when she was in the spotlight.

But even if Abby didn't mind the attention, there was still no way she would have chosen those seats. Jane was sitting in the first row, and she'd been giving Abby dirty looks ever since she arrived.

"Go right ahead," Abby said. "I'll meet up with you after."

Steph gave an exaggerated huff of disappointment. "No, Abs, the whole point is that I wanted to hang out with you tonight."

"Is that why you're not performing?" Isaac asked.

Abby and Steph exchanged a glance. "Uh...life's gotten a little hectic in the last few weeks," Steph said. "I just needed a break. I'm sure I'll be back up there next week, or maybe the week after."

"Good for you," Isaac said. "Burnout's the worst."

"I'll drink to that." Steph winked and sipped at her wine.

As they bantered, Abby reflected on how nice it was to see two people survive a flop of a date with no hard feelings. *Very adult*, she thought—and maybe not the worst way to make a good friend.

"By the way, Isaac," Steph was saying mischievously, "you'll never guess who else you'll be seeing up there soon."

"*Steph*," Abby warned.

Isaac looked between them with interest. "Really?"

"I said I'd *think* about it," she said, glaring at Steph.

"Mmm hmm," Steph said lightly. "Exactly. First you think about it, then you do it."

Abby gripped her cup so hard it began to split. "Then I strangle you in front of a bookstore full of people because you keep embarrassing me."

"I'm with Steph on this one," Isaac said, grinning.

"Of course you are," Abby sighed. "You know it's not too late for me to ditch you for Selwyn tonight."

Isaac covered his heart in mock horror. "You wouldn't."

"Who's Selwyn?" Steph asked.

"Abby's secret lover. You didn't know?"

"It's just a joke," Abby said hurriedly. "Something we, um, came up with to pass the time between stories."

"Huh." When it became clear she wasn't going be let in on the joke, Steph shrugged and moved on. "Well, anyway, Isaac—you'd love Abby's work."

"I have no doubt. Unfortunately, she's refused to let me read a word."

"Why am I not surprised?" Steph gave Abby a fond look. "I think Ben still has a copy the story she wrote for the very first Ships in the Night. I could—"

"Nobody wants to see that," Abby said hastily. "And you'd better move fast or you'll lose your seat."

"That's okay," Steph said slyly. "I'm starting to see why you like it back here—we can act up like the bad girls we are and Ben won't even be able to send us to detention."

Isaac snorted. "That gives me an idea, Abby—since you're working on a new piece and I've been having a hard time finishing the outline for my next book, what do you think of getting together this week to work? It'll keep us both accountable and force us to be productive for a few hours."

"Writing together?" Abby echoed, horrified...but also weirdly intrigued. "Like...in the same room?"

The corners of his mouth quirked up. "That's the usual definition of 'together,' yes."

But Abby had never written in the presence of another writer, not even in college. She'd never been the writing group type, and the thought of anyone watching her—much less a best-selling author—as she composed at the keyboard made her feel slightly nauseous.

"This is perfect!" Steph exclaimed. "I have to host a

consumer board meet-and-greet in Oakland tomorrow night, so Abby will be writing at the kitchen table anyway—you should totally come over, Isaac."

Abby stared at Steph, as if she could shut her friend's mouth by sheer will alone. *Calm down*, Abby ordered herself. Steph no doubt thought she was helping, finding a way to get Abby out of her rut and back on stage.

But that was the last place she belonged.

"I don't know," Abby hedged. "After all, we don't even know what book Ben picked for next time—it could be something we all hate."

"But Ben told me right before I came over here," Steph said enthusiastically. "It was sweet—he said he picked it just for you, Abs, for your big return."

"That doesn't sound like Ben," Abby said apprehensively, catching his eye at the front of the room where he was turning the lights on and off to signal for everyone to take their seats. To her consternation, he gave her an exaggerated wink.

"Sure it does...it's *Cyrano de Bergerac*," Steph said, looking immensely pleased with herself. "I didn't even know it was one of your favorites!"

That crafty bastard. Abby should have known—Ben had accepted her apology way too easily...and now he was getting back at her for meddling in his love life.

Well played, Abby thought, melting back against the shelves. Ben was a lot better at revenge than she ever would have guessed.

Chapter Twenty-Nine

In fairy tales when to the ill-starred Prince the lady says "I love you!" All his ugliness fades fast—but I remain the same, up to the last!

Abby had barely finished typing out the line from Edmond Rostand's play before she dragged her index finger across the keyboard and held down the delete button, feeling a strange mix of disappointment and relief as the cursor swallowed up the words. Who was she trying to fool? There was no way in hell she was getting back up on the Ships in the Night stage—and most definitely not for *Cyrano de Bergerac*.

Abby glanced up from her empty screen as the unrelenting beat of Billie Eilish's "bad guy" started up from Steph's bedroom. It was only ten minutes before Steph needed to leave for her event, and she still had to finish her hair and makeup.

In other words, right on schedule.

Abby wanted to get back to work, but that would have meant making a decision about what exactly she was working on. So instead, she'd spent the last half hour writing, deleting, and rewriting lines from other people's work. She'd tried to convince herself she was searching for inspiration, but really it was the writing equivalent of a kid pushing lima beans around on her plate, trying to make it look like she'd eaten a few.

It didn't help that Steph was blasting her going-out playlist, a high-energy mishmash of an ear-popping mix of genres. Abby would have asked her to turn it down, but that would mean leaving the sanctuary of the kitchen.

With only minutes to spare, Steph came sliding into the room like Tom Cruise with an imaginary mic, holding prim navy-and-bone spectator heels in one hand. "What do you think?" she asked, twirling in a circle.

Abby took in the simple dark blue pencil skirt and white fitted jacket with bracelet-length sleeves. "Surprising under-stated...distingué, even."

"Right? I mean, I'm not sure what you just said, but I walk in like this to set the tone, and then—" She whipped off the jacket to reveal a daringly low-cut wrap silk blouse printed with brilliantly-colored peacock feathers. "Vintage Pucci! They won't know what hit them!"

"Indeed," Abby murmured, pretending to concentrate on her screen. "Have fun."

"Will do. You too. I'll bring you a profiterole if—"

Abby winced at the sudden, shocked silence. *Damn*— she'd come so close.

"What. Are. You. *Wearing*!" Steph stepped into her

pumps and strode across the kitchen to poke a finger into Abby's wrinkled oxford shirt. "This is a *work* shirt!"

"And I'm working," Abby stated the obvious.

"And weren't you going to throw out those jeans?"

"Changed my mind. You're going to be late if—"

"I can help you put together an outfit if you want, something befitting the beginning of this new Algonquin Round Table," Steph thundered. "And what's going on with your hair?"

Abby touched one of the hairpins holding her curls more or less in place. She'd been aiming for a chignon but ended up with more of a...mess. "Enough already," she said testily. "You're going to be late."

"Mmm. I'm not finished with you, Abigail Margaret Reilly," Steph said, bending down and resting her chin on Abby's shoulder in a cloud of Chloe Nomade.

"Fine. Whatever. You're wrecking my concentration."

As soon as the front door closed, however, Abby dashed to her bedroom and yanked off her shirt, tossing it into the closet on top of the laundry pile.

Steph was right—the oxford cloth shirt only worked in an office setting. But none of the outfits she flicked through in her closet were any better. A dress was much too formal, a skirt too flirty. The wheat-colored ankle length pants were nice, but the waistband bit into her belly when she sat down, meaning that she had to constantly readjust.

Which was not only less than ideal in front of Isaac, but also distracting, which meant Abby would have trouble getting any writing done, which would suggest that she wasn't taking her work seriously, which might lead Isaac to wonder what she was playing at...and in the end, she gave up and pulled on exactly what she'd been wearing that morning.

And why not? Nothing communicated *I have absolutely no intentions or expectations about tonight* like beat-up old jeans and a sweatshirt printed with a penguin in a beach chair and the word "Chillin."

The moment she stepped out of her bedroom, there was a knock on the door.

Holy cannoli. One of Gramps' old sayings popped into her head. Heart pounding, she raced to the door, only to stand in front of it uncertainly, in case he thought she'd been waiting there...

Fuck it. Abby opened the door. "Hey."

"Hey, yourself." Isaac grinned down at her, dressed in jeans—not quite as broken in as hers—and a University of Miami T-shirt. A dark gray baseball cap covered his thick hair and there was a battered backpack over his shoulder. "I saw Steph leaving—she seemed to be in a hell of a rush. Is everything okay?"

"Yep." Abby stepped aside for Isaac to enter. "That's just Steph in work mode. She convinces herself that if she's not there to take care of every little detail, her event will go up in flames."

Isaac chuckled. "That sounds like Steph. When we went to the basketball game the other day, she had the whole night planned out in advance. I think..." He seemed to think better of what he was about to say.

But Abby couldn't stop herself. "You think...?"

Isaac's cheeks pulled up as his eyes swept down, his lips parting as he grimaced. He seemed almost embarrassed. It was an emotion she hadn't seen from him before, and one that went a long way to humanize him in her mind, taking him from Isaac the self-assured best-selling author to Isaac the man. "It's just that I feel like I might have disappointed Steph by not being...not having the same level of enthusiasm for basketball."

Abby's first instinct—one honed by years of playing family peacemaker—was to deny it, or at least smooth things over. But she was determined to be herself around Isaac, and that meant no more taking on roles that she'd never really asked for.

Which left one option: the truth. Which, luckily, wasn't a bad thing at all.

"I wouldn't worry about it," she said kindly. "Nobody gets over disappointment faster than Steph."

"Glad to hear it," he said with the lopsided smile she liked so much, the one that never showed up in public. The one which, come to think about it, Abby had only witnessed when the two of them were alone. "I had a feeling about that too."

Despite having sworn them off, Abby felt an entire swarm of butterflies take flight in her stomach. If she didn't do something fast, she was going to end up swooning like one of the Musgrove sisters in *Persuasion*.

"Coffee!" she blurted, bolting across the living room. "I mean, I could make some. Though it's probably too late in the day. So, water maybe? Or tea? Herbal tea? Or wine, I have wine somewhere—"

"Nothing for me, thanks," Isaac said, following her into the kitchen. He dropped his backpack on the table and unzipped it. "Besides, it looks like you're already hard at work."

Abby followed his gaze, wondering if he was being sarcastic—but luckily her screen saver hid the lone over-worked sentence. "Yes, that's me...real hard at work."

She slid into her seat and put her fingers on the keyboard and, when inspiration refused to strike, began typing the opening line of George Eliot's *Middlemarch*, the book currently on her bedside table.

Miss Brooke had that kind of beauty which seems to be...

She glanced up to make sure that Isaac wasn't watching, but he was busy arranging his laptop and notebook and pens in front of him on the table. He looked perfectly at home, as comfortable as a cat perched on a favorite windowsill. *Comfortable*: now there was a perfect word for Isaac, at least the version of him that didn't scowl from the back of his books.

He glanced up, and their eyes met. Isaac smiled.

Abby panicked. Her fingers flew.

...thrown into relief by poor dress.

. . .

Abby cleared her throat. "Do you like quiet to work? Because if I can put on music if you want. It's fine with me."

"Only if you want it. I can go either way. When I was writing *Alabaster Anarchy*, I listened to Elvis Costello's *Almost Blue* album on repeat." That crooked smile again. "But some books seem to call for silence."

Abby froze, unsure if she should share her opinion of Elvis Costello (meh) or if Isaac was asking her to shut up. Since she didn't know the second line of *Middlemarch* off the top of her head, she started backspacing, stopping when —to her enormous relief—Isaac started to type.

Abby stared at what she had written, tapping her chin to suggest she was deep in thought. Then she too started typing again.

Mr. Isaac Ferrer had the kind of ass that would make a nun forget her vows, its perfection impossible to overlook in perfectly fitting jeans.

Backspace, backspace, backspace. Abby sighed. "Is it hot in here? Should I open the window, or—"

"Abby."

She nearly jumped, because his voice had slid down to that low, suggestive register, like Barry White...but with a hint of wicked amusement, too. "Um...yes?"

Isaac seemed to be looking through her, haloed by the light from the vintage milk-glass ceiling fixture. "I'm fine.

Everything is good. If I need anything, I'll get up and get it myself."

"Sorry," Abby squeaked. "I'm not used to working around other people. Especially not—"

She bit her lip just before she said the quiet part out loud...but the damage was already done. Isaac's eyebrows lowered fractionally and he leaned forward, elbow on the table, chin in hand, and gazed steadily at her—the most dangerous, tortuous interrogation technique she could imagine.

"No, Abby. Finish that sentence. Especially not what?"

Abby felt like a deer in headlights. Or more accurately, like a deer in the headlights of an Italian sports car driven by a much bigger, sexier deer with hair she'd kill to run her fingers through. And the deer was getting out of the car, ducking to make room for his massive, masculine antlers, never taking his eyes off hers.

The words tumbled from Abby's mouth as if she'd mainlined truth serum. "Especially not like Number One *New York Times* Bestseller Isaac freakin' Ferrer."

The deer burst into laughter and morphed back into Isaac. The comfy version.

"I didn't realize you were expecting the official name-brand version of me tonight. I had to do that the other night with Steph, and it was exhausting."

"Oh...really?" Abby stammered.

"In fact, that's one of the reasons I've been looking forward to this all day. You're one of the only people I can really be myself around."

The smile he gave her this time wasn't one bit crooked,

and the butterflies started singing arias. Isaac had been looking forward to this all day…just as Abby had.

"That's great!" *Dial it down, Abby.* "Because I like your-self. I mean you. I mean the way you are." *Oh, for the love of God…*

"And I like yourself, the way you are, too. So how about we just be ourselves tonight."

"Works for me," Abby managed to get out.

"How about this. We'll write for a couple of hours and then take a break for dinner. Get some air, head down to the Mission, hunt down a giant burrito?"

Abby smiled shyly. "That sounds great."

Honestly, it sounded like heaven.

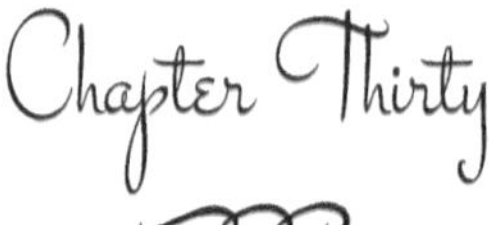

Chapter Thirty

Abby inhaled deeply, letting her eyelashes flutter at the glorious aromas of grilled meat and fresh tortillas. Behind her in the line that stretched out the door of the popular restaurant, a woman carrying one toddler and holding another's hand spoke rapidly in Spanish into the phone tucked between her ear and shoulder, and in front of her a couple of guys in paint-spattered work clothes ordered enough carnitas to feed an army.

When it was her turn, she fired off her burrito order with the gusto of a true aficionado. "Refried, rice, carnitas, pico-sour-cream-and-guac!"

"Damn," Isaac said as the guy behind the counter ladled ingredients onto a massive flour tortilla before passing it along to the next guy who folded and rolled and twisted it into a shiny, aluminum-wrapped cylinder. "I'm impressed... and a little ashamed."

"You should be," Abby teased. "Who orders a burrito with extra lettuce?"

"Someone who's been eating takeout for the last month because they're on deadline. I can't remember the last time I ate a vegetable."

"You still didn't need to ask for extra lettuce," Abby teased. "The pico de gallo counts for at least three vegetables. Not to mention the cilantro."

Isaac laughed and pulled out his wallet. "She's with me," he told the cashier.

"You don't need to pay for my burrito," Abby protested.

"Hush. I said I was taking you out to dinner, and I'm a man of my word."

Abby experienced a delicious little shiver. "Man of my word" was right up there with "I'll do the dishes" for sexiness. She hid her delight by filling their cups with ice and agua fresca, then followed Isaac through the busy restaurant to the only open table.

Oh, *hello* there. Isaac in broken-in jeans might just be her favorite Isaac of all.

They spread out their dinner on the colorful painted table. Like many of the Mission taco joints, the walls were painted with colorful murals, and the ceiling was strung with bright *papel picado* banners. Unlike too many of the trendy eateries in the city, no one here seemed to mind the presence of children and babies, and frequent laughter peppered the conversations around them.

"Thanks for coming all the way out here with me," Isaac said as he peeled back the foil on his steaming burrito. "I had a craving."

"You're welcome. It's a burden, I'll admit—being driven in your fancy Lexus with heated leather seats—"

"Hey, I picked that car for its safety rating," Isaac said, his gaze rolling down again in a move that Abby was quickly learning signaled slight embarrassment.

"—and getting to eat my burrito without my brother asking if I'm going to finish it or Steph freaking out when she gets salsa on her shirt."

"I thought salsa on your shirt was one of the rules," Isaac said, holding up a tomato-splattered cuff. "Gotta say, this city makes a damn fine burrito. We don't have anything that comes close in Miami."

Abby didn't respond until she'd finished chewing, Isaac being the kind of guy who didn't make a person feel they needed to rush. "What do you have there that you can't find here?"

"Arepas," Isaac said without hesitation. "Stuffed with shredded beef and cheese. And the other day I was craving guava pastelitos."

"I'm sure there's a Cuban restaurant somewhere in the city, isn't there?"

Isaac shrugged. "Yeah, but it's not the same. Close, but—you know how it is. Sometimes if you want the real deal, you've got to go to the source."

He held up his burrito in a toast, and Abby "clinked" it with her own. "Amen to that. So, do you miss living in Miami?"

"Sometimes. There's a few restaurants and cafes....a bakery a couple blocks from my parents' house. I miss all my nieces and nephews, of course. The way the breeze feels at sunset along South Pointe Park. But it's not enough to make me want to move back. I'm happy here."

"Please tell me to mind my own business if I'm getting too personal..."

Isaac snorted. "Says the woman who asked if I slept with her roommate. Go on, I'm dying to hear what you consider crossing the line."

Abby held up a finger in protest, even as her cheeks burned. "The way I remember it, I didn't want to ask that question. You goaded me into it."

Isaac's eyes glinted wickedly. "Oh, you wanted to ask, but you were afraid I'd be offended. Just like now...so ask."

"Fine. I'm just curious why you moved all the way to the other side of the country when you obviously love Miami."

Isaac didn't take his eyes off Abby, but something in his smile slipped. "It's...complicated. I guess there are two ways to answer that—the public version, and the private one. Which do you want?"

"The honest one."

Isaac didn't speak right away, his gaze shifting somewhere over her shoulder. "I do love Miami," he said at last. "My entire family is there. But the truth is sometimes it's easier to love a place—and everyone in it—from a distance. In this case, that distance ended up to be a few thousand miles."

Abby sensed that she was on delicate ground. "Why's that?"

"I come from a big family. Six brothers and sisters. Then there are all my aunts, uncles, cousins—it's a lot. Don't get me wrong, I love them all. But in a family that size, sometimes who you are as an individual takes a back seat to the role you play in the family. And I..." He chose his words carefully. "I couldn't always live up to their expectations. I wasn't the man they wanted me to be."

Abby studied Isaac, trying to figure out how anyone could know him and find anything lacking—and not just because he was gorgeous and successful. He was also funny and kind and generous and—

"I know what you're thinking," he said.

Abby's heart skittered. She could only hope that wasn't true. "That you're the kind of son who'd make any parents proud." At least it wasn't a lie.

Isaac sighed. He looked tired, as though this wasn't the first time he'd battled this disconnect—not just with other people, but with himself. "You don't know my parents. After coming to America, my dad worked two full-time jobs and did construction on the weekends until he and his brothers saved enough to buy a building that was literally condemned —and then he and his brothers rebuilt it themselves. Like every brick. And then he opened a tire store because he said everyone needs tires, they'll never stop making them."

Abby nodded slowly. "I get it. Believe it or not, my Gramps used the same reasoning when he decided to open a bar."

Isaac smiled sadly. "Our parents' and grandparents' generations worked hard. Blood and sweat and long hours— I'm sure I don't have to tell you—all so us kids could have every opportunity they never had. The only trouble was they never expected to have a son like me."

"Um...a world-famous author?"

"A nerd. A bookworm," Isaac countered, waving his burrito.

"Come on, Isaac. Your family has to be proud of you. You're wildly successful."

"Oh, sure. Just like back in your kitchen earlier this evening, everyone is proud of Isaac Ferrer the author. But Isaac the *person*? That's a different story. Boys from my neighborhood were taught to fight back with their fists when someone came at them, but I learned to talk my way out of conflict. Pá even took me down to the local boxing gym for lessons, but the trainer cut me loose after just a couple weeks. He said I just didn't have the fighting spirit.

"And he was right. I've always been interested in the reasons people attack and hurt each other, the reasons nations go to battle, even though I never felt a need to join in. I guess it explains why I write what I do."

"It kind of does, actually," Abby said. She bit her lip, wondering if she should say more. *What the hell.* "To tell the truth, I've often found myself wondering how to reconcile the warm, caring, funny guy in front of me with the dark and violent stuff you write."

Isaac's expression softened. He rested his chin on his hand to gaze at Abby. "It's nice to know that's the way you think of me."

Abby released a breath she didn't realize she'd been holding. Baby steps—she'd only shared the tip of the iceberg of feelings she had for Isaac, but now she felt emboldened to continue.

"I'm just trying to say that I think I understand now. I mean, I've experienced the same thing. The details and the culture around us might have been different, but I've never been comfortable in my body either, at least not the way that most girls are taught to be." Isaac appeared to be listening intently, so Abby pushed on. "I grew up absorbing the message that women are expected to be agreeable, especially with men, and that the highest praise they can receive is that they're beautiful...but the only thing I've ever wanted to be known for is the depth and breadth of my mind."

Isaac knit his brows, little crinkles appearing at the bridge of his nose. "That line, about the depth and breadth of your mind ...what's it from? I feel like I just read it somewhere."

Abby shrugged, unsure. She knew what he meant, a word or phrase tripping a memory of something she'd read. It probably happened all the time with people who read as much as she and Isaac did.

"Eh, I'm sure it will come back to me," Isaac was saying. "But anyway, I think you're right—that's one of the many reasons I have such a good time with you. We're both outsiders in our own worlds."

There went that little shivery feeling again, the thrill of connecting at ever-deeper levels.

"Even now?" she asked. "I'd have thought your family would have gotten over all that when you came home with your first royalty check."

"Yeah, but it's different now. I mean, before I got published, they gave me a hard time when my brothers and cousins were starting businesses and getting married. Like, when are you going to get this out of your system and grow up? But then I got that first book deal." He sighed and traced the initials someone had carved into the table with his fingertip. In a quieter voice he added, "And then I got rich."

"That...wow. Part of me wants to say 'that must be hard' but honestly, it's hard to react sympathetically to a statement like that."

"Yeah, I get that. And you're right, parts of it were great." His smile was tinged with sadness. "I could finally buy my mom a decent car. Pay for my nephews' braces, that kind of thing. But it didn't take long for things to get weird."

"Weird how?"

"Nothing terrible," Isaac said quickly. "We're not one of those families where suddenly everyone's got their hand out —though it happens, now and then. Mostly it was just that even though I was still the same person, they started to treat me differently. Like my cousins don't tell dirty jokes around me anymore. My nieces bring their friends around and make me sign their books. Even my mom—" He lifted his eyes heavenward, as if praying for patience. "My mom asked me if I could come to the senior center so she could tell everyone I'm famous, but she didn't want me to mention my books because they have curse words in them."

"No," Abby gasped in faux horror.

"I know," Isaac said ruefully. "I feel like I'm not getting at the heart of it. One day, I couldn't stop my family from criticizing every little detail about me, and the next, it was impossible to drag an honest, unfiltered reaction out of them. It was as if the pendulum swung from one extreme to the other, never pausing in the middle, on the person that I actually I am. And that..." He swallowed.

"It must hurt." Abby got it. "Not a day goes by that Owen doesn't give me a hard time about one thing or another. He still tries to give me wedgies, for God's sake—but if he ever stopped, I'd miss it. I mean, not the wedgies but...if Owen ever started treating me like—like a lady, I guess, it would be the end of the world as I know it."

Isaac managed a real smile. "Exactly. And that's why I moved as far away as I could get without leaving the country. Or at any rate the mainland—I wasn't quite ready for Alaska."

"And you got a blank slate. Right? You can be yourself here, at least when you're not mobbed by fans. Live where you want, eat what you want, stay up as late as you want—"

"Spoken like a woman who's still hoping for that herself."

An automatic denial hovered on Abby's lips, but she stopped herself. This was a different kind of conversation—a real and honest one. The kind that took place when she was alone with Isaac.

"Yeah, I guess so," she admitted. "You have to understand, I still live in the house I grew up in. Even though Mom's in Florida and Grams and Gramps are gone, most days it still feels like they're around me. And then there's Owen and Steph and Ben. They're always there. And it's not a bad thing—a lot of the time it's warm and comforting, but sometimes..."

"You worry that they somehow define you," he said, completing her thought. "You wonder if you'd recognize yourself if they weren't around."

Abby gaped at Isaac. He'd effortlessly put into words the uneasy feeling she'd been carrying around for years.

"I get it, Abby," he said softly.

For a moment the air between them seemed to shimmer—and then a nervous laugh overcame her. "Thank you."

But Isaac wasn't quite ready to move on. "To be honest with you, Abby, I'm relieved that I'm not the only one spilling my guts tonight."

It was like truth serum, that long-lashed, thoughtful gaze. "It's just that I've been pretending for so long," Abby blurted. "It's a family tradition. I had to pretend to be Irish starting in first grade. Gramps made me and Owen flashcards with stuff we were supposed to say, like 'top 'o the morning' and 'blarney.' It was ridiculous."

Isaac raised an eyebrow. "I'd pay good money to see thirteen-year-old you trying to convince a bunch of tourists from Ohio that you had shamrocks in your blood."

"It wasn't hard, really," Abby admitted. "The customers wanted to believe it. Also, they were drinking. The hardest part for me was that I was expected to be bubbly and outgoing all the time. I mean, I liked the customers, but unlike Owen I preferred doing chores in the back, like sweeping the stock room or even cleaning the bathrooms. And no one in my family got it, because I'm the only introvert. The only..." she hesitated, then added shyly, "nerd."

Isaac laughed and offered a fist bump. "Nerds rule!"

"How do you deal with it?" Abby asked. "I mean, I've seen you—you make it look easy, talking to complete strangers."

"It *is* easy. Or at least easy-ish, when I'm talking about books. If I can just get into that world—though you wouldn't know that, would you? Steph told me that you haven't read any of my books."

"That's not true," Abby said quickly, though Isaac didn't look the least bit bothered. "I've read the first one. I had to, for Ships."

Shit—Abby realized her mistake.

"But you didn't submit anything for that night. I would definitely have remembered."

"I was thinking about submitting," Abby lied, backpedaling furiously. "I never got around to finishing it."

"No?" Isaac's nose crinkled again, and Abby was struck by the horrible feeling that he might not completely buy what she was saying. "That's a shame. I'd love to have heard it."

"It's good to want things," Abby said lightly, turning it into a joke—the Reilly family's trusty default move.

The moment was over. Isaac was gathering up their trash. "You about ready to get back? I'd like to knock out a few more pages before Reggie Reynolds comes on."

"You're a late-night fan?"

"Not really. I mean, not at all, but the new season of the TV series is coming out next month so the publicist booked me on the talk show circuit. I have to fly to New York in the middle of the week and then down to LA."

Abby winced at the thought of all that publicity.

"Tell me about it," Isaac said, reading her expression. "It's been a year since I've had to do any TV appearances, so I guess I should consider myself lucky, but I'm rusty. I need to watch a few episodes to remind myself how to act in front of a camera."

"Better you than me," Abby said with feeling.

"There are worse things in the world."

"Name one."

"Let's see...how about spending three hours pretending to enjoy basketball so you don't embarrass your friend on the Jumbotron."

Chapter Thirty-One

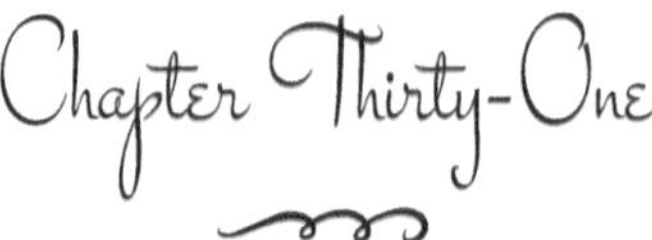

Abby wasn't much of a night owl, and the combination of a belly full of burrito and lounging on the couch in the glow of the television screen was making it hard to keep her eyes open.

"I can watch this at home if you want," Isaac said with a trace of amusement.

"No, no." Abby blinked furiously. "Stay. I'm awake."

But it was a losing battle after a long week. Besides, despite how nervous she'd been before Isaac arrived, now his quiet presence relaxed her.

"I'm taking up all the space on your couch." Isaac grabbed a throw pillow and patted it. "Here—why don't you lie down?"

On his *lap?* The offer was tempting, and he probably didn't mean anything by it, but—Oh God, she was over-thinking again, wasn't she?

Just freaking do it.

Abby gave in to the little voice for once and stretched out with her head on the pillow. The pillow on Isaac's lap.

Not all the way, of course. Abby rested most of her weight on the arm beneath her so that her head barely dented the pillow, terrified of making his legs go numb. It wasn't super comfortable, but she could handle it...until, during a commercial, Isaac started to laugh.

He rested his hand on her shoulder. "I'm not made of glass, Abby. Relax, you're not going to break me."

Abby eased up, but only a tiny bit. The fear of being burdensome was rooted too deep to simply let go. Especially with someone she really liked. What if Isaac changed his mind, and told her that she was too much, too big, too heavy? Abby would never get over it.

Soon Reggie Reynold's theme song started to play, and Abby's eyelids grew heavy again. Somewhere during the monologue, her mind started drifting in the sweet comfort of Isaac idly playing with her hair, twisting a curl around his finger and letting it go.

The sound of keys in the door abruptly woke her. On the screen, Reggie was interviewing his final guest of the night, and Abby realized with horror that she'd slept through most of the damn show. Even worse, she'd somehow become draped over Isaac, her face pressing against the warm landscape of his stomach.

Abby scrambled upright as Steph called out a greeting. "I'm home, Abs, did you miss me?"

She rubbed her face, wondering if she had pillow creases, if her mascara had smudged, if Isaac had been in silent agony but too polite to move her. Glancing at the pillow, she was horrified to see a spot of drool.

Two thumps in the foyer as Steph kicked off her heels, and then she strolled into the living room looking every bit as put together as when she'd left the house hours earlier. "Isaac," she said brightly, plopping into the armchair. "This is a treat. I thought that you'd be gone by the time I got home."

"No, no," Abby said quickly. "We wrote for most of the night. We were just catching some late-night. Did you know Isaac's going to be on Reggie Reynold's? And then the Late Show. You know, for the new season of *Evernight*."

Was she talking a lot? It felt like she was talking a lot. And fast too. Both Steph and Isaac were looking at her strangely. "Sorry," Abby added, feeling her face heat up. "I was asleep."

"I have to do the rounds before the season opener," Isaac explained to Steph.

"Oh, sure," Steph said, but she'd zeroed in on Abby like a hawk diving for its prey.

Abby snatched the pillow off of Isaac's lap and tucked it behind her back, but she was too late.

"So..." Steph said craftily, "...did you guys have a good night?"

Short and sweet, Reilly. Don't add any fuel to the fire. "Yep."

Isaac had returned to watching the TV. "Yeah, we wrote for a while then went out for burritos in the Mission," he said distractedly. "Damn good burritos."

Abby fiddled with the hem of her shirt as her insides twisted under Steph's scrutiny.

"Sounds like a great date," Steph finally said.

Abby cringed. Steph knew damn well this wasn't a date, just two friends working together, grabbing dinner, then watching a little TV.

But Isaac didn't seem to have noticed. "Yeah, it was."

The next five minutes felt like an eternity as Isaac watched the end of the show and Steph watched Abby and Abby tried to be invisible and no one said anything. Finally Reynolds signed off for the night and Isaac yawned and said he'd better get going and thanked Abby for a nice evening and she managed a weak smile and an "uh-huh" and even managed to stand up, though walking him to the door was out of the question.

The second the door closed behind him, Steph tackled Abby onto the couch.

"Why didn't you tell me you had a crush on Isaac?"

Chapter Thirty-Two

N o.

No no no no no.

"I'm not thirteen, Steph. I don't have a *crush*"—spoken with exaggerated distaste—"on anyone."

Steph folded her arms imperiously, which would have been more effective if she wasn't trying not to laugh. "Fine. What term would you prefer? Enamored? Smitten? Dying to ride him all the way to Poundtown?"

"Don't be gross." Abby made a face to show how appalled she was by the mere thought of having feelings for...him.

Steph's eyes widened. "Oh my God. You *do* have a crush on Isaac!"

"Stop being ridiculous," Abby said, attempting to fake a yawn. "I'm too tired. I'm going to bed. If you want to keep teasing me about Isaac, you'll have to wait until morning."

Except that Steph wasn't teasing, not anymore. "I can't

believe it," she whispered in a tone of awe. "You're in love with him."

"I don't want to talk about this," Abby snarled

She wasn't in love with Isaac—she couldn't be. Love didn't happen in a few days or weeks. It grew over time, with careful nurturing, trust and attention. Love was what her grandparents had after starting a family and building a business and making a home together. It was the other side of a million simple kindnesses and small favors and forgiven mistakes and forgotten disappointments.

Love was something you *did*—a verb for spending a lifetime showing someone they mattered. It was the act of choosing someone again and again.

What Abby felt for Isaac was nothing more than a tangle of emotions and hormones. It was infatuation, the same exciting yet insubstantial feeling that Steph herself had carried around for a while, until she realized that Isaac wasn't the man she'd built him up to be in her imagination.

Which was probably exactly what was going to happen to Abby. The version of Isaac that Abby had fallen for might be a different make and model, but the likelihood of it reflecting the real Isaac was just as small. Given a few more days or weeks, Abby was sure come to her senses too.

"That's not what's going on, Steph," Abby said tightly.

"Then explain it to me." There was a hint of irritation in Steph's voice that went beyond her usual unabashed meddling. "Why are you afraid to admit how you feel? Do you think I'd be—I don't know, offended or something?"

"Of course not," Abby snapped, tipping over into irritation herself. "Though if anyone should be offended it's me, since you seem to feel entitled to—"

She stopped herself before she could finish the sentence with "invade my privacy"—but Steph got there anyway.

"—to ask you about your personal life? Seriously, Abby, this is me, your best friend! We talk about everything!"

"We do, but—"

"Are you afraid I'll be mad? Because I'm totally over my own little Isaac thing, which you very well know because I told you all about it. I didn't sit there making you guess, or pretending it didn't happen, or—"

"Steph!" Abby put her hands to her temples, which were beginning to throb. "I seriously cannot do this right now. Please just let's go to bed and talk in the morning."

Steph was already shaking her head. "You're just trying to buy time to come up with an answer that I can't argue with. You know, to use all your words to say something clever that doesn't really say anything at all." To Abby's shock, Steph's voice had gone thick and wobbly, like she was about to cry. "I know you, Abby. What I don't get is why you don't want to talk about this with me."

Her words took the wind out of Abby's sails. Angry Steph, she could handle. But Sad Steph's appearances were so rare as to stop Abby in her tracks.

"Because...there is nothing to talk about," she said carefully. "Isaac and I went to dinner because we were hungry. I fell asleep on him because I was tired. That's the whole story. There's nothing else to say about me and him and there never will be."

Steph glared at Abby even as her eyes got shiny. "Just tell me how long you've had a thing for him."

Abby shook her head. She didn't want to lie, so the only thing she could do was just keep shaking her head and pray... for an earthquake, a fire alarm, the hand of God himself to come down and flick her into purgatory.

A tear slid down Steph's cheek and she angrily brushed it away. "Just answer the damn question. How long have you been in love with Isaac?"

Telling the truth was out of the question. It was too painful—not just for Steph to hear, but for Abby to admit, even to herself—that she had been nursing the same stupid, futile crush for over three months now. That like a fool she'd been carrying a torch for a someone who would never—could never—be hers. Because of that there was only one answer she could give.

"It doesn't matter."

Steph clamped a hand over her mouth. "Oh God...you been in love with him from the beginning, haven't you?"

Abby bit her lip. "Steph..."

There was no excuse she could give. No explanation that would make it better.

Steph covered her face with her hands and rocked back and forth. "How did I not see it?" she mumbled. "The way you were acting that first night at O'Reilly's. You were so weird and awkward. I thought you were just starstruck, but..."

"I didn't mean to," Abby blurted. "I'm sorry."

Steph took her hands away, angrier than ever. "You're

sorry? What the hell are you even saying? Tell me right now exactly what you're apologizing for."

"That I—" The words felt like giant rocks she was trying to swallow. "That I have...feelings...for Isaac."

"Wrong!" Steph smacked the coffee table so hard a book fell from the top of Abby's stack. "You can't apologize for the way you feel. That's not what this is about, Abby."

"Then...what is it about?"

The crease in the middle of Steph's forehead had never been deeper as she stared at Abby. "You were never going to tell me, were you?"

"I—I didn't see any reason to. It's not like anything was ever going to happen between him and me."

"Oh my God! That's not the damn point."

Abby struggled to find the words to defend herself, but she didn't really even understand what they were fighting about. "I, um, knew you had a thing for him, and..."

Steph waited for Abby to finish her sentence, but she couldn't. Some things were simply too painful to say out loud.

"And what? You thought you'd just bury your feelings forever?" Steph made it sound like Abby had decided to strangle a litter of puppies.

"Well...yeah. What other choice was there?"

"You could have told me!"

"And risked our friendship?" Abby shot back. "Over a guy that I had no chance with anyway? That would have been beyond stupid."

Steph reared back as if Abby had just smacked her across

the face. "Is that what you think of me? That I'm so shallow that I'd screw you over for some guy?"

"Well, no, but—"

"We're friends, Abby—best friends. I'm closer to you than to most of my family. At least I thought I was."

Abby's heart constricted painfully. "It's not like that, I swear."

She was really going to have to do this. She took a deep, ragged breath and dug her nails into her thighs hard enough to leave bruises and stared at the floor. "Okay. You want to know what I was really afraid of? That you'd laugh at me. Not just you, everybody—Ben, Dex, my brother, everyone at Ships. Guys like Isaac—" The words caught in her throat, but Abby forced herself to finish. "Guys like him don't go for women like me."

Steph was quiet for so long that Abby finally had no choice but to look at her.

"There are no 'guys like Isaac,' Abby," Steph said, not sounding so angry anymore...just sad. "He's his own thing. Just like you are. And that's why I don't buy that excuse. I've never laughed at you. Neither has Ben. Owen and Dex?—I don't know, maybe, but I doubt it. Not over anything important, anyway."

"And this isn't important," Abby tried. "Like you said, it's just a crush."

Steph gave her the look that said she'd be accepting no more bullshit today. "*I'm* the one who has crushes. Not you. For you, it's true love or nothing."

"Steph..."

"That better not be another apology about to come out

of your mouth," Steph said. "Because I'm not accepting anything of the sort until you admit the real reason you kept this from me."

Abby searched her mind, trying to figure out what answer Steph was fishing for, but came up empty. "Can you maybe give me a hint what that might be? Because I thought I already did."

Steph huffed, annoyed that she was to do all the heavy lifting. "You didn't keep your feelings for Isaac a secret because you were scared we'd laugh at you. You stayed quiet because you were scared we'd encourage you to go for it. You were afraid we'd assure you that Isaac wasn't out of your league, that you're perfect for each other, and then you'd have to do the one thing that terrifies you the most and put yourself out there. Be vulnerable. Be *seen*."

Abby froze. Every word that Steph said was true—painfully, terrifyingly true. She'd nailed the reason why Abby had stopped preforming at Ships. Why she stood behind the back row of seats. Staying in the shadows meant no chance of rejection...but it also meant no chance of joy.

"You're...You're right," Abby finally admitted in a whisper. "I'm sorry, Steph. I really am. I'm so sorry I kept things from you."

"Apology accepted."

"So...are we cool?"

"Not just yet." Steph's tone was flat. "I'm still really pissed at you for thinking I'd care more about some—some *fling* than about you."

Abby didn't bother to remind Steph that three months

ago, she'd been talking about wedding invitations. Because she understood what Steph was trying to say.

She and Steph were friends. Best friends. They would always have each other's backs—and Abby had almost broken something precious by forgetting it.

"I messed up." Not exactly eloquent, but from the heart. "I—I promise to do better. To trust you, even when it's hard, and...because I need you, Steph. Life's too messed up to do it alone."

Steph sagged against the couch. "Oh, thank God. I hate being mad at you."

"Well, I hate it too."

"Just don't ever do that again. Don't shut me out. And don't fall in love with someone and act like it's nothing. You promise?"

"I promise," Abby said.

Because after this, she knew she could never go back to acting like Isaac was nothing.

Besides, no one seemed to have been fooled in the first place.

Chapter Thirty-Three

Even though Abby had been a bookworm since the day she gnawed the corner off *Good Dog, Carl* as a toddler, she didn't start out wanting to be a writer. The adults in her life went to work in aprons and sturdy shoes or, in her mother's case, smart acrylic sweater sets because the bank branch where she worked as a teller always blasted the air conditioning too high. For a long time, it never even occurred to Abby that people could write books as an actual job.

When Abby and Owen started kindergarten, they confided to their teacher that they planned to work at the bar forever. But while Owen's career aspirations never strayed far from O'Reilly's, Abby moved on to dream of being an archeologist or zoologist or even an astronaut. She took a brief turn as a would-be pharmacist, but only because the Kovalenko twins' mom had tattoos of Frog and Toad on both arms and always waved at her through the glass at Walgreens.

It wasn't until Abby was mired in the miserable swamp of middle school that writing became a refuge. After spending most of her adolescence in the shelter of her family and the bar where she and Owen were beloved, once she turned thirteen her life took a nosedive.

Abby knew she wasn't alone, that lots of the kids at her school were suffering in their own ways, even if they weren't "the fat girl." But it was hard not to feel alone when everywhere she looked—movies, television, magazines, social media—all the women were thin.

No, that wasn't exactly true.

Every *admirable* woman was thin.

The handful of fat characters who made it into print or onto screens served as comic relief, foils, or villains. They were cautionary tales, victims of their own uncontrollable appetites, gluttons who lacked self-control. Which was ironic, since Abby almost never acted out, kept to herself, and did her best to make herself as small and invisible as possible.

So Abby absorbed media's cruel lessons in painful solitude. The fat buffoons were relatively easy to ignore, since Abby was a straight-A student. Foils usually faded into the background when they weren't needed to showcase the heroes. That left the most excruciating characters to watch: the transformational ones—ugly ducklings who bloomed into girls indistinguishable from the preening squad that ruled the lunchroom and dated the hot boys.

They seemed to be everywhere, these characters that started off fat, then after a two-minute workout montage shrank to half their size, proving themselves worthy of love and respect. As if fat was the worst possible thing a woman could be. As if her talent or wit or generosity or intelligence or skill in any of a thousand pursuits meant nothing compared to the only thing that could ever really define her value...her size.

Given the daily assault on Abby's fragile psyche, was it any wonder that she turned to books? Once a kind librarian introduced her to *Harriet the Spy*, Abby realized that she could imagine a book's characters looking any way she wished—even like her. She trained herself to skim over physical descriptions and cover illustrations and use her imagination to fill in the details. If the story made that impossible, if an author insisted on referring repeatedly to girl characters' slender necks or long, graceful legs or—the worst—her "small bust," then Abby shoved the book back through the library return slot with grim satisfaction and moved on.

Sometimes Abby saw other fat girls using the same tricks she did to disappear in school: doodling in the margins of their notebooks, staring at their assignments as if transfixed to avoid being called on, or the riskiest but most effective escape of all, which was to slide another book under a textbook and read it covertly.

One thing girls like her never did: talk about it. It was years before Abby realized that the reason she rarely became friends with these girls was because while most cliques have a single token fat girl, two fat girls together are subject to exponentially more—and more vicious—teasing. And so they drifted past each other in the halls, pretending not to see each other. Which wasn't very hard since all of them were experts at disappearing in plain sight.

Which might be why Abby was so good at seeing what she wanted to see in her books, which was girls like her—thick girls, sturdy girls, fat girls—playing sports and babysitting and running for school office and making out under the bleachers and sticking up for underdogs. And since she'd always been the introvert in the family, Abby was perfectly content with a book for a companion most of the time. Other girls' rowdy sleepovers and group shopping expeditions sounded exhausting to Abby, even if she often wished she had a friend—just one—who liked her exactly the way she was.

As the years passed and high school graduation loomed on the horizon, a new, dark shadow began to fall on Abby's days. Having mostly excelled without effort (funny how reading more than anyone she knew, including her teachers, reduced many of her classes to refresher courses), she suddenly found herself dreading the hours she spent at school more than ever—but the emotions took her by surprise.

Irritation. Impatience. Anger, even.

It came to a head when Abby sat down to draft a paper for Honors English. She'd read all of the books they were allowed to choose among, including one that stood out for its fat protagonist, who dealt with the experience of bullying by rallying the entire school to host a prom for the city's unhoused students and emerged a hero.

Abby had intended to skate through the assignment since she had the highest grade in the class and her A was not in jeopardy. Instead, many hours later, she had written a two-thousand word diatribe insisting that the systemic gender-based degradation of girls was not addressed by turning them into heroes, especially in the case of further marginalized groups and specifically fat girls. That by doing so, succeeding generations of authors reinforced the canonical practice of presenting female characters as collections of attributes rather than fully-imagined human beings.

The paper came back with a giant C at the top. Scrawled underneath it in red pen was not the point-by-point refutation of Abby's thesis that the grade called for, but a single sentence: "Glorifying obesity is dangerous."

Abby's fury was quickly overtaken by shame. She knew the grade was bullshit but told no one—not her mom, her grandparents, her school counselor. When the teacher—a forty-something graduate of a storied women's college, made a point of lavishly complimenting the next thing she turned in, Abby stared at the floor and didn't reply.

Glorified or demonized. Those were the two options available for girls like her even in her safe space. The books she loved, the ones in which fat girls dared to simply exist— to navigate ordinary family and friendship ups and downs, to make mistakes and learn from them, to fall in love—never made it into the books deemed worthy or literary, but were routinely dismissed as trash or, at best, "guilty pleasures." Fat girl characters got the stamp of approval only if they overcame their unspeakable shame through heroic sacrifice or resounding success.

And so, silenced by shame but fueled by this anger that refused to be snuffed out, Abby moved on from inhabiting other people's story worlds to writing her own.

It would be nice if this pivot had marked the beginning

of a crusade to right the wrongs of fat representation, but that hadn't happened. Or at least, the crusade part was buried so deeply in the layers of rejection and stigma and shame as to be almost invisible.

Abby soon learned how hard it was to shrug off early influences. That it was possible to love a problematic author or book, just as you could love someone who hurt you. And as with a woman making a decision to cut off contact with an abuser, it didn't happen all at once.

At first, the stories Abby wrote were imitations of the books she'd read, and her characters usually ended up being white, skinny, and outgoing, despite having hoped to make them Everywomen.

When Abby began to write fat characters, she found herself pulling her punches. The character was never *that* big, and she always had an excuse for being that way, a medical reason or trauma.

The acceptable kind of fat, in other words. The "good" kind.

Never the mind-your-own-damn-business-this-is-just-who-I-am kind of fat. Because when Abby tried—when she gritted her teeth and attempted to force that woman into existence, what came out was always dressed in camouflage and perfumed with apology meant to help her fade into the crowd.

Abby knew it was happening, even though she did her best to pretend it wasn't. Now, though, she couldn't put it out of her mind. In fact, she was pretty sure it was the reason she'd had so much trouble working on her own writing—and why she'd seized so eagerly on a project that borrowed other writers' characters and lifted the burden of her having to create her own.

No more.

Ever since the night Abby had fallen asleep on Isaac's lap and argued with Steph, she'd been writing up a storm. She wasn't entirely sure why, since there was no destination in mind, no book she was trying to write or point she was trying to make. She didn't even know, most days, what she was writing—short story, essay, prose poem, junk. It wasn't as if she could create something for Ships, since Steph couldn't perform her pieces anymore and Abby sure as hell wasn't about to get up on stage herself...and yet the stories kept turning into Ships pieces, at least in structure: beloved heroes and villains, turned upside down to upset every literary apple cart that had ever gotten under Abby's skin.

When she wrote something that especially pleased her, when she read over her pages and recognized the outline of something solid, Abby toyed with the idea of anonymously uploading the piece to a fanfic site, but always abandoned the idea. Eventually she understood that it was because Ships was hers from the start. Sure, the way it evolved, the joy people took from it, owed to Steph and Ben and everyone else who'd been a part of it, but the germ of the idea—short, ludicrous bits that both poked fun at and celebrated the concept of slashfic—was hers alone.

And now that she was writing with no one looking, Abby was producing comforting vignettes while at the same time building her storytelling muscles. She loved the thrill of the unexpected and the scandalous, but the day she made herself cry at the keyboard, Abby realized that something deeper had been happening all along. In the perceived safety of someone else's sandbox, with the ready dodge of abandoning a piece if it didn't land right, she'd begun to write from her heart.

Abby didn't know what to make of the fact that this was happening at the same time she was distancing herself from Ships. Her best guess was that the flurry of writing was a last, desperate grasp for the comfort and safety that Ships had provided. Because once she cut ties for good, Abby would have to face the fact that any future writing would take place in much more dangerous waters, where there would be no hiding behind someone else's themes or characters. That she would be forced to speak with her own voice and stand for her own beliefs.

And the trouble was that Steph had been right. Abby wasn't brave. If she'd barely been able to admit her feelings for Isaac to her best friend...how in the world could she expect herself to stand up and claim her voice?

Instead of going round and round with the futility of it, Abby just kept writing, a new Ships piece every day until her desktop was littered with them.

On the night that Isaac was to appear on the Reggie Reynolds show, Abby was typing "The End" once again as the theme music drifted in from the living room.

"It's starting!" Steph called. "Get in here!"

Abby glanced at the clock. It would take at least twenty minutes of monologue and commercials before the host got around to introducing Isaac. Steph had been buzzing with excitement about his appearance all week, inviting everyone she ran into to come over and watch the show with them.

Which was why Abby had retreated to her bedroom to work.

At least a dozen people were crammed into the tiny living room: Ben, Owen, Dex, a few of the bookstore employees, and a handful of Steph's work friends. Fortunately, no other regular Ships contestants. Abby really wasn't in the mood to have to listen to Steph lie about "taking a break to fill her creative well" again. Somehow keeping the lie alive only made the ache of losing Ships worse.

Steph loved a party, and she also knew that Abby didn't. They'd settled that long ago. But she'd made Abby promise that she'd come out for the main event, and Abby knew that if she didn't emerge soon, Steph would come drag her out.

She took a deep breath and forced a smile so her dread wouldn't show in her voice. "I'm on my way!"

Then Abby closed her laptop and opened her bedroom door and went out into the world, where people she loved could exist on a screen where terrible things happened to people just like her every day.

Chapter Thirty-Four

"Move, bro."

Owen shoved Dex hard enough to spill his beer, but he moved to the end of the couch to make space for Abby to sit between them.

"Waste of beer, man," Dex grumbled, wiping his jeans with one of Steph's elegant cocktail napkins.

Abby would have been happier in the back corner of the living room, with her potted parlor palm for company instead of Selwyn, as close to invisible as she could get in her own house.

But refusing to sit in the spot the guys had cleared for her would only attract attention, so she took her place with a pained smile and prepared to spend the next twenty minutes acting her ass off. How did normal people behave when someone they cared about appeared on live TV? Abby looked around the room and saw everything from giddy excitement to tipsy jousting to covert flirtation between Steph's office manager and one of her interns.

Unfortunately, most of the people in the room knew about her feelings for Isaac by now. Dex and Owen were unapologetic gossips and Abby was pretty sure that Steph's work friends also knew the whole story. Which meant that all these people would be watching her watch Isaac's interview, studying her for clues.

Someone handed her a bowl of popcorn. It was tempting to distract herself with a handful, but the risk of getting a kernel stuck in her teeth or butter on her sleeve was too great for someone doing her best to disappear. Abby passed the bowl to Ben, who was sitting on the floor with his back against the couch and his hand resting casually on Steph's ankle.

Which was interesting, and would have provided Abby gossip fodder of her own if she wasn't thoroughly distracted.

The energy in the room rose as the show went to commercial break. There was something about a casual brush with fame that struck a deep chord in some people, as if they were somehow elevated by proximity. Abby could guess at the conversations they'd be having tomorrow:

Did you catch Night Talk *last night? My friend Isaac Ferrer was on. Yeah, I know him. Great guy.*

But the guy they'd be talking about wasn't the one Abby knew. Her Isaac ordered lettuce in his burritos and hummed when he got lost in his thoughts and laughed from his belly. Trying to reconcile the celebrity with her own version of Isaac made Abby's head hurt.

Everyone raced to refill their drinks and grab snacks and hit the bathroom—everyone but Abby, who gazed woodenly at the bowls of beet chips and spiced pistachios on the coffee table while, in her peripheral vision, Steph pouring two glasses of red wine and piled two plates with snacks.

Everyone was back in their seats when the commercial break ended and the host introduced Isaac.

"Shut up, everyone!" Dex bellowed, as the host waited for the audience to stop screaming at the sight of tall, elegant Isaac taking his seat with an easy grace. His expression conveyed only eerily bland benevolence, but Abby had talked with him about visibility and exposure often enough to know that he was hiding considerable discomfort. Still, if she didn't know him, Abby would have been as clueless as everyone else about what was really going on in his head.

Isaac hadn't been kidding that first night when he'd told her that ninety percent of selling books was acting. Because the distinguished man who adjusted the creases in his black wool trousers with a sexy smirk, whose expensive watch glinted at his gray cashmere cuff, was no one Abby had spent time with.

"Nice audience," Isaac observed smugly, to another round of cheering.

"They love you, man," Reggie Reynolds, host of *Night Talk*, replied. "You're like the new George R.R. Martin, except you actually accepted our invitation to come on the show."

"For now." Fractional lift of the brow, to much laughter. "My dance card isn't as full as George's yet."

"Any day now, though," Reggie said, facing the camera for his segue. "The second season of *Evernight*, the blockbuster TV series based on your novels, debuts this week. Your books have sold over nine million copies in what, forty countries?"

Isaac gave a bored shrug. "Something like that."

"So while all of us are waiting for the show to drop next Wednesday on our very own network, we've brought you on to share some spoilers with us."

Isaac laughed, a short hard sound. "Wish I could, man."

"We won't tell anyone," Reggie said in an exaggerated stage-whisper, leaning across his desk with a wink.

Isaac raised his hands in mock defeat. "The lawyers have this wrapped up so tight I'm surprised they let me out of the cave to come here. I think they get my firstborn if I leak anything."

"Oh, come on," Reggie wheedled. "Just a clue, then."

"You do know," Isaac said, coolly drawing out the words, "that everything that happens in *Evernight* comes right out of the books, right? If you want spoilers, all you have to do is read them."

Reggie waited for the laughter to die down. "Speaking of which..." he reached under his desk and held up a hardback copy of Isaac's most recent book. "The ninth book in the series came out a couple of months ago. You had an interesting way of celebrating its launch."

In the corner of the screen, a photo of The City Bookmark appeared with a line out the door, and the living room crowd exploded in cheers. "Tell us about Ships in the Night, a monthly event at a San Francisco bookstore that I hear has become quite a local favorite."

"It's twice a month, actually, if you manage to get tickets. But there's a podcast, too, which is how I came to know about it." Isaac's voice warmed as he talked about getting hooked on the show, then watching the livestreams, about the hilarity and deftness of the entries and the diversity of the entrants. "It really gives a fresh look at books people have been reading for decades, even centuries. Which some of us think is long overdue."

"I never got through *Moby Dick*," Reggie admitted, scanning his notes. "And has anyone ever read an entire Dostoevsky novel from start to finish? I mean, isn't that what the internet is for? But Isaac, you've got your face in a book all day for work. Don't you like to, I don't know, shake it up in your free time?"

Isaac ignored the cheers from his female fans. "I'm still new to San Francisco," he said. "I only moved there six months ago so there hasn't been a lot of shaking up happening yet."

So much screaming. Abby half expected the stage to be pelted with lacy panties next.

"So you just called the bookstore one day," Reggie prompted.

"Yeah, I offered my latest up as a sacrifice."

"But you didn't just offer. You showed up in person—" The photo on-screen changed to a shot of Isaac on stage that first night. "—and judged the competition."

"Who took that photo?" Owen asked.

"Quiet." Steph reached across Abby and smacked his leg.

"I don't do things halfway," Isaac said slyly.

Abby knew she shouldn't be shocked by how well he knew—and played—his audience. After all, he'd had a decade of media training and plenty of practice. But it was still a strange and faintly unpleasant experience to watch his alter ego at work.

"Gotta say, I'm kind of surprised they took you up on the offer," Reggie said.

"Yeah?"

"Well, I hate to be the one to tell you this, but you're a little intimidating, my friend. I mean, there's the man-in-black thing, for starters. And the stuff you write?" He checked his notes. "Let's see: dismemberment, decapitation, disembowelment, defenestration...damn—damnation ad...?" Reggie frowned, making a show out of tripping over the Latin words, part of his good-natured-bumbling-fool act.

"*Damnatio ad bestias*," Isaac said. "Means 'condemnation to beasts,' like when the Romans used to execute people by feeding them to lions."

Reggie dropped his notecards with an exaggerated shudder. "Gotta say, Isaac, your mind comes up with some nasty, scary shit." Except, of course, "shit" was beeped, leading to much hilarity in the studio. "Should I be a little afraid of you, man?"

"Of course not," Isaac drawled. "As long as you behave yourself, that is."

"Well, the people in the audience at The City Bookmark are braver than me," Reggie joked as a new photo, this one of the audience on its feet in a standing ovation, appeared in the corner. "I personally wouldn't risk pissing you off by taking your seat or something. But anyway, how did it go?"

"It was…" Isaac paused, and Abby could see the assumed persona, the public version, cracking at the memory, the brightness returning to his eyes. "…one of the most memorable nights of my life."

"It must have been," Reggie enthused. "You've become a regular at the event, from what I understand."

"I have—but only as a spectator. I'd recommend it to anyone. And the bookstore is fantastic. Ben, the owner, does a remarkable job." He looked directly at the audience for the first time. "You're all supporting independent bookstores out there, right?"

The audience clapped enthusiastically. On the floor, Ben was beaming.

"Especially The City Bookmark in San Francisco!" Reggie chimed in, another plug for Ben. "Gotta say, your presence must bring in quite a crowd. Especially the ladies, if social media is to be believed."

"I don't know about that," Isaac said, and Abby could read the faint irritation that slipped through the mask.

"Maybe this will refresh your memory." Reggie waggled his eyebrows suggestively as a new photo appeared on screen: Isaac and Steph courtside at the Warriors game. "Isn't this lovely lady someone you met at the event?"

Abby lurched sideways on the couch as Dex jumped up to pump his fist in triumph. Owen clapped Steph on the back and her work friends hollered. Only Ben seemed unamused.

"That's my good friend Stephanie," Isaac said, his tone giving nothing away.

But that didn't stop Reggie from digging. "A very close friend?"

"She's one of the most amazing writers I've ever met," Isaac said, refusing to take the bait. "She can capture the essence of a writer's voice with only a few words. Sometimes she reads more like the author than the author themselves, to be honest. She has a fine ear for satire and a solid command of the short story form. If she didn't already have a career she loves, I have no doubt Steph could be an exciting new voice in contemporary fiction."

"Day-um," Reggie drawled. "That's mighty high praise from a guy like you. But I'm confused. I thought these were, like—I mean I don't want to get into trouble here, but isn't the idea that these stories are kind of X-rated?"

"They are," Isaac said. "But that doesn't mean they're not excellent. Genre-bashing has gone by the wayside, my friend."

The audience didn't miss the mild burn. Instead of being offended, though, Reggie laughed along with them. "Never bad-mouth a good dirty story!"

Abby's cheeks were beginning to hurt from the effort of keeping up a pleasant smile. She had to hand it to Reggie: he played his audience skillfully, riling them up and drawing reactions out of them that were sure to keep the audience at home engaged. She seemed to be the only one uncomfortable that he was doing it at the expense of the event she and her friends had built.

But at least he was promoting Ships...and the bookstore, Abby reminded herself. And that was the most important thing.

"Still, it's got to be tough when you've got such a high profile," Reggie was saying. "Not all of your fans seem to understand that you're just trying to enjoy the show. For every real—no, wait, what did you call her? Your 'good friend'?" A suggestive leer let the audience in on the joke. "Anyway, for every positive interaction you have out in public, you're bound to run into a situation like this."

He rolled his eyes as a new photo took up most of the screen.

Abby froze as the horror of what she was seeing sank in. All around her, the living room suddenly fell silent.

And then the audience started to laugh at the image of Abby appearing to lunge toward Isaac as he turned away, scowling.

It took her only a second to place it—the night Ben had discovered her and Steph's arrangement. Jane had been pestering Isaac at the refreshments table. He'd told her to back off, but Jane didn't listen. Upset, Abby had jumped in front of the camera to stop her.

But that wasn't the story the photograph told. The social media caption beneath read:

"Poor #IsaacFerrer trapped at #ShipsInTheNight #Evernight #stalkerfail

Even though the poster's handle had been blurred, the photograph hadn't. Jane's smiling face stared back at Abby from her TV screen.

Jane might not have gotten the shot she wanted that night…but she'd gotten her revenge instead. She'd managed to capture Abby at a remarkably unflattering angle in which the underside of her chin was exaggerated and her cheeks appeared to have taken over her face.

Even if the picture had been a good one, Abby would have been mortified by that caption, one the audience was making all too clear they agreed with. A desperate, pathetic fat woman making a fool of herself by chasing after Isaac Ferrer.

Abby's lip began to quiver and her eyes fill with tears. This couldn't be happening. She wouldn't survive it. As her body began to tremble, however, a strong arm wrapped around her shoulder and pulled her up.

Owen. Her brother looked like he wanted to smash something while at the same time trying to smile for her sake. A very specific kind of rage that Abby recognized as the same fierce sibling loyalty she felt for Owen whenever he was mistreated or taken for granted. Except turned up a thousand degrees.

"Abby...?"

Just her name, but in those two syllables Owen managed to convey fear that someone had hurt her, outrage that anyone would dare to, and determination to flatten them, along with the sweetest, most awkward tenderness, an assurance that he wasn't going anywhere.

For all of the thousands of times her brother had driven her up the wall, no one could comfort Abby like Owen could. Even when she could feel the ground slipping out from underneath her.

Before she could respond, Isaac's voice cut through the silence as if he was right there in the room, and everyone turned to look at the screen.

"I don't know where you got that photo, or why you'd show that hateful post," Isaac said in a voice like steel. "That's my girl, Abby. I cherish her as much as she cherishes her privacy. So why don't you take that trash down and move on, Reggie?"

Isaac's expression had shifted, his body suddenly tense, the tendons in his neck standing out. All his smug composure had vanished, leaving behind what might have been the terrifying countenance of his darkest villains. This was not a man who wore Bermuda shorts or recited lines from the original *Star Trek* or got a goofy grin on his face whenever he talked about his nephews.

For a brief second, the host seemed not to know what to do—but then he broke out a grin and shrugged. "All right, Isaac Ferrer, everyone," he said to the audience, and they began to clap. It was just a smattering at first, with none of the catcalls and shouting, but then it swelled briefly before fading away.

Abby had the fleeting thought that there were women in the audience who knew exactly how she felt right now. Who were dying on the inside a little for her. Whose friends and partners were pretending not to notice while they applauded to prove that they'd never do something so crass, so rude. Who were excusing themselves for laughing in the first place.

The photo vanished from the screen and Reggie joined in the applause. "Time for a break. When we come back, we'll have more with best-selling author Isaac Ferrer—and just maybe a sneak preview of the new season of *Evernight*!"

The band struck up the show's theme, the camera pulled back for a wide angle of the packed audience, and Reggie leaned in for a quiet word—or more likely an apology—to Isaac. And just like that they were watching a tire commercial narrated by a familiar actor who played presidents and generals. *Life throws all kinds of unexpected challenges your way. Your tires need to take what you didn't see coming and keep on rolling.*

Owen gripped her tightly. Steph fumbled for the remote and muted the audio. Somebody coughed.

But no one said a word. Abby didn't blame them. How were you supposed to respond after watching someone in the room be humiliated on national television?

Oh, dear God, you've just been humiliated on national television.

A sharp pain launched itself from the center of her chest, radiating out through her body, shattering her numb shock. A tear splashed on her cheek.

This is what happens when you open your big mouth, she scolded herself furiously. *You knew from the start that this would never lead anywhere good, and now look—it's even worse than you imagined.*

Abby could feel every pair of eyes in the room turning toward her in horror as the seconds ticked by. If she stayed there another minute, the pity was going to kill her.

"I think I'm going to call it a night," she blurted, wrenching herself free from Owen's arm. People stepped out of her way this time.

But Owen was right behind her. "I'm coming with you."

"Me too," Steph said.

Abby would have told them not to bother, but that

would have meant opening her mouth again, and she didn't think she could do that without sobs tumbling out. Besides, whether she wanted to admit it or not, she had never needed her brother and her best friend more than she did at this moment.

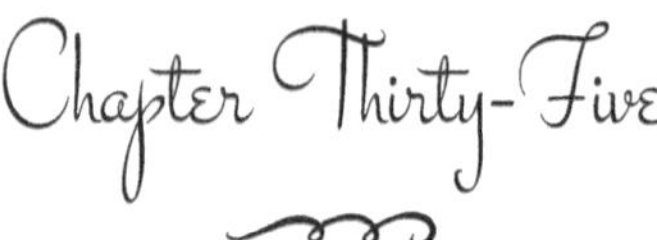

Chapter Thirty-Five

"Reggie Reynolds better stay the fuck on his side of the country because if he ever shows his face in California, I'll kill him with my bare hands."

Owen reached the far wall of Abby's bedroom and pivoted, his fists clenched. If he kept pacing, he was going to wear a path in the hooked rug Abby had found in a second-hand shop in the Haight, but she didn't have the energy to stop him.

Abby felt empty, like a balloon from which all the air had leaked…useless and ugly and utterly limp. All that pain—humiliation, shame, hurt, anger—had hardened into a dense knot deep inside her, the only external evidence a slightly quivering numbness and an inability to speak.

On the other hand, she hadn't actually tried to say anything, so that last one might be temporary. Given Owen's fury and Steph's distress, Abby didn't have anything to add to the conversation.

"Bet he's got security following him around like the

coward he is," Owen continued. Abby was pretty sure he was still talking about Reggie, but her brother had a few choice words for Isaac, too. The general idea seemed to be that Isaac had failed Abby by not punching the host instead of just verbally dressing him down.

Which was pretty ironic coming from Owen, who had never hit anyone in his life. Though he'd made the state wrestling finals twice in high school, he was fond of telling people that wrestling was a mind game that happened to take place in a gym. Owen was more likely to mock Reggie to the point of surrender than harm him physically.

Still, Abby had never seen him this upset. It was almost as if he was the one who had been attacked on national television instead of her. While Steph, on the other hand...

Though Abby seemed to have left her body in some sort of trauma-induced dissociation and was observing the drama taking place in her bedroom from somewhere up near the ceiling, she noticed that Steph's reaction to the on-air calamity was an unlikely combination of clumsy fawning and sheer, raw fury on a level Abby had never witnessed before.

Watching her brother and best friend rage on her behalf was both touching and deeply unsettling, but then again, Abby couldn't have predicted her own response to the worst moment of her life. Which was odd, because she'd been rehearsing it—or situations like it—since she was a teenager. Abby figured that the nightmare scenarios that plagued her were probably common among fat women: a chair collapsing at a dinner party, a skirt seam ripping while bending over, a fellow air passenger loudly refusing to sit next to her.

But that didn't make it any less awful when it happened,

especially since the other fat women in her living room had pretended nothing was wrong. Abby couldn't blame them, though...she probably would have done the same.

Steph had joined Abby on the bed and was patting her like she was made of glass and murmuring encouragement. She'd run through the easy ones like *this too shall pass* and the *darkest hour before the dawn* thing, and something from Winston Churchill, before branching into sayings Abby was pretty sure Steph had surreptitiously looked up on Instagram. At the moment Steph was plodding through some Tolkien quote having to do with snow and fire and dragons.

Abby was grateful, but nothing could erase what had been broadcast to the world. Nothing was okay, and it wasn't going to be for a while. She was a national punch line, a total joke—and the worst part was that Abby hadn't even done anything to bring it on. All she'd done was exist in front of a camera lens, and that was enough.

"I swear to God, that guy better make his will," Owen was fuming as he executed another pass, when Steph's arm suddenly shot out like a crossing guard's.

"Stop it," she barked. "Sit down, Owen. You're not helping. And you're making me dizzy."

Ordinarily Abby would play peacemaker, but she couldn't bring herself to care. She had no idea what she was supposed to do or think or feel, as if the responding and reacting parts of her brain had been blanketed by a dense, cold fog that blocked all emotion.

Where were the tears? The anger? Abby ought to be the one pacing, not Owen. Instead, she thought she might just stay in bed until she disappeared under dust and spiderwebs.

"Nothing in life is to be feared," Steph was saying, a tremor in her voice, "it is only to be understood—"

Abby abruptly yanked back the comforter and sure enough, Steph had been hiding her phone underneath. "You were reading those off the Internet!" she accused.

"That last one was Marie Curie," Steph said defensively. "I mean, I feel like the odds were stacked against her."

"Well, great," Abby snapped, though the flare of indignation was already fading. "Next time I'm dying from the effects of my research, I'm sure that quote will come in handy."

Owen cleared his throat. "You're, you know, going to get through this," he said tentatively.

Abby didn't know whether to laugh or cry. She almost told him how terrible he was at consolation—but was afraid she'd hurt his feelings.

Which was ridiculous. All of this, ridiculous. Of course she'd get through it. She'd get up tomorrow whether she wanted to or not. She'd shower and get dressed and put on makeup and head to work just like any other Thursday. Abby was hardly a novice when it came to putting on a mask to hide her hurt.

And in time the hurt would fade, not disappearing but sinking down to the dark, murky bottom of the toxic pit inside her, joining all the other assaults on her self-esteem, large and small, that had amassed over a lifetime.

There was a knock on the door, and Ben peered in apologetically.

"People are starting to leave, Steph. I thought you might want to..."

"Right." Steph gave Abby's hand a squeeze. "I'll be right back, Abs."

Owen flopped onto the bed and closed his eyes. Abby could hear people saying goodbye, the front door opening and closing. It wouldn't be long now until the house was quiet and she could pull the blankets over her head.

Her phone buzzed.

Abby looked down to see Isaac's name on her screen, and just like that, the fog evaporated and all the fear and pain came rushing back in.

She dropped the phone on her floor as if it was on fire and rolled away from Owen, curling into a fetal position. The bed creaked as Owen picked up her phone—and then he leaned over Abby and held it in her face, a question in his eyes.

"I-I can't."

He nodded and put the phone to his ear, his face tight with grim fury. Abby had never been so grateful for her brother.

"Isaac. This is Owen Reilly. You tell that son-of-a-bitch Reggie that if I ever cross paths with him, I'll—"

The bedroom door was flung open.

"Give me that," Steph demanded, grabbing the phone out of Owen's hand. Ben was right behind her. "Hey, Isaac." A pause. "Yeah, we saw."

Abby could hear Isaac's voice but it was tinny and far away and she couldn't make out the words. "She's not really in the mood to talk right now ... I'm sure she knows that ... Of course, I'll tell her ... Maybe tomorrow ... Yeah, I'll be sure to tell her, I promise ... Don't worry. It's going to be okay."

Steph clicked off, shoved Owen hard enough that he almost fell off the side of the bed, and wrapped her arms around Abby.

"You lied," Abby whispered, the tears finally coming. "Nothing's ever going to be okay again."

Chapter Thirty-Six

The alarm went off at 6:30, just as it did every weekday. Years ago, she'd started as a Communications Assistant II at the company. From the first day, she knew that if she ever wanted to be promoted out of the so-called Cutthroat Pool—only twenty percent of Communications hires stayed for more than two years—discipline would be the key.

And it had worked, Abby having been promoted to Senior Writer last year. But to get there she made a habit of arriving half an hour before everyone else and staying later, working in the evenings and on weekends, and had taken exactly one sick day, when a bug kept her chained to the bathroom for twenty-four hours.

But when she texted her boss at 6:32, Abby didn't even bother to check for typos before hitting send and tossing her phone on the floor.

I can't come in today. Taking a sick day. Sorry.

What Abby was suffering from was worse than being sick. It was safe to say that she'd prefer to spend the day in the emergency room or having a root canal or even passing a kidney stone over going to work today.

She hadn't anticipated how alarmed her team would be, probably convinced she was dying. One text after another buzzed, but the phone lay on the carpet just out of reach, and Abby simply didn't have it in her to get up.

It hadn't exactly been a restful night, and the tiny strip of early-morning light through the gap in her blackout curtains was evidence of the cruelty of the world beyond her four walls. Abby wasn't having it. She burrowed deeper under the covers, and eventually her phone fell silent.

Her bedroom door opened. "So this is the kind of day we're having," Steph observed. "Good thing I've got a light schedule."

Abby gave a pitiful moan from inside her cocoon as Steph curled up against her, big-spoon style, until her phone started buzzing again.

"Do you want me to answer those for you?"

"No." The blankets muffled Abby's voice. "They can leave a message. Or text me like a civilized person."

"It speaks!" Steph exclaimed, poking her gently. "That's a good sign. You'll be good as new in no time."

"Will not," Abby protested like a four-year-old. After a moment she added, "You think I'm being dramatic."

Steph laughed. "Dramatic? Sugar, you're being a total drama queen. But why is that a bad thing? Your problem is that you've never acted out. You don't have any experience, so you just assume you won't like it. But you need to give it a chance. You'll probably never have a better excuse to throw yourself a pity party, so why not dive in with both feet?"

"Mmmfp." A single syllable that meant *hell no* and *go away* but also *stay*.

"Like really go all the way if you're going to do it. What can it hurt? I mean, it's got to be better than stuffing it all down and pretending everything's fine like you usually do."

Abby pulled the covers down to her chin. She was running out of oxygen under there. "I don't do that," she protested sourly.

"Hmm," Steph said, distracted by her phone, which had started to vibrate. "It's Ben. I'd better take it. Hey, what's up?" She got up from the bed and went out into the hall, pulling the door shut behind her.

Abby had a feeling that Ben wasn't just calling to check up on her. Steph wouldn't have left the room for that. Which meant there was news...news that Steph didn't think she was ready to handle.

She burrowed back under the covers, but a few words reached her anyway. *...in bed...won't touch her phone...oh, God...for the best then...help you with a statement...give me an hour.*

Abby experienced a wave of nausea and fear as Steph

returned to the bed and rested a tentative hand on her shoulder.

"That bad?" Abby mumbled.

"Nothing Ben and I can't handle," Steph said with false brightness.

So, worse than bad. Abby took a deep, shaky breath and pulled down the blanket, blinking against the light from the hall. "Tell me."

A pause as Steph chose her words carefully. "Isaac's appearance last night sparked some...interest. Ben has received several media requests for statements and interviews."

Oh God. "About Ships, right? Tell me it's about Ships."

"Yes. Definitely." Another pause, just long enough for Abby to dare to hope. "Oh, and I think there was something about wanting to talk to you, too."

"Steph. Please. Tell me what people are saying."

Steph sighed heavily, and Abby could feel the brave front slipping away. "You sure you want to know?"

Of course she didn't. Wasn't it obvious? "No, but I need to."

"You really don't," Steph said firmly. "Let Ben and me handle this for a few hours. You need to take care of yourself today, which means I don't want to see your face outside this room. In fact, if I find you out of bed, I'm going to find some rope and tie you to it, and if you doubt me you might want to think about what I did to that catering rep last year when she sent me three hundred plastic champagne flutes." Steph shuddered at the memory. "I'll bring you something to eat, and if you need to go to the bathroom, just know that I'm keeping an eye on the clock and if you try to hide in there, I'll come in after you."

"You're being ridiculous," Abby protested. "You don't need to spend your day babysitting me."

"I'm your friend," Steph snarled. "Friends help. And I take offense to the idea that I'm just babysitting you—I'm a goddamn expert in dealing with press and social media."

Abby knew she should say yes, but the thought of turning over control to Steph made her feel like she couldn't breathe. It didn't matter that if the situation was reversed, she'd be saying the same things. That she wouldn't hesitate to help Steph—or Ben or Owen or even Dex. But being on the receiving end of this kind of help was different. Even the thought of it twisted Abby's guts into painful knots.

But not as painful as the thought of getting up and dealing with this herself.

"Okay," she whispered.

"Good," Steph said briskly. "We'll talk at the end of the day, and not one minute before—got it?"

Abby's only response was a groan.

Though when she peeked out of her nest of blankets to see Steph picking her phone up off the floor and slipping it into her pocket, Abby did maybe feel a tiny fraction of a bit less wretched.

Chapter Thirty-Seven

Abby fully intended to stay in bed for the rest of her life—or at least until Steph announced the end of her detainment—but it turned out that Abby wasn't really cut out for hibernation. While at work, she went for walks every hour or two—not just because getting her blood moving kicked her brain into high gear, but because she liked to move. She enjoyed the rush of getting her heartbeat up and stretching her legs, breathing fresh air and feeling the sun on her face.

Her cocoon, on the other hand, felt increasingly confining and oppressive and slightly rank as the day wore on until, in the early afternoon, she made a break for the bathroom and locked the door. After washing her face and brushing her teeth and running a comb through her hair, she helped herself to Steph's fancy hibiscus-scented hand lotion that she bought in a shockingly expensive boutique whenever work took her to New York City.

The bathroom fan served to mute Steph's voice, a

welcome relief from overhearing Lady Cobra, Abby's nickname for the frosty no-more-shit-will-be-put-up-with persona Steph saved for her most antagonistic work calls.

"My client is prepared...legal escalation is not out of the question...unprecedented brand capital damage..."

Abby stared at herself in the mirror and was surprised at how little external evidence there was of the train wreck of her life. Her eyes were a little puffy, and there were pillow creases on one side of her face, but otherwise she looked... fine. Or maybe not fine but at least vertical, and that was enough to get her to the living room, where Steph perched on the couch with her headphones on, furiously typing while she dressed down whoever was unfortunate enough to be on the other end.

"That *also* will not do, and I'm tempted to suggest we pick up this conversation when you've spoken with someone with the authority to do more than insult my client further. Excuse me for one moment." Steph muted her mouthpiece and glared at Abby, motioning her back to the bedroom. "Get back there now."

Abby stood her ground, nausea tempered by fascination. She'd never seen Steph work the phones with such fervor. Of course, the three discarded takeout coffee cups marked with her signature lipstick might have something to do with it.

Steph unmuted herself. "Must run, I have another call. Circle back when you have something worth discussing." She tapped the phone. "Stephanie Tran speaking. Yes...let me stop you there. As I said in my email, Miss Reilly has no plans to make a public statement at this time as she is not a public figure. I will emphasize—and suggest that you keep in mind—that she is a respected and award-winning communications professional employed by a top San Francisco company. Her family have been prominent members of the city's Irish American business community for generations, and she is a founding member of the popular weekly 'Ships in the Night' event at The City Bookmark bookstore that celebrates and promotes literacy with a media reach approaching nine hundred thousand and growing at a consistent two-digit rate month over month. But my client is also, and perhaps most relevantly, a private citizen who is understandably shocked to find herself thrust onto the national stage by a photograph published online without her knowledge or consent with clear intent to defame." There was a long pause, during which Steph fixed Abby with an icy, unblinking gaze. "On the contrary, if you own a dictionary I think you will find that the caption falls *precisely* in the legal definition, though of course I do encourage you to engage legal counsel if questions remain— after you publish a retraction making all relevant facts clear to *Times* readers. Failing to do so will result in further escalation."

Steph ended the call with a flourish, and Abby offered up a slow clap. "That was…"

"Brilliant and terrifying. Yes, I know. Why are you out of bed?"

"When you said 'The Times,' please tell me it was like the *Modesto Times* or the *Wasilla Times* or—"

Steph snorted. "Girl, I don't do things halfway, remember? At least it's not front-page news. If I had to guess, it'll be a couple paragraphs in the Style section."

Abby rolled her eyes. "Why does anybody even care? It's one unflattering photo of someone they've never met."

"Right. Yes. And that's where you should be focusing, Abby—that this story didn't take off because of you, but because Reggie Reynolds has been losing viewers for months. The show's had to issue retractions twice, he called that senator a 'desperate cougar' last month and his ex-wife just accused him of having an affair while she was pregnant."

"Oh. Wow." There was a reason Abby steered clear of so-called "entertainment" television.

"'Wow' is right. There's been grumbling at the network and a leaked report that they're considering a suspension, but Isaac is the first person to stand up to him publicly—and you just happened to get caught in the crossfire."

"Lucky me," Abby said, fighting the despair she felt at every reminder that her misery was in the public domain now. She went to the fridge and grabbed a soda, then put it back and opted for a beer, popped the cap and took a long, sustaining swallow before returning to the living room.

"So...how many of those calls have there been?" she asked, not at all certain she wanted to know.

Steph gave her an assessing look, as if trying to gauge her fragility. "A...few."

Abby plopped down on the couch. "Do I even want to look at my phone?"

"Absolutely not."

Abby's heart sank further into the morass. "That bad?"

Steph sighed. "Your mom called a couple times."

Yikes.

"Don't worry, I texted Owen, and he's going to call her for you."

"Good thinking. I don't think I could handle her right now."

"Yep. No worries. But Abs..." For the first time since Abby had left the bedroom, Steph's iron composure slipped.

"What?" Abby demanded. "Oh God, it's Isaac, isn't it?"

"He's worried about you," Steph said with grim determination.

"And you told him I was fine. Steph, tell me that you told him I'm fine."

"But are you?" she asked gently.

"I'm up, aren't I?"

Steph nodded at the nearly empty beer bottle in Abby's hand. "I'm not sure that's going to convince anyone."

Abby set the bottle on the coffee table and reached for the remote. "It's one damn beer. How do I get to those entertainment channels?"

"Abby. I'm not sure that's a good idea."

"So don't watch," Abby said, with a lot more conviction than she felt. This was probably a very terrible idea, but she had to face it eventually...and she might as well do it while Steph was there to pick up the pieces. And somehow, the television—with its sprayed and lacquered hosts and breathless banter and cheesy sets—seemed less threatening than the hellish landscape of social media and its anonymous armies of trolls.

"Fine." Steph grabbed the remote out of her hands and switched the channel. "But if you get triggered, I'm turning it off."

Three surreally beautiful human beings sat behind desks arranged like a newsroom, talking over each other about a celebrity divorce. Rumors of infidelity on both sides had apparently elevated the story to the level usually reserved for global conflicts and acts of God, and Abby stared glassy-eyed until they moved on to a story about an actor who'd been photographed puking his guts out behind a fast food joint in West Hollywood.

It was truly appalling, the things that passed for news— but Abby was overwhelmed with gratitude that the story of Isaac telling Reggie off wasn't scandalous enough to make the first half of the show. With any luck, everyone watching had gone to the kitchen for a snack.

An ad for hearing aids segued directly into That Photo, as Abby had begun to think of it. Taking up the entire screen, it was even more unflattering, but she forced herself not to look away as they played a brief clip from last night's show, then cut to Isaac's reaction.

"...the day that acceptance isn't reserved for people whose gender"—Isaac stabbed the air angrily with his index finger —"or *race*"—stab—"or *size* isn't the subject of thinly veiled mockery by unimaginative, insecure blowhards whose career..."

The shot changed as Isaac's rant continued, zooming in on Reggie. The pugnacious sneer melted into uncertainty, then something akin to fear before he slashed a finger across his throat in a signal for the control room to cut away, seconds before they did.

The three hosts all started talking at once again as social

media hot takes scrolled by on the screen, and Steph turned off the TV. As if on cue, someone knocked on the door.

"That'll be Ben!" Steph said brightly.

She jumped up and ran to the door, and Abby watched her two best friends embracing as though they'd just survived the Titanic. Which figured...while she was being pummeled by life's cruel curveball, Steph was finally getting around to recognizing the treasure laid at her feet.

Ben finally noticed Abby and untangled himself. "You're up!" he said with cautious enthusiasm. "Steph said she was keeping you in bed all day."

"No need." Abby sounded like a robot to her own ears, and tried again. "I'm fine."

Ben gave her a skeptical look. He came over and sat next to her on the couch, glancing at his phone before shoving it back into his pocket.

"I don't know how you do this, Steph. I didn't do anything at the store today but answer one call after another. Everyone wants a comment, but not just any comment— they have this idea of exactly what they want you to say."

"Mmm, welcome to my life," Steph murmured.

Ben was still picking up steam. "If you say what you really think, they just ask the question again in a different way. I seriously couldn't handle it. I told Minerva I had a dentist appointment and not to answer the phone while I was gone, and then I unplugged the landline so she wouldn't be tempted."

Ben's tone was light, but Abby could sense his genuine anxiety. The man could talk all day about books and authors and publishing and the neighborhood and a dozen other topics, but this episode had clearly shaken him up. Abby realized that she'd been so wrapped up in her own woes that she hadn't thought about the fact that she wasn't the only one affected.

"I'm really sorry, Ben."

He gave her a half-hearted grin. "Don't be. I feel weird saying it, but this whole shitshow has been great for business. There's no way I could buy press like this. The more often they run that clip, we keep getting more and more walk-ins. The next three Ships nights have already sold out! I'm going to have to hire an intern just to process all the submissions."

"I'm glad," Abby said, trying not to begrudge everyone their silver linings. Ben would enjoy a nice little bump to his bottom line, Isaac was being hailed a hero for standing up to Reggie, sales for his current book had hit a record, and Steph was knocking it out of the park on the national level, which definitely wouldn't go unnoticed by her clients.

As for Abby...she was willing to try, but it was hard to find anything positive in her situation. She usually lived by her grandmother's firm rule against self-pity, but today might be the exception.

"Um, Steph..." Ben said uncertainly. "There's something I need to talk to you about in private."

"Oh, for heaven's sake," Abby burst out. "Could everyone please stop treating me like I'm delicate? Things can't get any worse."

Ben gave her a worried look. "If you're sure...it's just that a *Buzzfeed* journalist sent an inquiry that—well, it's concerning."

"You should have forwarded it to me," Steph said,

sounding alarmed. "Seriously, Ben, whenever you're not sure of the right response, let me handle it."

Ben swallowed. "I would have, but in this case I thought that might make things worse. Draw more attention to it."

"To what?" Abby was seconds away from pummeling it out of him. "Come on, Ben, what the fuck did they ask you?"

"Okay, okay," Ben said hurriedly. "I don't know how they could have figured this out so fast—or why anyone would even bother—and I did my best to shut it down, but—"

Abby broke down and pinched his arm when he refused to get on with it.

"Ow! Fine. Some people are posting online about how you were Steph's ghostwriter for Ships. They're saying you only did it to lure Isaac into some kind of three-way."

"*Ew.*"

"But that's not the worst part," Ben added. "The thread's gone viral."

Abby grabbed a pillow and clutched it to her chest, holding back a whimper.

"Numbers," Steph demanded.

"Almost seven thousand retweets."

"That's not viral," Steph said. "But it's not good. Obviously."

Abby rocked, squeezing her eyes shut and hugging the pillow for dear life.

She'd been wrong: things could always get worse.

Chapter Thirty-Eight

Like most modern women finding themselves in an unusual etiquette quandary, Abby consulted the internet the next morning to find out if she was obligated to go to work. Unfortunately, no one who'd found themselves at the center of a toxic viral moment had gotten around to writing the definitive post on the subject, so she had to go with her gut.

And her gut said that while calling in sick the morning after being humiliated on national television was acceptable and probably for the best, hiding out any longer would only make matters worse, giving her detractors more fuel for their toxic dumpster fire.

So even though the thought of walking into the office made her light-headed, Abby showered and forced down some toast before submitting to an emergency styling session with Steph.

Flawless blowout. Understated makeup, with the exception of a dark berry-pink lipstick that Steph promised would make Abby appear more confident. Black pants, emerald silk blouse, carved statement bangle, block-heel sandals and, as a finishing touch, oversized sunglasses that felt like they'd swallowed her face.

"Okay," Steph said, stepping back to assess the final result. "Touch up your lipstick after lunch, and keep your hands off your hair."

"Aye, aye, Captain," Abby joked.

"So Ben told me you still hadn't submitted your piece for Ships yet," Steph said as she put all her pots and powders and brushes away.

Of course he'd told her—they were together now. Maybe not officially, no announcement had been made, but the two had been going out alone more and more in the week before the Reggie Reynold's incident...and on two of those nights, Steph hadn't come home.

"That's because I'm don't think I'm going to perform one this time." Or ever again, if she was being honest. "I think it would be better for everyone if I didn't show up even as a spectator for a while."

Steph stilled before turning around. "How would that be better?"

"Well, to start with, it would give everyone time to forget about me. For the gossip to die down. For life to go back to normal."

"Which normal? The one where you stand alone in the back of the store and listen to someone else read your words? I hate to break it to you, but that normal is gone and it is never coming back."

Abby sighed. "You're right. Maybe it's time to leave Ships altogether."

Steph rolled her eyes. "Why stop there, when you could just pack up all your stuff and move to Antarctica for the next few months?"

"You're being ridiculous."

"You are." Steph was silent for a moment, then rested her hand lightly on Abby's shoulder. "Listen, hiding won't help anything. You've done it for years and your worst fears still managed to find you. Maybe the answer isn't to retreat even deeper into the shadows, but to step into the light."

"Easy for you to say."

"Do me a favor and promise me that you'll at least think about it."

"Fine. I'll think about it," Abby lied.

Steph stepped back to give her one final top-to-bottom assessment. "Some of my best work," she murmured. "Now remember—head up, shoulders back, and be confident."

"Right. 'Be confident.'" Good thing Steph was here. She would have never have thought of that on her own.

"Call me if you need anything at all."

"I will," Abby promised, though if things got that bad, she already had a plan in place.

Screw Steph's pep talk about stepping into the light, the kind of platitude Abby would expect from the Strivers. It might work on the hundreds of thousands of podcast listeners, but Abby knew better. She was ready to bolt for a stall in the ladies' room and stay there all day if she had to.

If the walk to her bus stop was a test, Abby passed it with

flying colors. No one gave her a second glance, everyone sharing that same harried running-late-for-work expression.

Ordinarily, Abby resented the fact that fat women were treated as invisible. Somehow, she was always the one expected to make way on the sidewalk for people passing by. Today, however, she was grateful for the lack of acknowledgement. If she could just make it to the office without anyone recognizing her as the girl who blew up the *Night Talk* show, she had a feeling she could get through the rest of the day.

There was a brief panic at the card reader when the woman ahead of her turned around. "Excuse me," she said, and Abby froze.

"Do you happen to have any quarters?" the woman said apologetically, holding out a wrinkled dollar bill. "I forgot my card."

Abby was so relieved that she swiped her own card twice and told the woman to have a great day.

But the thrill of doing something nice for a stranger wore off by the time she found a seat, next to a man wearing a shirt starched within an inch of its life, talking loudly on his cell phone. "Then you tell him it's unacceptable...okay, but it's your job to *make* him listen. Come on, Hannah, how many times have I told you that you need to grow a pair?"

Abby rolled her eyes and switched seats.

When she finally reached her building and was riding up the elevator, Abby did what she could to erase the effects of exertion—pink cheeks and chewed-off lipstick—and mouthed a silent *thank you* to Steph's industrial-strength hair spray that had kept every strand in place. By the time she arrived at the twenty-second floor, Abby had restored her composure—at least on the outside.

Her heart sank to see that Anthony, the regular receptionist, was out for the day, and Mr. Hoover had sent his personal assistant to take over the job. Ochre, a frighteningly pale twentysomething with an anthropology degree from Barnard, considered reception beneath her and retaliated by dropping calls, failing to pass on messages, and leaving snarky notes for Anthony, which he took screenshots of and texted to Abby, things like "M: third call, must escalate" when there were seven people on the staff whose names began with M and none of them had any idea what was being escalated.

Abby had never missed Anthony as much as when Ochre fixed her with a fascinated, unblinking stare and said, "Look who's joining us."

Abby stopped cold, a terrible mixture of emotions gripping her heart like a vise, and took a deep breath before turning around to face her. "Good morning, Ochre."

"You weren't here yesterday," Ochre said accusingly.

"Yes. I called in sick."

"Are you feeling...better?"

For fuck's sake, Abby thought. "Better than yesterday? I suppose so. Is there anything else that you would like to ask me?"

"Like what?"

Abby wanted to scream. The conversation was like one of those woven straw finger puzzles which, the harder you tugged, became tighter and tighter.

"Abby!" Bruce from Marketing stood frozen between the copier and his desk, looking nearly as uncomfortable as she felt. "Hi. *Hi!* It's great to...see you. You look—I mean, how are you?"

"I'm fine, Bruce," Abby mumbled, nearly running him over in her rush to get away from Ochre. Bruce was a nice guy. And if this was the effect she had on him, it didn't bode well for—

"Oh my God!" Sharol Lee, a legal department admin who organized retirement parties and after-work happy hours that hardly anyone attended, stepped in front of Abby as if she'd been lying in wait. She grabbed Abby's arm and hustled her backward into the copy room, nearly toppling Bruce for the second time. "I've been dying to call you. I *should* have called you. Shit, I'm a bitch for not calling you. But seriously, I think you're so incredibly brave, do you know that?"

Abby's face burned. She couldn't do this. The room was too small to share with someone like Sharol on a good day, but today every shrieking syllable felt like a tentacle wrapped around her throat.

"Got to take a call," she gasped and shoved past Sharol so hard that she fell against the copy machine.

"Hey! Jesus, Abby, are you all right?"

Now she really *was* running. In her panic, she went the wrong direction down the corridor, which meant she had to pass every window office on her way to the Pasture. And since the higher-ups were committed to an open-door policy, she got to see everyone's eyebrows shoot up as she passed.

When Abby finally slid into her chair, six fellow members of the communications team gaped at her from their own desks in the green-carpeted center of the floor that had given rise to its nickname.

"Fuck," Abby whispered to herself, desperately trying to hold back the tears that were already stinging her eyes. It seemed like she was going to be visiting that restroom sooner rather than later.

Fortunately, five of the six remembered their manners and went back to pretending to be engrossed in their work, while Chetan dropped a box of tissues on the floor and used his foot to slide them over like a hockey puck before returning his eyes to his screen.

Chetan, seriously? The guy who stole a Cup O'Noodles that she'd written her name on and ate it right in front of her. This was the only guy who could bring himself to show her some compassion. Would wonders never cease?

Abby got to work. Or rather, she opened a document and scrolled through it slowly, erasing and retyping a word here and there. She did not allow her gaze to wander to either side of her enormous monitor.

The rest of the team were most likely trying to be considerate of her feelings. Abby knew that. If she was in their shoes, she would probably do the same thing...but the silence was suffocating.

When her phone buzzed, she was almost relieved. Until she looked down at the screen and saw that it was Isaac.

One ring. Two. Abby glanced up to see everyone watching, waiting to see if she would answer...which left her no choice.

She gave them a wan smile and headed for the conference

room where everyone took their personal calls, and tapped her phone.

"Hey."

"You picked up," Isaac said, sounding both relieved and apprehensive. "I wasn't sure you were going to."

"Mmm." Just a few more steps and she'd be out of earshot—except the conference room wasn't empty. Bruce was in there with Sharol, who must have cornered him and dragged him off to get the dirt after Abby shoved her. "Shit."

"Are you all right?" Isaac sounded alarmed. "Where are you?"

Abby dodged right and headed for the fire stairs. It was a risky move, because at least twice a month someone got locked in the stairwell, usually when they were sneaking a cigarette, and had to walk all twenty-two floors down to the lobby.

"I'm fine," she said, breathing hard. "Just at work so, you know, trying to keep my voice down."

"Oh. I...get it."

He didn't, obviously. "Look, Isaac, I'm sorry about yesterday. I just needed to block everything out for a while."

"You don't need to be sorry." His words came out in a rush. "I'm the one who should be apologizing. I should have seen where that bastard was going and shut it down before he...well."

Abby squeezed her eyes shut. This was even harder than she thought.

"I meant Reggie," Isaac clarified. "He's the bastard I was talking about."

The tension gripping Abby eased very slightly. "I knew

who you meant. Isaac, none of this is your fault. And it's really fine, or it will be. I mean, a story like this lasts what, a day or two?—before something else comes along and..."

Her voice had taken on a wobble, so she trailed off, leaning against the shiny cinderblock wall for support. Someone had scratched the words GOMER SUX ASS into the paint. Abby didn't know anyone named Gomer, but she wondered how he'd feel if he saw that.

Not very good, she suspected. Maybe they could form a little support group.

"You sound like my publicist," Isaac was saying. Abby could tell he was trying to sound upbeat, but he wasn't very good at it.

"Actually, it's Steph who keeps telling me that, so I'm not surprised. I just—" *I pray they're right*, she'd been about to say, but it felt too pathetic.

"Then you have nothing to worry about." Abby could almost hear Isaac wincing. "Jeez, sorry, Abby. That was a stupid thing to say. Steph knows her stuff, but you're not her, and I bet you're probably feeling like crap right now."

To Abby's surprise, she found herself smiling a little. For a guy who made his living with words, Isaac was remarkably clumsy in the reassurance department.

And that meant she was talking to the real Isaac, the dorky one in the old shorts, the one who disappeared when he went on stage and signed copies of his book and listened to his gushing fans.

"Yeah, but I'll survive," she said, realizing that it was true. "I even managed to come into work today."

"And how's that going?"

"Besides everyone staring at me like they're waiting for me to lose it?"

"I see," Isaac said gravely. "As it happens, I'm having one of those days myself."

Abby did a quick reset. She'd been dreading talking to him so much that it hadn't occurred to her to wonder how he was feeling about the whole episode. "I'm sorry. Are you still in New York?"

"I'm at LaGuardia—my flight leaves in an hour."

"Are you off to LA already?"

There was a pause. "I, um, take it you didn't turn on the TV before you left for work."

Abby never turned on the TV before work. It had never even occurred to her. "No..."

"Well, I was supposed to go on *Sunrise America*, but they wouldn't agree not to bring up what happened with Reggie, so I walked out."

Abby's eyes widened. "You...walked out? You just left?"

Isaac laughed. "I'm a grownup, Abby. I can do whatever I want."

"But—millions of people watch that show. This is your, your *career* and this tour is for publicity for your books and the show and—you know what you need to do?" The words were tumbling out of her mouth and she couldn't stop. "You need to go back there and apologize. I mean it, Isaac, get in a cab and—"

"No chance." Isaac sounded firm. "I made a simple request and they denied it. I refuse to give them more fuel to feed the fire. That's why I've canceled the rest of the tour."

Abby's mouth fell open. "You *what*?"

"It's fine, I promise. It'll just give people more to talk about. My publicist left me a voicemail saying that telling Reggie Reynolds to go fuck himself was the best thing I could have done for my career."

Abby was having a hard time keeping up. "But…"

"Hell, what does it even matter?" Isaac sounded a lot more like himself. "It's just money. I've got plenty. My sales go up, they go down, it gives the pencil pushers something to do, I guess, but it doesn't mean much to me."

"I just feel like…" Abby didn't know how to finish the sentence. What was she feeling? Nothing that she could tell Isaac. Nothing that she could afford to let him see.

And yet there was something so comforting about hearing his voice right now. It made her want to believe that he understood. But that was dangerous.

"You defended me, Isaac," she settled for saying. "On national television. Not many people would have done that."

And that was all it was. An incredibly decent guy doing the decent thing, and, if anything, it said a lot about the times that such a simple act was newsworthy. The rest…the things Abby yearned for…they were illusions she'd spun from thin air. Because there was no way that Isaac could know how she felt about him after she'd gone to such lengths to hide the truth. He'd opened himself up so completely, telling her things about himself that had never been said in public or printed in a magazine or tweeted by his fans.

And in return, Abby had hidden her truest self away from him.

"I'm just glad to hear you're doing better," he said. "But I was also calling to ask you about something."

Abby's stomach twisted in trepidation. She didn't like the tension that had crept into his voice.

"...Oh?"

"I hope this isn't too awkward, but I didn't just walk out on *Sunrise America* because they wanted to talk about Reggie. They also wanted my reaction to the rumors that you were the real writer behind Steph's stories."

Oh God. The tears finally spilled over. "And what did you tell them?"

"Nothing they could use. That if I wasted my time commenting on every ridiculous rumor connected to me, I would never get anything done."

"Oh." Abby slid down the concrete wall to the floor. An uncomfortable silence stretched between them, and eventually she couldn't take it anymore. "But do you believe it?"

"I...didn't want to," Isaac said carefully. "But it made me think. The night I went to the basketball game with Steph, I asked her about what inspired her *Great Gatsby* story. The way she answered made me wonder if she'd ever actually read the book. And her writing voice never sounded anything like the way she actually speaks. But it did sound like someone I know."

A vise was tightening around Abby's heart. She was sure of it, squeezing so hard could barely breathe.

"The other night at dinner you said something that seemed familiar, that thing about wanting to be known for your mind. I finally remembered where I heard it...Steph's *Dracula* story."

"Maybe...maybe I heard it there too and it stayed with me."

"Maybe," Isaac said, not sounding at all convinced. In the background, a crackling voice sounded over an airline PA system. "That's my boarding group. I've got to go, Abby. But my flight gets in early this afternoon. I have a call set up with my agent and editor when I get home, and I should probably take it. But I'd like to see you and talk more after that."

Tears streamed down Abby's face. She wasn't sure when she'd stopped fighting them. *Say something*, the voice inside her urged. But she couldn't.

Isaac had canceled his tour and left New York for her. Walked away from the spotlight. And now he wanted to see her.

Abby didn't deserve to see him. She'd tricked him, made him believe that she was someone else, and been so convincing that he'd upended his life for her. Abby wasn't at all sure how that had happened...only that it was her fault.

But Isaac was still waiting for her to say something.

"I'd...like that." She sounded like a recording of herself, shrill and tinny. "But since I didn't come in yesterday, I'm way behind on my work. I'm going to be here late. How about tomorrow instead?"

"Tomorrow? You mean—at Ships?"

Abby bit her lip. Right: tomorrow was Friday. There was no way she was risking another public humiliation, but Isaac didn't have to know that. In the time between now and the show, she'd figure out an excuse.

"That sounds good."

"Okay, then," Isaac said. Then, "And just so you know, you can tell me anything, Abby. Absolutely anything."

"Yeah. I know. Have a—have a safe flight home."

Abby hung up and hugged her knees, rocking gently. If someone came into the stairwell now, she'd never live it down.

She stayed a little longer anyway, wondering how much worse things could get.

Chapter Thirty-Nine

It wasn't gum that Abby managed to sit in, but powdery drywall dust from a patch the painters had missed. The brief wallow hadn't made her feel better, exactly, but at least she felt sufficiently fortified to return to her desk and bury herself in work—after a side trip to the ladies' room to clean up.

Unfortunately, one of the interns—she hadn't been there long enough for Abby to catch her name—arrived at the restroom door at the same time. Her eyes went wide and she started to back away, but then she stopped, stiffened her spine, and spun around.

"I just want you to know that I think you're very, very brave," she said in a low, urgent voice. "You speak for all of us."

Then she bolted back the way she'd come.

"Huh," Abby said, wondering what message the girl thought was conveyed by appearing in an unflattering photograph that was mocked on national television—and what part of that constituted bravery.

The question stayed in her mind as she rinsed and blotted her pants, touched up her smudged makeup, and headed back to her desk. Everyone was still glued to their screens, but this time Abby sensed more shades of gray in their emotional response to her return.

She was the elephant in the room, not because of anything she'd done, as the young intern had implied, but because of what she *represented*. It wasn't about her at all, but about society's rules about who got to date who, about celebrity and anonymity and bodies and the toxic culture of free-for-all online speech.

Reduced to its essence, breaking a social covenant was uncomfortable for everyone. But Abby didn't have to be. In all likelihood, she saw now, her coworkers weren't avoiding her out of judgment—they were just desperate for someone to make the whole thing go away. They didn't want to have to discuss or acknowledge it, and if she gave them permission to move on, she could release everyone from their misery.

Abby rapped Chetan's desk with her knuckles as she passed. "Is that a new jacket?" she asked breezily. "I like it. That shade of blue suits you."

Then she sat down and opened her document, resisting the temptation to check to see how her comment had landed.

"Uh...thank you?" Chetan said cautiously.

"No problem." She gave him a cheerful smile before addressing everyone else. "Hey, did they resolve the distribution issue for the fourth quarter mailing while I was out yesterday?"

Marilou blinked several times behind her oversized black glasses. "Yes. I think. Probably."

"Maybe check with Arthur?" Harris suggested.

"Or we could submit it for the agenda for Friday?" Gene added.

"Great idea," Abby said, and pretended to add a note to her desk calendar. Other than the fact that her colleagues were being weirdly tentative, things seemed to be moving in the right direction, the tension leaking out of the Pasture.

That was one problem down. But as the social awkwardness faded, the drumbeat of unpleasant emotions stemming from Isaac's accusations grew stronger. So Abby did what she always did when desperate to avoid getting pulled into the undertow of anxiety, and threw herself into work.

Which made it surprisingly easy to concentrate on the report she was composing for the marketing division. Trying to present a decline in projected fourth-quarter sales in a positive light gave her a welcome respite from her life drama, and Abby's fingers flew over the keyboard until, hours before she'd anticipated finishing it, the report was revised, polished, and sent.

When quitting time rolled around, Abby's inbox was cleared, her to-do list tackled, her calendar updated. In fact, it had been one of the most productive days she could remember. It certainly helped that no one had come by to chat or invite her to get coffee, or any of the other interruptions that usually peppered her day. But Abby suspected the real reason for her frenzied productivity was pure avoidance—anything to keep her brain from ruminating about her train wreck of a life.

Wait. Abby frowned and mentally backed up. "Train wreck" implied a disaster that was out of her hands, something that could have happened to anyone. The problem with that sort of thinking was that it kept her from seeing *her* part in a thing. And while she'd long practiced that sort of denial as a defense against pain, Abby's beliefs on the subject seemed to have shifted.

Not on purpose. Given a choice in the matter, Abby would have continued to delude herself indefinitely—but lately her issues kept hitting her over the head until she had no choice but to deal with them. And the very surprising result was that though the initial pulling-off-the-Band-Aid shock was awful, afterward things were...better.

Abby checked the time and was shocked to see that it was nearly six thirty, and the office had emptied out around her. She'd been so focused that she hadn't even noticed anyone leaving—or dropping off the thick stack of paper that was sitting on the corner of her desk.

The loopy red scrawl covering the top page tipped her off that her boss had been having a productive day as well. Sure enough, Mr. Hoover had already finished his revisions for the report and sent it back downstairs—in hard copy, because he clung to the belief that Track Changes robbed him of his creativity. As she flipped through the pages, red ink bleeding all over them, it became obvious that Mr. Hoover hated everything she'd come up with; she was going to have to start from scratch.

The rush of relief she felt at having something to keep her occupied a little longer probably wasn't a good sign, but

Abby pushed that thought away and texted Steph to let her know that she was working late.

She hesitated before hitting send...then took an eye-rolling selfie with the report, because there was a decent chance Steph would think she was lying, that in reality she was sitting alone in a movie theater quietly crying. When Steph texted back a picture of her and Ben snuggled up on the couch, Abby felt like she'd dodged a bullet.

She was delighted for her friends, of course, but she wasn't in the mood to be around their shiny new romance, especially in this early stage when they were high on pheromones and giddy with possibilities. And they deserved some time to focus on each other, without the burden of worrying about her, the heavy pall of her problems that had filled the house for the last couple of days.

But when Abby opened the report and started reading, she discovered that the day's work spree had exhausted her mental capacity. There was simply nothing left. The red handwriting, difficult to make out on a good day but nearly indecipherable when Mr. Hoover was agitated about something, made her temples throb. And he was going to be out of the office for the next few days so he couldn't even look at it again until next week.

Abby squared up the pages and placed them in her inbox and stared into space, wondering what to do. She couldn't go home. Couldn't stay at work. Wasn't in the mood to go shopping, and forget about subjecting herself to a solo table in a restaurant.

Which left the one place that felt as much like home as home.

O'Reilly's cheerful blinking neon shamrock was like a welcoming beacon as her ride share pulled up to the curb. A little girl held her mother's hand as she peered through the glass at the toy shop next door, while down the street, The City Bookmark's windows glowed golden and inviting. It was like a freaking Norman Rockwell scene, if he was the sort who enjoyed a nip now and then.

Abby stood under the kelly-green awning for a moment, gazing at the bookstore and wondering who was working tonight and if the phone was still ringing off the hook with media inquiries. She considered stopping by, casually managing to slip the question into a quick conversation—but the reality was that she might never have the nerve to set foot in the shop again.

O'Reilly's was packed with the usual after-work crowd, everyone from slick business-casual go-getters to day-shift workers from a nearby fulfillment center to construction workers in coveralls. Abby elbowed her way inside and spotted Dmitri behind the bar and Dex occupying his favorite stool in the corner. No sign of her brother. No doubt, he was in the back restocking.

Abby wasn't sure she was up for a heart to heart with her brother right now anyway. Too often, Owen's version of talking about her problems meant telling her what to do, and he wouldn't be dissuaded if she tried to change the subject. Maybe she could handle that after she had a chance to relax, but for the moment all Abby wanted was to blend into the background in one of the old wooden captain's chairs that Gramps had bought secondhand from an Italian restaurant that had been going out of business, decades' worth of graffiti carved into the arms.

Homey. Comfortable. Not everyone would use those words to describe the din and energy of the tipsy, enthusiastic crowd...but to Abby, they were as familiar as a favorite pair of old jeans. There was the plastic Budweiser sign that didn't light up anymore, but whose Clydesdales still cantered regally in formation. Above her hung the old fishing net and moldy buoy that added a mystifying nautical note to the Irish theme. A few tables over, Clive and Hank were continuing the argument they'd been having for the last five years.

Abby found an empty chair in the corner next to the narrow window ledge where she used to do her homework when she was a kid. She wouldn't exactly be invisible there, but it would take a while for Dex or Dmitri to spot her.

"Abby!"

She flinched as cool, bony fingers wrapped around her wrist. *Noooooooooo*, she silently wailed, cursing the cruelty of the Fates.

Abby slowly and deliberately pulled each finger off her arm as the hard kernel of anger she'd been carrying around burst into flame.

"Oh my God, Abby, I'm so glad I found you."

"Well, it is my family's pub, Jane," Abby said coldly.

Yesterday, in the funk of her misery, Abby had indulged in vivid fantasies of what she'd say to Jane if the bitch ever had the guts to stand in front of her again. Now she had her chance—but the all acid comments she'd come up with froze on Abby's tongue. Somehow the smug pleasure she'd imagined evaporated in the face of Jane's owlish glasses and "I

READ BANNED BOOKS" T-shirt and orangish lipstick, and all she felt was exhausted.

"It was hard to come here," Jane said, "but I had to take the risk."

Abby snorted. "That was pretty fucking brave of you, but maybe you should cut your losses and leave now."

"I can't." Jane twisted the strap of her NPR tote bag. "I need to talk to you."

Without waiting for Abby to reply, she headed for a table that had just opened up. The gall!—a prim voice in Abby's head remarked. She ought to turn around and head for the door.

Except that it was true, what she'd told Jane. This *was* her family's pub, and no one—especially not a backstabbing bitch advertising her lack of self-awareness in every detail of her being—was going to run her out of the place her grandparents had built with their own hands. Abby marched over and dropped into the chair across from Jane, not caring who she bumped into on the way.

"What do you want, Jane?"

Jane sat up a little taller. "I need you to forgive me."

A long pause stretched between them. Abby didn't know if she was more shocked by the audacity of Jane's demand or by the fact that the woman had two whole days to think up a decent apology and *that* was what she went with. "Yeah, that's not going to happen," Abby finally said, starting to get up.

Jane grabbed her hand to stop her. "But you have to," she implored. "Abby, you have to believe me. I didn't mean for any of this to happen. I didn't have anything to do with Reggie Reynolds using that picture on his show."

Abby shook her head in disbelief. "Seriously? You're going to look me in the face and deny that you took the picture? I saw you, Jane."

"That's not what I'm saying." Jane at least had the decency to look slightly flustered. "Yes, I took the photo and yes, I wrote that stupid caption and posted it. Okay? I'm not denying it."

"Then what are you saying?"

Jane took a breath. It was obvious that she hadn't been prepared for Abby to stand up for herself. "Okay. That post had like eight likes until a few days ago. To tell you the truth, I'd forgotten all about it. The first I heard about what happened on *Night Talk* was on Twitter the next day. Trust me, I was as shocked as you were."

Abby laughed. She couldn't help it. "Jesus, Jane. That's the best you can come up with?"

Jane's face turned red. "I'm trying," she said stiffly, "to apologize."

"That's funny. Because I haven't heard you use the word 'sorry' once."

"You know who else never got around to saying sorry?" Jane retorted, a bit of spittle collecting at the corner of her mouth. "You and Steph, for cheating. Yeah, I said it. I know it was you writing all those entries."

Abby stared at her, the pieces falling into place. "So you're the one behind those rumors too."

"Oh, please. We both know they're not rumors. And I'm

not the only one who figured it out. All the regulars knew, everyone who's been coming since the beginning."

There it was, the thing Abby had been afraid of so long... and all she felt was relief that it was finally out in the open.

"So this is...what? Your big revenge?"

"Don't be so dramatic," Jane snapped. "It's not like I was trying to come up with a way to humiliate you in front of millions of people."

"I think we're done here," Abby said.

"No, wait! Look, I was pissed at Steph for winning, and you for monopolizing Isaac. And then you didn't even have the guts to get up on that stage like everyone else. I—I posted that picture in a moment of weakness. It was a mistake, and I'm sorry."

It was a mistake, and I'm sorry.

Abby let the words roll around in her head for a moment. She hadn't realized how much she needed to hear them.

"Thank you," she said.

"So you forgive me?"

Why not? Abby would never trust Jane again—might not even talk to her again—but holding on to her anger and resentment wouldn't hurt Jane, only herself.

"Sure."

"Oh, thank God." Jane dug a business card from her purse and pushed it across the table. "I need you to write an email to this woman and tell her that everything is fine between us. That there are no hard feelings."

"I didn't say that." Abby picked up the card. It bore the

name Leslie Wannamaker and the logo of Jane's employer. "And who the hell is this?"

"My boss. Well, my former boss," Jane amended irritably. "They let me go today after issuing a statement on 'body positivity.'"

Said with air quotes, naturally.

"You're expecting me to help you get your job back?" Abby asked incredulously.

"I wouldn't ask if it weren't important."

Abby stared at her for a long time, abandoning one comeback after another. "That's the funny thing, Jane," she finally said. "You never once gave me the time of day. Not until now, when you need something."

Jane frowned. "Does this mean you don't accept my apology?"

Abby stood up. "You know what, Jane, I have no trouble believing that you didn't waste a single second considering the consequences of your actions. So yes, I forgive you—on the condition that I never have to see, hear, or think about you ever again."

Owen chose that moment to come out of the back—and naturally, he spotted her right away. "Abby!" he hollered, already on his way over.

"Maybe just keep the card," Jane said. "You might change your mind once you've calmed down."

"I doubt it, but one thing you could try is getting the hell out of my bar and never coming back."

Owen reached Abby in time to watch Jane's hasty departure. "*Your* bar?"

"A lie of convenience," Abby admitted. "She deserved it."

"If you think that's all she deserves then she's getting off easy." Owen slung his arm around Abby's shoulder. "Come with me. I've been stuck in the back all night washing dishes because Lowell had an emergency. I mean maybe not an emergency, but his girlfriend just called and told him she's pregnant, so he had to take off."

"Wow! Was it...planned?"

"Is anything in life planned?" Owen mused philosophically, maneuvering Abby toward the bar. "He's happy about it, that's the important thing. I guess life comes down to how you look at it. Sometimes what we think are disasters turn out to be the best things that ever happen."

Chapter Forty

Once inside the office-slash-stockroom, Owen gestured grandly to the chair across from his desk.

"The funny thing," Abby said thoughtfully, "was that it was actually kind of okay. Telling Jane off, I mean."

"Hmmm," Owen said skeptically. He was leaning back in Gramps' old desk chair, a beat-up fake-leather number that was missing two of its five wheels, and which Abby was pretty sure he'd never replace.

"I didn't say I *enjoyed* it, Owen. But I listened to her side of the story and, well...I believed her. She made a stupid mistake and posted something she never should have, then forgot all about it until it blew up. She was never out to destroy me."

"So you just—what, forgave her?" Owen said, outraged all over again.

"Well...yes, but I also told her that I would un-forgive her if I ever have to see, hear, or think about her again."

"Oh, Abs," Owen sighed. "We really need to work on your vengeance strategy. But hey, not bad for a girl who once apologized to the cab driver who almost ran you over."

"Not my finest moment," Abby agreed.

"So, listen. Mom's been calling."

A wave of guilt splashed over Abby. "I know, I know. Steph told me. I've been meaning to call her back, but..."

"But then she'd threaten to drop everything and jump on a plane in the middle of the night to smother you in person. I get it."

Was the world off its axis? Why was Owen being so understanding? "I'm a terrible daughter."

"No you're not. And I don't mind dealing with her, just as long as you remember you owe me."

Right—and just like that the world started spinning again. "Okay. So the next time you break up with some poor girl—"

"You'll tell Mom she had to move home to take care of a sick relative. Or moved to Des Moines for work. Or hell, that she entered a convent."

"Or I could always say that *she* broke up with *you*," Abby said drily.

"Except no one would ever believe that," Owen scoffed.

"Anyway, thanks for dealing with Mom," Abby said. "It's just...I'm so tired of people worrying about me, you know?"

Owen scratched his ear. "Uh, not really. I don't think people worry about me much, so I don't completely get it... but I can imagine it must be hard, especially for someone who's super-sensitive."

"Oh my God," Abby shrieked, looking for something to

throw at him. "I am *not* super sensitive. I'm average sensitive or even a little insensitive." She had to be to deal with the constant storm of shit that was shoveled her way, which made it all the more unfair that Owen always got a pass.

But those were the roles they'd been assigned by their family before they could even walk. Owen was Gramps' little tough guy, expected to shake it off, told he could handle anything. Gram gave him jars to open when his chubby hands barely fit around the lid, telling him she needed a big strong man to help.

Abby was the apple of both grandparents' eyes, but Gramps worried when Abby spent her free time reading instead of playing. He'd conspired with her mother to sign her up for activities meant to "bring out her moxie," activities Abby invariably hated.

"Fine." Owen held his hands up in mock surrender.

"I'm very okay. I mean it, Owen."

"I know."

"And you don't get to—wait, what?"

"I said I know you're okay. You're a badass, Abs. I've always known that."

Abby studied her brother, looking for the catch—but there didn't seem to be one. "Well, thank you. But you might be the only one."

"What do they know? It takes a Reilly to know one." He lowered the chair legs to the floor. "But I also know that in our family, 'okay' just means you're not actively dying. So tell me the honest truth: how are you really?"

"I'm…" Abby paused, realizing that she didn't know how to answer the question. Not when it was Owen asking. "You probably already figured out a lot of it. Like the fact that it took every ounce of energy to get out of bed this morning. That knowing people are talking about you feels like—like some big heavy humiliation blanket you have to drag around, and sometimes it makes you invisible and sometimes it's bright orange and everyone can see it from miles away."

"Yeah, I get that." Owen puffed his cheeks and blew out a breath. "I've actually felt that way myself, believe it or not, and no, I definitely do not want to talk about it."

Abby looked up sharply. She'd think Owen was lying to make her feel better if the admission didn't seem like it took so much effort. "It's all about me today," she said firmly, "but you'd better believe your humiliation blanket is fair game in future conversations."

"Sweet Jesus," Owen muttered, putting his face in his hands.

"The thing is," Abby said. She needed to admit something to someone, to say it out loud, and Owen might just be the only person who could hear it without immediately trying to fix it. Who'd understand that she wasn't asking for help and didn't want to be talked out of it. "Okay, here goes: I'm scared, Owen. I'm really, really scared."

Owen's eyebrows shot up and he looked ready to hit something. "Did some troll threaten you? Abby, you weren't supposed to go online, remember?"

"No, nothing like that," she said hastily. She knew better, at least for now when the sting was still so sharp. It was going to be a while before she dipped a toe in those waters again.

Owen didn't look reassured. "Is it something worse? Like worse than what happened with Reggie Reynolds?" He clutched his chest dramatically. "Come on, Abs, don't leave me hanging here!"

Rip off the Band-Aid. Abby took a breath. "It's gotten out that Steph and I were working together for Ships."

"Okay," Owen said after a beat, obviously confused. "And that means…"

"It means people knew that we were cheating, Owen! Not only that, but apparently lots of people figured it out a long time ago. And honestly, it's a relief in a way, not to have to pretend anymore, especially since I'm never going to show my face at Ships again. But now Isaac is asking about it and…"

Abby's words trailed off, the thought too horrifying to complete. Owen pressed his lips together and leaned back again, Gramps' chair groaning, and she prayed she wasn't about to hear an "I told you so."

But what Owen had to say was worse. "The truth always finds its way out."

No, no, no. Abby's mind whirled in an effort to stay in denial. "That's pretty rich, coming from the guy who spends hours every day pretending to be the Lucky Charms leprechaun."

"That's an impression, Abs. No one really believes it— it's just part of the happy fiction we all take part in at O'Reilly's. Completely unrelated."

"I don't see why," Abby retorted. The conversation was threatening to devolve into one of their ridiculous sibling arguments. "It's okay for you to be completely fake, but I'm not allowed to play the part of an anonymous spectator?"

Owen rolled his eyes. "'Completely fake' is what people

come to O'Reilly's for, and you know it. Gramps knew it instinctively, and I'm just carrying on the tradition. But nobody comes to Ships In the Night hoping to be ripped off."

"Ripped off?"

Owen refused to back down. "Sold a bill of goods. Pay to see someone read someone else's work. Plagiarism or whatever."

"If you think—" Abby hated the way her voice got high and wobbly.

"Hey, come on, Abs, I'm on your side here. I'm just saying it wrong. Look, you're right about me playing a character, and maybe part of it is, I don't know, a way of dealing with having to serve hundreds of loud strangers every day. The thing is, the real me—plain old Owen Reilly—can't give people what they're looking for. I'm just an average guy. There's nothing special about me."

"Don't," Abby blurted, surprising herself. But she couldn't bear it when Owen talked that way about himself. He was special, even if he couldn't see it—the one who had inherited Gramps' spark, his love of people, his ability to make them feel completely at home. Not to mention all the ways he'd improved the pub while still keeping it profitable.

Owen gave her a calm smile. "I know who I am, Abby. I like who I am. But I also know there's a gap between who I am and who I need to be to get where I want to go in life. And that's where good old Micky O'Reilly comes in."

"Micky? Oh, Owen." But she couldn't help returning his smile, because it was true—Owen was so much more comfortable with himself than she was. That's why he could come up goofy crap like that and get away with it.

Owen shrugged. "What can I say? Micky's got the charm. He loves attention. He makes the magic happen."

"I'm not sure I'm comfortable with you referring to yourself in the third person," Abby said, attempting to lighten the mood. "It's weird...even for you."

Owen laughed. "Face it, Abs, we come from a long line of average people with big dreams. Nothing wrong with that."

"I guess you're right. This time." The smile faded from her face as she added quietly, "I was only trying to protect myself."

"I know," Owen said a little sadly. "I hate that you read all those shitty comments people left and decided they were right. I hate that you thought the only way you could protect yourself was to run and hide from your dreams."

Tears gathered in Abby's eyes. Owen had never talked so openly about this to her before, and there was so much love in his eyes that it made her heart hurt.

"But you can't hide, Abby," he was saying. "You're too big; your dreams are too bright. The world was always going to see you, and nothing you can do will stop it."

He reached across the desk and squeezed her hand, and Abby squeezed back.

But there was something Owen was leaving out. "What about Isaac?" she whispered.

"What about him?"

Abby took a deep breath. "If I come clean and tell him everything, he's going to hate me for it. At the very least, he'll never want to see me again."

Owen gripped her hand so hard it hurt. "Then you have to tell him in a way he'll understand. Because if he knows why you did it—the *real* reasons, all the emotional crap and backstory and whatever—it'll remind him of all the reasons he likes you in the first place."

"How the hell am I supposed to do that, Owen?"

He released her hand and sat back in the chair with a smug grin. "I think you already know."

It took a moment for Owen's words to sink in, and then Abby recoiled in horror. "No way. No, no, no."

Owen tilted his head. "Your heart is free, lass," he said in his best Micky O'Reilly accent. "Ye must have the courage to follow it."

Abby blinked. "Did you just quote *Braveheart*?"

"It's very inspiring."

"It's also Scottish, you lugnut."

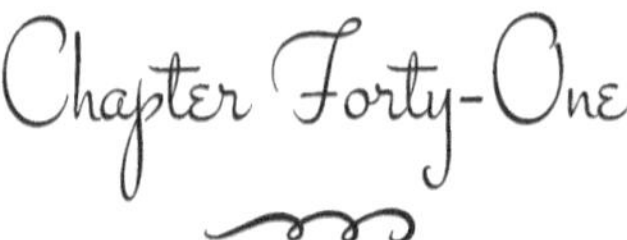

Chapter Forty-One

Abby replayed the line from *Braveheart* in her mind as she entered The City Bookmark the next night—though without Owen's cheesy accent. Her heart was free—the experience of being blown up in the worst possible way had burned through the shame and self-doubt that had bound it. Now she just had to find the courage to follow it.

The looks she got as she headed toward the back of the store didn't help. It was another sold-out crowd, and every folding chair was filled and people stood against the walls. The regulars seemed evenly divided between shock that Abby had dared to show up and excitement at the prospect of some good old-fashioned drama.

Jane was already seated onstage, wearing a pumpkin-colored angora cowl-neck sweater that overwhelmed her bony frame, an utterly unrepentant smile on her face. So much for never having to see her again for the rest of her life.

Ben was standing a few feet away, organizing the contestants. As Abby made her way up the aisle between the chairs, a hush fell over the crowd, but she kept her chin up and pretended she didn't hear the whispered comments.

"What the hell..."

"That takes guts..."

"I could never..."

Too late to turn around now. Doubts and second thoughts had nearly suffocated Abby on the ride over, and she almost begged the driver to turn the car around and take her home...but for once the voice in her head urging her to keep going was louder than the one shrieking in fear.

One foot in front of the other, she attempted to match Jane's serene expression though it almost hurt to stretch her face into a smile. By the time Abby reached Ben, he looked alarmed.

"Stop grimacing," he murmured. "You're scaring people. Are you sure you want to do this?"

Abby nodded, not trusting herself to speak.

"Okay," Ben said reluctantly, giving her shoulder an awkward pat. He was one of only three people who knew what Abby had planned, the other two being Owen and Steph.

She'd texted Ben early this morning, asking for a spot in the show and swearing him to secrecy. After spending most of the night at the kitchen table in her oldest nightgown, sipping chocolate milk and pouring her heart out onto the page, it hadn't been her most eloquent text, but it was good enough to get Ben to agree. Though he made sure to let her know that, as a last-minute entrant, she'd be the final contestant to perform.

Abby kept her head high as she took a seat at the end of the line of folding chairs. She ignored the other participants' curious looks, refusing to look any of them in the eye. She needed to ration her courage since she was staring down least an hour of marinating in her fears and doubts as one by one, they preceded her onstage.

Instead, she focused her attention on Ben as he stepped up to the mic to deliver his welcoming remarks. He was forced repeatedly to stop and wait for the cheering to subside. Abby could tell from the shy smile he couldn't quite suppress that he was enjoying the festival atmosphere.

The dress she'd chosen for tonight, a sleeveless A-line in a retro pink and yellow print, was cutting uncomfortably into her underarms, and her shoes pinched her heels. But that was nothing compared to the feeling of so many eyes on her. Even the newcomers seemed focused on what she would do.

The temptation to let her gaze wander to the corner—*her* corner—was strong, but Abby resisted. Still, it was impossible to miss Steph's parrot-green skirt in her peripheral vision, and she knew that Dex and Owen and Isaac were clustered around her.

Isaac. Abby didn't have to lay eyes on him to sense his presence. Maybe she was imagining it, but the air took on a different energy when he was near, as if all of her senses yearned to be close to him.

Abby was struck by a powerful urge to bolt, to run out the door and keep running until there was no chance of any of them ever finding her. What had she been thinking? She couldn't do this—she'd only make a spectacle of herself, one she would never live down. She'd become a legend, a cautionary tale, Icarus in a dress whose waxen wings melted in the sun.

That was the moment when the lights dimmed and the camera mounted on the tripod in front of the stage blinked red to signal it was streaming to the internet.

Abby's chance to chicken out had come and gone. There was no way out anymore...only through.

Chapter Forty-Two

Abby had been expecting the first contestant's scene, which featured Cyrano and Christian's discovery that they're much more than friends. Someone inevitably presented a piece about Roxane entertaining an entire battalion of Spanish soldiers. And of course there were way too many dildo jokes about Cyrano's nose.

But among the record number of submissions, there were gems such as an imaginative refashioning of Ragueneau's bakery into a sex toy factory, the skilled apprentice "cooks" obligingly testing each other's designs. An ambitious orgy scene at the Porte de Nesle among dozens of street thugs, police, actors and musicians.

Even so, as the standing-room-only crowd cheered and applauded and hooted, Abby could barely focus on the performances taking place a few yards away. Her hands were clammy and damp; her heart beat a staccato in her chest. Pinpoints of pain behind her eyes signaled the onset of a tension headache.

The passage of time had softened Abby's memory of the raw, numbing terror that was stage fright, and tonight was so much worse. As the contestants' chairs emptied one by one and her turn approached, she actually thought she might pass out.

But no such luck. Way too quickly, everyone had gone but her, and Ben was at the podium giving her an encouraging smile.

"All the way from County Cork, please welcome the savage Abigail O'Reilly, reading a piece titled *The Fool*! I'm lurred, so I am!"

Abby could hear Dex and Owen groaning at Ben's attempt at Irish slang. It was sweet that he'd remembered the County Cork thing—it was what Gramps used to call the broom closet where he stacked the cheap jug wine he sold as the house label—but it only seemed to encourage the already raucous crowd.

Or maybe they were just ready for the show to be over. Abby certainly was.

She knew without looking that the loudest cheering as she adjusted the mic was Owen. The extra lighting Ben had installed for tonight's performance had the effect of limiting her sight to the first two rows, which would have been welcome if it didn't feel like her eyeballs were burning as she looked down at the phone in her hand.

One deep breath.

You can do this.

"Cyrano was a fool."

Abby's opening line seemed to echo through the suddenly quiet room, the high-quality speakers amplifying the tremor in her voice. Her heart hammered so hard she was surprised the audio didn't pick it up, and beads of sweat popped out along her forehead.

Abby lowered her hand holding the phone. She didn't need to read the words; they were burned into her memory from the hours she'd spent fine-tuning them last night, agonizing over each line until it was as perfect as she could make it.

"Many people believe it was Christian de Neuvillette who was the fool," Abby recited, some of her fear receding as she found her rhythm. "But of all the cadets in their brigade, Christian had the deepest knowledge of his talents and short-comings. He knew he was brave and surefooted and strong, a man of principles as well as passion...but a poet he was not, and he never proclaimed to be.

"It should surprise no one that Christian fell for a glit-tering jewel of a woman. Many do, and though he was first ensnared by Roxane's beauty, it was her brilliant mind, her fine intellect, that set her apart from the many women who admired him."

Abby paused, and the audience seemed to be holding its breath. The weight of their judgement was crushing, but she had no choice but to continue.

"Some would argue that Roxanne was the real fool. That she should have figured out Cyrano's ruse much sooner, given the time the two spent together, how well they got along. But those people have it wrong too. They forget that Roxane only saw what Cyrano wanted her to, a curated version not only of Christian but of himself. That he hid the deepest part of him away, no matter how obvious it might be to those sitting in the front row watching him whisper his enchanting words beneath a window."

This time it was Abby who had to pause to take a breath, because with what she was about to say, she could never take it back.

"No, the truth was there was only one fool, and it was Cyrano. Because in trying to protect himself from a few moments of heartbreak, he ended up causing a lifetime of pain."

Abby's eyes had adjusted to the lights and she could see a few more faces in the audience looking back at her, their expressions giving little away. She couldn't tell if they were confused, or entranced, or bored. If she looked beyond them, Abby knew she would see her friends—encouraging, supporting—but she might also see Isaac and that could not happen. Not now, not until she got through the hard part.

"Cyrano believed himself to be clever and witty, and maybe he was; but more than any of that, he was a coward. He was afraid that people would mock him. And his fears were justified, because mocking is what some people do. They make cruel jokes at others' expense to deflect their own self-doubt, and the most skillful among them learn to identify a person's insecurities and focus their attacks. But not everyone joins them in their laughter. Though I can tell you from experience that it's much harder to hear that silence through the noise.

"The thing that made Cyrano a fool was despite all his intelligence he never realized until it was too late was that the mockery he feared was never his enemy. Laughter fades. Gossip dies. And there were so many people who never would have laughed at all. Which means that Cyrano's true enemy, the thing that robbed him of his happiness, was himself."

Now Abby did look up, her gaze landing on Steph's green skirt. Behind her, no one moved. "Tonight, I came here to tell you what I recently learned: that even if your very worst fear comes true, you can survive. You can remain standing."

There was a smattering of applause, quickly dying away as Abby gestured for quiet. Her eyes adjusted to the dimness of the rear of the crowd, and she found Isaac.

He stood behind Ben and Owen, watching her steadily, his soft brown eyes giving nothing away. Their gazes locked, and for a long moment Abby was frozen on a terrifying precipice, buffeted by fear and hope, desperate to look away.

But everything that she'd already said, the words she'd written with such care, would be meaningless if Abby didn't find the courage to face him as she said the rest.

"And...I know this because I am Cyrano."

The silence in the room seemed to take on a life of its own, pressing in on her like a dense fog. Her mouth was dry as she forced herself to continue.

"I wrote words for someone else to say. I willingly let them take credit just so I could feel safe. I thought I had to hide, to make sure no one knew that those words expressed the feelings that were in my heart, because I was afraid people would laugh at me if they knew. That I would be humiliated for revealing who I truly was.

"I've been a fool. Not just because I was foolish enough to believe that people who look like me don't deserve to be with glittering jewels, but for buying into the lie that we are not those jewels ourselves.

"I've been a coward. I've received the gifts of other people's honesty and compassion while never giving the same in return. In never allowing people see my vulnerabilities, I made sure they never saw me. In trying to protect myself, I only hurt myself more. Even worse, I hurt some of you too. And I'm deeply sorry."

Abby glanced at the other contestants who stood in a line along the wall, offering them a silent apology of their own. "I know there are people who think a celebration of fan fiction is nothing more than a joke. Some of you probably think the same thing of me. And maybe you're right. After all, we do tell jokes up here, some witty, some raunchy, and some—the best of them—both.

"But not all jokes are cruel, and not all laughter is mocking. We celebrate these stories because they've endured; we honor them because they spoke to us, even if we didn't love them. There are wonderful lessons to be learned by revisiting a work that challenged you. There can be healing in giving a stumbling character a second chance, or rewriting an ending that never rung completely true. There's a fierce kind of bravery in declaring that things can be different.

"And that is how I came back to Cyrano for another read and realized that while he was a fool and a coward, there was no need for him to wait until the end of his life to come to his senses. Some things are too important to be held back by fear.

"So tonight, I'm going to stop being a hypocrite and do what Cyrano couldn't. I'm going to stand on this stage, look my Roxane in the eye, and say, 'This is who I am, and this is how I feel,' accepting that everything that comes after is outside of my control. And though every word of that scares the living hell out of me, it's the truth, and in the end, that's the best thing a story could hope to be."

Abby's legs trembled as she closed her eyes for a moment. She waited until she felt a little steadier to open them, almost surprised to find that she was still standing.

No one moved as Abby walked back to her seat. She gripped her hands together tightly in her lap, the audience disappearing once again in the glare, and forced herself to keep her chin up high. Just a little longer, she thought—because for all her big words, there was only so much courage a person could fake in one day.

But as the silence stretched, a strange thing happened. Abby's breath came a little more easily; her muscles relaxed. She felt lighter, the burden of her fear dissolving now that it was done. If she'd made a mistake, so be it—because being on the other side of "I can't" more than made up for it.

And then Ben was back at the podium and the audience started to come back to life. "I think we can all agree," he said, glancing Abby's way, "that this has been one of the most surprising Ships in the Night shows in a long time."

There was a sprinkling of nervous laughter that was soon overcome by applause—not the raucous, contagious sort that had dominated the night, but something deeper and more resounding.

Abby had to smile. This might have been the last show that she would ever attend, but at least she'd made it memorable.

Chapter Forty-Three

Minerva turned off the bright lights and took her position at the register to start checking out customers. The cameras stopped recording. Around the room, people started doing the things they did after every performance—taking a final swipe at the picked-over crackers and cheese and the dregs of the boxed wine, chatting with the contestants, browsing the shelves, making plans for a bite or a drink.

Abby stayed seated on the periphery of all this activity, not quite ready to get up yet. A couple of the other contestants came over together to tell her that they thought she'd been very brave, and she nodded and smiled as if she didn't feel flattened by an emotional tsunami. Behind them, she could see a few other people staring at her with varying degrees of hostility.

Do I care?—she wondered, focusing on the strange, floating numbness that kept her from spreading into a puddle. It appeared that she didn't, not much anyway, at least for now. After all, Abby had known that not everyone would be pleased with her story. No—her *confession*. That her apology would fall on as many unsympathetic ears as forgiving ones.

Forgiveness wasn't something you could demand. And Abby had taken something real from the other competitors, though what that might be would have been different for different people. Some would resent her for hiding behind a presenter whose beauty gave her work an unfair advantage, others for lying, still others for getting off the hook for the discomfort they themselves had faced. And all of them would be right.

Complicating matters was the fact that there were some people whose forgiveness Abby didn't even want. Nothing about this was easy. A decision that seemed simple at first had grown tentacles that reached into other lives, other dramas, and now it seemed helplessly tangled.

"Are you okay?"

Ben had materialized in front of her, crouching so he could look Abby in the eye.

"Uh-huh."

"I'm proud of you, you know."

Proud. Of her. Those words got the floaty Abby's attention and she felt herself returning to her body with a solid landing. She studied Ben's face, his earnestly wrinkled brow, the spot on his chin where he'd missed shaving, and realized that it was just what she'd needed to hear.

"You are?" she said, with the sort of damp wobble in her voice that could turn into tears if she wasn't careful. "Really?"

He laughed. "Really and truly, but I'm not going to keep saying it until you believe me. For one thing, my knees are going numb."

"I believe you," Abby told him as he hauled himself up to his feet, his knees creaking alarmingly. "And it means more to me than you'll ever know."

His smile settled into a grimace as he took her hand and squeezed it. "Unfortunately, it's not over yet. If I could I'd transport us straight to my couch so we could watch TV all night, but your public awaits you."

Abby sighed and allowed herself to be pulled up. "I know. But thanks for coming to get me so I wouldn't have to walk into this alone."

"Anytime."

Abby felt like she'd fallen into another era as she took the arm Ben offered her and they walked stiffly through the mostly empty chairs toward their friends. Isaac stood slightly to the side, hands jammed in the pockets of an old, faded pair of jeans, watching her. Abby quickly looked away and immediately regretted it, but before she could do anything about it Steph came flying at her and nearly toppled her with a hard, long hug.

"Oh my God," she yelped when she finally pulled away. "I can't believe you did that. It was amazing. *You're* amazing."

Abby had to resist the urge to brush off the praise, to shrink from the attention, to change the subject to anything else. The spotlight had been her enemy for so long that inhabiting it now that she'd invited it was going to take practice, especially since everyone she loved was watching her, surrounding her. Including Isaac, who she was very carefully not looking at now.

"Yeah," Owen said, giving her an awkward slug on the shoulder. "I'm proud of you, sis."

"Me too," Dex said, grabbing Abby for a hug so brief she could've imagined it. The last time Dex had hugged her... yeah, Gramps' funeral. It occurred to Abby that was the last time she'd seen so many emotions on display from any of them, and now the tears really did fill her eyes.

"I'm confused, though," Dex continued, scratching his belly, which had the effect of an emotional emergency landing. Abby covertly wiped her eyes; there'd be time to cry when she was alone. "So that was fan fiction, right? Doesn't that mean it wasn't true?"

"Of course it doesn't," Owen said. Then he looked at Abby uncertainly. "Right?"

"Tell you what," Ben said, exchanging a look with Steph, confirming Abby's suspicion that they were colluding to take care of her. "Buy me a drink, guys, and I'll explain the entire genre to you."

"Buy *me* a drink and I'll change the subject to something you actually care about," Steph said drily. "Seriously, guys, head on back to O'Reilly's and we'll join you in a few. I'm just going to help Ben close up. If that's okay with you, Abs," she added, giving Abby a here-if-you-need me wink.

Which left Isaac and Abby.

"Hey, Ben," Isaac murmured without taking his eyes off Abby. "Mind if we borrow your office?"

"Um...sure? Yeah, no problem," he amended after Steph nudged him. "I can do the receipts tomorrow."

Isaac didn't look like he cared about Ben's receipts or about anything else as he gestured toward the door marked EMPLOYEES ONLY. Abby was painfully aware of the phones that appeared out of nowhere. Strangers didn't even bother to hide the fact that they were taking pictures of the two of them.

She reminded herself that she had deleted all her social media. Whatever people had to say about her, whatever nasty hashtags and offensive memes they came up with, they might as well be barking into a black hole for all it would matter to Abby.

Just keep telling yourself that. The old, critical voice had somehow managed to crawl out of the deep recesses to which Abby had banished it. But as the cameras flashed around her, she envisioned crushing the voice to a bloody pulp, then lighting it on fire.

It would be back, she knew. Inner critics were tough, wily bastards, always looking for an in. But every time Abby fought back, she found hers a little easier to ignore.

Ben and Steph, arms around each other's shoulders, stepped in front of Abby's would-be paparazzi. "Take all the time you need," Ben said cheerfully. "You can leave out the back. The door locks automatically."

Before Abby could thank him, Isaac whisked her into the office and shut the door as if he were slamming the lid back on Pandora's box. He stood between her and the door, grim-faced, fists clenched as if ready for a fight.

But when nobody tried to come after them, the wind went out of Isaac's sails. His shoulders untensed and his hands hung limp at his sides as he turned to face Abby with an utterly blank expression.

Neither of them said anything. It was their first awkward silence, Abby realized sadly. Then she saw that his expression wasn't completely empty after all. Deep in his soft brown eyes was the hurt he'd tried to hide from her.

"Isaac, I'm so sorry," she began, but he held up a hand to stop her.

"Just tell me if it was you the whole time. All those stories that Steph read. You wrote all of them?"

She winced at the hardness at his voice. "Yes," she said reluctantly. "I wrote the words and she performed them. We'd been doing it for a little over a year before you showed up."

"And that makes it okay?"

"No. No, of course not. I just—" Abby forced herself to stop and settle the panic threatening her. She owed Isaac the truth. "I just wanted you to know that it wasn't about you. At least not at first."

Isaac nodded. He took his time looking around the room, taking in Ben's old adding machine and stacks of advance copies of new books and scrawled sticky notes stuck to the wall, even though Abby doubted he was really seeing any of it.

"I'm not saying I approve," he finally said, "but I can understand how it happened. Now that I know you, I'm not really even all that surprised, given how you feel about public exposure. But at some point you stopped just being Steph's ghostwriter and became...well, Cyrano. To Steph's Christian."

Leave it to Isaac to just put it all out there. It was one of the things Abby loved about him, his refusal to avoid difficult truths. It just wasn't making things any easier tonight.

But tonight wasn't about easy. It was about setting things right.

Abby shut her eyes. "Yes."

"And you were fine with that?"

Oh, God. He was going to make her say it…all of it. The urge to flee was like an electric current running through Abby, and she had to swallow past a lump in her throat to speak. "I thought….I thought it was the best option."

Isaac looked baffled. "Explain that to me."

"Steph was…" How to say it, without betraying either of them? "She was into you. Head over heels for you, really, before we ever met you."

"I'm not interested in what Steph was thinking. I asked you about you."

Why couldn't he see what was so painfully clear to her and everyone outside that door? "I knew…well, it was obvious that you showed up every week to watch her. And I mean, who wouldn't? She's gorgeous, and smart, and—"

"You don't get it, Abby. I came every week to hear Steph's stories." Isaac seemed incredulous. "Stories that I now know weren't even hers. That they were written by the *other* person I came to see every damn week. The one I stood next to, the one I laughed with, the one I defended on TV."

Abby flinched at the reminder. She'd been so focused on her humiliation that she hadn't spent nearly enough time considering what it had cost Isaac. He might appear perfectly composed in front of an audience, but she knew that was as much of a front as the one she put up in public.

"I'm so sorry, Isaac. I—I never imagined this would blow up the way it has."

"That's what you're sorry for?" Isaac shook his head. The corners of his mouth dipped down in disappointment. "Not for deceiving people, including your closest friends—including *me*—but just because people found out?"

The weight of shame pressed down on Abby. "I'm sorry for all of it," she mumbled. "For the hurt I've caused, the embarrassment, for ruining our friendship, for being such a coward."

"But that isn't all of it, Abby. You're smarter than that. If you'd just—" He bit off his words in frustration before trying again. "What about the fact that you sold me short? That you insisted on believing that I could only be attracted to a flirt in a short skirt? I thought you were different, Abby. I thought that for once, someone saw me for who I really was. But just like my entire family, you decided who I was without ever bothering to ask me."

It was the longest and most impassioned speech Abby had ever heard Isaac make, and the worst part was that he was right. She'd been spinning assumptions about him from the moment she laid eyes on him. And she could have asked him —she'd had so many opportunities, and wasted them all.

"Isaac, I—"

"Why did you think nothing happened between me and Steph? It was her words that attracted me to her, but when we were together, she was different. There was no spark. And besides, it never would have worked, not when I was falling for you."

I was falling for you. The words that Abby had dreamed of hearing...but not like this. Not when she'd destroyed the fragile thing that was growing between them.

"Isaac, I'm—"

"You're sorry. I know. You know what, Abby? You should try being something other than sorry for a while. I'm going back to Miami for a few days. If you grow a spine while I'm gone, maybe you can tell me who you really are and what you really want when I get back."

Abby couldn't move. She watched Isaac walk out the back door into the night, feeling as though a part of herself was being torn free, unable to do anything to stop it.

But that wasn't entirely true. Isaac had given her one last chance...if only she could find the courage to take it.

Chapter Forty-Four

On the fourth day of Isaac's absence, Abby discovered that the project she'd thrown herself headlong into was taking her places she'd never expected to go.

Not literally, of course. A little after one o'clock that afternoon, she was sitting on the same bench where she and Isaac had shared a sack of empanadas only a couple of months ago, eating an ice cream cone. She was savoring every bite while thinking about the maddening unspecificity of the word "few"—as in Isaac being gone "for a few days."

It could be anything from three to...a week? A month? Maybe he was enjoying his nieces and nephews so much that his visit would stretch indefinitely. All Abby really knew was that he wasn't taking up as much room in her head as she'd expected after their painful parting. And if that was due to the distance, maybe it was a good thing, in a way.

After Isaac left the office Friday night, Abby had collapsed in Ben's chair in a stunned fugue. She wasn't sure how long she sat there until she finally gathered herself sufficiently to leave. The shop was locked up and there was no one out front, so she was able to make her escape unseen.

Once home, she turned off her phone and shut herself in her room and slept almost eleven hours...and when she woke, refreshed and reinvigorated, Abby made her decision.

She was going to grow a spine.

Unfortunately, the process wasn't exactly something she could look up online or study in a book. There were dozens of titles in Ben's store devoted to changing oneself—becoming fitter or more outgoing or richer, finding a partner or a passion or a retirement home...but no one seemed to have written a book about how to let go of a decades-old habit of apologizing for one's existence. Nothing to teach a person who'd spent her life trying to make herself smaller to step out of the shadows and take up space.

But when the man you were in love with packed up and left for an indefinite amount of time, it seemed pretty obvious that the first thing you needed to do was figure out how to be okay with waiting.

And so Abby had taken a hard look at herself, at the hours and days and weeks and years she'd spent waiting—for texts and calls that didn't come, for designers to figure out how to make clothes for real human bodies, for her boss to start promoting people based on the work they did rather than who talked the loudest in meetings.

She didn't like what she saw. It suddenly struck her as ridiculous to keep waiting for things that were completely out of her control. So Abby decided to focus only on things within her power to change.

It was hard at first. It turned out that when you'd been settling for less for so long, even knowing what you wanted seemed like an impossible puzzle. After wandering around the house for a while, trying to figure out what she could buy or get rid of that would lead to increased happiness, Abby gave up and decided to take Muhammad to the mountain, so to speak.

Abby put on her favorite outfit, because what else would you wear on a day when you were going to change your life? —and then, in her comfy denim skort and vintage Care Bears T-Shirt and lavender glitter Converse sneakers, she took the bus to an outdoor market where she strolled the stalls, admiring the hand-dyed scarves and fragrant soaps and sampling kettle corn and hot sauce and helping a young mother chase after her twins and getting into a conversation with a man selling carved wooden flutes about how he'd hitchhiked to San Francisco as a seventeen-year-old in the late sixties and never left. Hours later, all she'd bought was a secondhand copy of *The Horse And His Boy* and a perfect peach, and the secret of life seemed as distant as ever…but on the bus ride home, the colors seemed a little brighter, the other passengers less annoying, and she spent a perfectly pleasant evening reading her book and eating her peach with a wedge of Point Reyes bleu and a cold Belgian beer.

Since then, Abby had begun each day by asking herself what she would do if she was allowed to enjoy herself. And slowly, the but-I-couldn't-possibly side of the scale started to give way to the discovery that, no matter how unnatural it felt to do what she wanted with no thought to others' opinions, the world continued to turn and nothing terrible happened. Sure, people still gave her dirty looks for everything from buying a cupcake to trying on four different shades of nail polish at the Bloomingdales counter to seeing a matinee by herself.

Whenever Abby felt the shame bucket beginning to tip above her head, she forced herself to step out of the way. *Take up space*, she reminded herself, saying it out loud when there was no one around. A few days wasn't enough to remake herself into someone new, but it was enough for a tiny shift in the way Abby saw the world, and she was content simply to see where it led next.

A seagull swooped down to land on the railing in front of Abby, eyeing the last of her cone and squawking.

"No way, buddy," Abby said, flapping her hand. "This is all mine."

The gull grudgingly hopped away, leaving Abby to enjoy the view. Tourists and day-trippers boarded the ferry moored in the choppy waters of the bay, while not far away, cars glittered in the sun as they crossed the Bay Bridge and midday crowds flocked to the food stalls inside the Ferry Building.

And because Abby continued to enjoy mostly uninterrupted focus at work, she'd completed everything on her calendar and could sit there as long as she wanted. Hell, she could take off the rest of the week and still not fall behind, but Abby wasn't going to do that. Because as the mental picture captioned "The Life I Want" slowly started to come into focus, work was definitely a part of it. She loved her job, especially now that she wasn't trying to please everyone else who worked there.

The rest of the picture was still pretty damn fuzzy,

however. It was becoming easier to leave the house every day, to go out into the world alone. But she was still mulling over all the things Isaac had said, with no conclusions in sight.

Which, Abby decided, meant it was probably time for the other thing she'd promised herself she would do. She popped the pointy last bit of the cone in her mouth, wiped her hands on a napkin, and dialed her mother.

She picked up on the second ring, sounding alarmed. "Abby, darling. I've been so worried about you."

"I know, Mom. I should have called you earlier, but things have been a little weird around here."

"A little *weird*? Your face is all over my TV!"

Abby held the phone away from her ear as her mother's voice rose.

"Come on, Mom, you're exaggerating." The story had lost steam fast, just as Steph had predicted. There hadn't been a blip for days. "How much television are you watching? Maybe it's time to take a break."

"Well, they're definitely still talking about Reggie Reynolds."

Abby laughed. "Let them. The guy's a jerk."

"But honey, every time his name comes up, you know people are talking about you."

"There's nothing I can do about that, Mom. And I've decided not to waste any more of my time and energy worrying about it." It was only when the words came out of her mouth that Abby realized it was mostly true. Sure, she still had her bad moments, and she'd probably never be able to look at Reggie without cringing, but the horror of the episode had receded in her mind enough to give her some perspective.

"Oh, my sweet girl," her mother sighed. "Good for you, putting on a brave face."

Abby rolled her eyes. She loved her mother deeply, but as with Isaac and his family, a couple thousand miles improved their relationship immensely.

"But how are you doing, Mom? How's Jerry?"

"Fine and fine. His back's been giving him some trouble lately, but he wanted me to send his love. He's devastated that this happened, you know."

Abby doubted that very much. "Tell him I appreciate that."

In the dozen years that her mom had been with Jerry, he couldn't have said more than a hundred words to Abby. She didn't take it personally; they had almost nothing in common. But while she couldn't share his love of easy chairs, deep sea fishing, and football games, Abby was grateful for the fact that Jerry made her mother happy.

"So what are you doing right now?" her mother asked.

"I'm sitting outside the Ferry Building enjoying the sun, and I just had the most delicious vanilla ice cream cone."

There was a long pause. "Do you think that's a good idea, Abby?"

"Obviously," Abby said, barely ruffled, "or I wouldn't have bought it."

"But honey, people might see you."

"Yeah, mom. It's the city. I can pretty much guarantee that a lot of people have seen me." Abby resisted the urge to laugh. Why had she ever let her mother's sniping bother her so much? "No one cares."

That wasn't completely true; there had been a few pointed stares since Abby sat down, some whispering. Though really, she might have been imagining it. Even if anyone recognized her from the photo on Reggie's show, they'd probably already forgotten the reason for all the drama.

"But what if someone takes a picture of you eating dessert outside by yourself?" her mother said, giving up on Abby connecting the dots on her own. "They could send it to one of those gossip shows, and then what?"

"Then they'd be an asshole, Mom. And I refuse to let assholes run my life anymore."

There was a sharp intake of breath on the other end. "Are you sure you're okay, Abby? You don't sound like yourself."

Or maybe I finally sound exactly like myself, Abby thought. "What can I say? A lot has happened in the last week."

"I just want to make sure...honey, you have to know that eating your feelings isn't going to help."

"It's an ice cream cone, Mom, not a moral failure."

"I just worry about you, sweetheart," her mom said, mournful in defeat.

Abby understood. She'd inherited her mother's fear of strangers' judgement, after all. She'd been brought up to believe that others' opinions were more important than your own. Abby had wondered if it was some sort of reaction to Gramps' boundless confidence, or maybe the opposite, that from his running con her mother had picked up the idea that the price of success was changing yourself to fit other people's expectations.

Peggy Reilly had never wanted to run a pub. Abby didn't either. But both of them wanted to fit in, and so they'd sanded down everything that was special or exceptional about themselves until there was almost nothing left.

Somehow, her mother had made it work. She truly seemed to love her cookie-cutter townhome in their senior community, her discount store décor, bridge club, and cruises with Jerry.

But that wasn't for Abby. She missed the parts of herself she'd kept hidden for so long. She didn't want to be quiet any more. And all her attempts to hide herself away had only caused more trouble than if she'd just put herself out there from the start.

"I know you worry, Mom," Abby said as kindly as she could. "But I really am okay."

And for the first time in her life, she meant it.

Chapter Forty-Five

By the time Friday rolled around, Abby felt ready to stop by The City Bookmark to pick up next week's selection. Since she was taking a break from social media, and Steph had been working frantically to prepare for an upcoming event at the Philippine Consulate, she didn't know what book Ben had finally settled on, only that he'd been worried about choosing a title that could hold its own after the "Cyrano Spectacle," as he'd taken to calling it.

But when Ben was finished ringing up his customer, he pulled a copy of *The Code of the Woosters* from under the register and handed it to Abby.

"Oh, I love P. G. Wodehouse!" she exclaimed.

"On the house," Ben told her with a grin. "Read the inscription."

Abby flipped the book open to find Ben's familiar, spidery handwriting taking up most of the title page.

.   .   .

To Abby —

As Wodehouse himself once said, "There is no surer foundation for a beautiful friendship than a mutual taste in literature." But I'll always be grateful that we share a mutual taste in friends. Don't ever change!

Love, Ben

Ben seemed slightly embarrassed. "Now that I think about it, that last bit reads like an eighth-grade yearbook."

But Abby thought it was perfect.

She started the book on the bus ride home, and decided that *The Code of the Woosters* was the perfect chaser for Cyrano. After a quick break to pull on a pair of comfy pajamas and brew herself a cup of herbal tea, she settled into the cushions of the couch and dove back into the world of 1920s England as twilight descended outside the living room window. With the wonderfully named Gussie Fink-Nottle and Stiffy Byng joining Bertie and Jeeves in a madcap plot involving a stolen cow-creamer and the blackmail of a designer of ladies' underclothing, nearly every page found her nearly laughing out loud.

The buzz of a text interrupted the parade of scenarios that was running through Abby's mind. She checked her phone screen absently...then made an involuntary choking sound when she saw that it was from Isaac.

> Got back today. I'm headed over to the Little Skillet if you want to get a cup of coffee and talk.

"You okay?" Steph asked from the dining room, where she was working on a vast seating chart that took up most of the table. "Did another creep get your number somehow?"

"No, nothing like that." Abby took a deep breath. "It's Isaac. He's back in town and he wants to meet up."

"When?"

"Well...now, actually."

Steph jumped out of her chair and spun in a pirouette, hooting like she'd won the lottery. "I told you he'd come around. Nobody can stay mad at you, Abs."

"He might still be mad," Abby said worriedly. "All he said was that he wants to talk."

"Gimme that." Steph grabbed the phone out of Abby's hand and studied the text. "That is not all he said. He asked you to meet at the Little Skillet!"

"Yeah, a diner around the corner from Oracle Park. Super romantic," Abby said sarcastically.

"A diner that also happens to have an intimate bar," Steph said. "One that's never busy except on game nights, so you can linger as long as you want. This way he can pretend he's inviting you for coffee but hoping it might lead into drinks. Come on, you need to get moving."

"I'm pretty sure you're overthinking things," Abby

grumbled, but she allowed Steph to pull her up from the sofa.

"Look at it this way: if things go badly, at least Little Skillet makes fantastic chicken and waffles. Now let's find you something to wear."

Twenty minutes and a terse text later—

sounds good, see you there

—Abby was on her way to the restaurant in a ride share driven by a blessedly silent driver. Steph had promised that the red peep-toes she'd loaned Abby added a confident, sexy touch to the simple white Peter-Pan-collar blouse and pinstriped wide-legged trousers she'd chosen to signal contrition. Abby had to admit that the matching red lipstick and perfectly winged eyeliner Steph had applied in record time looked pretty damn great...unless she was headed for a breakup, in which case she'd look like she was trying way too hard.

Or not a breakup, exactly, since they weren't dating. They weren't anything, really, other than friends who'd apparently missed each other's cues from the start.

But that didn't quite capture it either, because one of those friends had been honest about the way he felt, even when it threatened his career, while the other one was a big, lying coward.

By the time Abby got out of the Prius, she was feeling even more apprehensive. She spotted Isaac sitting at a table by the window and when she walked into the restaurant, he started waving despite the fact that the place was nearly empty.

He wasn't smiling, exactly, but he didn't look angry either. Abby tried to strike the same balance and ended up with a frozen grimace as she walked to the table, her heels making way too much noise on the scarred wooden floors. She reminded herself that she had been preparing for this moment ever since Isaac left, and that no matter what happened next, she would be okay.

On the table in front of him were two steaming cups and a paper sack. "I got you a coffee to go," Isaac said in lieu of a greeting. "I hope that's okay. I've been on a plane most of the day, and I thought it might be nice to walk along the Embarcadero."

"Sure." So much for Steph's fantasy scenario. But Abby didn't mind, since it would be easier to control her nerves if they were moving than if she had to face Isaac across the table.

"So...you just got back today," she said once they were outside, the silence awkward between them.

"Yeah, a couple hours ago. Just enough time to drop off my bags, grab a shower, and come down here."

"Ah." Abby's heart fell. Whatever Isaac had to say, he was burning to get it off his chest.

There were plenty of people out enjoying the South Beach neighborhood that surrounded the Giants' home stadium on three sides, and the Embarcadero separating it from the bay was busy with cyclists and joggers and strollers and couples holding hands, taking advantage of the mild evening. In the modern apartment buildings that had sprung up between the old brick buildings heralding from the neighborhood's days as a warehouse district, lights glowed from windows and barbecues were started up on balconies, and people sat outdoors at café tables in front of restaurants and bars.

"None of this was here when I was a kid," Abby said impulsively. "Well, I guess they were starting to build the office buildings during the dot-com boom, but my mom always said it was dangerous and run-down, so we never came here. But I can remember when I was in kindergarten, Gramps brought me and Owen to see the stadium construction site a couple times."

"That's something we have in common," Isaac said. "I got to watch Marlins Park going up from my parents' roof. Or a corner of it, anyway—the rest of it was blocked by the church at the end of our block. It's less than half a mile from the house I grew up in."

They lapsed into silence again, this one more comfortable. Abby hadn't realized how much she'd missed being together like this. If only things could stay like this forever, strolling along and chatting about nothing in particular. If only she could have met Isaac now, with her newfound courage and confidence.

But she couldn't change the past....and Abby refused to hide from the truth anymore.

"How was your time with your family?" she asked, nudging the conversation back in the direction it needed to go.

"Good," Isaac said, "and bad. Just like always. My cousins are doing well, my siblings are as exasperating and also wonderful as ever, and my mother is certain that I threw my career away by telling Reggie to go to hell."

"That sounds familiar," Abby said, "with a few minor substitutions."

Isaac shrugged. "Life, right?"

Life, indeed. Abby took a steadying breath before she asked the question she'd rehearsed.

"Did you get what you needed out of the trip?"

Isaac glanced at her, his expression hard to read. "Yeah, I think I did.'

"Good. That's good." She was nodding too vigorously. "If I'm being honest, I was surprised to get your text. After eight days, I'd pretty much given up on hearing from you again."

Another glance, a longer pause. "I needed some time."

"I get it. As it turned out, I needed some too."

"Did you come to any big revelations?"

"I guess that depends on what qualifies for 'big.' It was all in front of me all along, if I'd had the guts to look. And I probably should have figured it out a lot sooner than I did." Abby realized that all this confessing wasn't as bad as she'd feared. Maybe that was because the truth never was.

Okay, here goes. "Isaac...I'm hoping that we can find a way to stay friends."

She'd taken a few more steps before she realized that Isaac wasn't with her. Turning, she found him stopped in the middle of the path, frowning.

"Yeah, that's not going to happen."

Oh.

Abby thought she was prepared for this moment. She

knew it was the most likely outcome after their last conversation, and had spent much of the last week trying to convince herself she was okay with it. Truly okay. And yet the reality still hit her like a punch to the gut.

She managed a weak smile. "I understand."

Isaac took a step toward her. "No, I don't think you do. Let's go sit over there for a minute, okay?"

They were walking past the playground in the South Beach Community Park, empty now that night had fallen. Isaac sat on the low concrete wall and patted the spot next to him. Abby reluctantly sat, leaving extra space between them, not at all sure she wanted to hear what was coming.

But since she'd been the one to screw things up, she knew she owed him the chance to tell her how he felt.

"I had some time to myself this past week," Isaac said. "I thought about the reasons I moved here in the first place. The pressures that came with success, the expectations I couldn't live up to, all those unwritten rules I'd never been able to follow.

"Being home made me realize how much I've changed since I came here. I don't like admitting it, but a year ago, I probably wouldn't have confronted Reggie the way I did. I would have been too worried about what my publicist would think, my editor, my readers...my family. A year ago, I would have taken my cues from other people instead of doing what I knew in my heart was right."

He watched her, and Abby had the terrible feeling of not knowing what he was expecting of her. "I'm not sure I know what that means," she said uncertainly. "I'm sorry."

Isaac reached for her hand, folding it in his big, warm

one. "I'm saying I get it. I know I was lucky to have the freedom and the means to pull up stakes and move across the country, away from my family's expectations. Not everyone has that chance. And I also see now that some things are too big to ever really get away from, no matter how hard you try. What I'm trying to say is that I hate the fact that you thought you couldn't trust me with your feelings, Abby...but maybe now I understand why."

He was telling the truth. Abby could see it in his eyes. "Then why can't we stay friends?" she blurted.

"Because that's not how I feel about you, Abby."

He didn't want to be her friend.

But maybe...

Abby's heart was pounding so hard she could barely get the words out. "H-How do you feel?"

"Like this."

Isaac reached for her, pulling her into his arms. He was so close, so real. He was everything she'd ever wanted.

Taking it exquisitely slow, Isaac tipped her chin up with his fingertip, and lowered his mouth until their lips brushed, a butterfly kiss, the flutter of an angel's wings. Every bit of Abby's will vanished in this moment she'd dreamed of for so long.

And then Isaac kissed her for real.

It was everything she'd imagined and more, soft and yet unyielding, hungry but also knowing, exciting and also like it had always been there between them. They kissed and kissed, and Abby didn't care at all who might see them. When they finally pulled apart, Isaac was grinning like a kid.

"*That's* how I feel."

To hell with it, Abby thought. She wasn't going to miss another chance to tell him the truth. "I can't even tell you how good that is to hear. Because I feel the same way."

Isaac reached into his jacket and pulled out a flat parcel wrapped in brown paper. "I got you a little something."

"Isaac! You didn't have to—"

"Just open it."

Abby tore off the paper and found herself looking into a dear, familiar face. She turned the book over, and there was the faded photo of the Great Pyramids of Giza.

"You bought me Selwyn's book!"

Isaac dipped his head modestly, but he was obviously pleased at her reaction. "You're back up on stage now," he explained. "And that means you can't visit him like you used to. But this way, you can take Selwyn with you whenever you need a little extra support, or just someone to talk to."

Tears welled in Abby's eyes. "This is the best gift anyone ever gave me." Because no one had ever made the effort to understand her as well as Isaac did, she realized.

"Well—good. But you'll have to explain to Ben why you needed a budget travel guide to Egypt. He seemed really confused when I asked him to gift wrap it."

Abby hugged the book to her chest. "Nah, I'm going to let him try to figure it out for himself. This one's just for me."

"Damn right," Isaac growled, pulling her closer.

Abby stayed there for a while, enjoying the feeling of his arm around her, of resting her head on his shoulder. "So what happens now?" she murmured.

Isaac put his hands on her shoulders and turned her back

toward the stadium. "You see that brick building behind the fake-Art-Deco-y one with the fancy balconies?"

"Uh-huh..."

"I live there."

"You live in a warehouse?"

"Well...the top floor, anyway."

Abby goggled at him, trying to imagine how much the penthouse of a restored landmark would even cost. That television deal must have been pretty damn sweet.

Isaac had a slightly pained expression, and Abby realized he was embarrassed. "Nice," she said, "though lacking the pedigree of Casa O'Reilly."

Isaac relaxed. "I guess we can't all be San Francisco royalty. But if you can lower your standards enough to come upstairs, I make a mean cafecita.""

"I suppose I could make the time, but—" Abby lifted her paper cup. "I already have a coffee."

Isaac grabbed it and tossed it into a nearby trash can. "No you don't."

Oh my God, were they flirting? No—this definitely went beyond that. Abby couldn't pretend she didn't know what Isaac was asking her.

"If I drink any more coffee this late, I'll be up all night," she said suggestively, feeling both ridiculous and pretty pleased with herself.

Isaac stood and pulled Abby up and into his arms, leaning down to press his forehead to hers. "Even better. And I'll make you another one in the morning."

Abby felt her eyelashes flutter against him. "Then yes," she whispered. "If you're sure."

"Never been more sure about anything in my life. By the way, remember that first night at Ships? That thing you wrote that Theoden does to Mistress Gray on her alchemy table?"

Abby's face grew hot. Oh yes indeed, she remembered that.

Isaac nuzzled her neck, his stubble rough against her skin. "Yeah...we're totally doing that."

Oh God. Abby wriggled out of his arms, feeling dizzy. "I —I think I'm ready for that cafecita."

Isaac held her hand all the way back. They made out in the freight elevator. They made out in the vast, two-story entry to his apartment. They made out in front of the arched windows that were taller than he was.

"Be right back," Isaac told her, and went off to make the coffee.

Abby set her book down carefully on a glass-and-iron coffee table strewn with books and newspapers in three languages, and gave herself a tour of his bookshelves and his fish tank and the photos of his family lined up on the windowsill. When Isaac returned with two white china cups, she was bent over examining the carved detail of a rustic antique bench. Before she could straighten up in embarrassment, he gave a low whistle and set down the cups.

"God, you're beautiful," he said—and Abby believed him.

They started kissing again. Isaac led her to his bedroom, and there they stayed until, just as he'd promised, he made her a fresh cup in the morning.

Coming Soon

Look for Dex's story

Roll for Initiative

Coming Winter 2023

About the Author

Bell Fyfe is the pseudonym for writing partners Adrienne Bell and Sophie Littlefield. Sidelined in 2020 in the same pandemic pod, these two old friends and best-selling authors decided to join forces to create stories of hope, humor, and heart.

www.ingramcontent.com/pod-product-compliance
Lightning Source LLC
Chambersburg PA
CBHW031001190726
48285CB00004BB/1417